MARCH
OF WAR

MARCH OF WAR

BENNETT R. COLES

TITAN BOOKS

March Of War
Print edition ISBN: 9781783294275
Electronic edition ISBN: 9781783294282

Published by Titan Books
A division of Titan Publishing Group Ltd
144 Southwark Street, London SE1 0UP

First edition: October 2017
2 4 6 8 10 9 7 5 3 1

Visit our website: www.titanbooks.com

A CIP catalogue record for this title is available from the British Library.

Printed and bound in the United States.

Did you enjoy this book? We love to hear from our readers.
Please email us at readerfeedback@titanemail.com or write to us at
Reader Feedback at the above address.

To receive advance information, news, competitions, and exclusive offers
online, please sign up for the Titan newsletter on our website:
www.titanbooks.com

TO MY MUM
AND TO ALL MOTHERS WHO HAVE WATCHED THEIR CHILDREN
GO OFF TO WAR

DRAMATIS PERSONAE

ASTRAL SPECIAL FORCES PERSONNEL
Brigadier Alexander Korolev (head of Astral Special Forces)
Katja Emmes
Suleiman Chang
Ali al-Jamil
Shin Mun-Hee

ADMIRAL BOWEN CREW MEMBERS
Commander Hu (captain)
Lieutenant Perry (executive officer)
Lieutenant Gillgren (combat officer)
Lieutenant Jack Mallory (Hawk pilot)
Lieutenant John Micah (anti-stealth warfare director)
Sublieutenant Thomas Kane (strike officer)
Sublieutenant Wi Chen
Sublieutenant Hayley Oaks
Master Rating Daisy Singh

OTHER PERSONNEL
Admiral Eric Chandler
Commander Sean Duncan
Valeria Moretti (covert Centauri agent)
Vijay Shah (Minister of Natural Resources, Progressive Party)
Charity Shah (Vijay Shah's wife)
Christopher Sheridan (leader of the Federalist Party)

GLOSSARY

AAR	anti-armor robot
AAW	anti-attack warfare
AF	Astral Force
AG	artificial gravity
APR	anti-personnel robot
CO	commanding officer (or captain)
FAC	fast-attack craft
XO	executive officer

OFFICER TRADES

Line officer	in charge of the general operations of the Astral Force warships, this trade is exclusive to the Fleet
Strike officer	commanding AF ground operations, this trade is exclusive to the Corps
Pilot officer	operators of the Astral Force small craft, this trade exists in both Fleet and Corps, depending on the craft being piloted
Support officer	divided into three distinct sub-trades—Supply, Engineering, and Intelligence—this trade fulfills the Astral Force non-combat roles for both Fleet and Corps

EXTRA-DIMENSIONAL

Brane   a region of spacetime which consists of three spatial dimensions and one time dimension; humans exist in one of several known branes

Bulk   an area of spacetime which consists of FOUR spatial dimensions and one time dimension

Peet   the unit of measurement to describe how far away into the fourth dimension something is from the brane in which humans exist

SHIPBOARD

Aft	toward the back of the ship
Bow	front of the ship
Bridge	the command center of the ship
Bulkhead	wall
Deck	floor
Deckhead	ceiling
Forward	toward the front of the ship
Flats	corridor
Frame	an air-tight bulkhead which divides one section of the ship from another
Galley	kitchen
Hatch	a permanent access point built into a deck (as opposed to a door which is built into a bulkhead)
Heads	toilet
Ladder	a steep stairway leading from one deck to another
Main cave	main cafeteria
Passageway	corridor
Port	left
Rack	bed; also a verb meaning to sleep
Starboard	right
Stern	back of the ship
Washplace	sink, shower

1

Burning up in the atmosphere was becoming routine. It was the crossfire that made him nervous.

Lieutenant Jack Mallory nudged his control stick to the right. The Hawk shuddered as the thunderous vector of superheated air fought the movement. Visual reckoning was useless through the orange halo enveloping his ship and flight controls did little to warn him of the relentless exchange of firepower between the Terran warships in orbit and the rebel batteries on the surface.

The battle for control of the Asgard system wasn't going well, and Jack seemed to find himself at the center of these situations with an increasing frequency, which alarmed him.

"Altitude one-seven archons," Master Rating Singh shouted. The tactical operator was in the seat over his left shoulder. "Still on full descent!" The panic in the young woman's voice echoed vaguely in Jack's ears. The Hawk was dropping like a stone through the planet's thick atmo, and he was still pushing the throttle forward.

"Send to flight," he ordered. "Break at archons ten to scatter delta and regroup at rally point one."

She repeated his command to the flight of five other Hawks descending in mad obedience, flying in wedge formation astern. They'd started their drop thirty seconds ago, and Jack knew the ground batteries were already starting to track them.

"Fire control shining," she cried. "They're locking us up!"

Jack held the stick steady as his altimeter flashed through ten kilometers.

"Break formation!" he cried as he wrenched back the throttle to idle and leaned the stick forward. His stomach lurched into his throat as the Hawk dove and pounded without thrust into the wall of thickening air. On his flight display he watched as the rest of his flight fanned out and dropped their speeds, just as they fell into range of the rebel anti-aircraft weapons.

Bolts of energy flashed ahead of him, dimly visible through the fading heat cone. The scatter had foiled the initial targeting by the ground batteries, but Jack had come under fire too many times to underestimate the abilities of his enemy. Another glance at his display showed the other Hawks vectoring outward in a classic delta pattern, and he hoped their pilots knew enough to get low.

"Archons five," Singh warned.

As fire control radars locked on again, Jack did a random jink to port, changing his vector, but he kept the throttle idled and let gravity accelerate him downward. His target landing zone was only sixty seconds away at maximum thrust, but it was currently under a maelstrom of orbital bombardment, and his flight had just three safe routes in. If they didn't adhere to the Fleet's battlespace management plan, the rebel ground weapons would be the least of his worries.

Not that he wasn't scared shitless by the fifty thousand rebel troops located in the hills ahead of him, each squad carrying some kind of anti-aircraft weapon, and each of them linked into that damned Centauri uber-mind which seemed to reveal every Terran movement.

Air resistance slowed the Hawk to hypersonic speed, and as he dropped below one kilometer he pushed the throttle forward again, watching the rolling landscape rise to meet him. The other Hawks flitted in and out of sensor reach among the mountains. They cruised at two kilometers altitude, staying below the approaching peaks but giving themselves some room for error.

They were probably low enough to stay under the rebel tracking systems, but he didn't want to give the enemy a chance for pot-shots at his own bird. He nudged his vessel down, feeling the rumble of ground resistance in the air beneath him.

Ahead, he could see the rain of fire pounding away at the rebel positions that encircled the Terran base. He flashed over a ridge and scanned the wasteland of military equipment that had been the battle of New Trondheim barely a week ago. A flash to the left caught his eye, but the weapon was already falling astern. He heard Singh report it and launch countermeasures, but he kept his eyes on the mayhem coming into view ahead.

At least twenty orbital batteries were hammering down on the rebels, but the rain of fire was countered by dozens of mobile defense guns, their energy weapons lancing upward to intercept the Terran meteor swarm. The sky crackled with explosions seen through thick smoke, and the ground was barely visible amid the mad dance of scattered light and shadows.

"Project battlespace," he ordered.

A faint hologram flickered into existence, projecting onto the canopy as an overlay to the world before him. Rally point one glowed as a beacon off the starboard bow. Beyond it was the narrow corridor of extraction route one, straight through the maelstrom. In his peripheral he noted the symbols of his flight of Hawks as they emerged from the hills and converged, local anti-aircraft fire trailing their hypersonic passages.

"Time to corridor sweep?"

"Sixteen seconds."

"Send to flight," he said, leaning his stick to the right and lining up on rally point one. "Formation alpha—execute."

Singh relayed the order and the vectors of the Hawks changed as they altered to close him. Holding his own course steady put him at the greatest risk, out here on the open plain, but for these few seconds he needed to give his flight a target toward which to steer. The glowing hologram of rally point one loomed ahead of him, and beyond that the desperate rebel ground defenses countered the bombardment.

As he flashed through rally point one and nudged left to aim at the extraction corridor, Jack saw a sudden dimming of the sky as all orbital bombardment momentarily ceased. An eerie calm settled over the battlefield, but Jack knew what was coming next. His flight remained in formation behind him, single file, extraction corridor entry ten seconds away. He kept his eyes down, away from the sky.

The curtain of fire that suddenly burned down from orbit was brighter than Asgard itself. This was no new super weapon attacking the rebels—just the concentrated, coordinated fire of every orbital battery, all at once, all targeting the extraction corridor ahead of him.

For nine long seconds the Terran weapons slammed into a single line of rebel forces, overwhelming any defenses and smashing any exposed positions. Jack didn't slow his approach, aiming directly for the center of the fire.

A second before he entered the corridor, the focused bombardment ceased. The Hawk bucked as it slammed into the furnace of tortured air. He eased upward just enough to clear the thick smoke. His passage cut a wake through the debris that from orbit would look like God's finger pointing at his position, but the rebels below him—those still alive—would spend the next few minutes digging themselves out. By the time they succeeded, he and his flight would be long gone.

They were through the main rebel line. Ahead of him he could see the blackened, smoking remains of a Terran base. Eyes narrowing, he pushed the throttle forward even more. There were troopers in those remains, and it was his job to get them out.

"There's no way out!"

Behind his visor, Sublieutenant Thomas Kane winced at the distant words of Sergeant Bunyasiriphant, his senior surviving soldier, as she clambered back toward him. Smoke was filling the half-collapsed hallway too quickly, and there was no time to try to dig or blast through the blockage.

Escape through the hangar wasn't an option.

"Get back down here," he barked at Buns—as the sergeant was known—before turning back to the rest of his "troop." A motley gang of Terrans, but they were alive, for the moment, and they were his fighting force. More important, they were his responsibility. He checked his forearm display, scrolling through the internal structure of the base. He needed an area large enough for the Hawks to land, but one which wasn't yet controlled by the advancing rebels.

One of the section weapons thudded to life. His rifle snapped up even as he crouched and moved forward, pushing past the wounded and the terrified civilians. He heard Buns scrambling to follow him.

Trooper Furmek was on the section weapon. She leaned over a mound of collapsed wall and loosed another short burst of heavy rounds as Thomas approached. Through the constant ringing in his ears he heard the ripple of destruction as the explosive rounds hit their distant marks. He crouched next to Furmek, glancing around the wall into the wreckage of what had been the main control center.

"Another probe," she growled, eyes not wavering from her scan outward. "I discouraged them."

"Another milly?"

"Nope, just humans."

The millies had been chewing up Terran troopers of late. Their official designation was UCR—urban combat robot, or something—but they looked for all the worlds like mechanical millipedes, and Thomas hadn't ever heard one called anything but a milly. War simplified things. He remembered once upon a time when the primary rebel infantry robot had actually been called an APR, rather than an "appy," and the flying "airy" had been referred to by its official designation of AAR.

Thomas glanced out again. No movement among the debris. He checked his map, reorienting himself. This was a big establishment, designed to be the planetary headquarters both for the Terran campaign here on Thor and for the Asgard system in general. Too bad the rebels had found it before it had been garrisoned properly.

Fucking Army.

The hallway to his left headed toward the workshops and some storage bays. Not much there. He scanned the tactical center again. Furmek might have forced the rebels to duck their heads down, but there was no way he could get this group of wounded and civilians across that large an open space.

"Sir." Trooper McDonald tapped his shoulder, still pressing one hand over an ear. "Fleet says the extraction force is on final approach. Request our location for pickup."

Thomas scanned his display. The Hawks would be coming under heavy fire—he couldn't leave them loitering. All he needed was a flat space they could access. He scrolled up through the base diagram... The roof. It was dangerously exposed, but it was open and flat. He traced back the path from one of the rooftop guard posts, and saw that the stairs that led upward were only twenty meters away.

"Tell them we'll be on the roof, near guard post seven," he said, before tapping Furmek's armored shoulder. "We're going to move the group across this opening and back into the hallway, heading for the first set of stairs. We're going all the way to the top."

Furmek flexed her grip on the trigger. "I got you covered, skipper."

Thomas edged back and motioned for the group to rise. There were five troopers still in fighting form, and four others being carried between the six civilians.

"Hawks are inbound—we're heading for the roof. O'Hara, Unrau, and I will lead. Stay close." He hefted his rifle again and nodded to Furmek.

She opened up with the section weapon, pounding the far side of the tactical center with sweeps of explosive rounds.

Thomas dashed across the exposed opening where part of the wall had collapsed, eyes already on the dim hallway which angled off to the left. Emergency lamps cast narrow arcs of light through the thin, drifting smoke—enough to see by in natural vision as Thomas loped forward, rifle up at his eyeline.

At the junction to the wide stairwell he paused, fist held up to signal a stop. Still behind the corner he activated the infra-red in his visor, scanning through the wall and up to the next floor. No heat signatures. He motioned his team forward and rounded the corner, rifle sweeping up the stairs.

He took the steps two at a time, reaching the landing and swinging his rifle across the next climb. No visible resistance. He dashed up again. The clatter of boots behind him indicated the team following, loud enough for the dead to hear. Speed was more important than stealth, though, and without pause he scanned the corridor in both directions before charging up the next flight of stairs.

At the fourth floor he paused, signaling Subtrooper O'Hara to cover the left corridor while he covered the right. Unrau had kept pace, emerging up the latest set of stairs, but the civilians were lagging under their burden of carrying the wounded. Thomas glanced back, grimacing as the clutter of gasping figures extended back more than a flight of stairs.

"Hold here," he ordered O'Hara. He motioned for Unrau to move back down, and then followed, keeping against the outer wall to make room for the wounded. To their credit, none of the civvies were complaining, their faces fixed in grim determination as they helped their charges to climb.

The metal panel of a ventilation duct exploded from its frame and smashed into the group on the landing. A silvery machine lashed out from the exposed duct like a giant metallic snake. Thomas snapped his weapon up and fired. Explosive bullets thudded into the dust-covered armor, knocking the milly in mid-air as the impacts dispersed over its armored form. The robot's forward claws clamped onto the head of a civilian and wrenched.

The human was dead even before he hit the floor.

Unrau leapt back and fired at the milly slithering at his feet, but the robot's long body rippled to the side as its hundreds of tiny legs reacted with inhuman swiftness. In a heartbeat the robot was up to strike, grasping Unrau's helmet and launching multiple tungsten darts from its underbelly. The point-blank shots punched through Unrau's lowered weapon, and his armor. He dropped the rifle as smoke and coolant leaked from the multiple holes, grabbing the milly with his armored hands and throwing them both down the stairs.

"Go, go, go!" Thomas shouted, gesturing up the stairs.

He aimed at the milly, but Unrau's massive frame blocked the shot as he kept the robot beneath him for the fall. Man and machine crashed into the lower floor. Thomas heard the muffled bangs of further darts punching into Unrau's torso. He motioned for the rest of his charges to keep ascending as he leapt down to aid his trooper.

The milly shuddered free of Unrau, the trooper rolling off as blood began to flow freely. Thomas fired. The bullets exploded against the robot's armor—enough to knock it back but still doing no real damage—and the thing was so damn fast. Already it was scuttling back on itself and moving to strike against him. Before Thomas could jump aside he saw the puff of darts and felt the sting of impacts against his chest.

He fell backward from the sheer force.

Even before he hit the landing floor he squeezed the trigger for his grenade launcher. From beneath the rifle's main barrel the shot rocketed outward. The explosion hurled the milly backward. Thomas crashed down into the floor and wall, vision blurring.

In the corridor below, the milly skittered up, an entire section of its feet either missing or hanging limply amid the charred wreckage. Its forward claws still operated, though, as did the lower half of its body.

Thomas tried to focus.

Another explosion tore into the milly's lower half, flipping it backward. Sergeant Bunyasiriphant stepped into Thomas's view and fired a final grenade into the milly's head. It collapsed in a smoldering heap. Thomas righted his vision as Buns crouched over Unrau, tearing a wound-sealant pack from his belt and reaching repeatedly into the shattered armor. Trooper McDonald appeared next to her, followed by Trooper Furmek swinging the section weapon in a slow, covering arc.

Thomas leaned against the wall and pushed himself to his feet. The civilians and wounded were clustered at the top of the stairwell above him, watching anxiously.

"Is he alive?" he called down to Buns.

"Yes," Buns replied, not looking up as she continued to apply first aid. Thomas checked his forearm display. One more floor up to the rooftop guard post.

"McDonald," he said over his helmet radio, "take point with O'Hara, and get everyone up the next set of stairs. Find guard post seven and get everyone inside. Hawks are inbound to land on the roof."

Trooper McDonald hustled up the stairs past him to comply.

Thomas descended and helped Buns lift Unrau's heavy form. Furmek maintained rearguard as they struggled to ascend.

2

Jack checked his descent vector. His Hawk would bottom out at thirty meters before leveling on final approach, but the billowing clouds of black smoke rising from what had once been the base's main hangar were problematic. He couldn't climb—not unless he wanted to re-enter the shooting gallery of the scattered rebel forces which continued to evade the orbital bombardment blasts—but flying through zero visibility toward a structure that wasn't really maintaining its official shape was just begging for a crash.

The rest of his flight had loosely formed up in the forgiving echo pattern which allowed each Hawk the flexibility to dodge individual ground attacks. To the right of his approach was the rest of the base, a tortured pile of rebel-occupied wreckage he wasn't going anywhere near. To the left was open ground, but it was covered by mobile anti-aircraft batteries that continued to evade the slower-reacting orbital bombardment. A fist of tanks would have made short work of those bastards, but the whole point of this operation was to get Terran troops *off* the surface.

His flight had to avoid the smoke, and that meant taking on the AA batteries. So he calmly ordered the flight to shift vector left, instinctively dropping his own Hawk even lower. Ground resistance was a steady force rattling his craft, but he fought it almost absently as he scanned ahead for the two enemy defenders. At this altitude they'd have big trouble tracking him, but likewise his own sensors couldn't pinpoint them.

"Relay orbital ground picture to my projection," he said.

His holographic battlespace lit up with hundreds of contacts—an overwhelming array of tactical info as every single contact being tracked by the ships in orbit flooded his display. He ignored everything except for the two hostile symbols on the ground in front of him. He reached up and tapped the camera on his helmet, locking onto one symbol, then the other.

"Clear orbital ground picture."

The galaxy of symbols disappeared, except for the two he'd personally targeted. The orbital feed continued to update his holographic image as the rebel batteries moved. His flight wouldn't be able to get past those weapons without taking casualties, unless the weapons were taken out first. Bombardment clearly couldn't do it, and there were no Terran ground assets that could help.

His Hawk, however, had two self-defense missiles tucked up under its stubby wings, and there was nothing that said he couldn't employ them for *aggressive* self-defense. He leaned forward in his seat and smiled. In training, he'd always wanted to be a strike fighter pilot.

"Troopers say they're at the roof," Singh reported. Jack checked the relative position of the landing zone and the smoke from the hangar. His flight had a clear run now.

"Send to flight," he said. "Commence landing run, Axe-Two leading. I'm taking out the AA batteries."

There was the briefest of pauses from behind him, but Singh dutifully relayed the order. Above him, the other Hawks broke right and headed for the extraction. Jack armed both his missiles and linked their targeting to the orbital feed. They growled *ready* in his ear. He designated one each to the rebel batteries, which were even now repositioning.

"Tell Fleet to hold fire on surface hostiles alpha-two-eight and alpha-two-niner," he said. "Axe-One is taking them."

Orbital bombardment was a blunt instrument, and was as likely to hit his Hawk as the enemy at these ranges. Assuming the ships above him would comply, Jack closed on the first battery. The rolling landscape flashed beneath him as a pale blur. He fought to keep the Hawk steady, then pressed the trigger.

The first missile burst forth, ringing in his ear with its positive lock.

Jack nudged his stick to the right and pressed the trigger again. The second weapon blazed ahead, just as an explosion on the ground to his left erupted upward, instantly flashing astern. A second later another explosion lit up a shallow depression ahead.

He pulled back to gain altitude and hard right to head for the extraction.

The heavy thud of the section weapon was a beautiful sound to a trooper. It meant somebody was covering your ass.

Thomas knew Furmek was still holding off the rebels in the corridor, and he stayed focused on his task of getting his troop out onto the roof. He heaved Unrau's massive form up through the gun port of the guard post, where two of his troopers took the limp body and struggled forward onto the open surface. Buns was already topside, arranging the few combat-ready assets they still had in a thin perimeter around the weak and wounded.

The thudding of the weapon abruptly died.

Thomas swung around, raising his rifle at the door. Beside him, Subtrooper O'Hara followed suit. She'd held up well throughout this entire incident, but he could see the strain on her too-young face. She was barely old enough to drink—she wasn't old enough to die.

Trooper Furmek dove through the door, snapping it shut behind her. The section weapon was nowhere in sight.

"Ammo spent," she gasped.

"How many approaching?" Thomas asked.

"Probably a dozen. Humans, small arms only."

He glanced up through the gun port. His troop was hunkered down, waiting, and completely exposed if the rebels could gain access to the roof.

"We hold them here," he said. He snapped out his pistol and handed it to Furmek. She took it in one hand and hefted her own pistol in the other.

O'Hara, beyond Furmek, crouched lower and pointed her rifle at the door.

He spoke into his comms. "McDonald, what's the ETA on the Hawks?"

"*Two-zero seconds.*" And another twenty seconds to load the wounded, he knew. Something pounded against the door, and he heard shouting on the other side.

"Once the packages are aboard, get the troopers back here to cover our withdrawal. Heavy fire imminent."

"*Roger.*"

There wasn't much to offer cover in the small, round room, but Thomas crouched behind a status board. Another, larger thump impacted the door, buckling it against its reinforced frame.

"Don't fire until you see a target," he called out. "Our own rounds will blow a hole open in the wall."

A mechanical roar echoed through the door, and something massive struck it so that it cracked inward. A rifle poked through the gap. Thomas fired. A wet explosion mixed with shouts, and the rifle fell back. Amid the cacophony he made out a single word being repeated beyond the door.

"Grenade."

If a single grenade got dropped through that opening, it was over for him and his troopers. They had no choice but to attack.

"Open fire!" he shouted.

His own assault rifle burst to life on automatic, the reinforced wall of the guard post crumbling backward under the hail of explosive rounds. O'Hara's own fire joined his, thundering into the crowd of stunned rebels located beyond the shattered wall. Limbs and blood flew in all directions as dust choked the corridor.

His rifle clicked silent. Quick check—empty mag. He jettisoned the magazine and slapped in another.

O'Hara and Furmek both advanced, firing into the chaos.

"Get back!" Thomas roared.

A flash of silver rose up from the rubble, bowling into Furmek. She tumbled backward even as the milly rolled in mid-air and stabbed out at O'Hara with its main claws. The young trooper screamed as blood splashed out from her shoulder. She dropped her weapon and clutched at the gash in her armor, dropping instantly.

Furmek pulled herself to her knees and fired with both pistols, the rounds bouncing harmlessly off the milly's back. It spun again, firing darts even as Furmek threw herself down.

Thomas reached for his grenade trigger, but the milly was scuttling right over Furmek's slumping form. He switched back to bullets and charged forward, looking to bury his rifle into the fucker's underside. He fired on automatic, relishing the power as the explosive rounds thundered into the milly's legs and knocked it backward.

The robot staggered back against the wall, flailing against the onslaught. Thomas felt darts slamming into his front torso armor, felt white-hot burning mixed with liquid next to his skin. But he stepped forward again, emptying the last of his magazine into the milly's head. The robot slumped down and was still.

Something hard hit him from behind, and he vaguely heard the sound of a gunshot. He turned to face the wreckage of the wall and corridor, and saw rebel troops advancing. Another impact-only bullet pinged off his helmet, shaking his vision. He brought his rifle to bear and squeezed the trigger, but heard only the awful click of another empty mag.

More rounds struck him, knocking him back against the wall and burning his torso. The rebels closed in. O'Hara and Furmek lay motionless at his feet. His hand dropped to the grenade launcher and he started firing. As his vision faded, he wondered if the rest of his troops had made it to the Hawks.

As he slowed for landing on the roof, Jack spotted three of his Hawks already lifting off. Wounded and non-combatants were loaded, and the first wave of the flight were bugging out.

"Tell Axe-Two to use the primary exit corridor," he ordered as he thrusted to a hover and swung around to point his stern loading ramp toward the guard post. "We'll use the secondary."

His bird thumped down and he started to lower the ramp. A rush of heat swept through the cabin and the distant sounds of battle penetrated through his helmet. He looked back over his shoulder, and dimly saw two troopers hustling with a limp companion carried between them. He leaned to scan out of his port canopy and saw two others carrying another casualty.

"Get back there," he barked at Singh, "and help them get on board!"

She unbuckled and hurried aft, taking the load of the casualty as the troopers staggered up the ramp and swung their rifles back toward the base. One of them fired off a few rounds toward the guard post, the other watched their companions climb aboard the other Hawk. Jack caught the motion as that Hawk's ramp started to rise, and he turned his attention back to the troopers. They were climbing up into his main cabin.

"That's everyone," one of them shouted. "Go, go, go!"

He started closing his own ramp and pulled up into a hover, drifting forward and turning so that the other Hawk could take station on his port quarter. The ramp sealed. He pushed the throttle forward and started to climb. His wingman followed.

The abandoned base disappeared astern as he increased to hypersonic speed, and he surveyed the tortured landscape looming ahead of him again. Orbital bombardment pounded down on all sides, but the rebel forces continued their determined defense.

"Tell Fleet to open the secondary exit corridor," he said. He heard a brief exchange by Singh, then a report back.

"Fleet ready to clear secondary corridor, but be advised orbital battle is intensifying."

Jack frowned. Apparently a surface battle wasn't enough of a challenge for one day, and he'd already expended his two self-defense missiles.

"Tell *Frankfurt* we're going to need cover on our approach."

His own mothership, the destroyer *Frankfurt*, needed to clear a path that would enable him to sneak through the orbital battle. Hawks were flexible, nifty little craft, but starfighters they were not.

As before, the ominous silence fell over the battlefield, and Jack nudged his course to starboard to line up with the secondary exit corridor. Then Fleet once again came together to lay waste to the narrow path through the main rebel line, and he followed the firestorm through. He and his wingman emerged and separated into the rising mountains, cutting individual paths out to a range where enemy fire was minimal. Jack pulled back on his stick and pushed the throttle to maximum power, activating his external boosters to assist in the climb.

The gray atmosphere of the planet Thor began to fade into the blackness of orbital space. After barely thirty seconds the boosters expended their fuel and fell silent. He jettisoned them and continued to climb with his own engines.

"Bring up orbital battlespace," he gasped. A moment later the darkness beyond his canopy lit up with a new galaxy of contacts. He found *Frankfurt*'s unique beacon and pulled hard over to point for home.

Right away, he could see trouble.

The blue symbol of his destroyer was in the middle of a cluster of red hostiles, and even at this distance he could make out the flashes of combat, if not the combatants themselves. Other Terran ships were scattered across the near sky, and he could see them starting to pull back from low orbit. Their bombardment batteries were going silent, but their defense weapons blazed.

Jack made sure his own beacon was shining, knowing that at this speed *Frankfurt*'s sensors could easily interpret his direct approach as a missile threat. Off the starboard bow he could see the big cruiser *Admiral Bowen* closing *Frankfurt*, weapons already firing at the hostiles.

"Do we have an approach vector?" he asked.

"Negative," Singh replied. "She's all over the place."

Jack maintained his speed, reckoning it was the only thing that might keep his Hawk out of the enemy crosshairs. *Frankfurt* wasn't yet visible, but the rapidly changing vector of her blue symbol indicated heavy, erratic maneuvering. Jack took a deep breath. He'd landed his bird during combat before, and at least this time he had functioning thrusters. No problem.

In the darkness ahead, he saw a bright series of flashes. The blue symbol of *Frankfurt* blinked, then disappeared.

"What the hell?" Singh cried out behind him. Jack just stared ahead at the empty space where his mothership, his home for the past year, had been. This, he realized as a cold pit formed in his stomach, was a problem.

Alarms flashed, and he spotted several enemy contacts vectoring toward him. He jinked automatically. No missiles inbound yet, but his Hawk was awfully alone out here. He scanned the battlespace—the nearest friendly was the cruiser *Admiral Bowen*, which was even now engaging the closest rebel ships. Without thinking, he hauled his stick over to point at the blue symbol and tapped in Fleet Craft Control to his own comms.

"Windmill, Windmill, Windmill," he said clearly, using *Bowen*'s callsign, "this is Axe-One, Axe-One, Axe-One, three k off your port quarter, inbound. Request emergency recovery, over."

There was only a slight pause before the steady voice of the cruiser's small craft controller came over the circuit.

"*Axe-One, this is Windmill, roger. I am disengaging hostiles and closing your position. Take delta for port-side automated recovery.*"

"This is Axe-One, wilco."

He killed his throttle and angled to starboard, swinging slowly around to match the cruiser's course and speed as she closed, weapons still peppering the rebel forces as they fell astern. Her charcoal hull was impossible to see against the blackness, but Jack watched the relative vectors converge as he bled off his own velocity and lined up. Just as the dim hull of the Terran warship started to emerge against the background, he felt the shudder of the gravity beams grab his Hawk and start to pull him in.

Killing his thrusters, he let the computers do the rest of the work.

As soon as his Hawk set down inside the airlock, he requested a medical team to meet them in the hangar. Receiving acknowledgement, he unstrapped and climbed past the exhausted Singh, patting her shoulder with a smile, then moving toward the troopers. One of them was laid out on the deck, the effects of first-aid packs still bubbling all over the armor. The other two sat slumped against each bulkhead, just pulling off their helmets. Two women, they cast heavy, exhausted eyes up at him.

"Lieutenant Mallory," he said, crouching down at the feet of the casualty. "We have a medical team en route."

"Sergeant Bunyasiriphant," the older woman growled before nodding at her peer, "and Trooper McDonald."

Jack glanced at the wounds on the casualty, realizing quickly that he had no way of knowing how serious they were.

"What ship are you from?" he asked the troopers.

"*Admiral Bowen.*"

Jack saw the dents and cracks in the casualty's helmet, and through the broken visor he could actually see the man's pale face—and his heart clenched. He pressed his fingers against the man's neck, then was relieved to feel a faint pulse.

There was a knock at the side airlock hatch, and he stepped up to open it for the medical team before looking back down at the casualty and speaking.

"Welcome home, Thomas."

3

Apparently some citizens of Terra thought the war against the rebels was going badly. Parliament didn't like that fact, but until now they'd only employed gentle measures to try to dissuade those few citizens of their misconceptions.

A sterner lesson needed to be taught.

Operative Katja Emmes felt the icy breeze across her uncovered face as she strolled across the dark boulevard. The soft rustle of the snow-covered pine needles masked her gentle footfalls, but there was no particular need for stealth. Her targets were inside the pub just ahead, and even from this distance she could hear the faint voice of the orator, interrupted by occasional cheers.

This group of dissidents planned to settle upon a name for their movement this evening, and that the footage from their little gathering would be sent out to all the news networks. It was a group just on the cusp of causing real trouble.

Strolling up to the pub entrance, she noted the attractive young woman minding the door, as well as the two burly men standing just inside the threshold, eyes toward the interior but their attention on the entranceway. They hardly worried her—big men never considered small women a threat.

Wearing her thick winter jacket, Katja knew she looked almost portly. This made her appear even less threatening, and easily hid the array of weapons tucked into her belt. A black tuque was pressed down on her head, long blonde hair spilling out haphazardly. Contact lenses transformed her dark-brown eyes into brilliant blues, but more importantly they gave her infra-red and quantum-flux vision as needed.

"Hi," she said shyly, looking at the woman then peering through the door. "Is this where the meeting is?" Her accent wasn't perfect, she knew, but it had enough of a local twang to make her sound as if she'd lived some years in Scotland. With all the noise coming from within, she doubted the pub's greeter even gave it a thought.

"It sure is," the woman replied. "It's already started, but come on in."

Katja stepped inside, noting the quick glances from both burly men as she paused to take in the scene. She waited for any sudden or unusual moments from either of them, but neither paid her more than a moment's attention.

Noting that many people near her were standing on chairs to see across the crowd, she climbed up on one herself, smiling as a young man offered a hand and then climbed onto the chair next to hers. He grinned back with youthful excitement before returning his gaze to the speaker. Katja peered over the rows of crowded tables to the small stage where a handsome, middle-aged man had just paused in his speech as a new roar of approval erupted from the assembled crowd.

She clapped absently, scanning the room.

The man on the stage was one of her targets, a local businessman who had the wealth to fund a considerable smear campaign against Parliament. He was well-known as a generous community member here in Inverness, and was involved in many local projects to help the poor.

The second target she spotted to the right of the stage—a stern, middle-aged woman who had for years been a State lawyer but who recently had set up her own practice in this, her home town. Her recent articles on the "quasi-legality" of Parliament's position on the war could become quite embarrassing, if they received wide distribution.

The third target wasn't immediately visible. A woman of no significant professional history, intelligence suggested that she was little more than a rabble-rouser capable of using the social networks for recruitment. There were no confirmed images of her on the nets, which by itself raised considerable suspicion. Katja also doubted she would speak at this gathering—her role in the movement was that of connector, not leader.

Personal devices abounded as people recorded what they assumed was a great beginning to their glorious revolution. Katja reached out tentatively into the Cloud, quietly probing the various accounts for any unusual signals or encryptions. It took several long moments for her to work her mind through the crowded electronic space, but nothing jumped out as odd. She recorded each user ID anyway, just in case Parliament felt it necessary to track any of these people after tonight.

What was that?

Among the cacophony of noise, she noticed something different. Something encrypted. It was barely a pulse within the waves of energy, with no repeats. She focused her mind in the Cloud, listening, but detected nothing else. She might have imagined it, but experience with the enemy had taught her more than enough about paying attention to "imagined" things.

She would need to move fast, as soon as opportunity allowed.

Target One thundered on for at least fifteen minutes more, rallying the crowd. Katja continued to clap as appropriate, even cheering once toward the very end. His words were socialist drivel, but she played her role of excited naïf, even returning the occasional grins of the kid next to her. But the speech eventually came to an end.

Target Two joined her companion on the stage just long enough to explain that there would be a half hour of mingling time, when everyone was welcome to come forward and cast their vote on the three names which had been put forward to identify this movement. She pointed up at the pub's menu board where the three options appeared.

The two leaders stepped down, a band took the stage, and a general hubbub of excited chatter rumbled through the room. Katja glanced around again from her perch, assessing the likelihood that she would be able to get close to her targets amid this throng of admirers. Both seemed to be positioning themselves near the bar, where the open floor space gave them room to mingle.

A hand gripped her elbow, and she almost jerked away. The boy next to her had stepped down and was reaching up to assist her.

"Can I help you down?" he asked.

She placed her own tiny hand into his, and stepped down to the hard floor. The noise from the band crashed over them and he leaned in to her ear to speak.

"Isn't this awesome?"

She gave him a shy smile. "It's really exciting. I've never been to anything like this before."

"Me neither," he admitted. "But it's great to be part of something so worthwhile."

"I've never met the leaders—I was hoping to tonight, but there are so many people here!"

He looked over the crowd toward the bar, then grinned again, taking her hand and pushing forward between the tables. She tucked in behind him and followed, letting him take all the notice as they gently pressed through the mass. Soon enough they'd made it past the tables and jostled in among the crowd of admirers.

He let go of her hand long enough to grab a couple of beers from the line of free drinks being offered on the bar.

"Thanks," she said.

"I'm Will," he said, clinking glasses with her.

"Kelly," she replied, holding his gaze and giving him a wink with her right eye. The wink activated her quantum-flux vision and she dropped her gaze, scanning the long wooden panels of the bar for any hidden weapons or devices. There was nothing of note beyond the usual plumbing and cold storage. A glance up to the ceiling revealed the usual network and power connections.

Target Two was almost within arm's reach. Katja dropped her gaze again and unzipped her thick coat.

"It's roasting in here," she said, making a show of being hot before taking another big gulp of beer. "I think we're going to need more of these." Her pet teenager willingly obliged, downing the last of his own drink and stepping away to fetch more.

Katja made as if to loosen her coat, and in a quick motion reached inside to her belt. Her palm pressed against a tiny square, and she felt the patch adhere to her palm, then slip free of the belt.

Target Two was wilting under all the attention of her admirers, her severe face looking less friendly with each person who pressed forward to speak to her. She wasn't going to last much longer, Katja thought as she slipped through the last row of admirers and right into the target's face.

"I know you're so busy," Katja gushed, reaching out and clasping the target's hand in both of her own, "but I just wanted to thank you for everything you're doing."

The patch needed less than a second to take effect, but Katja held on tightly for as long as she could. The target managed a faint smile and thanked her.

The poison from the patch would leave her dead within six hours, with no visible symptoms. She would appear to have died in her sleep. Nothing could ever be traced back to Parliament.

Katja stepped back and turned toward Target One, but young Will stepped into her path with another pair of drinks. She had no choice but to stop and accept, and flirt away with the eager pup amid the noise of the band. After a few minutes she noticed that Target One was retreating from the well-wishers, surrounded by a serious group of citizens who appeared to be some sort of inner cadre. Getting close to him now would be impossible.

Time for a less direct method.

"I am *totally* roasting," she said. "I might just step outside and get some air for a moment."

"Yeah, good idea," he said. "Let's get out of here."

Katja sighed inwardly—she should have thought that through better. She needed to shake this kid.

"Just give me a sec," she smiled. "I need to visit the little girls' room first." He pointed her in the right direction, assuring her he'd be there when she got back.

It was early enough in the drinking that a line-up for the ladies' had yet to form and in the sudden quiet, as the door shut behind her, Katja scanned the small room. Three stalls to the left, one occupied. Three sinks, with a lone woman drying her hands. A window was high on the far wall, closed against the chill.

Ignoring the hand-drying woman as she left, Katja winked on her infra-red to scan the stalls. Judging from the way she was seated, the woman on the toilet wasn't going to move for at least thirty seconds.

The door shut behind Katja, and she had her opening.

Leaping upward, she grabbed the lip beneath the window. Bracing one foot against the nearest sink, she freed a hand to snap the latch up and push the window open. A quick push from her foot and she squeezed her small frame through the opening, clutching the outside of the frame with one hand as she wormed her legs through and let them swing downward. A short drop and she thumped down on the pavement.

A wave of noise burst from the pub as another patron entered the ladies' room, but Katja was already out of sight.

The area behind the pub was dark, dim light shining through a frosted window to her left. No movement among the recycling bins. She pressed up against the cold wall and reached out into the Cloud, searching for any security sensors. Clear. Staying in the shadows, she moved silently along the wall toward the collection of parked cars beside the building.

All vehicles had an ID beacon that was attached to their owner. These beacons only radiated when the cars were activated, but they were also designed to respond to a direct security query, even when dormant. Katja peered around the corner of the building and quickly interrogated each beacon—the white, luxury sedan belonged to Target One. It was two rows away from her, farthest from the road. Fully exposed.

She glanced around the parking lot, then swept in infra-red. No contacts—everyone was still inside.

Stepping out into the dim pool of light cast from the street, she moved with casual purpose through the two rows of parked cars, reaching under her coat again. Against her left hip was a fist-sized metal box, flat on one side and ergonomically rounded on the others.

Activating quantum-flux, she slowed to a casual stroll and scanned the white sedan. The inner workings of the vehicle were hard to make out, but the ventilation system was by necessity quite large when compared to the intricate electro-mechanical systems. It didn't take long to spot the main air feed that led into the sedan's cabin. Its trunking was difficult to access from outside, however, and Katja followed it back to the filters, and then traced one of the smaller ducts which fed air through to the driver's side.

She crouched down just behind the forward levitator and reached up under the car's casing, still gripping the box. In quantum-flux she watched her own hand reach up to bump against the secondary ventilation duct, and saw the asphyxiator clamp on, punching a tiny rod through into the air passage. As soon as it sensed air flowing past the rod, the device would release an odorless, fast-acting poison.

Target One would be killed within minutes, and the resulting crash would probably be blamed for his death.

"Kelly?"

She froze at the voice. It was very close.

"Are you okay?"

She withdrew her hand and looked up from her crouch. In the dual input of normal and quantum-flux vision, it took her a moment to recognize Will, staring down at her with a mixture of curiosity and concern. His breath was controlled but quick, like he'd been running and was trying to hide the fact.

"Hi, Will," she said, opening her eyes wide and smiling broadly. "I just dropped something and it slid under this car. I got it, though."

"I didn't see you leave," he said. "How did you get out here?"

She stood up, keeping her big eyes locked on his. She casually drew her coat shut as she stepped forward, letting her smile turn playful.

"I didn't see you when I came out of the ladies'," she said. "I figured you'd already come outside, so I came out looking for you."

Puzzlement clouded his young features, but his mouth twisted into a sort of smile as he watched her approach. With the quantum-flux still feeding her vision, she had trouble reading his expression, but the slow wink needed to deactivate the sensor would seem very odd.

He was taller than her, and probably stronger, but if she could get in close she'd have the advantage. She licked her lips and held his gaze, taking another step forward, coming within arm's reach.

He laughed nervously, dropping his eyes and blinking twice.

Something activated inside his skull. Encrypted communications skirted the edge of her senses. He raised his eyes and stared back at her.

They froze, a pace apart. This was no innocent kid. Via the Cloud she shot a Special Forces interrogation at him.

Nothing came back.

His fist flew toward her. She blocked it, but the force knocked her back against the sedan. Staggering against the metal she raised both arms in defense as he lashed out again. Falling onto the car's trunk she reared both legs and slam-kicked him in the chest. He staggered back but enough of his charging momentum got through to send her sliding off the car.

Katja crashed down on the ground, rolling onto her back to again block his flurry of blows. He loomed over her, raising one leg to strike, and she kicked out his supporting knee. He grunted in pain and staggered. Rolling backward and onto her feet, she reached for the pistol against her right hip.

She loosed the weapon and brought it up to aim at his center of mass, but his leg swept round in a kick as her finger reached the trigger. A single shot cracked in the dark air, flying wide. She stepped back out of reach, but he pressed forward again, swinging completely around to deliver another flying kick. Her hand smashed against the cold, hard polymer of the car. The pistol slipped from her grip and clattered down.

His eyes darted toward the weapon. That moment was all she needed.

Katja's left hand lashed out, through his blocks and up against his nose. Cartilage crackled under her palm strike and his head snapped back. Her right hand followed through, knuckles hammering into his exposed throat.

When his powerful arm knocked both of her hands away, she stepped back, limbs burning from the impact. He staggered, strained coughs wheezing from his partially collapsed windpipe. His feet shuffled against the pavement, his whole body sagging against an unseen weight. She crouched, arms up in a guard, waiting.

He stumbled back, eyes still on her. She ducked down and retrieved her pistol, bringing it to bear once more.

<Who are you?> she demanded in the Cloud. There was no response, but she knew from his expression that he'd received her message.

The distance between them had opened too much for quantum-flux to be precise and she finally disabled it with a long wink, focusing her mental energy on interrogating the various artificial devices she knew were implanted in him. The standard Terran ID in his chest looked legitimate, but there was nothing normal about the enhancements in his limbs or his skull. She pressed harder, and met a wall of sophisticated, elegant encryption. She knew well what that meant.

"Not this time, Centauri," she said quietly.

She pulled the trigger twice.

His body crashed backward, the special slugs bursting on impact to scatter microscopic bullets in a flash of intense heat. The wide cone of tiny projectiles cut a swathe of destruction through the body, but rapidly lost momentum. As the Centauri spy tumbled backward in a heap, no exit wounds clouded his back and no blood seeped from the cauterized entry point.

Katja scanned the parking lot for movement or witnesses. All was quiet. She holstered her weapon and activated her visual recorder, then crouched down over the Centauri, her vision drifting over him as she captured images of his face. In the pain of death his features had lost their youthfulness, and in the new, cold clarity she guessed he was actually as old as she was.

It was time to disappear. Grabbing the body, she dragged it across the cold pavement and heaved it into the dark bushes. Pocketing the recorder she wrapped her coat tightly around her, hands holding it closed for quick access to the weapons within. She walked across the parking lot to the street and away from the bustling pub. As she did, she reached out with the Cloud to watch for any alarms, or for personal devices suddenly moving rapidly as their carriers pursued her. No one reacted to her departure.

Yet he'd been communicating with someone nearby, which meant there was at least one more Centauri agent in the vicinity. Perhaps the mysterious Target Three, the invisible leader of this misguided group of civilians. If she was an enemy agent, it would certainly explain why she was impossible to pin down on the Terran security nets.

Turning back, Katja forced herself to calm down, using all her senses to search the dark parking lot and the heaving pub. Nothing unusual stood out, though no doubt her enemy knew exactly where she was. This wasn't a good tactical situation.

Her secondary retrieval point was three blocks away, and she forced herself to walk at a brisk pace, rather than break into the run her adrenalin screamed at her to employ. She took deep breaths of the cold air, in through her nose and out through her mouth, sending oxygen to her brain and forcing her heart to slow and her body to throttle down.

Was it luck that had handed her a Centauri agent, or was it something more dangerous? He'd latched onto her almost immediately, and appeared to have anticipated her movement to the parking lot. It would have been difficult indeed to have picked him out amid all the electronic noise of the pub—yet had he somehow recognized her?

Had she just been sloppy, or had she been expected?

While the mission was a success, Katja felt a cold pit in her gut to match the wind against her face.

4

When he'd been just a subbie, Jack hadn't garnered much attention aboard ship. Crew members had slipped past him in the passageways with nary a glance, and the other officers had carried on conversations right over him. Ever since his promotion to lieutenant, however, people had started to notice him.

"Morning, sir," the umpteenth crew member said, hurrying past him. The ship was preparing for departure for another patrol in one of the colonies. Everyone was focused, but Jack was still just trying to learn his way around his new vessel.

The flats of the cruiser *Admiral Bowen* were wider than those of a destroyer, and people didn't actually have to turn sideways to pass each other. The bulkheads were a dull gray, interspersed with the black glass of computer interfaces and the crowded alcoves containing damage control equipment. Jack glanced down at the nearest rack of halon backpacks, designed for firefighters to don if the ship's atmo-purge system failed and a fire had to be fought by hand.

"Excuse me, sir."

He looked up and saw one of *Bowen*'s resident sublieutenants approaching. Jack figured they were the same age, but he suddenly felt years older as he saw the subbie's imploring expression.

"Sir, do you know when the departure briefing is?"

Seriously? Did this kid not know how to read a flex? Then

Jack remembered how, not that long ago, he wouldn't even have known what a "flex" was, or that there was such a thing as a departure brief.

"Oh-nine-hundred. On the bridge."

"Thank you, sir." The subbie hurried off.

Jack laughed to himself. Now that he'd reached the lofty rank of lieutenant, it seemed he had become the fount of all useful knowledge—and he was just the pilot on board.

This morning, however, his own quest for knowledge was taking him down to the engine room. *Bowen* had suffered damage to her starboard-side recovery system and no one in the hangar seemed to know if it was fully back on line. The equipment was all repaired, but power to some components remained intermittent. Jack figured a quick visit to engineering would solve the mystery.

Eventually he found the correct hatch and descended the steep set of stairs which the Fleet called a "ladder," emerging into a machinery control room frantic with activity. At least half the consoles were manned, steady chatter into headsets punctuated by the odd shout. Getting the mighty cruiser's systems powered up was no small task, but he sensed an edge of tension in the voices that didn't fill him with confidence. He glanced at his watch.

Ninety minutes until scheduled departure.

He spotted a nearby petty officer, and approached.

"Morning, PO," he said, "I need to confirm the readiness of the starboard recovery system."

The middle-aged petty officer looked up sharply, then spotted Jack's rank and swallowed down his instinctive response. Instead, he indicated toward a door on the forward bulkhead.

"Better talk to the chief, sir. He's in the ADE with the departure officer."

Jack nodded and walked forward, wondering idly who the departure officer was today. It was a tough job, running around the ship ensuring that all departments were ready, and having to report to the captain. As a pilot he was never trusted with such responsibility—only qualified bridge watchkeepers were burdened with that particular duty.

He stepped through into the accretion drive enclosure, the

beating heart of the ship, though there was nothing much to see. Both accretion drives were hidden behind their massive containment units, and it didn't take much imagination for Jack to sense the raw power barely contained behind the featureless tanks that towered on either side of him. A dull, nagging hum assailed his ears and he immediately grabbed for one of the sets of ear defenders hanging just inside the door.

As he walked along the grated catwalk between the accretion drives he could feel his entire body tingle. Beneath him, engineers scurried among a jungle of ancillary equipment. Above him, two more catwalks gave access to the containment tanks and still more equipment. Up ahead he saw a bank of control consoles around which the catwalk weaved, and over the muted hum of the ADE, he heard raised voices. Slowing, he glanced around the consoles and saw two figures squared off at the central control station.

"This ship is departing her berth on schedule at ten-hundred," Thomas Kane said, holding a tablet in his hand. "Yet you're not filling me with confidence, Chief." Thomas faced a tall, burly man who threatened to bulge out of his dark-blue coveralls. His round face was red under wisps of white hair and small eyes glared. Chief Petty Officer Ranson.

"Sir." That word alone carried with it enough bile, venom, condescension, and outrage to send many a subbie running, but Jack wasn't at all surprised to see Sublieutenant Kane stand his ground. "I've got an entire department scrambling to balance the feed between two accretion drives, because dockyard maintenance didn't finish their job last week. I have four new engineers who still don't know their asses from a circuit board, and we're still cleaning up the mess in the starboard recovery system."

Well, that answered Jack's question, but he remained riveted in place.

"Chief." That word from Thomas carried with it the heavy weight of resignation, fading tolerance, and a distinct lack of patience. "Your failure to plan ahead is not my problem. Stop whining at me and tell me if we're going to be ready to depart on schedule or not."

"Did you not just hear me?" The thick muscles in Ranson's neck bulged dangerously.

"Yeah, you're busy. So's everyone. So am I—so stop wasting my time. This ship is departing in eighty-five minutes, and if you're not capable of making that happen, I'll find someone who is."

Ranson stepped forward, moving his considerable bulk right into Thomas's space. "You cause one bit of disruption down here, Subbie, and I'll go straight to the captain."

Thomas didn't budge, looking up to meet the chief's eyes.

"You won't need to, because I'll have already done so and been given permission to come back here and arrest you."

Ranson took half a step back, his expression shifting into a sneer.

"This isn't the Corps, sir."

"You're right. If it was, I'd have already shot you." The pistol at Thomas's hip was still holstered, but his hand rested easily only inches away. Even from his perch, Jack could feel the cold certainty of Thomas's words.

So, apparently, could Chief Petty Officer Ranson. He stepped further back, dropping his gaze.

"We'll be ready, sir, but I'll have to skip the departure briefing."

"I'll send the captain your regrets."

Thomas turned abruptly and strode aft. Jack jumped backward to clear a path. Rounding the consoles, Thomas spotted him and smiled.

"Helping out with flash-up operations, sir?" Being called "sir" by Thomas Kane was almost as disconcerting as realizing how close the ship had just come to needing a new engineering chief. Jack fumbled to find the words as he fell in step behind Thomas.

"Ah, I was just down here looking to see if they'd sorted the problems with the starboard recovery system, but I found the answer."

"The port system is fully operational," Thomas called back over his shoulder, "so starboard isn't essential for departure. They'll have it fixed prior to us reaching the jump gate."

He was right, Jack realized, just like always. He wondered how many other crew members had made the mistake of doubting this enigmatic Corps sublieutenant.

* * *

Life in the Fleet was more or less the same, no matter what ship you were on. In the two years since finishing flight school Jack had served on most classes, from tiny fast-attack craft to hulking invasion ships, and while *Admiral Bowen* was his first cruiser, he hadn't needed much time to settle in.

The Hawk maintenance crew was friendly and efficient. His three fellow pilots were decent folk, although they each held the rank of ship's petty officer, which meant that they didn't hang out in the wardroom with Jack and the other officers. Only one of them had actually been a pilot before the war started—the other two had been senior technicians who had recently completed pilot training.

The officers themselves were the usual collection of hard-nosed, perpetually tired line officers with a few support officers thrown in just for irritation. The small herd of subbies were driven hard by the lieutenants and mostly kept to themselves in Club Sub, the four-bunk mess deck they called home.

As captain, Commander Hu remained a distant figure, but in their few interactions Jack had gained every confidence that *Bowen* was in good hands. Hu seemed very grounded, with none of the political aspirations which all too often seemed to affect a captain's thinking.

By contrast the executive officer, Lieutenant Perry, was new to the ship and apparently new to his role as XO. Jack had never once seen him in a good mood. To Jack he represented the growing number of mid-career officers being rapidly advanced due to the casualties of this war.

And then there was Thomas.

As the sole strike officer on board, he naturally stood apart from the rest of the wardroom, even though he chose to wear the blue coveralls of the Fleet rather than the green of the Corps. Among the fifteen officers on board, Thomas was quite possibly the oldest, making his rank of sublieutenant all the more odd. Most of the crew assumed he'd been commissioned from the ranks and thus gave him a wide, respectful berth. As the senior sublieutenant he carried the amusing honorific "Bull Sub" and was in charge of the herd, but his relationship with the other officers was more complex.

Jack munched away at dinner at the crowded wardroom table, listening idly to the usual banter between his peers, but without taking part. The XO was at the head of the table, eyes down as he wearily shoveled in food, but a spirited discussion had broken out between the anti-stealth warfare director, Lieutenant John Micah, and the supply officer, Lieutenant Ashley Kaneen. Jack gathered that they'd attended the Astral College together, but their friendly debate seemed focused on the inanities of line versus support rivalries.

"Hey, Shades," Sublieutenant Wi Chen piped in at Jack's side, "why don't we just get right to it. Between you and Pay, who's senior?"

John paused, glanced at Micah, then smiled indulgently. He was newly qualified in his anti-stealth director role, and he enjoyed the nickname "Shades" as *Bowen*'s hunter of the shadowy stealth ships.

"That's actually a good question. Ashley and I were promoted at the same time, so no advantage there. So really your answer comes from whether we're in battle or not."

"How so?" Chen asked.

"Think back to your ship organization req, subbie. In the functional organization, Ashley's a head of department and I'm just a director, so I bow before her."

Jack was intrigued by that. He was the head of *Bowen*'s flight department—did that make him senior to most of the line officers?

"But in the fighting organization, the line of command goes down through the bridge watchkeepers. So if something happened to the captain and the XO, if you'll pardon me, sir"— John nodded to Lieutenant Perry at the head—"then the senior watchkeeper takes command." He glanced up and down the table, populated mostly by subbies and non-line officers. "So if we here at this table were the only officers left alive, then I'd be in command."

"Not quite," Perry commented.

"Sir?"

"You forgot about Sublieutenant Kane."

John laughed. "My apologies. The line of command goes captain—XO—bull sub. Then the rest of us scrap it out below that." He gestured down the table to where Thomas was eating in silence. "My respects, Mr. Kane."

Amid the scattered laughter the XO put down his utensils.

"No," Perry said firmly. "In battle the line of command descends through all command-qualified officers first, then through the qualified bridge watchkeepers."

Silence descended. John cast a puzzled look up the table.

"Yes, sir, that's true…"

"And Sublieutenant Kane is, according to official records at least, command qualified."

Jack watched as half a dozen pairs of eyes whipped around to stare at his old colleague. Thomas didn't look up, trapping the last vegetables on his plate and popping them into his mouth. The XO returned to his meal with a scowl.

The silence extended into awkwardness.

"So what you're saying, Shades," Jack jumped in loudly, "is that most of the time Ashley can kick your ass all she wants."

John forced a laugh and turned his eyes back to the supply officer.

"Pretty much, Jack. I'd say that's par for the course."

The table conversation picked up again on other topics, and Jack forced himself to join in, getting the discussion moving as far away from lines of command as possible.

Jack stared at the clock on his cabin bulkhead for a third time. He'd almost managed his regulation eight hours of rest after the last sortie, and had intended this morning to get some admin done. Yet somehow he was due at the pre-flight briefing in ten minutes.

Slipping on his boots, he grabbed the warbags from their netting on the back of the cabin door. The emergency vacuum suit folded down easily into a pouch on the belt, next to the power unit and emergency beacon, but the helmet couldn't be compressed so he clipped it to his hip.

The flats were quiet. Now that *Bowen* was through the jump gate and patrolling Valhallan space, the crew were focused on their grueling watch routine, and few spent their off-time anywhere other than the mess decks. The stealth threat level was low, so gravity was still activated, but the cruiser was maintaining a constant ASW picket with her four Hawks. Very wise, Jack thought. Stealth ships were known to get very close to inattentive warships, and the first warning would be the detection of a gravi-torpedo seconds from impact.

Still, the captain had ordered that at least some training continue, and today that meant one of the subbies was riding in the Hawk for ASW familiarization. Jack walked aft from his cabin and knocked on the door of Club Sub. He opened the door, bracing for the smell typical of a junior officer mess. To his surprise, he was greeted by a pleasant, clean fragrance and a huddle of subbies gathered on the pair of couches just forward of the bunks.

Wi Chen rose to his feet, an excited smile playing across his face.

"Hi, sir," he said. "I'm ready."

"You don't have to call me sir," Jack said, sighing and stepping in to shut the door behind him. Not only were the subbies awake—that alone was astonishing—but they appeared to be engaged in a training discussion, tablets out and open to multiple references. Jack was impressed... and then he noted Thomas sitting back against the bulkhead.

"The XO doesn't like us addressing the lieutenants by their first names," Thomas explained. "He wants us to maintain proper wartime discipline. Sir."

"Yeah," Jack said, rolling his eyes, "but I'm a pilot. I don't count."

"What's the usual nickname for the head of the flight department?" Alex Celi asked, looking over at Thomas.

The bull sub thought for a moment.

"'Wings,' I think."

"Can we call you Wings?" Alex asked.

The only people Jack had ever heard called by that nickname were senior commanders of entire fighter squadrons, but if it would make the XO happy...

"Sure." He jabbed Chen. "But I'm going to be called late if you don't get your ass in gear."

Chen strapped on his warbags, and with subbie in tow Jack headed forward to the bridge. Usually he stayed clear of the ship's command center, as it was there that the line officers really became stress-monsters, but he truly did enjoy stepping onto the transparent deck and into what he sometimes called the sphere of the heavens.

The entire bridge was encased in a spherical, armored shell, and on the inside of that sphere was a permanent projection of the view outside the hull, cluttered with military symbols like the blue friendly that indicated the Hawk currently on patrol. He'd been told it helped the line officers maintain spatial awareness in the three-dimensional battlespace, but to Jack stepping onto the bridge was like stepping among the stars themselves. It was a better view even than what he got in his own Hawk.

These days each ASW mission carried a second qualified crew member, which not only reduced the burden on the pilot but also gave Jack someone to whom he could delegate his part of the briefing. Master Rating Singh was already set up by the command position at the center of the bridge, and she did an admirable enough job detailing the status of the Hawk. John Micah, who would be directing the mission from the bridge, then took over and briefed the rest of the ASW team, the two officers of the watch, and Jack.

It was a routine patrol, the latest in dozens since *Bowen* had arrived in theater, but Jack was pleased to see that John kept his tone professional, even going so far as to explicitly remind everyone that no mission was ever routine.

Briefing complete, Jack made his way aft to the hangar, followed by Chen and Singh. Upon arrival he conducted his walkaround of the Hawk, pointing out to Chen various critical things he watched out for among the craft's various engine ports, weapon fittings, and sensor arrays. Chen asked surprisingly intelligent questions—stuff Jack himself might not have thought of when he was a subbie.

As usual everything looked good, and the maintenance team helped them into their full spacesuits. The extra weight made climbing into the Hawk a nuisance, but it was just part of the routine, and soon Jack was strapped into his seat at the front of the cockpit. Master Rating Singh conducted internal flash-ups, and Jack scanned his checklist as he powered up the Hawk and brought his main systems on line. He found the routine almost therapeutic, clearing his mind of anything except the Hawk, and the mission.

As the Hawk rolled into the airlock and waited for decompression, Jack took a moment to study the navigation display and once again familiarize himself with the Valhalla system. It was a binary, but the two stars were so far apart from each other that they each supported full planetary systems with terrestrial and gaseous worlds. The Roman and Greek pantheons had long-since been exhausted by the time this system was explored, so the names from Norse myth had been given new life. The stars themselves were named Asgard and Vanaheim, with their respective planets named for the gods from each of those mystic houses.

Bowen was patrolling high above the ecliptic of the Asgard system, about halfway between the star and the Terran-built jump gate that led back to Sol. The Astral Force and the Army still maintained a presence among Asgard's worlds, but it was an increasingly perilous one as more rebel forces slipped past the blockade. The Centauris had constructed their own jump gate to Valhalla—indeed, to every colony—but the Fleet had yet to pinpoint the location of any of them outside of Terra. Most rebel incursions came from south of a system's ecliptic, but part of *Bowen*'s mission was to actively search for any signs of new jump gates here in the northern sector, as well as tracking for any suspicious vessels.

Once clear of the airlock, Jack felt his stomach churn as the Hawk thrusted clear of *Bowen*'s artificial gravity field. Zero-g was his least favorite aspect of ASW, but since the enemy hunted for gravity signatures, he had to forego it in the interest of survival.

He pushed his throttles forward and moved with speed to gain separation from his mothership. The view of the stars ahead didn't budge, nor did his astrographic position relative to Asgard and Vanaheim. The best reference point he had this deep in space was *Bowen* herself, and he watched as the cruiser tracked quickly astern. At his command Singh projected their patrol sector onto the display, and he adjusted course to aim for a far corner of it.

"Do you have a set pattern for patrol?" Chen asked.

"We have a few standard patterns, but we only use them when multiple Hawks are working in concert. If we were to start flying the same patrol patterns every time, enemy stealth ships would eventually get wise and use them against us."

"So you make it up for each patrol?"

"Unless I have something interesting I'm investigating, I fly on whim."

"Can I quote you on that?"

"Only after I've received my Terran Medal of Honor."

An appreciative snort was the only reply.

The tactical display was clear, the previous patrol having detected nothing of interest to hand over to Jack. He noted the inbound symbol of the other Hawk, Spinner-Four, as it left its patrol sector and began to approach *Bowen*. He watched the bird's progress for a few moments and, satisfied that all was well, returned his attention to his own patrol.

"So," he said to Chen. "Any idea what we're doing out here today?"

"Looking for enemy stealth ships."

"Always, but the stealth threat is considered low right now, so that actually isn't our primary concern. What else are we looking for?"

"Rebel ships trying to get close to the jump gate and cause trouble."

"Rebel warships?"

"Maybe, but lots of the colonies use converted civilian ships to do surprise attacks. Here in Valhalla it's quite common."

Smart kid.

"Any idea how we search for ships here on the brane?"

Chen thought for a moment. ASW detection gear was designed primarily to search deep into the Bulk, the fourth spatial dimension where stealth ships lurked, but while Jack knew how to manipulate his sensors for searches on the brane, he'd be very impressed if a line officer subbie knew.

"I heard a rumor in training," Chen said finally, "that just before the war started one of our pilots spotted a ship by eye, way out in deep Sirian space."

"Yeah, I heard about that, too. It's true, but it's not our standard technique."

"So… you use your ASW equipment in a different way?"

"Yup." Jack tapped the panel of hunt controls next to his right hand, then called over his shoulder to Singh. "You got the barbells primed for a brane search?"

"Ready to deploy."

Jack noted that his Hawk had entered the inner boundary of its search sector. He maintained course for the farthest corner.

"Sow the line."

Singh tapped to activate her controls. This was followed by a slow series of gentle thumps as the passive gravimetric sensors known as barbells fired from the Hawk. Within minutes a line of twenty were deployed, after which Jack altered course sharply and accelerated to open the distance. After a short sprint he cut the engines and deployed the Hawk's own main gravimetric sensor, called the big dipper.

"I've got my barbells positioned here," he explained to Chen, pointing out the features on his 3D hunt display, "and by placing us this far away, we should be able to crossfix anything of interest."

Chen leaned in to peer at the display. Jack watched patiently. Except for the symbols of the Hawk, the barbells, and the more distant *Bowen*, the display was completely empty.

"So," the subbie said finally, "anything interesting?"

"Nope," Jack said. "Tacs, you got anything?"

Singh, as tactical crew member, used the enhanced processing equipment to study the readings at a much finer resolution.

"Nothing big. I have a slight indication of bending from barbell one-zero, and possibly a complement from zero-niner."

Jack glanced at Chen. The subbie's face was blank.

"Our mid-line barbell is reporting a possible bend in spacetime," he explained, "and the next nearest sensor might be confirming that, but it's too weak to tell."

"So…" Chen looked back at Jack. "There might be a mass bending spacetime?"

"Might be." Jack checked his big dipper readings. "I don't have anything on our local sensors, but we're a lot further away. Whatever it is, it's small."

"Like a rebel ship?" Excitement was plain in Chen's voice.

"Or a comet fragment. But worth checking—it's not like we have anywhere else to be." He activated his voice link to *Bowen*'s bridge. "Windmill, this is Spinner-One. Poss-low brane contact, design zero-one, investigating."

"*Windmill roger,*" John Micah replied, "*nothing held here.*"

Jack brought the Hawk up to cruising speed and steered in the general direction of barbell one-zero, near the center of the sown line. He pointed his nose up to ensure adequate separation between his craft and the sensor line, knowing that these new generation barbells were sensitive enough to detect even his own Hawk, despite its tiny size and lack of artificial gravity. If he got too close to the line, his own presence might disrupt the readings.

He cut the engines and let the Hawk sail past the barbell line at a hundred kilometers, activating the big dipper again. After a few moments his hunt display lit up with a possible curvature, low and to starboard.

"Tacs, prep a rapid sow of five."

"Roger."

"Sow the line."

A series of thumps mere seconds apart indicated the new line of five barbells being deployed. Jack already was getting a sense of where in space his quarry might be, and he pushed the Hawk's nose down for another short, perpendicular sprint, easing closer to his original barbell line.

"Four of five barbells indicating curvature," Singh reported.

"Give me bearings," Jack said, even as he activated the big dipper.

His hunt display zoomed in, and four red bearings suddenly extended from the symbols of his new line. Lighter red cones appeared from the two barbells which had originally noticed the curvature, indicating direction based on the weak readings. The big dipper immediately reported curvature, and Jack dropped another line onto the display.

"Windmill, Spinner-One. Reassess zero-one as poss-high brane contact, request permission to go active."

"*Spinner-One, this is Windmill. Go active.*" There was excitement in John's voice.

At Jack's command, the big dipper fired a directional burst of gravitons at the area of space where the cluster of intersecting lines said an object would lie. If there was indeed something there, the gravitons would interact with it in a tell-tale way.

They did. Jack's eyes lit up as the report came back of an object matching the mass profile of a mid-sized spaceship. His eyes darted up to check the visual, then down to his flight controls and back to the hunt controls.

"Windmill, Spinner-One. Positive brane contact, assess prob vessel. Request permission to close and challenge."

There was a slight pause, and when John's voice came back, *Bowen*'s general alarm was sounding behind him.

"*Spinner-One, this is Windmill. Close target zero-one and challenge.*"

The contact had been upgraded to a target, Jack noted. The Astral Force didn't take chances these days.

"Countermeasures to auto," he ordered Singh, "I'm retrieving the big dipper." Jack eased the throttle forward as his main sensor retracted into the hull. With his right hand he flicked off the safeties on the Hawk's weapons.

"What's going on, sir?" Chen asked.

"Not now."

"*This is Windmill,*" John's voice reported on the encrypted channel, "*I am closing to support, Spinner-Four will launch in two mikes.*"

Jack did a quick calculation on his approach. At his current speed he'd intercept in seven minutes. The Hawk just returned from patrol would be ready to assist in two plus transit time… say six minutes. *Bowen* could easily engage a target from her current position, if required.

All things considered, he was covered. Switching his unencrypted voice circuit to standard civilian navigation, Jack focused the transmitter on his target.

"Unknown vessel, this is Terran warship Spinner-One at six hundred kilometers and closing. Identify yourself immediately, over."

The distant crackle of solar wind was his only reply. After a few moments he repeated his hail. Again no response. As he closed within five hundred kilometers he switched to his more threatening standard hail.

"Unknown vessel, this is Terran warship Spinner-One. I

am targeting you with military weapons. Identify yourself immediately or I will fire upon you, over."

He listened through the static for even the faintest of voice or beacon response. Nothing.

Spinner-Four had re-launched, he saw, and was rocketing toward him at high speed. The target was now only two hundred kilometers away. The barbells were detecting no accelerations or energy outputs—it was completely unresponsive. He repeated his threatening hail, adding the phrase he hated most.

"Unknown vessel, this is Terran warship Spinner-One. I am targeting you with military weapons. Identify yourself immediately or I will fire upon you. This is my final warning, over."

The Hawk carried short-range planetary missiles. Not ideal for space combat but effective enough at these ranges, against a soft target. Jack activated their seeker heads and locked onto the unknown vessel.

"Uhh, sir…" Chen said behind him.

"Not now."

"Sir, look!" Chen tapped Jack's shoulder and pointed ahead.

Jack's eyes snapped up to the visual, and immediately spotted a tiny section of blackness dead ahead where once there had been stars. Something was visible against the galactic background. He snapped down his helmet visor and locked on to where his eyes were focused.

"Tacs, ID this object!" The Hawk transferred to Singh's console the image captured by his helmet-cam. "Windmill, this is Spinner-One," he snapped. "Missiles locked on target. I have a distant visual—currently assessing."

"This is Windmill, roger. Stand by to engage target zero-one."

Spinner-Four was now within five hundred kilometers, low to Jack's starboard side, and reporting weapons lock on the target.

"Visually assess target as a warship," Singh said.

Jack activated comms to send the report, but stopped as Singh spoke again.

"Assess as *Terran* warship!"

Jack slapped his weapons safeties back on.

"All units, Spinner-One. Hold fire, hold fire. Reassess target zero-one as friendly zero-one. I say again, *friendly* zero-one!"

5

The reflection of yellow warning lights flickered off the dark surfaces of the strike team's armored spacesuits. Thomas completed his quick inspection of their gear. As usual his troopers were suited without error, and he nodded his approval to his second-in-command, Sergeant Bunyasiriphant, before turning to watch one of the Hawks rotating into position. The sergeant turned her attention to the line of eight troopers and began barking the standard pre-mission spiel.

A Terran destroyer had been discovered nearby, dead in space. Thomas and his strike team were going to board and investigate. A second set of warning lights flashed to life at the port-side airlock, and the doors began to slide open as another Hawk returned from the scene.

Bowen's XO, Lieutenant Perry, approached Thomas across the hangar deck, moving awkwardly in his full spacesuit. The emergency suits worn during battle stations only had a few hours of life support in them, but they were thin enough not to impede regular movement in the close confines of a warship. The full suits were designed for extended excursions into open space, and while much better at keeping their occupants alive for long periods, they were bulky.

The strike team's armored suits had servo assists to reduce their weight, if not their bulk, but Thomas was so used to wearing his now, he barely even noticed the soft whirrs as he stepped forward to greet the XO.

"It's *Toronto*," Perry said without preamble. "No power emissions, no life signs—but no obvious battle damage, either." The destroyer *Toronto* had been reported missing in action some months ago, Thomas recalled, a suspected victim of a lucky stealth attack. Since gravi-torpedoes usually left nothing but a thin cloud of plasma, no one had ever expected to find any wreckage. A fully intact ship, seemingly abandoned, made no sense.

"Did the lifeboats jettison?" Thomas asked.

"No." The XO, a man three years younger than Thomas, suddenly looked much older as the strain showed on his features. "This isn't going to be pretty."

Fleet personnel didn't see death up close and personal very often. Thomas felt his first glimmer of sympathy for the man who stood before him. Any XO had to act like a tough bastard in order to enforce discipline, and showing weakness was anathema to line officers in general. But the pressure was wearing on Perry.

"I'll give you a heads-up before you arrive," Thomas offered.

"We'll be on station within ten minutes of your boarding—don't search beyond what you need to in order to assess the threat."

"Yes, sir."

Sergeant Bunyasiriphant appeared at his side. She was tall, and her wiry frame was surprisingly strong. Small eyes against dark-brown skin revealed little, and after nearly a year of serving with her, Thomas knew almost nothing about her personally. But she was competent and loyal.

"Sir, our ride's ready."

The just-returned Hawk had rotated on the deck and was now pointed back toward the airlock, doors open for the troopers to climb in. He nodded farewell to the XO and followed his sergeant to the small craft.

He paused at the doors to let Wi Chen climb down. The youngster's face was flushed with excitement.

"Quite a famil ride, Chen?"

"I'm heading straight to the bridge to see how the rest of this goes!"

"Glad to be part of the entertainment."

Chen laughed as he stepped clear. Thomas climbed through the Hawk's airlock and squeezed past his troopers, who were in the process of snapping down the passenger benches on either side of the craft's main cabin. He stepped forward into the cockpit and patted Jack Mallory on his suited shoulder.

"Hey, Wings. What have you got me into this time?"

Jack glanced up, raising an eyebrow.

"Hey, Guns. I got you a dead friendly. Maybe we can salvage it and take command." It was a joke, Thomas knew, but it stung. Thomas took his seat behind Jack's right shoulder.

"Just get me there in one piece, Jack."

"Troopers ready," Buns called from back aft.

Thomas listened as Jack spoke quietly with flight control, and the Hawk rolled forward into the airlock. Just as they passed through the doors he glanced to starboard and saw that Spinner-Two had completed pre-flight checks and the second boarding party was loading up. The XO's job would be to thoroughly assess the cause of *Toronto*'s demise, but no one that valuable was setting foot on the destroyer until Thomas and his jarheads had made certain it was safe.

The Hawk was through the airlock quickly and flying free. *Bowen* had taken station off *Toronto*'s stern, ensuring that her own weapons arcs were maximized and the destroyer's were minimized, just in case there was a nasty surprise waiting. Reading Jack's 3D display Thomas could see Spinner-Four still patrolling at close range.

"We're going in as if hot," he said over his strike team circuit. "Sensors report no activity from *Toronto*, but the rebels have used local stealth fields before to hide defenses. Stay sharp."

"Where do you want to board?" Jack asked.

Thomas surveyed the charcoal metal of the destroyer's hull, searching for any signs of blast damage or weapons fire. As far as he could tell, the ship looked perfectly intact.

"The airlock at top-part midships," he said. With no hints, they might as well start at the middle and work outward. Jack maneuvered his craft smoothly into position, sliding to port to mate his airlock with *Toronto*'s hull. Thomas heard the usual series of clicks and hisses as the airlocks connected.

"Watch for gravity shift," he called out as his troopers started to push off their benches. "We're entering down into top-part."

Once the airlock was secure and atmosphere confirmed within the destroyer, the hatch was opened. Even in the cockpit Thomas felt his ears pop as pressure shifted rapidly, and he instinctively dropped his faceplate to switch to suit support. Jack did likewise, followed a moment later by the Hawk's tactical crewman.

"*This is Bravo-One,*" Buns reported over the strike circuit. "*Through the door. Zero-g. Atmo pressure low but breathable; oxygen content normal.*" So the ship had lost air, but in equal parts. That suggested a hull breach somewhere, rather than a fire or a chemical attack.

"*This is Alpha-One, roger. Proceed on suit support,*" Thomas ordered. Any faceplates that hadn't already been lowered snapped down. The eight troopers followed their sergeant through the airlock, and Thomas brought up the rear.

The interior of *Toronto* offered no gravity, and they pulled themselves along the short tubing "down" into one of the main corridors of the ship. Helmet lights danced across the black interior bulkheads as they spread out fore and aft along the passageway. Thomas checked his forearm display to ensure comms with *Bowen* were still clear, and spoke on the command frequency.

"Mother, this is Alpha-One. Touchdown, ops green. Environment at entry point is zero-g, atmo at seven-zero percent, temperature at"—he double-checked his display—"two degrees Celsius."

"*This is Mother, roger. No changes in power levels detected, assess your entry has triggered no responses.*"

Thomas glanced at his sergeant. She nodded her agreement.

"Alpha-One confirms, commencing standard search pattern." He switched to strike frequency. "All units, Alpha-One. Standard search procedure: Alpha Team to bridge, Bravo Team to engine room. Record and report on sight any signs of battle, of survivors, or casualties. Bravo-One, over."

"*Bravo-One,*" Buns replied. She immediately pushed her way aft as her team of four troopers formed up around her.

Thomas watched as his own lead trooper, Alpha-Two, took point and started moving carefully along the passageway, weapon pointed forward with one hand while the other grabbed at the regular handholds. Alpha-Three followed, and Thomas obediently stayed behind his designated bodyguard. Alphas Four and Five brought up the rear.

The helmet lights cast an uncertain, yellowish field of view ahead, but there was no doubt that they were moving along the familiar lines of a Fleet warship. Thomas felt unsettled as he watched so many recognizable landmarks appear out of the utter darkness. This didn't feel dangerous, he realized. It felt uncomfortable, almost as if something had been violated.

The bridge of a city-class destroyer was two decks down from their entry point and two frames forward. Alpha Team moved efficiently through the darkened spaces without incident or opposition. A single report from Buns indicated a similar ease of movement for Bravo Team toward engineering.

Thomas pulled himself through the airlock door of the second frame when he heard his leading trooper speak.

"This is Alpha-Two. I can see damage to equipment here… but it looks weird."

He could see the light cone of the trooper up ahead, no longer moving forward but scanning slowly along the bulkheads. Alpha-Three paused, but Thomas edged past him. The big trooper moved to stay at his side.

"Be more specific, Alpha-Two," Thomas said.

"Things are broken, but it doesn't look like battle damage. I don't see any blast marks."

Thomas floated up alongside Alpha-Two and shone his own helmet lights along the metal frames of the passageway. He also saw no sign of impacts, but firefighting equipment was floating half-loose from its brackets, and one corner of a bulkhead panel had ripped open. There was no damage behind the rip, just another layer of interior bulkhead.

He swept his lights around the passageway. Starting from about where he floated, and becoming more obvious as he continued forward, Thomas saw weakened fixtures, equipment missing from mounts and, eventually, the absence of handrails. Casting his light forward, he saw the end of the corridor where he knew the airlock to the bridge should be. In its place was a ragged outline of the frame opening, and darkness beyond.

"All units, Alpha-One," he reported on both circuits. "Mild structural damage sighted aft of the bridge, contained within a single frame and worsening as we move forward. From my position I assess the bridge will be significantly damaged. I am advancing on thrusters to investigate, over."

"*Mother, roger.*"

"*Bravo-One, roger.*"

With the handholds gone there was no way to move forward now without using his suit's thrusters, but they had limited fuel and didn't offer much speed. Thomas unreeled the safety line from his belt and handed it back to Alpha-Three. He pointed at the nearest handhold.

"Is that handle secure?"

Alpha-Three pushed over to grab it. With his powerful tug the handle snapped free of its base. The trooper's eyes were wide as he held up the broken metal.

"Try the next one back," Thomas said.

Three handholds aft, the troopers finally found secure anchors they could use to affix the safety lines for Thomas and Alpha-Two. Thomas motioned Alpha-Two to lead the way forward. Under thruster power, they approached the blasted opening to the bridge.

All Fleet bridges were contained within an armored sphere, designed to protect the ship's command center even from attacks which penetrated the outer hull. He'd spent years working in spaces like this one, but as he approached now, both his lights and those of Alpha-Two were swallowed up by darkness.

Alpha-Two entered the bridge first. Thomas watched as the trooper floated through the opening and swung the light mounted on his assault rifle. It moved in a swift, steady arc. Then the arc faltered.

An armored hand grabbed desperately for the frame.

It was out of reach, and Alpha-Two scrambled in mid-air, legs flailing and weapon arm tucking in close as he grabbed for his safety line.

Thomas locked his own line and heaved on Alpha-Two's taut safety wire. The trooper sailed back, thudding against the bulkhead as he grabbed hold of something solid.

"Report," Thomas barked.

Alpha-Two was close against the bulkhead, but to his credit he responded immediately, quick breaths punctuating his words.

"Sorry, sir. I lost my bearings. The whole thing's gone!"

Thomas unlocked his line and thrust forward carefully, surveying upward into the bridge from just inside the frame. What he saw made him reach down and lock his line again.

There was no bridge.

There was no central deck, no outer sphere of armor.

There was nothing but a vast, completely empty space bordered by the ragged edges of bulkheads and decks. Twisted remains of fixed equipment gave some spaces a nightmarish image, but most of the openings in the vaguely circular space were completely empty. Thomas spotted what looked like half the communications control room to port, and a pair of forward storage bays on the far side from his position.

Leaning to his right he realized he was looking into the very after end of what had been the captain's cabin. The dining table was still there, bent and twisted, but all the chairs were missing.

The bridge was gone, and he realized suddenly that everything near it had been pulled violently inward. No outer damage to the hull. No survivors. And this.

"Mother, Alpha-One," he said. "Recommend anti-stealth warfare condition red: attack imminent."

Any sense of boredom which might have settled upon *Bowen*'s crew was gone.

Thomas returned to the cruiser as the fourth and final Hawk was being prepped for launch, a full load of torpedoes and detection gear aboard. More people moved with purpose through the flats, floating instead of striding now that the AG was doused. All training manuals in Club Sub had been abandoned, replaced by tactical reports from the various theaters of war. The junior officers pored over them to look for records of similar incidents.

Thomas knew he should sleep, but his mind spun with scenarios on how the attack on *Toronto* could have played out. His subbies should sleep, as well, since they all had bridge watches to stand, but the excitement was fevered. All lights were on as they read reports and discussed what they found. He was hooked down into his usual corner of the big couch, watching as Chen floated freely, looking as if he wished he could pace. Alex scrolled through yet another list of reports, and Hayley absently munched away at a free-floating bag of fries.

He'd trained them well. There was a time to sleep and a time to focus, and these kids all seemed to know the distinction.

"I don't get how anyone could control a singularity," Alex commented. "Aren't they by definition beyond known physics?"

"No, they're totally possible," Chen countered. "We studied them all the time at the college. They just don't tell you artsies, so you don't go trying to order one from your engineering department."

"Did you make them in class?"

"No, but we weren't conducting stealth warfare, either—and from what I've seen so far, those ASW guys are mad geniuses. Like totally insane."

"*You're* fucking insane," Hayley growled, "just to have majored in physics in the first place." She was short and cute with bright-blue eyes, but she easily had the foulest mouth and worst temper of anyone Thomas had ever met. He liked that.

"What's so insane about ASW?" Thomas asked.

"Just the ability to think in four spatial dimensions," Chen said, excitement growing on his face as he started to maneuver his hands like ships. "Like with Wings, he dropped a line of barbells here, and with nothing more to go on than a curvature eddy any sane person would have dismissed as space dust, he cuts across here, drops another line—boom-boom-boom—and cuts over again to do the big dip. And voilà, we were sitting practically right on the target. Close enough that I could see it!"

"That's his job," Alex said.

"But I asked Master Rating Singh afterward what procedure Wings was using and Singh just threw up her hands. She said she's learned to go with her pilot's instinct, because it's never wrong."

"Jack *does* have a crazy ability to see the entire picture as a whole," Thomas acknowledged. "Some of the ideas I've seen him come up with—"

The comm panel chirped. Hayley reached for the headset.

"Club Sub—Sublieutenant Oaks." She listened for a moment, then glanced at Thomas. "Yes, sir." Another moment of listening, and she hung up. Blue eyes assessed him. "Somebody's in shit."

"Why?" he asked.

"You just got summoned to the CO's cabin. By the Old Man himself."

"What, right now?"

"Yeah, fucking jarhead, right now."

Thomas unhooked and pushed past Hayley and Alex.

"Get that out of my face," she said, smacking his butt.

"At least I didn't drop a line of barbells as I went past…"

He appreciated the laughter as he exited his little corner of subbie security and re-entered the real world. The captain wanted to see him. In a year on board, Commander Hu had *never* wanted to see him.

The CO's cabin door was closed and the do-not-disturb light was shining. Thomas buzzed for entry. The door opened immediately, and he spotted the CO hooked down at the head of a briefing table in the center of the large space. Every seat was occupied by members of the second boarding party. The XO and Chief Ranson flanked the captain, both looking up indignantly at the interruption.

"Mr. Kane," Commander Hu greeted, gesturing him forward, "please join us. Chief, continue."

Thomas pushed himself over and hovered discreetly, listening as Ranson carried on with a discussion concerning the engineering systems in *Toronto*. To Thomas's surprise, the destroyer was salvageable, although without a functioning bridge it would likely have to be towed home. The captain surveyed his table of guests grimly.

"Good work, everyone. That'll be all."

Hu was a man of few words. Perhaps ten years Thomas's senior, he'd already been long in his command of *Bowen* when war broke out. During the initial panic of the rebel attacks, it had been Hu's order which had seen the newly demoted Sublieutenant Kane assigned as a crisis replacement to *Bowen*'s strike team. Over the past year, though, he rarely addressed his strike officer directly, and never had he invited Thomas to his cabin.

Yet as the assembled team unhooked themselves and pushed away from the table, Thomas saw Hu place a hand on the XO's arm, the other hand rising to motion Thomas to take a seat. Hu gave him a bland expression that somehow carried frightening authority.

Thomas hooked into the chair Ranson had just vacated, and listened as the door shut behind the last of the departing group.

"We're breaking off to continue our patrol," Hu said quietly, "but we'll leave a secure beacon here, in case anyone decides to return. XO, how much time do you need to set that up?"

"No more than thirty minutes, sir," Perry replied.

"Make it so." He turned deep-set eyes to Thomas. "What's your take on the damage to *Toronto*, Mr. Kane?"

"It looks like a gravi-torpedo, sir, but I've never seen one that small or precise."

"Because there aren't any," Perry snapped. The captain ignored his XO's comment, and after a moment of silence, it seemed as if Thomas was being invited to continue.

"The damage pattern clearly shows a violent force directed inward toward the center of the bridge," he added, "and the complete lack of debris suggests a singularity which destroyed everything within a certain radius."

"You've seen this before?"

"No, sir, but I've been in a ship which had a near miss with a gravi-torpedo. The way it pulled us, I'd expect to see this sort of damage."

"That's right," Perry muttered. "There isn't anything Sublieutenant Kane hasn't seen."

Thomas dropped his gaze, pushing down anger. He was just a strike subbie now, he reminded himself firmly. Arguing with a cruiser's XO wasn't what strike subbies did.

"Sir," Perry continued, "our scans indicated no unusual gravimetric readings."

"It could have faded by now," Hu replied.

"Even this many months later, there would still be some evidence of a singularity."

"How do you know?" Thomas blurted out. "We've never seen anything like this before."

"Because my last staff job was at the ASW school on Astral Base Four, Mr. Kane," the XO replied, "and before that I was an ASW director. I don't recall seeing any ASW experience in your files. Or did I miss something?"

Thomas pursed his lips together, biting down his reply.

"Stay focused, gentlemen," Hu said.

"It might have been a regular torpedo which failed to activate properly," Perry offered.

"I don't think so, sir," Thomas said. "For one, the target is too precise—that singularity was placed directly in the center of *Toronto*'s bridge. For two, if a regular torpedo had misfired, we'd have found some evidence of the rest of the crew. Either they would have taken to the lifeboats, or they would have been killed in the attack. Each of those scenarios would have provided us clear evidence which just isn't there."

"The same thing goes for your mini-torpedo, Kane," Perry snapped. "Where are the survivors? Or did your magic weapon suck up all the crew and leave the rest of the ship intact?"

That was a good point, Thomas conceded silently with a nod.

"Perhaps, then," Perry suggested, "it was some kind of singularity bomb planted before the ship left port."

Hu turned at that, expression newly thoughtful.

"Why not just blow the entire Astral Base, then, XO?"

"Perhaps they wanted to test it small scale, away from any large gravity wells."

"The Centauris are nothing if not patient," Hu mused. None of the other rebellious colonies really mattered in this war. Centauria was the leader—both technologically and politically— and it was their culture which Terrans needed to understand best.

"XO, sweep our ship for any gravimetric anomalies," Hu ordered suddenly.

"Yes, sir."

"Any other recommendations?"

"Maintain our augmented ASW status," Perry replied immediately. "While I may not agree with Mr. Kane's assessment of the attack, there may be a higher stealth threat in this sector than Intelligence suggests."

"Mr. Kane, your recommendation?"

Thomas started. He was being asked to give a command recommendation. Perry's face darkened, he noticed, but the XO remained silent.

"Inform Astral Command of the incident, sir, and recommend that all future patrols consist of at least two ships. *Toronto* may have been vulnerable because she was alone. Others might be, as well."

6

Out in deep space, far from any of the planets, the only way to guess where in the solar system you were was to look at the sun. If it was big, relatively speaking, you were among the rocky inner worlds. If it was small, you were in the realm of the gas giants.

This single reference point always told Katja that Astral Special Forces Headquarters was somewhere in the inner solar system, but otherwise she had no idea of its coordinates—and that suited her fine. As an operative she was at highest risk of capture by the enemy, and the less she knew about her own organization, the better.

Simplicity of knowledge was her new best friend, in fact. Although she was a member of the most sophisticated intelligence organization in Terran history, and could herself tap into the Cloud at any time, she'd found that the less she kept tabs on the worlds—the less she thought—the easier her job became.

She was an amoral instrument of the State, and the State told her everything she needed to know to do her job effectively.

Since her last mission she'd had more than a week of downtime. As she slipped on her boots she absently glanced around her quarters, making certain everything was in its place. Her eye caught a rogue plate on a side table next to the couch, the remnants of a snack the previous evening. She collected it up and placed it in the washer. SFHQ would have provided someone to do her cleaning, but she preferred to be responsible for her own quarters.

These five rooms were her own private empire, her sanctuary. She maintained complete control over them. It was a coping mechanism to counter the madness of an operative's life, but it worked and she was happy.

Her front door slid open and she stepped out onto a wide, stone terrace, breathing deeply, taking in the soft cool scents of the trees, the water, and even the stone itself. She strolled forward to the wide railing and gazed down at the park below. Many hectares of well-tended grass stretched away, dotted by natural clusters of trees and broken by meandering paths and gardens blooming in vibrant colors. A stream bisected the entire park, widening into a pool bordered on one side by sand and on the other by a wooden gazebo.

A brilliant panel of white light shone down from the dark ceiling of the cavern, its angle indicating mid-morning as it cast its shadows across the landscape. There were people scattered throughout the park, some enjoying the landscape while others worked quietly at maintenance.

Katja took a moment each day just to take in this vista, thankful again to the State for taking such good care of her. Then she turned and strode along the stone walkway, past doors which fronted the quarters of other operatives, toward the lift which would take her to the briefing rooms. It was time to start working again.

On the terrace she saw only one other person, a fellow operative named Shin Mun-Hee, and beyond a smile and a nod there was no need for further communication.

At least, until Shin decided to speak.

"Hi, Katja. Still on vacation?"

"Actually," she said, glancing down at her military issue coveralls, "I'm just heading back to work today."

"I heard about the Centauri spy—nicely done sniffing him out." Shin was quite a bit taller than Katja, but the way she looked down always suggested more than just a difference in height. Even her compliments sounded ever-so-slightly superior.

"Thanks. One less spy for us all to worry about."

"Shame you couldn't take him alive—I'd love to have deconstructed his mind."

"He was a legitimate target," Katja said, feeling a familiar anger start to rise. "My orders were clear."

"Yes, of course, and you're very good at what you do."

The subtleties of wordplay had never been Katja's strength, and not even all her augmentations had made her feel any better equipped for this sort of combat.

"We all have our strengths, Mun-Hee," she said, and she started walking again, quickly reaching the lift. When it arrived, she found herself sharing it with a maintenance tech she'd seen before. He was about her age, and quite handsome in an intelligent way. SFHQ staffed their facility with the very best of Terran citizens, and Katja was reasonably certain that intelligence and skillset weren't the only requirements for his employment.

However, the lift arrived at her floor before she could figure out how to engage the tech in casual conversation. Still, she tucked the idea away for future exploration.

The operational level was hard and metallic, with square corridors and soft artificial light which cast no shadows. Uniformed personnel strode by purposefully, nodding politely to her and staying clear of her path. Katja felt her entire mindset shift, as dormant parts of her brain activated, and she sifted through the gentle waves of information on Terra and the colonies.

The door to Briefing Room Three loomed on the right. She mentally transmitted a clearance request and the door hissed open in response. Inside, seated at the large conference table, was her frequent mission partner, Suleiman Chang.

He nodded to her in greeting, deep-set eyes giving only a glint of comradeship in his otherwise stoic expression. His broad features were plain, his skin the common, deep brown of so many humans. It was his size that made him stand out in a crowd, and even seated his vast bulk dominated the space. They had led a strike team and a platoon together at the outbreak of the war, and had forged the kind of fellowship considered necessary for an operative team.

"Good morning, Katty," he rumbled.

"Morning, Sules. How long have you been back?"

"Ten days. It's been nice. I finally tried out the climbing wall."

"We exercise enough by decree—why would you choose to do more?"

"Would you rather hear me sing?"

Katja's main form of recreation was to polish her skill as a coloratura soprano. She eyed him up and shrugged.

"You might have a wicked bass hiding in that barrel chest of yours." His features shifted marginally into what she'd come to recognize as amusement. Other than a slight dip of his eyelids, he offered no further comment.

The door hissed open again, revealing Brigadier Alexander Korolev, the head of Special Forces. Katja instinctively rose to her feet and heard Chang doing the same.

"Relax," Korolev said, waving them back to their chairs. He sat across from them, glancing at each of them with his usual, mild expression. "Are you ready to receive?"

"Yes," Katja said, and Chang echoed her reply.

She withdrew those parts of her mind which had been surveying the information flow, and focused her attention on the commander. He began with high-level data, framing a scenario, then drilled down deeper into specifics. Katja queried when necessary, asking multiple questions along different paths and listening to Chang's questions while still receiving the main feed.

Korolev seemed to partition as he addressed multiple questions simultaneously, drawing connections between dispersed facts and revealing the patterns of the situation. It was enough to require a three-hour briefing, yet in real time it took about ten seconds.

Katja sat back, feeling sudden tension.

Centauri spies were still active in Terra—no surprise there, since espionage was their most effective weapon—but a changing pattern was emerging. They were becoming more aggressive against Terran soft targets, focusing on key figures who supported the war behind the scenes. Two wealthy businessmen with large government contracts had recently died under mysterious circumstances, and an accident had befallen a senior advisor to the Minister of Defense.

Any bureaucracy was vulnerable to inertia and incompetence, if not properly led and directed by key individuals. Now the

Centauris seemed to be trying to cripple the Terran government by removing those who kept it functioning effectively.

Disparate sources suggested where the latest Centauri cell was operating, and another attack was expected soon, this time against a senior advisor to the smallest Parliamentary party in the government coalition. A lucky intercept of Centauri data had given an exact time and place. At least two agents were involved, although how they planned to carry out their assault remained a mystery.

Katja and Chang were assigned to protect that advisor, a middle-aged woman named Sarah Goldberg, and capture or kill the Centauri spies.

7

Mars loomed large in the cockpit screens as Katja strolled forward from the main cabin. The pilot was engaged in routine chatter with orbital control, identifying them as a courier ship from one of the major Jovian delivery companies. She stood behind his seat and cast her mind out, getting used to the style and flow of the Martian infosphere.

People spoke faster on Mars than they did on Earth, using words much more efficiently and wasting little on pleasantries. They weren't abrasive or rude, like the majority of Mercurians, but they spoke and wrote as if they were constantly in a rush. Life moved fast on Mars, and the society prized efficiency. Born of the first colonists to survive on this once-hostile world, their dedication to precision and conservation had built the undisputed industrial powerhouse of Terra.

Off to both sides of the shuttle, thousands of lights moved within and through the orbital control zone. The distant bulk of Astral Base Two was visible near the edge of Mars' ruddy horizon, the security zone around it noticeably clear of traffic. Military sensors reached out from the base, linking into a ghostly web that included the discreet satellites orbiting around the entire planet.

No less than seven Fleet warships were active in planetary protection, and even at this altitude she could hear the routine transmissions from atmospheric sentries guarding against surface incursions.

Only once had the rebels attempted a surface attack on Mars. They had breached several points in the outer walls of the city of New Longreach, and the resulting depressurization had done more damage than any weapon. Those Centauri war machines which survived the blasts had run loose for weeks before they were all hunted down. The civilian death toll had been tremendous—so much so that Special Forces concluded that another rebel attack on Mars would be unlikely.

The Centauris, more so than any other colony, abhorred civilian deaths. No, Katja thought as she returned to the main cabin and took her seat for landing, the military aspects of war had moved back into space—the surface was now the battleground for spies.

Chang glanced up at her. He wore nondescript, slightly shabby civilian clothes, looking the part of a laborer who couldn't afford to care about his appearance. She'd colored her hair brown and cut it back to an efficient length that didn't quite reach her shoulders. She wore an inexpensive pant suit typical of any mid-level shopping concourse, with high heels and a large bag. Her role was to be a middle manager who dreamed of one day being a senior manager.

The descent through the thin Martian atmosphere was always smoother than on an Earth-like world. A few subtle bumps gave encouraging hints to the slowly increasing air density that centuries of terraforming had achieved, but no human could survive outside the pressure domes for long.

The shuttle passed through one of the airlocks and settled down within a large commercial hangar. As the cargo door opened and a Special Forces team carried on their charade of delivering courier packages, Katja grabbed her bag and headed for the passenger door on the side of the vessel.

"See you at the RV," she said quietly to Chang. He nodded, staying in his seat as planned to allow for a clear separation of their departures from the ship.

Katja stepped down to the hard floor of the vast hangar, breathing in the faint chalkiness of the air unique to Mars. All of the oxygen in the human settlements was produced artificially, but enough of the actual planetary atmosphere got mixed in to give Martian air its distinctiveness.

Listening with her ears to the bustle of a civilian port, she discreetly searched for any surveillance devices. There were the obvious ones installed by the port authority, of course, but a passive EM sweep looked for anything else that might be actively investigating her brisk stroll toward the security gates. Nothing was focused on her, but she did notice an unusual scanner on one of the freighters to her left. Glancing casually toward it, she noted that its corporate markings suggested an origin on Triton, and captured an image. Turning her eyes forward again, she packaged the image with her sensor data and stored it for later.

The security lines to enter the city of Ares were as long as usual, and she passed the time first by scanning all the personal IDs of the people around her, then by hacking into the Martian border security system to look for any signs of unusual activity lately. Centauri spies were very good at covering their tracks, but Katja had learned to search for a specific structure in data packets.

The Centauri Cloud technology was much more sophisticated than standard Terran, and very occasionally she would find something which had an architecture far too complex to be legitimate. The enemy was incapable, it seemed, of dumbing down its own technology entirely.

There.

Three days ago, a woman had entered Mars through the main passenger terminal at Olympus Mons on a seven-day tourist itinerary. Katja traced the name, Paula McGee, back to her home on Ganymede and searched her record. It was clean, unremarkable, and entirely believable. That she had no spouse, children, or siblings gave the first indication of a false ID, and when Katja looked underneath the data itself, she saw the tell-tale sophistication of Centauri insertion.

She'd found an enemy spy. No telling yet if it was the person she was after, but further analysis should determine that. She glanced up with her eyes, noting that she'd almost reached the security counter, and retracted her links. She'd need to play the innocent State functionary for the next few minutes.

Then it would be a long ride on public transit to her reserved quarters. She was confident she'd have found her target by the time she met Chang at the RV.

The pink sun shone through the translucent upper walls and ceilings of most of the city, augmented by artificial white light that faded to orange as the orb dropped toward the dusty horizon. Centuries of human existence on Mars had created an interior environment which produced a tremendous likeness to nature, but it was still just a likeness.

Chang's utility bag rustled behind her as he shouldered it and followed her across the plaza. The tram had carried them through one of the close-in connecting tunnels, but the dome enclosing this cluster of buildings soared above them now. It was far from the largest dome in Ares, only stretching far enough to contain the frontages of the buildings. Each of those extended out into the Martian landscape. There were small commuter shops clustered near the tram stop, but otherwise the artificial floor was interrupted only by the carefully spaced trees in their individual pots. Katja spotted the modest entrance to the Ministry of Industry building and motioned for Chang to follow.

The guards outside the building watched them with vague interest as they approached. Only the time of day made their arrival unusual—few civil servants actually worked at this hour. So Katja pursed her features into a frown and offered a State-issue tablet with a message displayed brightly on the screen.

"Data Manager Watkins," she snapped in a typical Martian accent. "There's a series of faults causing intermittent link breakage within the unclass system. We need to watch it when the network's quiet, so"—she jerked a thumb back at Chang—"we're going to start this evening."

Choosing the unclassified system meant no additional security checks would be required, and data management maintenance was generally considered just about the unsexiest thing in the world, unlikely even to be remembered the next day.

One of the guards looked at her tablet, then checked his own forearm display. His eyes lit up when the corresponding confirmation appeared.

"How long will you be?" he asked.

She shot a look back at Chang.

"Hopefully less than two hours," Suleiman replied.

"Hopefully *much* less," she growled, taking back her tablet.

The guard indicated for them to enter. "You know the way, I assume?"

"Yes," Katja replied, already past him and through the doors.

As they had anticipated, the building was quiet. The only sounds were their soft footfalls and the jangle of Chang's tool bag. Katja scanned the network around them, and Chang did likewise. She quickly isolated a pair of terminals active on the third floor.

<Our prize is working late,> she commented through the Cloud.

<As expected.> Chang's ghostly voice whispered in her mind. <I love it when intel gets things right.>

The "prize" was Sarah Goldberg, the State official they were here to protect. She was busily reading messages, responding to some and forwarding others to a person who occupied the office beside hers. An executive assistant, most likely.

Katja suddenly felt a momentary sting in her ribcage. She glanced back at Chang and returned a signal of her own. He nodded. Both of their entanglement implants were functioning normally.

Someone had tried to explain the physics to her once, and she thought she understood it. Both she and Chang had been implanted with tiny devices, each of which held a group of individual elementary particles. Each set of particles had been entangled, and then separated in such a way that they were held in isolation from the rest of the surrounding environments.

Because the particles were entangled, what happened to one set would affect the other, and vice versa—instantly and no matter how far apart in the universe they were. Albert Einstein had first called it "spooky action at a distance," more than five hundred years ago.

It gave the two operatives the ability to keep tabs on each other's bodily status, to the point that each would know instantly if the other was alive or dead. Every time a signal was sent, however, that entangled pair of particles "collapsed" and could not be used again.

They boarded an elevator and, after a swift rise, the door opened and they stepped out onto the third floor. The corridor was at half-light, a broad, square window at the far end shining pale pink in the last flames of the sunset beyond. She reached out to sense for any surveillance equipment, while Chang found the network maintenance closet and stepped inside. She heard the soft clink of "tools" as he began assembling them into a pair of energy weapons. She would have preferred something more traditional, but State buildings employed scanners that could detect the unique inner mechanisms necessary for modern projectile weapons.

At least their opponents would be equally disadvantaged.

As Chang expertly constructed the weapons, he tapped directly into the network to begin a rapid sweep of the building. Katja activated her quantum-flux and walked slowly along the corridor, scanning a pair of offices. She saw the forms of the two people, each at a desk, and the quantum glow of their terminals. A single, thin wall separated them, but it was likely that there was a door open between the two rooms.

<There's movement of the elevator,> Chang reported.

Katja turned and slowly retraced her steps, switching to infra-red. The hot elevator shaft blazed, as did the air ducts which pushed new air to these outer offices in an eternal war against the Martian winter. It swirled in a maelstrom of eddies, some funneled upward into the office of Goldberg's assistant, while the rest fluctuated along the duct and toward the corner room. There seemed to be more turbulence than was necessary, and she turned, walking slowly back toward the window as she studied the flow of heat in the ducts beneath the floor.

Something wasn't right.

<Katja, the elevator.>

Her ears picked up the whoosh of the door sliding open and the rattle of a hovercart being pushed out and turned sharply in the corridor. It was guided by a middle-aged man, thinning gray hair, strong frame clothed in a cleaning staff uniform. In no way a fit to the description of the Centauri target, but her instincts still pushed her into fight mode.

She winked off infra-red and strode toward the cleaner.

"Who are you?" she demanded. <Male, south Asian,> she reported to Chang, still in the closet. <Mid-age, strong.>

The man stopped between the elevator and Goldberg's suite. He looked up in surprise, but quickly brought a smile to his face.

"Good evening, ma'am," he said amiably, glancing at the insignia on her work uniform. "Working late tonight?"

She didn't slow, trying to close the distance. Chang still had both of the energy weapons. Five paces to go.

"Are you authorized to be here?" she barked, watching his expression carefully. His eyes widened, but not with the sort of fear she'd expect from a low-pay civilian.

<Poss high target,> she reported.

<Roger,> Chang replied, <tracking.>

Just as she reached the hovercart, the cleaner reached down.

"Hands up!" she shouted.

His right arm began to rise.

She dropped to a crouch and slammed her shoulder into the hovercart. It surged forward into the cleaner. She heard his feet stumble backward, and then the thump as he fell to the floor. She pushed the cart toward him, spotting an energy pistol in his hand. Launching her weight off the cart, she hurled against the door to the suite, grunting as it snapped open and she sprawled across the floor.

Scrambling forward, she stumbled as a burst of fiery pain exploded in her leg. Falling to her knees she rolled to clear the doorway, coming up against the desk and spotting the wide-eyed face of a very young man in a suit, half-risen from his chair behind the desk.

Energy blasts hissed in the corridor behind her. With her good leg she vaulted across the desk and tackled the man, taking them both down as his chair crashed away.

"Police emergency," she hissed as she lay on top of him. "Stay down."

He nodded weakly.

She pulled herself up, peeking once over the desk before ducking down again. The firing had stopped.

<Suleiman!>

<Target contained,> Chang replied.

She hauled herself up and limped to the open door into Goldberg's office. Her left leg was unable to take any weight. She looked down and saw the blackened flesh of her calf mixed with the charred tatters of her suit leg. Her body had shut down all pain receptors to allow her to focus, but she wouldn't be in the action for much longer.

Sarah Goldberg had abandoned her chair for the floor, and her eyes were barely visible over the solid wooden desk top.

"Senior Advisor," Katja called out, "this is a police emergency. Please stay down."

"Who are you?" Goldberg answered in a frightened but still commanding voice. Katja propped herself against the doorframe, rapidly scanning the room. The walls were secure, no surveillance kit, no hacks detected on Goldberg's network. Two large windows formed the corner, and through them the last pink glow of sunset was fading beyond a dark landscape.

She switched to quantum-flux. All clear. She switched to infra-red. The river of heat sweeping along the air duct below the floor was moving smoothly. In fact, she noted suddenly, there was hardly a ripple. The hot air was plumed unhindered into the room, and from within the plume, a figure emerged.

<Strike on prize!> she roared into the Cloud.

"Goldberg," she shouted, "behind you!"

The woman turned and raised her arms in defense at a figure leaping in her direction. Katja broke into a run, stumbling as her left leg collapsed beneath her. She caught her own fall and rolled up into a fighting stance, just as a blade struck down and Goldberg screamed.

An energy blast sizzled into the dark form, enough to stop another stab. Chang came charging in behind her, but even as a second blast hissed forth, the assassin hefted Goldberg's slumped figure as a shield. The energy scorched through the prize's clothes and burned into her back.

Katja charged forward, only to collapse again. Her skin was slick with sweat, her breath coming in quick gasps. She couldn't feel the pain, but her body was suffering.

Chang's massive form leapt into the air, taking both Goldberg and her attacker in a flying tackle. The floor shook as all three slammed down. Katja scrambled to the desk and pulled herself up in time to see Chang on his feet, grappling with a much smaller form in what was clearly a black pressure suit. The helmet was clear on three sides, and Katja caught a glimpse of the woman's snarl as she took a step back and braced against Chang's push.

Through blurring vision Katja realized what she was seeing. This woman, not much bigger than her, was fighting Suleiman Chang in a test of strength, and winning.

A sudden surge by the enemy knocked Chang back on his heels. She wrenched her hands free, recoiled into a perfect side kick to his midsection. Chang was knocked clear off his feet, crashing against the far wall.

The assassin turned to Katja, eyes burning with murderous intent. She pulled the blade free of Goldberg's limp body and stepped forward.

<You're next, Emmes.>

Katja heard the malice in the voice even through the Cloud. She struggled to hold her defensive fighting stance, favoring her uninjured leg. Alarms began sounding in every room, indicating a security alert on the third floor. Chang pulled himself to his feet.

The Centauri's eyes flickered between Katja and Chang, then toward the doorway. With a snarl she stepped back, rearing to deliver a kick to one of the picture windows. The glass cracked on the first impact.

Katja dove to the floor and clutched the solid leg of the desk. The sound of another crack was followed by an ominous shattering. A breeze began to blow, transforming in seconds to a torrent of air as the pressurized room bled out into the Martian atmosphere. Katja hung onto the wooden leg and shut her eyes, pulling her suit jacket over her face in a desperate attempt to trap a last gasp of air.

A metallic slam brought the windstorm to a sudden, silent halt. Katja glanced up and saw that the safety barrier had activated and sealed over the breach. Her lungs burned as they gulped in as much oxygen as they could, but she forced herself to let go of the desk and roll across the floor.

Sarah Goldberg was dead. Of that there was no question. The body lay almost within arm's reach, but Katja made no move to examine it. Instead she struggled to her hands and knees to regard Chang, slumped against the wall, hands clutching the handles of an emergency fire equipment station.

<Suleiman?>

He moved a hand, although his eyes didn't open.

<Here.>

<Can you walk?>

<Probably.>

<I can't.>

His eyes snapped open. She shifted her leg to reveal the burn. He looked off toward the outer office and frowned.

<Authorities are here. Act like the damsel in distress and I'll carry you out.>

She hadn't heard anything, and suddenly realized that her entire world was silent. She lay back down and touched fingers to her ears. There was blood on both sides. As Chang loomed over her and scooped her up in his arms, she saw that his ears were bleeding, as well.

A group of guards appeared and poured into the room.

<Remember,> he said, <you're the damsel in distress—look weak and injured.>

<Easy,> she said, letting her body go limp.

In the chaos around the death of Goldberg and the unconscious Centauri "janitor," the young assistant made it clear that Katja and Chang weren't the assassins, so most of the police ignored them as they slipped out into the corridor. One armored officer did a quick medical check, and escorted them down to one of the ambulances in the central dome.

Chang placed Katja onto a stretcher and heaved himself up next to her in the back of the ambulance, firmly dismissing any attempts by the medic to assess him.

"Take care of her leg first," he growled, pointing at the mangled calf.

<She knew my name,> Katja said, staring up at Chang. <My real name.>

<Not good,> he responded, eyes on the medic who was

expertly applying anti-burn dressings. <Once we're clear of this scene, we'll take control of the ambulance and disappear. Until then, just relax.>

The mission had gone to shit. Their prize was dead and the enemy had escaped. Katja wanted to get angry, wanted to give chase to that Centauri bitch, but her injured leg was completely unresponsive and she doubted she could even walk. Chang slumped in the seat as the ambulance swayed along the roadway, and was probably much more badly injured than he was letting on.

But he'd been doing this for years. He'd get her clear, she knew.

He always did.

8

The hangar was bustling with activity, even though only a single Hawk was present. Thomas walked against the bulkhead, keeping clear of the craft as it swung around to face the airlock through which it had just landed. Even before the ramp had lowered, the ground crew began their efficient movements to rearm and resupply it.

He gave the crew a minute to do their jobs on the bird, ignoring the restless shifting behind him as his strike team waited impatiently. Like him, they wore their armored spacesuits, loaded with weapons and extra ammo. Everyone was still haunted by the dark, empty tomb that had been *Toronto*—now they had the chance to stop that from happening again, and they wanted to move *now*.

Finally, the flight chief waved at the troopers to approach. Thomas stepped off in his heavy suit, hearing the steady thumping of his team moving in single file behind him. He clambered up into the Hawk, passing the newly installed benches in the main cabin and nodding to the young operator seated at her side console.

"Master Rating Singh," he said.

"Sir," she murmured, unable to hold his gaze as her eyes swept over the armor and weapons piling into her ship. Thomas stepped forward and tapped the Hawk's pilot on the shoulder.

"Hey, Wings," Thomas said. "Captain wants to get my team over to *Singapore*—looks like the rebels are trying to board her."

Jack barely glanced up. He cycled through a series of displays on his console and tapped in quick commands.

"Okay." He leaned over his shoulder to make sure Singh could hear. "I've tasked Spinners Three and Four to cover. I'm going to do a straight, fast approach, no jinking, and get the strike team locked on. What entry point do you want?"

His words were so clipped and efficient, it took Thomas a second to realize the question was aimed at him.

"Top-part midships."

"Your team strapped in?"

Thomas glanced back to the main cabin. All the troopers were squeezed down on the benches. Buns gave him a thumbs-up.

"We're ready to go, sir."

Jack nodded and initiated departure procedures. The Hawk began to roll forward into the airlock even as Thomas took his own seat behind the pilot's right shoulder. The flashing lights of the hangar gave way to the muted airlock, and then finally to the starry blackness of deep space. Thomas felt the gentle push as the Hawk thrust clear of *Bowen*.

Then he gasped as Jack threw open the throttle and hauled to port. The view ahead swung and then straightened with a hard jerk, and Thomas saw his distant target—the Terran destroyer *Singapore*. Flashes indicated anti-attack fire, most likely to keep the pack of rebel ships at bay. The line officer in him immediately began assessing the symbols on Jack's 3D display, and experience suggested that the Hawk had a clear run to target.

That could change quickly, he knew, but it wasn't his problem. *His* problem would be the rebel troops fighting their way through *Singapore*'s interior.

The dark form of the destroyer loomed against the blackness. Thomas gritted his teeth and gripped his seat as the Hawk decelerated and moved to a hover next to the hull. Jack nudged his bird in, clamping to the destroyer's airlock.

"We're secure," he said.

Thomas unstrapped from his seat and floated into the zero-g environment, noting that his troopers were already moving to open the Hawk's side airlock and make room for Buns to glide through. She activated the controls and did so.

"*This is Bravo-One,*" she reported on the strike circuit. "*Entry point clear. Gravity in place, full atmo. No hostiles.*"

"Deploy," Thomas ordered.

"I'm going to lift off," Jack said as the troopers began moving through the airlock. "I'm too much of a target here, and I reckon you don't need an escape route like you usually do."

Thomas's strike instincts screamed at him to maintain the extraction point, but he knew Jack was right. Better to have the Hawk nearby in one piece, rather than splattered across *Singapore*'s hull.

"Agreed," he said. "Just don't stray too far."

"I got your back."

He patted Jack's shoulder and moved to follow his troopers. The Hawk's tactical operator, Singh, offered him a nervous smile as he passed.

"See you soon," he said, giving her a friendly wink. Then he swung around to slide feet-first into the airlock, feeling the destroyer's gravity field tug at him and create a "down" as he dropped through the tubing and thumped onto the deck.

His rifle was up to the guard, and he swept his eyes both directions down the familiar-looking passageway. His troopers had spread out behind what little cover was afforded, also watching both directions. The way aft was sealed off by an airtight door, but the route forward was much more exposed. The nearest exit had been buckled and torn free of its structure. Further ahead, another door had been blown completely out of its combing.

There was pounding and clanking in the distance.

Buns activated one of *Singapore*'s bulkhead panels to display a diagram of the ship's interior.

"Mother, this is Alpha-One," Thomas said on the command circuit. "Touchdown, ops yellow. Ready for orders, over."

"*This is Mother,*" Bowen responded, "*tactical control of your team is now shifted to callsign Raffles on this circuit. Break. Raffles, go.*"

"*This is Raffles actual,*" a new voice replied on the circuit— the captain of *Singapore* himself. "*My crew are in lockdown at their battle stations, mostly unarmed. The enemy force is currently contained on deck four, but they are breaking through our frames and moving forward."*

Thomas studied the destroyer's layout on the display. The enemy was on the same deck as they were, six frames forward. If he could get access to one deck below, he could easily outflank them, but the ship was completely locked down.

"This is Alpha-One, roger," he said. "Request access to hatches... 47F and 42D to position my troops."

"Roger, we'll unlock hatches 47F and 42D."

Thomas signaled his troopers to close in on him as he strode forward. Hatch 47F loomed in the deck ahead.

"Alpha Team with me," he ordered, "going down a deck and positioning ourselves forward of the hostiles. Bravo Team will hold position here until we're ready, and then hit the hostiles from astern." Buns nodded, and he scanned his troopers for any questioning looks. There were none. "Open that hatch," he ordered.

Moving through, Alpha Team dropped to deck three and hustled forward. Thomas linked his forearm display to the helmet-cam of Alpha-Two up front, but kept his own eyes up to stay focused on one heavy step after another. It almost felt like an exercise, running in full armor through the familiar, well-lit passageway of a Terran warship. It was a dangerous illusion, he knew.

Alpha-Two reached hatch 42D and headed up the ladder to wrap armored hands around the handle, waiting for the order to open it.

"All units, Alpha-One," he said on the strike team circuit. "Don't be fooled by our familiar surroundings. This is not an exercise. This is not a simulation. We are engaging actual hostiles and there are actual friendlies around. Watch your fire. This is a Terran warship, and we want it to stay intact."

He heard a deep chuckle beside him, and glared down at the grim amusement on Alpha-Three's face. Then he motioned for the hatch to be opened.

The moment it did his team scrambled up the ladder back onto deck four, and moved toward the sealed door that lay aft. It was still intact, but the first blast to loosen it had already warped the top starboard corner. He could hear taps against it as the hostiles prepared another charge.

"All units, this is Alpha-One, in position. Bravo-One, over."

"*Bravo Team in position*," Buns replied.

"Faceplates down," he ordered. "Assume vacuum conditions."

Switch freq.

"Raffles, Alpha-One. We are go to take hostiles, over."

"*This is Raffles. Take hostiles.*"

Switch freq.

"All units, Alpha-One. Alpha Team will commence the strike. Watch your fire—only shoot if you can positively identify the hostile."

Thomas raised his rifle, reaching for the grenade launcher. A Terran warship door was designed to take a heavy pounding before it gave way. If he wanted to surprise the hostiles, he needed an overwhelming first strike.

"Alpha Team: target the door, one grenade each."

Four more rifles lifted up, troopers settling into crouches.

"Fire."

Even through the filtered audio of his helmet, the blast was deafening. The pale gray metal of the door vanished in a fireball that swept through the passageway, boiling over Alpha Team before vanishing into the sudden clouds of thick, chalky smoke. Thomas staggered at the force of the blast, but kept his feet and followed his troopers into the fray.

Even before he stepped over the twisted wreckage of the door he spotted the first dead rebel, reinforced spacesuit shredded by multiple scraps of charred metal. A pair of shots rang out ahead. He saw a heavy splash of red against the deckhead as the result of one of the impacts.

"*This is Bravo-One*," he heard on the circuit, "*visual on Alpha Team.*"

"*Visual on Bravo Team*," Alpha-Two replied. "*Hostiles clear.*"

"*Bravo Team clear.*"

Thomas did a quick sweep of his position at the destroyed door. Through the smoke he could make out nearly a dozen bodies splayed around him. None of them were moving.

"Alpha Team clear," he reported.

His troopers emerged like golems through the blasted passageway, weapons swinging slowly over the dead hostiles as they checked for life signs. Thomas scanned the scene again, reassuring himself that the battle was in fact over.

Just like that, it was over.

"Raffles, Alpha-One," he said on the command circuit. "Hostiles neutralized. Strike team assessing damages."

"This is Raffles actual. Roger, Alpha-One, victor-mike-tango."

Thomas smiled. The Astral Force had a saying, *Line officers eat their young.* And while it was usually verbal abuse toward the subbies, it also showed in the reluctance of line officers to acknowledge good work done by others. The coveted "bravo-zulu" was often cited as the highest compliment a line officer could pay anyone—dating back nearly a thousand years to the signal flags sent between sailing ships.

But a "victor-mike-tango"... Translated as "very many thanks" it was reserved as a personal message of appreciation from sender to recipient. If he hadn't been a line officer himself for nearly twenty years, he doubted he'd have understood the depth of gratitude *Singapore*'s CO had just displayed.

Thomas scanned the bodies near him, then stepped back through the shattered door to give his troopers room. He listened as the captain made an update to his crew over the main broadcast, indicating that the internal threat had been eliminated. Even so, the attacking rebel ships still posed real danger to *Singapore*.

When Buns reported to him that the bodies had been secured, Thomas found himself strangely lacking in orders. He passed on the report to *Singapore*'s command team and requested further instructions. Word came back that the rebel ships were still harassing *Singapore* and *Bowen*, and that a Hawk transfer would be unsafe. With nowhere else to send them, the strike team was told to report to the hangar.

Alpha-One was invited to report to the bridge.

Thomas ordered his team to report to the hangar, then told Sergeant Buns and Alpha-Three to join him. If any more kudos were going to be handed out, Thomas wanted *some* of his troopers there to receive it.

Movement through the destroyer was slow, as every airtight bulkhead had to be opened and then resealed. With the ship at battle stations, the main passageways were deserted. Thomas and his troopers passed only one trio of *Singapore* crewmen, wearing emergency suits with helmets strapped to their waists. The trio gave Thomas a wide berth and hurried on their way.

Singapore's bridge was much like any other—smaller than *Bowen*'s, with fewer consoles and crew, but the basic format still seated the captain and officer of the watch in the center, with the three warfare teams positioned around them.

Thomas weaved his way forward and stood before the center chairs. The captain was looking the other way, in conversation with his anti-attack warfare director, but the officer of the watch nodded to the troopers. Thomas saluted.

"*Bowen* strike team reporting, sir."

The captain turned, and Thomas saw for the first time the face of *Singapore*'s commanding officer. His stomach twisted in a sudden vortex of emotion as Commander Sean Duncan's face lit up in recognition and surprise, then a smile spread across his face.

"So that's where you've been hiding for the past year."

He glanced at Thomas's suit, and Thomas breathed a silent prayer that it carried no rank insignia. He'd made his peace with his demotion and banishment, but meeting a career-long friend and peer… it still hurt. He and Duncan had done their initial line officer training together, and had maintained a friendly rivalry for years. When last they'd met, Lieutenant Commander Kane had been leading the race over Lieutenant Duncan.

Oh, he realized with a sickened heart, how much things could change.

"It's good to see you again, sir," he said aloud. "Congratulations on your command."

Duncan reached down a hand, which Thomas gently shook in his armored glove. Thomas's two troopers looked confused at the friendly exchange.

"I had no idea you were back in the Corps," Duncan said. "Or that you jarheads had created some sort of elite unit." Then a sudden flurry of symbols on the bridge sphere stole his attention. He barked commands and Thomas watched as the swarm of rebel ships scattered under *Singapore*'s defensive fire. Duncan turned back.

"Wasn't I lucky to get boarded when you were nearby," he said, glancing down at Thomas before watching his display again.

"Just doing our job, sir," he replied carefully. He glanced instinctively at the nearest display, looking for the hostiles and *Bowen*'s relative position. "As soon as you tidy up the mess outside, we'll get out of your hair."

"Looks like the rebel ships are starting to pull back. On their previous swarm attack, one of them looked like it was trying to clamp us, but then one of your Hawks engaged it point-blank with missiles. Ballsy move, Thomas."

"Spinner-One?"

"Yeah."

"That's our boy Jack Mallory, sir. Still as crazy as ever—and a lieutenant, now." Duncan nodded with no small amount of pride. He'd been Jack's first XO.

"I trained that cocky, talented little punk, turned him into something useful, it seems."

"I was happy to finish the job, sir."

Beyond Duncan, flashes of fire erupted from the rebel ships. *Singapore* easily deflected the desperate attack and Duncan gave the order to back off, putting distance between his ship and the enemy. *Bowen* was inbound at speed and was already taking over the front line of defense.

"I can't believe how quickly these kids are growing up," Duncan mused. "I guess war does that. Bloody war and sickly season, eh, Thomas?" The old naval toast, wishing for senior officers to die so that there'd be promotions all round. The entire conversation was getting very uncomfortable.

"I should head back to the hangar, sir," Thomas said suddenly, "so that we're ready to depart as soon as there's a window for the transfer."

"Great to see you, Thomas. I'll look for you when we're back in Terra—what's your home unit?"

Thomas was already turning to go, but the innocent question stopped him. Again he saw his troopers watching him, and knew that truth was the only answer.

"*Admiral Bowen*, sir. We'll see you back home." He shooed Buns and Alpha-Three ahead of him, and kept walking even as he heard Duncan give an order to the officer of the watch.

"Contact *Bowen* and arrange for a transfer of Commander Kane and his team as soon as the hostiles disengage."

Buns' eyes snapped over to him. He forcibly gripped her suit and kept her moving.

"Keep walking, Sergeant."

9

The Hawk's hull shuddered again, but this time Jack heard a sharp *bang* beneath him. Atmo pressure warning lights started flashing and he slapped down the faceplate of his helmet. The moment of silence gave him a chance to take a single, deep breath, then the suit's audio system connected directly to the Hawk's computers and his ears were awash in alarms.

"Windmill, this is Spinner-One," he signaled as he plunged his stick to starboard, "I am aborting my approach to hostile one-seven."

The small rebel ship fired another volley at him as he veered away, but otherwise didn't pursue. In his display Jack could see the cluster of rebel craft forming up in a protective perimeter around the one he'd just nailed with missiles. Not enough to destroy it, but enough to divert the rebels away from their main target for a few minutes.

He assessed his own craft. Losing atmo, one engine down, empty of missiles and low on fuel. There was nothing more he could contribute to this fight.

"Windmill, this is Spinner-One. I am heavily damaged and empty weapons. Request immediate recovery."

"This is Windmill, roger. We're closing Raffles to cover so no set course. Just get close and we'll pull you in."

Jack acknowledged, pushing his single engine to maximum as he cleared the battle zone. *Bowen* was ahead, visible only for the constant flashes of weapons fire she lobbed into the fray of rebel ships swarming the Terran destroyer *Singapore*. Her weapons would be far more effective than the Hawk's had been.

Bowen was approaching at speed, so her relative distance to the Hawk shrank surprisingly fast. Jack steered wide for a few seconds, then reversed his turn to swing through a long arc and come up behind his mothership. Flashes of battle lit up the starry darkness ahead, but Jack focused on the charcoal-colored bulk of the cruiser as he matched vectors and sailed into a recovery position alongside the open hangar airlock.

Feeling the tug of the ship's gravity beam, he killed his engines, letting the computers do the final work of pulling his Hawk into the barn. As it settled on the deck and the airlock pressurized, he finally let go of his controls and sat back in his seat, taking another deep breath.

"That one was nasty, eh?" he said into his internal circuit. Singh didn't reply. Jack didn't blame her, and took another few moments to focus on slowing his heart rate down.

The inner airlock doors opened and the Hawk was pulled through. The hangar looked very empty, Jack noted, with all three other birds still out in the action. He hoped they were doing better than he had. Unstrapping from his seat, he pushed himself up, swinging around to face Singh.

The master rating was still motionless in her chair, strapped in and staring at her controls, but her arms were floating free, hands open and limp. Almost...

Jack thrust himself over to Singh's seat, staring into what he suddenly realized was an open helmet.

...Lifeless.

Singh's face had barely had time to register the shock before her life was swept away by the slug which had penetrated the Hawk's deck and shot up through her chair, her torso, and out through her head. An exit blast out the top of her helmet matched the hole in the Hawk's deckhead, through which he could see the bright lights of the hangar glaring through.

Jack floated back, shutting his eyes tight against the sudden tears. What a fluke shot, and what a waste of an excellent human being.

A hard series of thumps against the hull startled him, until he realized it was the maintenance crew requesting entry. He released the airlock controls and also lowered the aft ramp. They were going to need some heavy equipment in here.

The first of the crew floated in, dressed in the emergency vacuum suits of battle stations, bright expressions greeting him.

"Hey, sir," one of them said, "you took some damage on that one."

He lifted his faceplate and stared numbly back at them.

"Singh's dead. Get the chief up here, and get a body bag."

Without waiting for a response he pushed clear and out the open ramp into the hangar. It wouldn't do to have the flight department head burst into tears in front of his men.

The fueling crew was already hooking up and turned to address him, but he waved them off. Another pair of techs guided a rack of replacement missiles up to the wings, and he gestured for them to stop.

"This bird is grounded for repairs," he called out loudly enough for everyone to hear. "Secure that gear and start your damage assessments."

His maintenance chief floated over, grabbing the edge of the Hawk.

"You okay, sir?"

"Yeah, thanks," he lied. "I better report to the captain."

"Recommend you tell the XO, too, sir—he's just forward of here in DCC."

Jack floated forward into the main passageway and quickly found the hubbub of the damage control center. A crowd of engineers manned a series of displays with various flavors of holographic depictions of *Bowen*. Many red symbols on those displays—accompanied by steady chatter into headsets—suggested there was a lot of damage control underway. Prior to deployment Jack had seen a large group of spare crewmen lined up against the forward bulkhead, on call to go wherever extra bodies were needed to shore up damage or replace downed operators. Now only a few very junior crewmen floated nervously in silence.

In the center of DCC, floating tethered in front of the largest display, Jack saw the XO. Lieutenant Perry's back was to him, but even from here Jack could see the sweat glistening in beads on the pale skin, a drop or two breaking loose as the man gestured sharply toward different crisis points on the diagram.

Keeping clear of the crowd, Jack slid along the after bulkhead and then pushed across the open space toward the XO's station. He thudded into the end of the main display, catching a surprised look from Perry and, beside him, Chief Ranson.

"XO, sir, flight commander," he said without waiting for comment.

"What is it?" Perry shifted his gaze back to the damage control board.

"Spinner-One is recovered, but inoperable. Unknown repair time. One casualty."

Ranson shook his head, his jowly face sagging in regret. He turned and spoke quietly to one of the engineers. Jack noticed the status board change to indicate one of the four Hawks was now red for operations. Something changed on the section dedicated to the ship's medical teams, as well, but Jack didn't pay attention.

Perry paused, looking over for a moment, then turned back to his display. His eyes moved quickly to take in the info, but Jack could see a blankness in the expression. Finally, the XO's lips pursed in frustration.

"Chief, how does that affect us?" he asked.

"It doesn't, sir," Ranson replied. "The bird'll be parked and"—he turned menacing eyes toward Jack—"I *assume* not refueled or rearmed."

"That's correct," Jack responded.

"No additional risks from the broken Hawk, sir."

Perry nodded, still scanning his display. He tapped a nervous finger against his lips.

"I'm still worried about that hit we took on deck five. If they don't secure that breach, we're going to lose the compartment."

"Sir—"

"...*and* we'll lose too much air. They're taking too long."

"There's an entire damage control team doing structural repairs. It'll be complete as soon as the last of the panels are brought aft from stores."

"That's the delay, then," Perry snapped. "Get two more bodies down there to help transfer the panels."

"Yes, sir." Ranson turned and growled at one of the engineers. The situation was tense, and Jack had nothing more to contribute.

"I'm heading to the bridge to brief the CO, sir," he said.

"Very good," the XO replied, still not looking over. Jack pushed off and cleared DCC, hugging the bulkhead again as a pair of youngsters from the manning pool were given orders and sent scurrying forward, snapping on their emergency helmets and activating their vacuum suits as they did.

Jack was still in his full spacesuit and he wasn't worried about exposure, but the damn thing made it difficult to move easily down the flats in zero-g. Either Commander Hu anticipated an imminent stealth attack, or the ghost of *Toronto* was still spooking everyone.

He passed through the airlock that led to the bridge, quickly tethering himself to one of the anchor runners inside the door. As he moved into the open space the tiny runner slid magnetically up the inner surface of the sphere, tracking with him and keeping his tether clear of all the others.

The view in the sphere was both spectacular and frightening. Ahead, Jack could see the dark shape of a Terran destroyer, blue symbol naming it as *Singapore*, and weapons fire lashed out from every turret and battery. Red symbols revealed the invisible shapes of the swarming rebel craft—little more than Hawk-sized, in Jack's guess, but each packing a wallop with their energy and kinetic guns.

Flashes in the corners of his vision indicated *Bowen*'s fire, but the tiny enemy ships were proving hard to hit. Elsewhere in the sphere he saw three more blue symbols—his Hawks—as they kept clear of the fray and maintained an ASW guard.

Pulling himself along the railing, Jack made it to the command station where the CO was strapped into his seat and the ship's combat officer, Lieutenant Gillgren, stood beside him as officer of the watch. Hayley Oaks, as second officer of the watch, was hooked to her station immediately forward of the command chairs. All around them, the arced panels of the circular bridge were alight with activity and manned by calm professionals. The quiet of the bridge stood in stark contrast to the chaos of DCC.

Hayley glanced up at his approach, but went immediately back to her console. He moved into the CO's view.

"Captain, sir, flight commander."

Hu looked down at him sharply.

"Jack, are you hurt?"

"No, sir, but I lost Singh, and Spinner-One is inoperable—multiple hull breaches and only one engine."

"Not inoperable, Wings, but not ideal. I've tasked Spinner-Two to collect our strike team."

"Yes, sir."

"Stay on the bridge. I might need you."

"Yes, sir."

Hu looked up and past Jack again, eyes on the battle raging outside. He spoke quietly to Gillgren, who in turn spoke into his headset. The view of the starscape shifted as *Bowen* altered course. Jack instinctively grabbed for the handrail, even though the inertial dampeners protected everything inside the hull and carried them with the ship through space.

He looked around at the bridge crew. Anti-vessel warfare was to starboard of the captain, and that crew were frantically engaged with the ship battle. Anti-attack warfare was forward, and all stations were primed to repel anything the rebels threw at *Bowen*. Anti-stealth warfare was to port, and all was quiet among those consoles. Jack glided over to where John Micah floated at his director station, in the center of the ASW section. Wi Chen hovered behind Micah.

"Gents," Jack greeted. "How goes the battle?"

"Nothing in our warfare area, although we're maintaining threat condition yellow."

"Are the Hawks tracking anything?"

"No. There was that sniff of something two hours ago—that's when we started closing *Singapore*—but nothing's been detected since, by either ship or any Hawk."

Jack nodded.

"But we don't want the brane attack," John continued, and he gestured forward at the ship battle, "to be a distraction in case there actually is something. So we're maintaining yellow."

Jack nodded again. A destroyer like *Singapore* wasn't designed to fight a battle on all three fronts at once, but a cruiser like *Admiral Bowen* was designed to do *precisely* that. Maybe that's why things were so calm here on the bridge.

"How's the brane battle going?"

John considered, glancing up at the sphere projection before reflexively bringing his eyes back down to his ASW displays.

"Not great, but not bad, either. Those little rebel ships are hard to hit, and they're really pressing *Singapore*. They can do damage, as you found out, but not enough to really hurt either warship."

"The XO was pretty concerned about a hull breach on deck five."

"Oh, yeah?" Micah glanced at Chen inquisitively.

"One of the rebels charged us," Chen replied, "and put some holes in the main cave. It's a big space and we lost some air before containment fields kicked in, but damage control's on it." He shrugged. "Talking to second officer of the watch, command doesn't seem too fussed by it."

The main cave—or crew's cafeteria—was hardly a critical space for the ship's ability to fight. Jack wondered at the XO's concern. Or perhaps over-concern.

"Maybe if the slugs penetrated the beer machine…" John smiled. "But the biggest concern we'd have then would be a mutiny."

Chen couldn't quite subdue his laugh.

Jack didn't share their mirth, but the easy rapport suggested that the battle was going well, at least from *Bowen*'s point of view. A flash of light from behind him suddenly illuminated the faces of his colleagues.

"Got the bastard," John said.

Jack turned and saw a blinking red symbol disappear amid the last glitter of an explosion. One of the rebel ships had finally been destroyed. Moments later, he saw the vectors of all three remaining hostiles alter together and disengage from *Singapore*.

Pulling himself back to the command station, Jack guessed that the disposition of his Hawks was likely about to change. He eased up to Hayley, who was exhaling loudly.

"Holy fuck," she said, "that was intense."

"What's the status of the Hawks?"

"Can I have a fucking moment to catch my breath?"

She was smart, he knew, but way too much of a line officer for his liking.

"No, subbie," he replied. "We're still at battle stations, so do your fucking job."

She glowered down at her displays, bringing up a flight status board for him to see.

"All three Hawks are fully operational. Spinner-Two is departing *Singapore* with the strike team, and the others are maintaining close ASW picket."

He turned to look up at Commander Hu, just as the combat officer announced over the broadcast to secure from battle stations.

"Captain, sir, flight commander."

"Captain."

"Recommend we recover Spinner-Two and prep her for a later ASW patrol. Based on the current threat level, I recommend we maintain Spinners Three and Four on station until I can assess the damage to Spinner-One."

"Very good."

Jack glanced at Hayley, who nodded and began issuing orders into her headset to the Hawks and the hangar maintenance crew.

All around the bridge, crew members began shedding their emergency vacuum suits and stuffing them back into their warbags. Jack actually started to feel a bit silly in his bright white spacesuit. He was about to depart the bridge when he saw the XO making his way into the spherical space. Perry's face was flushed and shining, but he was smiling. He swiftly pulled his way up to the command station.

"Captain, sir, XO. Hull breach on deck five is fully contained. No other damage to report," he nodded at Jack, "other than Spinner-One currently inoperable."

"Very good, XO."

"Shall we schedule the evening briefing for thirty minutes from now, sir?"

The combat officer paused in his movement to unstrap from his seat.

"You still want to have an evening brief, XO?"

Perry's smile faded into a hard line.

"Yes, Combat. Even amid the chaos of a war patrol, we can still maintain our regular routine. In fact, it's essential that we do so. Discipline and routine shall not be compromised by the effects of fatigue or adrenalin."

Lieutenant Gillgren looked as if he disagreed, but he held his tongue. Jack glanced at the captain, noting just the briefest flicker of impatience as it crossed his stony features.

"The XO's right," Commander Hu said, loudly enough for everyone to hear, "but honestly, tonight, I think I'd personally like to skip it. Number One, just have the section heads each report to my cabin when they have a moment."

"Yes, sir," the XO said.

The group broke up at that point, with the XO departing, Hayley burying herself in her duties at the console, the combat officer turning the watch over to John Micah, and then gathering the other two warfare directors off to the side for a debrief. The captain stayed in his chair for a few minutes, stoically observing the scene around him. Jack figured he should probably be somewhere himself, but he was content to simply float in his warm spacesuit and watch the line officers scurry.

Once he seemed satisfied with the status of his realm, the CO unstrapped and climbed out of his seat, informing John that he'd be in his cabin if needed. Hayley glanced up from her station and watched the captain's retreating form.

"The XO wanted a fucking evening brief," she muttered up at John. "Does he want spiffy dins after that, and a parade in the hangar tomorrow morning?"

"Shut up, Hayley," John said, his tone mild.

She shook her head and looked over at Jack.

"What's up, marshmallow man?"

Jack couldn't help but laugh, realizing just how stupid he must look in his spacesuit.

"Ms. Oaks," John said with mock seriousness, "I require you to say 'what's up, marshmallow man, *sir*.' Discipline and routine shall not be compromised by the effects of either fatigue or adrenalin."

"Yes, sir," she snorted.

"So it's okay if I just sleep here?" Jack asked.

"If we can bounce you around the bridge like a beach ball," John replied, "sure."

Jack took hold of the railing and started moving for the airlock. The playful banter of line officers never went away, not even after the stress of battle, but it was more than he could stomach right now.

"Have a good watch, kiddies."

10

As he made his way aft through the ship, Jack kept clear of the damage control teams and their cleanup. It looked as if nearly every piece of emergency equipment had been pulled for use. As he passed through each frame Jack had to weave around crew members stuffing halon hoses back into racks, replacing emergency breathing kits, securing fire extinguishers and carrying unused breach panels back to storage.

At least the hangar was in good shape. As he entered the wide space Jack realized that he'd really begun to think of this part of the ship as his own domain—not one which he owned so much as one for which he was responsible. There were four fully kitted Hawks and their crews who put their lives in his hands, and a team of twenty maintenance crew who took direction from him without question. As Spinner-Two was shunted into its parking bay and technicians climbed over the damaged Spinner-One, he thought of all the sensors and weapons his department commanded, all the resources of war entrusted to his hands.

Yet he was just Jack Mallory, barely six months in rank and not even two years out of flight school.

"Hey, Wings!" He heard a familiar voice behind him. "You can take your suit off any time." Looking over his shoulder was fairly pointless with his big helmet blocking the peripheral, so Jack turned fully around. Thomas Kane was regarding him with a wry smile, out of his armored suit and coveralls matted with sweat.

"I've been busy," Jack said simply.

Thomas moved forward and reached for his right glove.

"Let me help you get out of this. Your team will want to air it out."

With Thomas's help he struggled out of his suit, by which time his maintenance chief had floated over and was ready to take possession of it. The chief gave him a sad smile.

"We're all glad you made it back, sir." He hesitated for a second, then added, "Singh wasn't your fault. Just bullshit bad luck, sir."

His flight crews trusted him with their lives, none more so than those who flew with him.

"Thanks," he whispered. The chief retreated, spacesuit bundled in his arms.

"First time losing someone?" Thomas asked.

"No," he said, "but first time losing someone to bullshit bad luck."

"Yeah, those hurt for a long time."

Jack glanced over at his companion. Once upon a time Thomas had been his XO, and briefly before that his captain. He was the rare kind of line officer who led with grace and courage, and now he'd been dumped in the garbage by the Astral Force and banished to lowly security detail.

"War sucks, Thomas."

"Tell me about it."

"Do you still keep a bottle of scotch in Club Sub?"

"Not after the kids found it. You think Hayley's rude now, you should see when she's loaded. Chen just giggles, and Alex likes to dance."

Jack smiled at the image. "So it's all gone?"

"Yup." Thomas motioned for him to follow. "But I think I might have some in the strike storage locker."

Strike storage was across the flats from damage control. Jack quickly followed Thomas in through the reinforced door. The space was crowded with racks of weapons and gear, not least of which were the ten armored spacesuits floating in their netting like massive dark corpses. There was a single trooper in the process of counting items on a shelf.

"Hey, Collins," Thomas said. "How much more do you have to check?"

"I'm about halfway, sir."

"It can wait. Go get some chow and finish up after. I'll guard it for you."

A surprised smile lit up the trooper's features. He locked down the open shelves, stowed his tablet, and slipped past, slamming the door shut as he went.

Thomas floated behind a desk stuffed into the forward end of the space and unlocked one of the drawers. He pulled out a bottle of dark amber liquid and a pair of bulbs, filling them skillfully despite the handicap of zero-g. Jack accepted one of the bulbs and hefted it ceremoniously.

"To Master Crewman Daisy Singh."

"A good woman," Thomas toasted in return, "taken too early."

Jack sipped at the plastic straw, coughing as the liquid burned his throat.

"It takes practice," Thomas laughed. "Sip easy."

Jack took a deep breath, only to cough again as the fire in his throat crawled up his nose. Through the hacking he compared himself to his composed, serene companion, and his coughs gave way to laughter.

"Honestly, Thomas, this is the story of my life. I don't know how to do anything well, because everything's always new. I'm such a kid..." He flicked at his lieutenant's rank insignia in disdain. "...but they seem to think I'm this boy genius who can handle anything."

"Most officers in the Fleet—and the Corps for that matter—wish for their entire career to have your problem."

"You didn't," Jack said. When they'd first met, Thomas had been a rising star.

"No." He took a sip of his scotch. "And look where I am now."

"With all respect, that's hardly an inspirational speech."

Thomas stared up at him, his face a hard mixture of amusement and thought.

"Is that what you want right now? Inspiration?"

"You've been in command, Thomas. You've led troops and ships into battle. I'm just a junior department head, and I'm struggling. I'd appreciate *something*."

Thomas sipped again, paused, then nodded.

"You're not struggling because you're incompetent in your job, Jack. You're struggling because you care."

"What?"

"The chief was right. Singh died because of bullshit bad luck. It had nothing to do with your skill or your decisions at that moment. You didn't do anything wrong, but Singh was a nice lady who didn't deserve to die, and it's eating at you because you care."

"Who says I didn't do anything wrong? Were you there?"

"A single slug happened to hit a weak spot in your hull, and who knows where those develop, with the kind of pounding your birds take. Unfortunately there was a living person in its flight path. How many hits have your Hawks taken over time, Jack? Hundreds? And every other hit has been absorbed by the hull or impacted against non-living matter."

"Yeah, but we were in pretty close…"

"Your Hawk is designed for close combat—it has those armor plates the Fleet slapped on six months ago. You were doing your job, which was to go into harm's way."

"I was actually bailing at the time."

"Because"—Thomas gestured at him to emphasize his words—"you knew it was a bad idea to proceed, and there was no value in risking yourself, your crew, or your bird. You did the right thing, but bullshit bad luck finally struck."

Jack nodded, dropping his gaze and taking another sip. It didn't burn so much this time.

"It's just… I got a whole department of people who are relying on me, now, and I'm one of the youngest in that entire hangar."

"I haven't heard a single complaint."

"Like they'd tell you. Everyone on board is scared shitless of you."

"It's useful."

"Do you ever doubt yourself?"

"Sometimes, but never in the moment. That'd be the quickest way to get people killed. You?"

Jack considered.

"Never in the cockpit. On the ship, hell, all the time. But never when I'm flying."

"Good." Thomas sucked more scotch into his bulb. "You're a great pilot and a smart kid. All this leadership stuff will come to you in time."

"So I'll grow out of my incompetence, then?"

Thomas laughed. "You care, Jack, and that's the most important part of leadership. It means you'll watch out for your people and you'll find the smartest way to accomplish your missions." He reached for Jack's bulb and refilled it.

Jack took another pull. The scotch was going down smooth, now. He glanced around at the racks of trooper gear. It was a world he'd never wanted to see again, after his obligatory summer of strike training at the Astral College, but his career as a pilot never seemed to take him far away from it.

"Do you think Katja cared?" he asked suddenly.

Thomas looked up at him in silence.

"As a strike commander," Jack persisted. "Do you think she cared about her troops?"

Thomas stared at his bulb for a long moment, then blinked a couple of times.

"Yeah, I think she cared. Way deep down."

"I miss her. She was kind of crazy, so I guess I'm not surprised she died in combat, but I still miss her. Terra could use a few more like her."

"You guys were good friends, after all that, weren't you?"

"Yeah, we were." He looked down at Thomas. "How come you two never got together?"

"Because I'm an idiot."

Jack laughed out loud. "I'm pretty sure that's what she always thought I was. I guess she didn't understand my boyish charms."

Laughter rumbled from Thomas's chest. Jack took another sip, enjoying the warm peace and quiet. Through the bulkhead he could faintly hear the last of the damage control equipment being stowed.

Thomas must have heard it too. He gestured toward the distant sounds.

"Now the XO, *he's* struggling because of incompetence. He's overwhelmed, but he won't accept any help."

"I didn't think XOs were allowed to ask for help."

"Anyone can, Jack. Even captains. It's just a matter of knowing how and when to do so."

"When I was in DCC earlier, I saw the XO ask Chief Ranson about the impact on the ship of my Hawk being grounded."

Thomas rolled his eyes.

"That's proof right there that he's overwhelmed. Even Chen would have known that a Hawk parked safely in the hangar is completely irrelevant to damage control."

"Well, at least he asked, and the chief gave him a good answer."

"Ranson's smart, even though he's an asshole, but he chews officers up for breakfast. I bet he's telling all the chiefs and POs right now what an idiot the XO is."

Jack never thought much about the politics aboard a ship. The flight department mostly kept to itself and as a pilot he'd never had to worry about anything beyond his own job. He considered the incessant mockery that took place between the line officers on the bridge.

"I think the XO's making it hard on himself," he suggested, "by sticking to all this peacetime routine stuff."

Thomas shrugged. "It can have its place... *sir*... but Perry just clings to it because he understands it and feels like he's in control. He doesn't seem to get that the rebels don't give a shit if it's time for our evening briefing."

"You heard, then?"

"Oh, yeah. Chen came all the way down here just to gossip. There were troopers around so I shut him up and sent him packing, but he wasn't wrong." Thomas closed his eyes. "The XO's over his head and he doesn't know how to swim."

"How did he even get the job?"

"Because we're taking losses and people are getting promoted quickly." He opened his eyes and stared at Jack's rank insignia. "Wouldn't you say, Wings?"

"I didn't ask for this."

"You're right, sorry—and besides, the Astral Force also has a counter-plan to tactically bury senior officers in junior positions, waiting to pounce." Thomas lifted his bulb in salute again. "And here I wait."

"You're our ace in the hole, Thomas."

"Way, way, waaaaay down in that hole. Yup."

11

Katja sat back in her chair, suddenly uneasy under the stares of her colleagues. Neither Chang nor Korolev displayed much emotion, but the new intensity of their gazes was discomfiting. Operatives Shin and al-Jamil failed to hide their new interest in her.

"Oh, the tangled webs we weave," Korolev said mildly.

The Terran attack on the Centauri homeworld, Abeona, was an experience Katja would never forget, even if it seemed like a lifetime ago. She and Chang had led their platoon on a mission to pinpoint the enemy's forward artillery spotters and the resulting battle had seen Katja nearly killed by orbital bombardment, and Chang's first true taste of military command. Their mission had succeeded in destroying the spotters, and had been a significant turning point in those early hours of the invasion.

It had also had other consequences.

"How well did you know Kete Obadele?" Shin asked, her eyebrow arching.

"Not well," Katja replied. "He was supposedly a journalist, and the boyfriend of some bitch, so I didn't make much time for him until I knew he was a Centauri spy."

"And then you shot him."

Katja felt a rush of anger.

"I'd have done the same," Chang rumbled. "He was an enemy spy leading an attack against Earth."

"I just thought," Shin said, and she shrugged, "that being able to interrogate him would have been more useful."

Katja took her anger and honed it into a weapon. No one was allowed to question her judgement, not anymore, and not even another operative.

"There was no other option," she stated flatly, staring at Shin and willing her to argue. "I made the call."

Shin shrugged again and dropped her eyes.

"Obadele is dead," Korolev said, "and is no longer our problem—but his friend Valeria Moretti very much *is* our problem."

Katja's eyes flicked up to the wall screen beyond her commander, and the collection of images that had been captured of this elusive Centauri woman. Coupled with the visuals captured in Goldberg's office, they told the ASF exactly who to look for. An all-consuming search of the Terran visual records for the past six months had revealed less than half a dozen hits anywhere in the solar system. These included a single glimpse from the Inverness pub, captured by a random personal device sweeping the room and then posted to social media.

Middle height and slim build, she usually wore her hair brown and styled unremarkably. Her face was long and angular, not particularly attractive or memorable. But Katja had stared her down. Moretti was betrayed by her large eyes, and the intensity of their gaze. It was unmistakable.

"She likely has muscular augments," Chang said, "which would have been easy to create when they regrew her limbs." Moretti was another casualty of the attack on Abeona. She'd been Obadele's neighbor, and her family had been killed in the battle.

Until then she'd been a support worker in Centauri intelligence, but after the battle she'd applied and been accepted for a field agent role. Any reliable information on her ceased at that point, but threads of anecdotal evidence suggested that in the space of a year she had become one of Centauria's most effective spies. Katja had followed the links created by her colleagues between more than a dozen unexplained, highly improbable attacks which had been pulled off by enemy agents. Now that the ASF had a positive visual on Moretti, it was child's play to search security footage from across Terra and catch glimpses of her.

Child's play to search, Katja noted, but actually finding Moretti's image was proving exceedingly difficult. The small collection of images displayed before her represented the bulk of what they had.

"Her list of successful missions is worrying," Shin said, "and we assess that another attack is imminent."

"Too bad I didn't kill her, as well," Katja muttered. "Or would you prefer that she has another shot at us?"

"Dead agents garner zero intelligence."

"Dead agents do no damage."

"What do you think our job is?" Frustration twisted Shin's features. "We're trying to win a war, not a schoolyard scrap. Centauri intelligence is a hydra, and for every agent you kill without interrogation, two more slip into place unseen. Then we have to start all over again, searching for random clues, guessing at patterns, trying to predict where the next attack will be."

"Centauri agents don't play nice," Katja said. "I'd rather they die instead of me. Or even you."

"There are ways to subdue them without killing them—or did you skip that section in combat training?"

Katja sensed a voice in the Cloud, but it wasn't directed at her. She guessed it was al-Jamil, based on his intent gaze toward Shin. The woman's expression tightened. Her glance flickered then returned.

"You do not have a free hand, Katja, to just kill whoever you feel like," she pressed. "We have a very specific job to do, and it is for the good of Terra." Her finger suddenly stabbed out toward Chang. "And I don't want to hear one fucking word from you."

Chang stared back stoically.

Katja started to rise from her chair, every muscle tensing.

"Enough," Korolev said.

Katja pressed down her anger. Under Korolev's firm gaze she retook her seat.

"We have a mission to plan," he continued. "Against the most dangerous threat we've yet faced. Get your heads in the game."

A long moment of silence hung over the table.

"I suspect Moretti's still in Terra somewhere," al-Jamil said. "She's clearly a master of avoiding surveillance, and once she's inside the net it would be easiest for her to stay inside."

"So we'll have to find her," Katja said, mind already racing as she assessed hunting strategies.

"If her next target is indeed Christopher Sheridan," Shin said, "we get close to him. That way we don't need to find her. She'll find us."

"But just to be sure," Korolev added, "I want you, Katja, to be at Sheridan's side at all times."

"Why?"

"It's pretty clear that Kete Obadele had a personal vendetta against you, and I'm sure Moretti does, too. She knows you're not dead, despite the official records, and no doubt she'd like another shot at you."

"You think she'll come after me?"

"Probably not directly, but if Sheridan is her target and Moretti finds you right next to him, it might rattle her judgement—she might make a mistake."

"So I get to be bait?" Katja felt the slow burn of anger and aggression rising in her again. Let the foreign bitch come. She'd die just like her buddy Kete had.

"Yes, and you three"—Korolev indicated Chang, al-Jamil, and Shin—"are the trap."

It helped that she was small. At thirty years old Katja was still young by Terran standards, but even so her battle-hardened skin had long ago lost that baby-smooth quality of youth. Anyone truly perceptive would be able to spot the wisdom in her eyes and the confidence of her movements. So while she could play the role of innocent intern to some degree, spending all day every day with smart, ambitious young colleagues would make it challenging to come across as ten years younger than she was.

No, being short and petite was her best weapon in not being taken too seriously. The politician for whom she now "worked" barely even noticed her among the herd of interns. Christopher Sheridan was the new leader of the Federalist Party in Parliament, the largest political group outside of the ruling government, and therefore the official leader of the Opposition.

Unusual for a leading politician in being of only average height, Sheridan made up for his lack of stature with a lightning wit, a commanding voice, and a force of personality that washed over any room like a tidal wave. He was very busy making waves all across the Terran networks as he established himself publicly.

Like any politician, Sheridan preferred to have a backdrop of beautiful people whenever he gave an important speech, and as one of the interns on staff Katja dutifully stood in the front rank behind her boss while he orated for the cameras. Her hair was black and cut in a short bob, but she knew that Centauri recognition systems would identify her facial features easily.

Political speeches bored her, but she forced herself to listen as Sheridan thundered away against the policies of the current government. At times his words struck her as openly treasonous, until she reminded herself that he was himself a senior member of Parliament, and that it was his job to demonstrate to the people the healthy debate over policies.

This Denver speech addressed the war against the rebel colonies. Public opinion wasn't as supportive of the war as once it had been—despite the fact that Katja and her colleagues had snuffed out various dissident groups. Sheridan's words echoed the vague unease felt by many. He was quick to praise the courage and dedication of the Terran Army and Astral Force, but he openly criticized the strategies employed by the government.

Sheridan criticized the use of violence against colonial populations, and demanded a return to focused, military-on-military engagements. He decried the rebels as a small group of armed dissidents, led by the criminal leaders of Centauria, and claimed that the vast majority of colonists were victims of the war, as much so as Terran civilians.

"Strike at the heart of terror," he said again—it had become his catchphrase, and his target was the Centauri government. He called for a withdrawal from the far-flung colonies, and a concerted attack on Centauria itself.

No matter how eloquently he delivered this message, Katja found it ridiculous, yet he gave voice to that certain sector of Terran society that was frustrated by Parliament's policies, and made those people feel heard. It was the classic role of the leader of the Opposition, and Sheridan played it beautifully.

Following the inevitable question-and-answer period, Sheridan was whisked away from the stage by security, the broad, suited form of Suleiman Chang among them. Sheridan's recent election as leader of his party had been the perfect excuse for additional security, and if Centauri intelligence recognized Chang as Special Forces, then his presence would seem perfectly natural.

What Valeria Moretti and her colleagues wouldn't recognize was SF's hidden presence—Shin Mun-Hee as a researcher and Ali al-Jamil as a driver.

The entourage of interns followed Sheridan to his waiting transport. The big bus hid heavy armor beneath the bright outer paint of the Federalist Party, and an array of sensors tracked movement all around. Armed guards waited discreetly inside the main doors, away from the media. A security scanner interrogated Katja's embedded ID chip as she stepped up into the transport's interior, and she offered a nervous smile to the motionless guards.

The vehicle was large enough to comfortably carry four dozen people, and had served as the leader's mobile ground headquarters during an election campaign. Terra was years away from the next election, and the interior seemed cavernous for the small staff it currently housed. Katja couldn't see al-Jamil up forward in the cockpit, but she sensed him easily in the Cloud.

Shin sat at her research terminal and didn't glance up as the interns moved past, but Katja heard a voice in her head.

<First media images have already been transmitted. You're clear as day in them.>

<Good,> she replied without breaking stride as she headed aft. <I'm going to make first contact on this ride—can you give me some solid polling data?>

<Within the hour.>

Since the mission began, Shin had been pure professionalism. Katja, however, was struggling to shake the effects of their heated exchange. Anger wouldn't serve her here, as she had to maintain a polite, pretty facade for the civilians, and Shin was an ally—one of the few she had in this universe. Fighting with her was the last thing Katja wanted, but the words from the briefing room haunted her.

Did the other operatives disapprove of Katja?

It was an idea that threatened to bring tears to her eyes, and she pushed it down firmly.

Sheridan retreated to his private office toward the rear of the bus. Katja took one of the soft chairs in the central lounge and pulled her Baryon from her purse. Every intern was expected to jump on social media in the wake of a major political speech, and she dutifully sent out messages echoing the thrust of her boss's agenda. The other interns did the same, and she idly tracked their transmissions for any suspicious patterns.

Although she'd only had three days on the team, thus far all seven interns appeared to be legitimate, over-privileged kids eager to jump-start their careers. A perfect mix of racial and planetary backgrounds, each one of these four men and three other women was smart and savvy enough, but their social media patterns revealed an identifiable lack of experience. None of them had yet dared to approach Sheridan himself, but the jostling for position within the herd had already started.

Katja played it cool, giving the impression of a cute but empty-headed dilettante who posed little threat.

With a slight lurch the transport departed for Atlanta. Most politicians would have headed for the nearest skyport, but Sheridan's message hinged on his very visible ground travel. It gave the impression that he was a man of the people, and it made his Federal Party bus into a physical presence as it zoomed along the public highways. It also created a unique security challenge, but even this weakness was part of the plan.

The bus left Denver behind and headed out onto the great central plains of North America. It was several hours of uninterrupted travel to Atlanta and a busy work day for all. Katja watched as several senior advisors came and went from Sheridan's office, and by linking into Chang's audio feed she could listen to the conversations. It was typical administrative details and political speculation, but it gave her a sense of Sheridan's mindset.

Shin sent her a preliminary report, and Katja quickly scanned the effect Sheridan's recent speech had made on the Terran networks. The results had been positive, and Katja looked forward to being the bearer of good news.

Making herself appear to be busy, she waited for a moment when Sheridan was alone with Chang.

<Suleiman,> she reached out. <I'm ready.>

<Execute,> he replied.

Rising from her seat, Baryon in hand, she strolled aft past her fellow interns. One glanced up, but otherwise her passage went unnoticed. Even the one glance faded away when she paused at the snack trays and popped a quarter-sandwich into her mouth before pouring some water. Downing the liquid, she walked further aft, past the washrooms and the cubicles of the senior advisors. Just as she reached the entrance to Sheridan's office the door slid open. Chang looked at her in a moment's assessment, then stepped aside.

Sheridan was seated behind his desk.

"Excuse me, Mr. Sheridan?" she said from the doorway. "I have some initial analysis of your Denver speech." The politician glanced up at her with mild surprise, which melted quickly into sudden interest. He glanced at Chang, who nodded curtly, then motioned Katja inside.

"I'll be right back, sir," Chang said as he stepped outside and closed the door. He'd be gone long enough for her to make the required contact, and he'd stop anyone else from interrupting. She opened her eyes wide and smiled.

"It's a pleasure to meet you, sir," she said.

He rose from his chair and extended his hand to shake hers. His handsome face wore an expression of indulgent charm.

"I'm sorry I haven't learned the names of all my new interns, Miss...?"

"Laurent. Sophie Laurent." If she was going to play the role of flirtatious little vixen, her best example to follow had been French.

"Miss Laurent." He retook his seat and offered her the chair facing him across the desk. She sat down and held the Baryon between them, leaning in just enough that he'd be able to sense her subtle perfume. He leaned in slightly as well, powerful gaze taking her in.

"The initial reaction by the networks has been both widespread and positive," she began. In two minutes she gave him a detailed analysis of the reporting tone and priority given to the speech. Thanks to Shin's research skills her report achieved the analytical level of a briefing from a top campaign staffer, and Katja forced herself to skip some of the details. Nevertheless, they were clear to a smart observer, and Sheridan proved his acumen with his own comments.

She made a show of being very impressed.

"I didn't see that, sir." She took a deep breath and met his gaze. "I'm looking forward so much to learning under you."

"Don't sell yourself short, Sophie," he said, holding her eyes. "This is a great analysis. I'm impressed."

"Really?" She grinned, then forced it down into a smile. "Thank you, sir."

He sat back, quickly looking her up and down. She took another quick breath, ensuring her chest swelled as she did.

"Do you think you could do another report like this after the Atlanta speech?" he asked. "I'll be curious to see the follow-on reaction."

"Yeah, of course!" she responded. "I could have it for you this evening." She paused, glancing down as if embarrassed. "I mean, if you want it that soon."

"Don't worry, Sophie," he replied. "I work late. I'm at a dinner this evening but you can come by afterward to the hotel suite."

<Objective achieved,> she sent to Chang.

"Yes, sir, Mr. Sheridan. No problem."

"Call me Chris," he said, waving away the formality. "At least, when the other interns aren't around." She laughed, and heard the door open behind her. Holding his gaze for just a moment longer, she rose, thanked him for his time, and slipped past Chang out of the office.

12

"Are any of the interns giving you trouble?" Chang asked.

Katja laughed as she slipped off her shoes and rubbed her heels—standing for hours at a time in these fashion necessities was becoming torture.

"The tall one—the redhead from Mercury—threatened me this afternoon. Told me she'd kick my ass if I didn't back off from Sheridan." Chang handed her a soda water from the hotel room's mini-bar and dropped down in the chair across from her. The curtains behind him were drawn, but a sliver of darkness revealed the night beyond.

"The redhead?" He nodded. "Yeah, she's been pretty busy asserting her dominance over the other females. I haven't seen her talking to Sheridan much, though."

"Classic mistake in warfare." Katja shrugged. "She's too busy fighting peripheral battles, and she's lost sight of her main objective."

"Is that how you women consider romance?"

"As warfare? Oh, yeah. I was just never very good at it, until I stopped caring."

"I take it the redhead doesn't know that you've been invited to Sheridan's room the past two evenings?"

"No, it hasn't even occurred to her. In her mind, no one could move that fast."

"Another big mistake, underestimating the enemy."

Katja shrugged again. Maneuvering her way into Sheridan's

confidence hadn't been that difficult, and engaging in psychological warfare with a bunch of interns really didn't task her. Much greater concerns occupied her thoughts.

"Sules," she said suddenly, "what did Mun-Hee mean back at HQ, when she said she didn't want to hear another word from you?"

To his credit, Chang didn't try to evade the question. He met her eyes with his usual stoic gaze.

"There are a few operatives who feel that you're a little too trigger-happy," he replied. "I've defended you."

Exactly as she'd feared. She couldn't describe the emotion that washed up over her. Anger was there, as always, but it was weakened by something much older, more primitive—a sense of failure. She closed her eyes, fighting down the frustration at her own emotional vulnerability.

"How many people think that?" she asked.

"A few... but we all bring different strengths to the ASF."

"Why don't they say it to my face?" she gritted. "I thought we were supposed to be open with each other."

"They're afraid of you."

That stopped her cold. Afraid of *her*? A flicker of pride burned through the chill of her emotion, but it was dampened by a ghost of a thought—what had she become?

"They shouldn't be. You guys are my family."

"I know, but like I said, we all bring different strengths. Mun-Hee is like me—a background operator who keeps an eye on the big picture. You're more like Ali—you lead the charge. Even then we're all different. Mun-Hee is the investigator while I'm the guardian. Ali just slips into action like a ghost, patiently waiting for the perfect moment to attack."

"And me?"

"You're the executioner. You strike hard and fast."

"And without remorse, I suppose."

"That's up to you, Katty."

She glanced up at him. "Do you feel remorse for what we do?"

"Do I *look* like I feel remorse?"

She had to laugh. His moon face revealed nothing, as always, but deep down she knew his humanity was there, and strong.

After a year as an operative, she was afraid to think about how much of her own humanity had been sacrificed. But now wasn't the time, she told herself firmly. They were on a mission, and what needed to occupy her thoughts was a Centauri spy.

"Still no sightings of Moretti?" she asked.

"No—and I mean, not *anywhere*. She's vanished from the Cloud."

"Suggesting extra care on her part to remain invisible. I think she's close."

"Ali's monitoring all foot traffic into the hotel, and Mun-Hee is positioned on the roof. I had sensors installed in the air conditioning ducts of every hotel we're planning to stay at in the next week."

"She won't try that again," Katja said. "Not after we caught her red-handed."

"Doesn't hurt to cover our bases. I'm also checking staff movements to flag any sudden replacements of personnel." He pulled up his suit sleeve to reveal the sleek forearm display that was wrapped around it. "And I have dark-energy detectors deployed in case she tries to open a local jump gate."

Katja sipped her water and sat back on the couch.

"It's nice to feel protected."

"Just doing my job, Katty, so you can do yours."

She nodded, taking another long drink. They were all just doing their jobs, but that didn't make it mean any less. She didn't allow herself many emotions these days, but loyalty to her new family was one indulgence that made her feel stronger.

Finishing the soda water she rose, smoothing her dress. From her open suitcase she pulled out a pair of stylish flats and slipped them on her feet.

"Well, Mr. Sheridan will be waiting for me to deliver his evening report."

"Not changing into something more comfortable?"

She cast her gaze back over her shoulder to where Chang was rising to his feet.

"He hasn't actually propositioned me yet," Katja replied. "I just know he appreciates no heels—he's a bit sensitive about his height."

"I'll remember to stoop."

She laughed and transferred her pocket energy weapon to her

purse. Chang exited to the hallway and nodded back to her that all was clear.

Sheridan was staying in the penthouse suite on the top floor, just a single flight above Katja's room. She climbed the stairs, easing the door shut as she stepped into the upper corridor and reached out with all her senses. Nothing was within quantum-flux range, and with infra-red she peered through the wall to the left and made out his seated form. To the right was the other penthouse suite, currently unoccupied, and ahead the corridor led less than ten meters before ending at a broad window. Above her was the roof, but other than the dark flow of cooled air through the ducts she could see nothing.

Shin was up there, so her topside was covered.

One of the regular security guards was on duty outside Sheridan's doors. He noticed her approach and regarded her without expression.

"Working late again, Miss Durant?"

She smiled at him, as always. On the first night she'd offered a shy expression, and last night she'd practically grinned. Tonight she allowed a touch of smugness to flicker across her lips, indicating a woman who knew she'd succeeded.

"Mr. Sheridan is very demanding," she said.

The guard knocked sharply on the door and opened it, announced her arrival, then stepped back to let her pass. Sheridan was seated in the armchair facing the door, feet up on the table and his suit jacket tossed on the couch to his left. The penthouse's sitting area was nearly as large as Katja's old apartment, and beyond she could see the undisturbed dining area, then a pair of doors leading to bedrooms. The curtains were drawn, but she knew there was a patio beyond the glass. She quickly scanned the room before turning her most radiant smile toward her patron.

"Evening, Sophie." He rose slowly from his chair, reaching to clear his suit jacket from the couch before inviting her to take a seat.

"Good evening, sir." She heard the door shut behind her as she sat down on the couch, and leaned toward him earnestly. "How was your dinner?"

He flopped back down and shrugged. The busy public schedule

was wearing him down. His handsome face sagged with fatigue.

"Fine," he said. "The usual glad-handing and scheming."

"I have the initial report on your media coverage from this evening." She handed him the tablet.

"Thanks," he said, taking it and, to her surprise, actually scanning the first few pages. His eyes were alight with intelligence, and shone in contrast to his haggard features. Katja couldn't help but be impressed by this man. In the few days she'd been on his team she'd watched him work longer hours than anyone on his staff. His discussions with officials very often contained real substance, and amid all the chaos he'd maintained a cool, steady demeanor, treating all his staff members—from his senior advisors right down to his transport driver—with respect and courtesy.

He wasn't at all what she'd expected in a politician.

"You do excellent work, Sophie," he said finally, leaning back in his chair and holding her in his gaze. "I'd like to keep you closer to me."

Finally. To his credit, he'd not tried to get her into bed right away—he'd at least had the decency to wait a few nights. Katja leaned forward slightly, letting a touch of eagerness burn in her eyes.

"I'd like that too, Chris."

"I want to make you my official executive assistant."

"Of course," she purred, reaching out to rest a hand on his knee. "I'd be honored."

His eyes held hers for a moment, then flicked down to her hand. He sat up suddenly, pulling his legs down off the table and shaking her hand free.

"And Sophie," he said, looking into her eyes again, "that's *all* I want."

She nodded automatically, then paused as his words registered, smiling to cover her confusion.

"You're a beautiful, intelligent woman," he said, sitting straighter and moving away from her, "but I'm happily married, and I'd like to stay that way."

Katja sat back, pushing down any emotions that threatened to well up, but knowing that her cheeks were reddening. His smile was kind, and that only made her feel patronized. A big part of her was relieved that she wouldn't have to expose herself so intimately, but honestly—he could have at least been tempted.

"Are you okay?" he asked.

"Yes, of course," she said, forcing an amused smile to her lips. "I'm flattered that you thought that was my intention."

"So are you interested in being my EA?"

"Absolutely. When do I start?"

<Ops red! Ops red!>

His quiet answer was drowned out in her mind by a sudden shout in the Cloud. She pressed a hand to his knee again, motioning for silence. Her eyes pointed at his surprised features but her perception reached out in all directions. She couldn't even tell from whom the alert had sounded.

<With prize,> she shot out. <Location of threat?>

Metal and plastic clattered on the patio beyond the curtains. She snapped over with infra-red—two bodies grappled outside. An incoherent message hissed through the Cloud.

She launched herself into Sheridan, tipping his armchair backward and sending them both to the floor. He thumped down on his back, staring at her in shock. She climbed on top of him, watching for movement through the curtains.

"Sophie," he gasped, "I'm serious—I'm married."

<Threat in corridor,> Chang transmitted.

"Quiet," she hissed in his ear, fumbling into her purse for the energy pistol. "Into the bedroom, move!"

"I appreciate your sense of fun," he growled, pushing her off and attempting to sit up. "But this is too much." She pulled out the pistol and pointed it toward the curtains. Rising to a crouch she grabbed his elbow and pulled him up.

"I'm Special Forces, assigned to protect you."

He stared at her, mouth open in silence.

The curtains billowed as glass shattered behind them. A wall of hot air flowed into the room. Katja heaved Sheridan to his feet and hustled him toward the bedroom door on the far wall. A figure emerged through the curtains, but seemed to be facing away from her. The figure collapsed through the fabric—the broken form of Shin Mun-Hee.

Through the bedroom door, Katja heard a faint crackling noise. Someone had just materialized from the Bulk. She grabbed

Sheridan in mid-stride and pushed him down toward the dining-room floor.

"Get under the table!" she snapped.

He scrambled over the hardwood and between the chairs tucked around the small dining-room table. Katja crouched in front, senses scanning all directions.

A dark figure rushed through from the bedroom. She fired. The energy blast crackled over the intruder, causing him to stumble, but he pressed forward. Katja unleashed rapid-fire blasts into what she recognized as a Bulk-suit, clearly Centauri in design. Each energy bolt staggered her target until he fell backward, finally letting out a scream of pain.

His form thumped down against the floor.

The tinkle of glass alerted her to movement back at the patio and she swung to face the new threat. Another Bulk-suited attacker stepped through the billowing curtains. She fired, feeling a quick pulse from the pistol against her hand, indicating it was almost out of power. Her attacker strode forward, brandishing a heavy rod in one hand.

<Flashbang!> she heard.

Throwing herself to the floor she covered her eyes even as she heard the door crack open. A wave of light and sound burned over her as the flashbang grenade from Chang detonated in the room. Then everything went silent and dark.

She looked up and saw the intruder staggering from the blast. Chang ran into the room, throwing his huge form in a body tackle, crashing down on top of the Centauri. The enemy's rod slipped loose, rolling under the table. Chang pinned his opponent and Katja turned to cover her first target.

The body was still lying in the bedroom door, but even as she approached another form appeared, bent over her target, and activated a device on his forearm. The fallen figure disappeared into the Bulk. The second Centauri rose and stepped through the door, his—no, her—face visible where the face shield had been retracted.

"Valeria Moretti," Katja said.

Moretti's large eyes snapped over. Surprise flashed into recognition, and then into rage.

"Emmes."

Katja raised her pistol and fired, but Moretti was already in motion. A single blast struck her torso before she knocked the weapon aside and grabbed Katja by the throat. Katja tried to gasp, but no air moved as the iron fingers closed, her feet left the ground, and pain seared her neck. She smashed her forearm upward into Moretti's elbow, but the grip held.

Clutching onto her enemy's wrist, Katja tried to swing her leg up into a kick, but her bare feet struck against unyielding armor. Her vision began to fade and sparkle as Moretti's face glared up at hers.

A flash of energy crackled across Moretti's Bulk-suit. Two more struck the Centauri, the energy tickling Katja's cheeks. The pressure on her throat lessened and she felt herself collapse to the floor. Ears ringing from the impact, she desperately tried to suck air through her windpipe, vaguely hearing a high-pitched squeak with each attempted breath.

Another blast dropped Moretti to her knees, and then Chang was upon her. The big Terran kicked the Centauri's bent form. She reeled back but kept her footing, struggling into a standing position and blocking his heavy fists as they came down. He pressed his advantage with a flurry of blows, none of which struck home. Then she unleashed a kick, sending Chang stumbling backward.

Drawing a heavy baton from her belt, identical to the one her fellow Centauri had wielded, Moretti shuffled forward, raising it to strike. Chang moved in, blocking the expected swing and landing a jab to her face. Moretti took the blow and carried her baton through into a backswing. Chang threw up his right forearm, and the club shattered it. He roared in pain and staggered back.

Katja grabbed her pistol from the floor and fired twice into Moretti's back. The bolts crackled over her Bulk-suit and she staggered. Katja fired again, but to no effect. A quick glance told her the weapon was out of charges. She forced another tortured breath into her lungs as she scanned for Chang's pistol. It wasn't visible, but another weapon was. The dropped baton lay just a body-length away, leaning against one of the chair legs.

Moretti glanced back as Katja scrabbled across the floor, but paid for the distraction as Chang's roundhouse kick smashed into her unguarded ribcage. Moretti staggered to her knees, turning back to Chang as the Terran unleashed a devastating barrage of one-handed blows.

Katja grabbed the baton, noting quickly that Sheridan was still under the table. Far from cowering, the politician had his personal communicator out and was using it. With at least three Centauri agents in the room, however, Katja doubted any outside help was still standing. As she hefted the baton she saw Shin's body among the broken glass, her face shattered by an impact trench where her skull had caved in from chin to forehead.

The baton was surprisingly light, but as she swung it experimentally Katja felt the mass shift down the length of the rod, increasing the force of each swing.

Moretti was still holding her own baton, but she was in full defense as Chang pressed forward with powerful blows. He was on full attack, Katja knew, which could only be sustained for a few seconds before exhaustion drained his muscles. But Moretti was entirely occupied with defense.

Diving into a roll, Katja quickly closed the distance and swung the baton into Moretti's knee. Even through the armor she heard the snap of the joint, and her foe sagged with a cry of pain. Katja tumbled clear and watched as Moretti crashed down on her back, Chang's great bulk slamming down on top of her. Katja rose up, raising the baton to strike down.

Moretti's weapon lashed out, striking Katja's shin. Katja instinctively staggered back, but snarled through the pain and advanced again. Across the room, Ali al-Jamil burst through the door, Corps assault rifle up at the ready.

Then Moretti dropped her baton and wrapped a mighty arm around Chang's body. With eyes burning into Katja's, she reached for a device on her forearm—the same device which had sent her companion back into the Bulk.

"No!" Katja swung downward with the baton.

And smashed the floorboards where a heartbeat before two bodies had grappled. Her chest seared as her entanglement connection to Chang exploded in agony.

<Where the prize?> al-Jamil demanded.

<They're in the Bulk!> she screamed. <They're in the Bulk!>

"Where's Sheridan?" al-Jamil shouted out loud.

"Here," he responded, his reply muffled.

Katja dove for the Centauri agent lying still near Shin's fallen form. She pounded at the controls to release the Bulk suit from the body. Sheridan climbed out from under the table and al-Jamil covered the room with the assault rifle.

"Help me get into this suit," she shouted. "Chang's in the Bulk!" The Centauri's body was a dead weight as she struggled to rip the suit clear. It was an impossible task on her own. Why wasn't al-Jamil helping?

"Help me!"

Lowering his rifle, al-Jamil held her with cold, sad eyes.

"It's too late, Katja."

"No!" She tugged at the suit, freeing another section of the Centauri's torso.

"Katja," al-Jamil said quietly, "there is no oxygen, no pressure, and no temperature in the Bulk. Sules was dead the moment he went in."

"He was my *partner*," she snapped.

He held her gaze for a moment, then nodded past her to the other casualty on the floor.

"And Mun-Hee was mine. There'll be time to grieve, Katja, but not now."

He raised the rifle suddenly, then relaxed again. There was the familiar thump of armored police entering the room. She switched the settings on her implanted ID chip to reveal her Special Forces identity, even before the scan washed over her. There was no way she was answering questions in the guise of an intern. Not tonight.

She sat back, releasing her grip on the Centauri Bulk-suit. She heard al-Jamil speak firmly to the police, heard Sheridan's voice as well. No one bothered her. After a moment she reached for the baton by her feet and moved toward the pale and injured Centauri agent.

Somebody was going to pay for Chang, and it might as well be this piece of shit.

Then al-Jamil placed a firm hand on hers.

"No, Katja. We need the prisoner." His voice was soft, but his grip was like steel, and his other hand still held the assault rifle. She took half a step forward, eyes still on the unconscious prisoner, and felt al-Jamil's fingers dig into her forearm.

Glaring up at him, she wondered for just a moment if she could take him, but the still point of his gaze cooled her anger, allowed her brain to take control again.

"Then let's get this prisoner home," she said, "and find out how to kill Valeria Moretti."

13

"**A**re you comfortable in front of the media, Mr. Kane?"

The captain's question made Thomas turn, pulling his eyes away from the looming shape of Astral Base One as projected on the bridge sphere. *Bowen* was on initial approach to the giant station, a dark silhouette against the dazzling backdrop of Earth. The lights of other craft teemed in the orbital space. Apparently at least one of them carried a news crew, and more reporters had been authorized into the base.

"Not particularly, sir," he replied. Once, not long ago, he would have jumped at the chance to appear on camera, but journalists were sharp, and had long memories. Thomas didn't relish the prospect of explaining his demotion on interplanetary news.

Commander Hu shot a questioning glance down to him. Seated in his command chair next to the busy officer of the watch, he wore the expression of a man concentrating on a dozen things at once. Yet still he had capacity to interrogate his strike officer.

"The request," he said firmly, "is to interview the officer who led the initial search of *Toronto*." *Bowen*'s discovery of *Toronto*, a ship thought lost, had ignited a firestorm of attention back home. The fact that the crew were missing suggested that they might still be alive. At the same time there was the inevitable gnashing of teeth over the fact that the vaunted Astral Force had suffered such a defeat.

"In that case, sir," Thomas said carefully, "I think that honor clearly belongs to the executive officer. He led the search—I simply conducted the initial security sweep."

Hu regarded him in silence for a long moment, dark eyes revealing nothing.

"Very well, Mr. Kane," he replied. "That's all."

Thomas stepped back from the command chair, retreating to the after section of the bridge as the captain called over to the XO. Jack sidled up to him, and Thomas offered a smile to his young friend.

"Got any plans for shore leave?"

"No," Jack replied. "I think I might head up to Vancouver to see my folks. They worry."

"Yeah, I reckon mine do, too, but they stopped saying so years ago."

"Are your parents veterans?"

"No, I'm the first."

"Really?" Jack looked thoughtful. "Something about you suggested a long line of family service."

"I think it's my wife's money that gives that impression," he said with a wry smile.

"How is she?"

Thomas considered. His wife Soma was absolutely thrilled to be pregnant with twins, but quite irritable at having to significantly reduce her recreational drug habits. She'd been keeping busy, however, preparing the nursery and hiring additional staff, and spending money always cheered her up.

"On balance, quite content."

"She must be due any day, now."

"Another month, although with twins you can never tell."

"You must be excited."

"How so?" he asked.

"Well, to be a dad."

"Oh…" The comment caught Thomas by surprise. His focus had been on preparing himself for the inevitable onslaught of social and financial demands. The way Soma spoke of the impending children, they seemed more like assets than offspring. In fact, when he'd heard the news his first thought had been that the babies would need to be DNA-tested, to prove who the father was.

"Yes," he acknowledged. "It's going to be a big change." At least there would be more servants around.

Jack looked at him strangely, and he didn't like it, so he turned his attention back to Astral Base One. The station filled the entire forward view, the beckoning lights of the docking spar blinking in response to *Bowen*'s approach. The line officer in Thomas immediately began to assess the ship's vectors, but he shook off the thought.

Not my problem anymore.

"Are you going to see Amanda this time?" he asked.

If possible, Jack's face fell even more.

"No, her ship is deployed. She can't even tell me which system she's in, let alone when she'll be back."

"Good for you two, though, making it work."

"Don't get the wrong idea," Jack said. "When we're together we're together, but the rest of the time I'd hardly call it a real relationship."

"Shame she isn't here," Thomas offered. "You look like you could use a friend."

Jack's face hardened, but he just wasn't the type to clam up.

"What's the point of having friends?" he spat. "Bullshit bad luck can snuff anybody out, any time. For all I know Amanda's ship took a torpedo this morning."

"Jack..."

"I mean, look how amazing Katja was, and even she got killed. What chance do any of us have?"

It was too big a question to try to answer, Thomas knew, and it was one every soldier eventually asked. He could try to respond, but anything he said would just be empty words, especially since in his heart he'd accepted his own death months ago. He didn't know when he was going to die, but he doubted very much that he'd ever have to worry about growing old. Or being a good father, for that matter.

This war was taking its toll.

"All you can do," he said finally, "is look out for yourself and your shipmates."

"What about the mission? Aren't we supposed to sacrifice ourselves and our shipmates to accomplish the mission?"

Classic Astral Force doctrine. Thomas could hardly argue with the philosophy, but, looking into Jack's hollow gaze, he knew it was time to share a hard-earned truth.

"As officers, Jack, part of our job is to know which is more important to sacrifice—our troops or our mission. Every situation is unique, and you have to trust your own judgement."

"And what if my judgement's wrong?"

"Then the wrong people will die."

Jack sighed heavily, closing his eyes and fighting down emotion. Thomas looked forward just as *Bowen* linked up to the spar for docking. He patted Jack on the arm.

"We'll be secured in a minute, Jack," he said. "Why don't you get out of here and head ashore. Catch the first flight to Vancouver and forget about all this for a couple of days."

"Yeah," Jack agreed, offering a fist-bump. "Thanks, Thomas. See you in a few days."

Thomas lingered on the bridge for a few more minutes, idly listening to the chatter between line officers as shore connections were made and systems began shutting down. The XO hurried past him, face alight with excitement, and through the broad windows on the spar he could see a crowd of civilians gathered to welcome the crew home. Somewhere in that crowd, he knew, was his beautiful wife and her entourage.

He glanced down at his uniform.

Time to change out of one role, and into another.

The house had been transformed. An entire section of guest rooms had been redone as a nursery, a playroom, a green room, and a pair of residences for the incoming nannies. Contractors were still finishing off the adjustments, but the baby rooms were ready to receive.

Soma herself had also transformed. Her sleek, tiny frame had been carrying the baby bump well when Thomas had left on patrol, but now her limbs had thickened and her entire frame widened to carry the massive womb which her belly had swollen to contain. Her face had rounded out and her breasts, he couldn't help but notice, were enormous. She waddled instead of walked, and sat heavily whenever chance offered her a seat.

She looked, Thomas realized, absolutely beautiful.

Soma obviously didn't agree, and as they prepared for the dinner party that evening she spent twice as much time as he remembered on her hair and make-up.

"Are you wearing your uniform this evening?" she asked as she applied mascara.

Thomas was impressed at the new selection of suits she'd bought for him while he was away. His uniforms with their sublieutenant rank, he noted, were pushed discreetly to the far end of the dressing room.

"No, I want to try one of these gorgeous new suits," he replied. "Do you have a preference?"

"I think the dark blue would go nicely with your medals," she called back, "if you wanted to wear them."

Before the war, Thomas would never have worn his military decorations with a civilian outfit, but apparently that had become the style. Quite a few civilians had been honored for various services to the State, and a new galaxy of awards had started appearing at formal social gatherings. As a genuine veteran, Thomas was welcome to display his own honors, even in a civilian setting.

"Sounds good, darling," he said.

As he slipped into the dark-blue suit, he marveled at her subtle ability to discourage him from wearing the uniform, with its rank insignia, while keeping medals and awards prominent. As always, the world just seemed to fall into place according to her advantage. If only, he mused as he made certain his rack of medals was straight against the dark-blue pocket of his jacket, he'd mastered that skill to the same degree.

Nevertheless, he had his role to play in Soma's game. He took his wife's hand and guided her down the hall to the glass-sided elevator which gently lowered them to their waiting cluster of guests. The doors slid open to a hearty round of applause, and Thomas gestured for his wife to precede him into the ballroom. Winters in Longreach never got that cold, but the sun set too early for an outdoor party, so Soma had decided to host a dinner inside.

She reintroduced him to several Jovian business magnates, all long-time friends of her family, as well as a pair of senior State officials based here on Earth. There was a distinct lack of fops or dandies present, Thomas noticed, suggesting that this particular dinner was intended for serious business. It was just as well. Soma's dilettante friends and their floozy girlfriends tended to make his blood boil.

Before long he found himself standing, drink in hand, in a conversation circle with the gentlemen. Then came the inevitable question.

"And what are you doing with the Astral Force these days, Thomas?"

"I've been assigned to *Admiral Bowen*," he said easily, adding, "one of our modern cruisers."

"Oh, yes, weren't you the ones who discovered poor *Toronto*?"

"Yes, I was on the initial team who searched her."

"Damn shame, that business."

"I saw an interview today," one of the Jovian magnates commented, "with a member of the *Bowen* crew. I think he was the… executive officer? That's not the captain, is it?"

"No," another joked, "that would be the *chief* executive officer."

Thomas joined politely in the chuckles.

"The XO," he explained, "whom you saw being interviewed, is the second-in-command."

"So you report to him?"

The idea of being subordinate to Lieutenant Perry made Thomas want to roll his eyes. Time for a mostly truthful statement.

"Actually, I report directly to the captain."

"I see. In what role?"

Thomas borrowed an expression Jack had used. He'd quite come to like it. He leaned in slightly, lowering his voice.

"I'm the ace in the hole."

The gentlemen all nodded conspiratorially. The cluster of medals on Thomas's chest spoke for themselves, he knew, and his enigmatic answer would stop any further questions. Each gentleman would now tuck away his own bit of delicious information, having dined with a military man who was more than he seemed.

"And what about that Centauri terrorist," someone commented. "Do you think she'll be captured?"

The face of a female Centauri spy had been splashed all over the media lately. She was the sole survivor of a failed assassination attempt, and while her co-conspirators had all been killed or captured, she was still at large.

"I'm sure she will," Thomas said. "Having been so clearly identified, there's no way she can escape our borders, and it's only a matter of time before someone recognizes her."

Thomas's earpiece sounded softly.

"Sir, madame. Minister Shah and Mrs. Shah have arrived."

"Excuse me," Thomas said, bowing slightly, "our next guests have arrived." He joined Soma in the middle of the room and strolled forward to where the new arrivals would emerge from the front hall.

"I'm impressed," he said quietly to his wife. "We don't often host senior members of Parliament."

"I met him through his wife," Soma replied. "Lovely lady."

They paused near the entrance, watching as the new couple entered. Thomas pushed a welcoming smile to his face and turned his eyes to Vijay Shah. The Minister of Natural Resources and a member of the largest party in Parliament, he was a tall, slim man with a mane of gray hair over his angular features. His eyes flicked down to the medals, then he reached out to grip Thomas's extended hand.

"Vijay Shah, sir."

"Minister Shah, it's an honor to have you in our home. My name is Thomas Kane."

"Modesty is not required. What rank do you hold in the armed services, so that I can honor you with a proper salutation."

Thomas was about to modestly dismiss the query when he heard Mrs. Shah's voice beside her husband.

"He's a sublieutenant, if memory serves."

He looked over at the politician's wife, and his smile froze in place.

Standing elegantly on the arm of her husband, one of the

most powerful men in Terra, was a woman he knew only too well. Dazzling blue eyes embedded in porcelain features framed by long black hair, hourglass figure wrapped in a stunning silk dress and jewelry to shame a queen.

Charity Brisebois.

"Mrs... Shah."

"Hello, darling," Breeze said as she leaned in to accept his cheek kisses. She held him in the embrace just long enough to whisper, "Did you miss me?"

14

It was irritating to be in the presence of a man who knew her former life, but Breeze had known that Thomas Kane would be skulking around at the edges of her new social circle. His wife Soma was extremely well-connected, and the months spent cultivating that friendship were certainly paying off.

This dinner party was vivid proof.

And now that Soma was heavily preggers, Breeze had no competition as the most beautiful woman in the room. Scanning the Kanes' ballroom, she quickly sized up the other wives—as they did her—and a preliminary pecking order was wordlessly established.

They were all ten to twenty years Breeze's senior, and to their credit beautifully turned out, but Breeze held the advantages of relative youth and the arm of a Parliamentary minister. She also had her own military career to fall back on, if necessary. Yes, it was going to be an enjoyable evening.

The guest list was surprisingly intimate, which suggested an agenda. The business magnates each ran mining conglomerates in the outer solar system, and the two junior state officials both worked for her husband in the Ministry of Natural Resources. The other senior politician was Christopher Sheridan, the leader of the Opposition and the most prominent Parliamentary figure representing Mars. Nothing happened in Parliament without the consent of the Martian voting bloc.

Sheridan was unescorted, Breeze noted immediately, and as

soon as the Kanes had completed their hostly welcomes she moved in.

"Good evening, Mr. Sheridan," she said, offering her hand for him to kiss. "I'm Charity Shah." His eyes lit up appraisingly, but he couldn't quite hide the fatigue weighing him down.

"Mrs. Shah, a pleasure," he said smoothly. "I'd heard that Vijay's young bride was the most beautiful woman in the worlds, but now I see that the description was inadequate."

"And I've heard that you are an exquisite orator," she laughed. "Please, continue your fiction."

"How are you enjoying life in the public eye?"

"I'm mostly leaving it to Vijay," she said. "I'm not sure I'd welcome that much attention." It was a half-truth, she knew. There had been a fair bit of coverage of this glamorous new power couple, but she'd hung back, largely to help his public image. It would be better to keep her head down until worlds had forgotten about the court-martial which had ended her career.

The incident was just a little too recent in public memory.

"I understand—it's why my wife stays at home," Sheridan agreed. "Public life is getting a bit too risky these days."

"The war has endangered so many people."

"Yes. Almost makes you wonder if it's worth it."

Breeze pressed her lips shut. Those were dangerous words, even in an intimate setting like this. Then he laughed and gave her a wink.

"My role as Opposition leader requires me to say things like that."

She returned the laugh, but felt a twinge of discomfort. Getting on the wrong side of the State might be his official role, but it was something she never wanted to do again. Relief coursed through her as she heard her husband stroll up to her side.

"Hello, Christopher," Vijay said. "I suppose you and I should sit on opposite sides of the table tonight."

"Yes, and I'll be sure to stand and address our host first, whenever I want to speak to you," Sheridan replied with an easy smile.

The two politicians shook hands, the conversation easily flowing into a casual exchange about life on the road while the new Parliament building was being constructed. The original Chamber of Parliament had been destroyed in the opening attack of the war, and other incidents had claimed the lives of nearly a third of Parliament's members, including the President herself.

This past year had seen an uneasy shifting of alliances among the political parties as they jockeyed for position amid the chaos of elections which saw many seats change hands. Vijay, as one of the longest-serving government representatives still alive, had maneuvered his way quietly into the low-profile but extremely powerful Ministry of Natural Resources. Sheridan had led the movement to consolidate the Martian mandate and, while still excluded from government, was gaining popular support.

As she watched the two men chat so amiably, she wondered idly if she was witness to a precursor to the next presidential election.

Breeze had no problem with her role as charming consort. Vijay was a man of quiet, resolute power who had built his life on succeeding without making waves. It was rare for a resident of distant Triton to walk the halls of power—especially one who had grown up in a ward as poor as Vijay's. He was, Breeze had discovered, a master behind the scenes, and her admiration for him grew more with each success he achieved.

Her own political ambitions would be well-served at his side.

Glancing around the room at the various clusters of conversation, Breeze admitted that there was still one threat she needed to neutralize. Watching subtly, she noted when Thomas excused himself from a group and spoke to one of the servants. With a quick touch to Vijay's arm she slipped away.

Thomas saw her approach, and she noted the subtle tension that rippled through his powerful body. It thrilled her that she could still frighten such a man with her mere presence, but she damped her instincts and instead greeted him with an earnest expression.

"I'd like to declare a truce," she said simply.

Surprise flickered over him before his features hardened into bland neutrality.

"I'd be happy with that," he said, "if I could believe it."

She conceded with a nod. He was nobody's fool, and she knew her charms were useless on him. She grudgingly admitted to a great deal of respect for him as an opponent. He could be a powerful ally, but she doubted that would ever happen. So he needed to be disarmed.

"Fair enough," she said. "I'm not going to say that I've changed, or that I want us to be friends, but I don't see any benefit to fighting with you."

"Because you have what you want, and you can kick a sublieutenant whenever you feel like it?" It *had* been a cheap shot, revealing his rank to Vijay. Damn her predatory instincts.

"I'm sorry about that. I'll make it up to you at dinner."

"No thanks."

"I promise, and you don't need to say a word."

"You'd like that," he sneered. "Or maybe I'll just casually mention your court-martial. You may have been let off, but we both know that was the lawyers. You still aided the Centauri invasion, and I don't think your new husband would be well-served by having a wife accused of treason."

"Just as I doubt your wife would like to learn that you were fucking me," she countered, "while you were engaged to her."

To her surprise, his expression hardened even more.

"Do I look like I give a shit, Breeze?"

Honestly, he didn't. This wasn't his world, and he knew it. Threats to it no longer mattered to him.

"Please..." She took a deep breath. "What do you want in exchange for your silence?"

"To be left alone."

"Done."

"And..." he hesitated, "I want my career back."

There it was. Thomas the soldier.

"Let me see what I can do," she said. "I may be out, but I still have friends in uniform."

"You and your kind make me sick," he muttered.

"I know. So you stay in uniform and do what you're best at, and I'll stay in my silk dress and do what I'm best at. We both want success for Terra, and for ourselves—we're actually on the same side."

His laugh was bitter, but some of the hostility drained from his eyes. Wordlessly he guided her back to the collection of guests.

Dinner was exquisite, and Breeze was newly impressed at Soma Kane's ability to throw the perfect party. Despite the ever-present threat of rebel stealth ships, she'd managed to acquire

Martian potatoes to complement the sun-grown, organic salad, and with dessert she even had two bottles of the latest ice-wine from Triton. Thus she ensured that her position—as heiress to one of the largest trading companies in Terra—remained intact. And all the while she played the happy expectant mother with an enchanting grace.

Genius.

Chatter around the table meandered as it did from topic to topic, starting with the innocuous—the latest entertainment and fashions—and moving to sports and the inevitable bragging about children. Breeze rode the currents with ease, watching for opportunities. As the ice-wine was poured, one of the magnates leaned forward and looked up to the head of the table.

"Thomas, I'm dying to hear more about what happened to poor *Toronto*," he said. "Where are the crew, now? Are you planning a rescue of them?"

Thomas dabbed at his mouth with a napkin. Breeze tuned in.

"There's still some mystery around *Toronto*'s fate," Thomas said. "I can't really say what the overall plan is."

"Thomas is only a sublieutenant," Vijay chimed in innocently. "You can't expect him to know top strategies." Before anyone else could speak, though, Breeze laid her hand on her husband's.

"I think I may have misled you earlier, darling," she said with a bit more volume than normal. "Thomas is far more than a sublieutenant."

Vijay's brow furrowed, and she noted the interested expressions from around the table. She assumed a look of modesty.

"I don't know if everyone was aware, but I recently retired from Astral Intelligence."

Surprise and new interest focused upon her.

"I obviously can't give details, but I supported Thomas on many occasions. His official rank changes from time to time, depending on his mission. He may be wearing a sublieutenant's rank right now, but that hasn't always been the case. I myself have served under him, and my rank," she paused for emphasis, "was commander."

The magnate smiled and nodded, turning a respectful gaze back to Thomas.

"I'm sure you understand," Thomas added, "why I'm not always at liberty to discuss my job."

"Of course, of course. You're the, ah, ace in the hole."

"And I think Breeze," Thomas gave her a friendly glance, "has said all that needs to be said."

"Who?" Sheridan asked.

"It was a nickname for me," Breeze laughed. "My maiden name was Brisebois, but everybody called me Breeze."

Sheridan nodded amid the polite laughter.

"And what did you call Thomas?"

"Mostly," she said, smiling to the head of the table, "I called him sir."

Amid the renewed laughter, she saw his tiny nod of gratitude.

The truce had taken hold. She'd happily fulfill her promise to get his career kickstarted again. With luck he'd stay out on the front line, get himself killed, and she'd finally be rid of him.

15

It was hard to imagine the world changing much, for the loss of a single person.

Jack laughed to himself, lifting his head and breathing in the cool sea breeze that rushed over him. The waters of the strait sparkled in the brilliant sunshine, and he glanced around the park. It was a good thing none of the passers-by could read his thoughts—that last one sounded a bit suicidal.

But what difference did a single person make, anyway?

His hometown hadn't changed much since the war started. Some things were harder to find in shops, but in general people in Vancouver just lived their lives like always. They went to work, raised their families, worried about taxes. The usual. His folks were thrilled to see him, as always, but this time he just couldn't stomach being paraded around to all their friends. He wasn't some hero—he was just a tired guy who wanted a rest.

Coming down to Bridge Park had been a good idea, he decided. Leaving the crowded mass of the city behind, he'd ridden the train south through the razed land and out onto the delta. Rice paddies stretched to every horizon, blurring the line between land, river and sea. And then, in the shadow of the ruined supports of the bridge, the park rose like a garden oasis. He wasn't the only person who'd had the idea today, either, and the park was lifted by the shrieks of children playing on the fun zone behind him.

Sitting on his bench, Jack took in the sights and sounds of his little corner of the world. In the distance over the water he could see the dark, low shapes of the islands, and there was the constant movement of skycraft heading to and from Vancouver's big sister Victoria, the city located on the largest island. He sometimes wondered why the State didn't build a new bridge to the islands, but then he glanced up at the massive towers of ancient concrete looming over him, and realized that a new bridge might cheapen the sacrifices symbolized by the old.

A man sat down at the other end of the bench. He returned Jack's polite nod.

"Beautiful day," he said.

"Welcome to the West Coast summer," Jack replied. "Should be like this for the next, oh, three months or so."

A smile stretched across plain features, eyes casting around in appreciation before returning with a sudden interest.

"We've met before, I think," the man said, turning slightly. "Is your name Jack?"

"Uhh, yeah." He studied the man anew. Middle-aged, middle-build, nothing remarkable about his face—but he did look vaguely familiar.

"I'm Sasha Korolev," he said. "We met in *Normandy*, during the Sirius campaign." His face split in a good-natured smile. "You stole my seat for a briefing, I think."

Jack laughed as the memory came rushing back. He really had been the personification of a "dumb subbie" in his day. He made to rise from the bench.

"Am I stealing your seat now, sir?"

Korolev chuckled and waved him back down.

"There are no uniforms here, Jack. I'm just another citizen enjoying the day. I don't mean to disturb you, either, if you were looking for solitude." He shifted as if to leave.

"No, no, please." Jack motioned for him to stay, realizing suddenly that a fellow veteran to talk to might be just what he needed. "What brings you to Vancouver?"

"I travel all over Terra with my job." He shrugged. "I had a meeting here and figured I'd come down and see the great bridge."

Jack cast his eyes up again at the massive stanchions towering up out of the waves. Any sign of the old bridge deck had long since fallen away or been removed, and all that remained was the pair of towers that had once supported the soaring arc stretching from here all the way to the first of the islands on the horizon.

"It's a beautiful place," Jack said, "and I've been here tons of times, but it still moves me."

"It's hard to imagine such a peaceful place being the site of such a great sacrifice," Korolev agreed.

"From what I've seen, most places are peaceful until we get there." It was a cheeky statement, Jack knew, and he was relieved to see this senior Corps officer simply nod. They sat in silence for a long moment, the breeze gusting over them.

"Are you with one of the ships right now?" Korolev asked.

"*Admiral Bowen*. I was in *Frankfurt*, but she was destroyed over Thor."

"Sorry to hear that. Lifeboats aren't fun."

"Oh, I wasn't even on board when it happened. I was extracting some of your troopers from the surface."

"Did you successfully retrieve them?"

"Yes."

"Thank you."

The quiet earnestness of Korolev's expression made Jack pause. He thought back, trying to recall if Korolev's name had been listed as one of the senior commanders in the Valhalla theater.

"Were they your troopers?"

"No... but every soldier is valuable, Jack. Any time one lives instead of dies, it's a good day."

Jack's mind flashed back to images of Master Rating Daisy Singh. She'd had a great laugh, but every time he tried to remember it he was flooded by the image of her dead face, frozen in mouth-open shock from the slug that had torn through her.

"I wish we had more good days."

Korolev was gazing up at the bridge, but he turned at that.

"Do you want to talk about it, my friend? No ranks, no roles. Just two guys shooting the shit, as they say."

"I guess you've seen your fair share of shit."

"Yeah, I was a troop commander in the Dog Watch, and I did a bit of time in Special Forces."

"Really? Can I ask what you did in the ASF?"

"You can ask…" Korolev's grim smile said the rest.

"I get it," Jack said, leaning in. "Not so much the details, but can I ask you another question about it?"

"Go ahead."

"How did you deal with it? I realize that it's our job to go into harm's way, and I guess I'm okay with that. But the shit we do sometimes… And lots of people die."

Jack already guessed that he wasn't going to get the standard *hoo-rah* speech from this Corps officer, but even so the response surprised.

"It sucks, Jack. It really sucks."

A cloud drifted over the bridge towers, and the wind suddenly carried a chill.

"But how do you deal with it? You've been in for what, thirty years?"

"Thirty-seven."

"How have you not taken your assault rifle and put it in your own mouth at some point?"

Korolev pulled his jacket closed, nodding thoughtfully.

"I've had enough troopers do that, Jack, and it makes me want to do it myself every time, but I never have." His eyes rose to hold Jack's with their quiet intensity. "Because I've always had other troopers who are still alive and relying on me. I could never turn my back on those people who are relying on me to get them home."

Images of the wild descent to the shattered base on Thor flooded Jack's memory. Of taking out the ground batteries, of dodging fire, of landing on the roof and getting the troopers on board. He hadn't known it at the time, but Thomas had been one of those troopers he'd saved. Thomas Kane had been relying on him—Jack Mallory—to get him home.

Yet so had Daisy Singh.

"I guess what really gets me," he said suddenly, "is just how much we rely on luck. We get all this training, and all this equipment, but even if we do everything right, sooner or later some lucky shot snuffs us out."

"When I was a young officer I heard my troops call that

'Athena's Whim'—named for the bitchy Greek war goddess."

"We pilots just call it bullshit bad luck."

"Well, I guess you don't get the same training in classical literature as the Corps."

Laughter burst forth from his throat. It must have been audio books, since it was widely assumed most troopers couldn't read. Although, he considered, his old friend Katja had been an opera singer before joining the Corps.

"All that good training, gone with a single bullet." Korolev sat back. "The war is such a huge thing—it's hard to think that any one of us can actually make a difference."

Jack couldn't believe how similar his own thoughts were to this senior officer's. Maybe he wasn't crazy… or traitorous… after all.

"But rising to a senior rank must help," he said. "Now your decisions can affect much bigger things than just a lone grunt in a trench—or a pilot in a Hawk."

"In one sense, yes, but in another, I'm powerless because I'm not the one who actually takes action—I just direct others to do so. I might set events in motion, but I can't control how they turn out."

"Great, so if I survive my time in the cockpit, then I have years of second-hand guilt to look forward to."

Korolev sighed, but his expression was sympathetic.

Jack looked out at the bridge again. It was a monument he'd seen since childhood, but now he looked at it with new understanding.

"I wonder if they knew just what they were doing when they blew up the bridge."

"You mean, did they know they were saving the entire human race?"

"Yeah. I wonder how those people felt when they actively killed their fellow citizens and doomed millions more to death."

"I think they knew that they weren't dooming anyone, Jack. The mainland was contaminated, and the virus was spreading fast. Cutting off the islands was the only way to ensure that anybody survived at all."

"I know, but I wonder if they knew."

Korolev glanced up at the bridge, then back to Jack.

"They were probably scared to death and hating themselves,

but it was an act of tremendous courage that they knew was the right decision, no matter how hard."

Jack had always been proud to live near the site of the event where humanity's battle against the MAS outbreak had finally turned. Blowing up the bridge had isolated Victoria and the essential bio-research centers, and allowed work on the vaccine to continue. The act had shocked an already panicked world, but it had given others the courage to do the same. The guns of Kristiansand in Norway had stopped the thousands of boats fleeing continental Europe, and the pilots of Hokkaido had cleared their skies of refugees. Because those sacrifices had been made, the vaccine had been developed in time to deploy and save the lives of billions.

"At least," Jack said thoughtfully, "the bridge sappers knew why they were doing what they did. It isn't always the same for soldiers like us."

"That was definitely the best part of being Special Forces," Korolev replied. "We knew we were making a difference, and why. Even if the mission was simple and isolated, we knew why it would make a difference. That helped a lot."

"If only I knew how to apply for Special Forces," Jack scoffed. Nobody knew where these elite, secret soldiers with their amazing powers came from. Jack had only ever met one—that he knew of—and Suleiman Chang had been one scary individual. He wondered idly if he could find Chang in the network.

"No one applies," Korolev said. "They're selected."

"Oh, well, I'll just wait then." It was a joke, but Korolev didn't laugh, or look away. He continued to regard Jack with that same steady, kind expression. A dawning suspicion swept over Jack.

"So... does anyone ever *leave* Special Forces?"

"Not really. Sometimes we go back to the regular Fleet or Corps for career postings, but it depends."

"You were a colonel the last time we met. Has that changed?"

"My rank changes weekly, Jack, depending on what I'm doing, but my real rank is brigadier."

"What rank is the highest member of the ASF?"

"Brigadier."

Jack wasn't sure whether to feel flattered, suspicious, or afraid.

"What was your meeting here in Vancouver?"

"To talk to you, Jack."

"Why?"

"Special Forces has kept a file on you ever since your little science experiment in Centauria. Your ability to think laterally is remarkable—you have a knack for making connections between things that no one else can see. And, let's not kid ourselves, you're just about the most unorthodox pilot in the Fleet."

Jack stared at the man sitting next to him. Dressed in regular civilian clothes, graying brown hair over nondescript features, with the gentle expression of a professor or a favorite uncle, he was the head of Astral Special Forces—perhaps the most powerful individual alive. And he had come looking for Jack. The surreal nature of this conversation sent a chill through Jack's body.

"Am I in trouble, sir?"

"Not at all. I just wanted to meet you in person. I wanted to get a sense of who you are."

"Sorry I've been such a downer. This last patrol was tough."

"I know."

Of course he did—he was the head of Special fucking Forces. Anger suddenly burned through Jack.

"What do you know?"

"I know that your ship discovered the *Toronto* derelict. I know that you personally saw some close-in combat with rebel ships. And I know that you lost your crewman."

"Do you know her name?"

"Yes. Do you want to talk about her?"

"No," he said firmly. "It's not like she was my sister, or my friend, or my lover or anything. But she was my responsibility!"

"And bullshit bad luck took her."

"How the fuck do I deal with that?" Jack suddenly realized that he was shouting, and he noticed the glares of nearby parents. His hand gripped the wooden back of the bench. He felt like screaming at those self-righteous civilians. What the fuck did they know? About *anything*.

"I was tortured nearly to death," he whispered, "and all the worlds saw it in their living rooms. I've killed hundreds of rebel sailors in their stealth ships, and I created the Dark Bomb—and somehow, sir, I can live with that. But I've lost too many people who put their trust in me, because they thought I was capable of keeping them safe. Singh wasn't the first, but I hope to God she's the last because if she isn't, I might be the next one putting an assault rifle in his mouth."

Silence fell over the bench as Jack stared down at his hands. He could see Korolev's knee where the brigadier sat facing him.

"I don't think," Jack said finally, "I'd be a very good Special Forces person."

"On the contrary," came the soft reply, "I think you're exactly what we need."

Jack blinked tears from his eyes as he looked up.

"Special Forces," Korolev continued, "isn't necessarily what you think. You wouldn't have to storm enemy positions, set bombs, or assassinate people—leave that for the movies. I need people who have the ability to do remarkable things, and the convictions to make the right decisions for Terra." He gestured over his shoulder at the bridge monument. "I wish I could have had some of the folks who blew this up."

"But instead, you got me."

"I have the entire Terran population to choose from, Jack, and I chose to speak to you."

"Why would I want to listen to you?"

"Because I'm offering you the chance to make a difference. As just one man, to *really* make a difference. This war is out of control and too many people—across all human systems—are dying for no reason. I have a plan to end the war, and to help me you won't need to kill anyone. I need someone with your unique abilities, and you'd be part of an elite team who are as talented and dedicated as you are."

Jack brushed the moisture from his eyes.

"Are you interested, Jack?"

16

Despite the State's best efforts, it was impossible not to notice the anger among the crowds lining the streets. Breeze stared through the window of the limo at the faces beyond, as the car trundled far too slowly along the narrow secure lane. Glancing the other way, she noted that Vijay wasn't even looking out, focused instead on his tablet. She placed her hand against the soft material of his trousers.

"Why did this event have to be in the outer city?"

"Because that's where the factory is," he replied without glancing up.

"But look at this place."

He did, lowering his tablet and gazing out both windows, and then up through the transparent, tinted roof. The dark gray apartment towers stretched high, leaving only a thin strip of pale sky at the very top. The facades were grim and showing their age, nets protruding every ten stories to catch stray garbage or brickwork. Many of the lower floors were dedicated to commercial ventures, signs in windows advertising various inexpensive services, while at street level reinforced doors were rolled back to reveal stands of goods for sale.

In front of those, pressed behind barriers manned by armored police, were the local citizens of Terra. They dutifully lined the streets, watching with grim stoicism as the long parade of cars slowly passed.

At no time did Vijay's expression change from one of casual interest.

"It's a typical city on Earth," he said finally. "Could be Miami, could be Baghdad, could be Longreach, but it happens to be Munich. They all kind of look the same."

"Wretched is what it looks like," she replied, frowning. "I'm sure even Munich has a gated section."

"Yes," he said, taking her hand and squeezing it affectionately, "but the gated section doesn't have any factories in it. And that's what we're here to celebrate—the revitalization of Terra's industrial might. Hopefully the new factory will bring some life back to this ward."

Breeze couldn't see how a scattering of new jobs made a difference to this monolithic slum, but she knew that it was the hope. And hope was what politicians had to sell.

Central Europe as a whole had been particularly hard-hit by the rebel disruptions to trade, and ever since the Civil Defense Headquarters had been destroyed by a Centauri surface sneak attack, there had been little law and order to protect what businesses still survived. The result had been a year of rapid decline for the whole region and a swelling of Munich's population as the destitute trundled into the city looking for work.

Looking at the heavy police presence outside, Breeze wasn't worried about civil strife. What frightened her most were the rumors of new cases of the Gray Death. Another outbreak might deal with the overcrowding, but she wasn't going to be part of the cull. She'd been sure to visit the booster clinic before making this trip.

"So who do you need to speak to today?" she asked, "and when do you want me at your side?"

"I always want you at my side," he said with a smile. "But today I need to try to talk to Sheridan alone, and I'm sure a few of the Triton-based miners will want to corner me to discuss import channels."

"Why do you need to talk to Sheridan? He's not even in government."

"He has a lot of influence, both in Parliament and with the general population. He's been making concerted efforts to raise his profile here on Earth, and it's working. If he can influence both Earth and Mars, he's a man I want on my side."

"I thought you two were political enemies."

"In Parliament, yes." Vijay shrugged. "But in the real world we have to get the job done."

Breeze sat back against the leather seat, admiring her husband anew as he returned his attention to his tablet. Brilliant, hard-working, and above all practical. He lacked charisma, but she was happy to provide that at his side. As a team, they were unstoppable.

The car finally pulled up to the main gate of the new factory. The grim crowds were noticeably further away, barricaded on the far side of the square, and security was overt. Armored police thumped between fixed gun positions, and patrol cruisers traced slow orbits overhead. A red carpet had been laid out through the factory gates to the road, and on either side, behind velvet ropes, crowds of cheering citizens waved Terran flags. Through the car windows Breeze spotted the locations of the news teams and considered where to position herself when walking alongside Vijay. Huge screens had been placed on the factory walls to project the arrivals to the public, a live feed that was visible clear across the square.

The door opened and a wave of hot, stinky air washed into the cabin. Breeze was thankful that the tinted windows hid her face and she busied herself with sliding across the rear seat as gracefully as possible while Vijay stepped out into the lights. She gave him a moment to be imaged on his own, then reached out to take the hand he extended back to her.

Getting out of a limousine in a form-fitting dress was an art she'd been practicing, and with relief she planted her feet on the carpet without incident, then stood up at her husband's left side. There was a roar of approval from the cheering crowds, which she answered with her most winning smile. It seemed as if the PR machine was still working hard to cultivate the idea of Minister Shah and his wife as the new power couple in Terran society.

A shy little girl was led forward to present Breeze with a bouquet of flowers. Breeze bent down to accept them, smiling radiantly at the child's nervous features.

"Thank you so much," she gushed, although her words

were muted by the roar of a police cruiser ascending overhead. "They're beautiful."

The girl managed a smile in return, bravely standing her ground and accepting Breeze's fingers against her cheek. The moment lasted long enough for the media to grab their images, then the girl was led away. Breeze straightened with the bouquet and took Vijay's arm to stroll past the cheering crowds.

There was a schedule to keep, and even higher-ranking politicians still to come, so the moment on the red carpet was short-lived. Within moments Breeze found herself through the factory gates and into the relative quiet of the main manufacturing floor.

A large central space had been cleared, many of the production machines jammed against the outer walls of the vast room. Breeze scanned for security points and any possible hiding places where assassins might lurk. Too many public figures had been killed in the past few months, and today's gathering would be a prime target. There was no pattern to the assassinations, though, and Breeze wondered if the killings were secretly ordered by the State, and not the rebels.

On an impulse she gripped Vijay's arm tighter.

One of Vijay's staffers relieved her of the bouquet and offered a drink. Another staffer stepped up to Vijay's other side, her tablet discreetly in hand to support him in his upcoming discussions. Most of the guests had already arrived, so it wasn't long before Vijay was introduced to the CEO of a local mining corporation. Breeze smiled along at the standard chit-chat about government support for the protection of local exploitation, and listened to Vijay's smooth reassurances which ultimately lacked any solid commitment. An agreement was made for the CEO to meet with a senior official in the Ministry, and the interview concluded.

"Ah," Vijay said, leaning in, "there's one of the Tritonian magnates I need to talk to. Would you excuse me, dear?"

Breeze noted the dour, pale little man whose entire appearance screamed that he was from Triton, and was suddenly glad to be freed from the next conversation. She glanced around the room.

"Of course. Is there anyone you think I should talk to?"

Vijay scanned the room. "Wes Taal has just arrived. This

event has nothing to do with Defense, and I know he's irritated to be here. Maybe you could brighten his day?"

"Thanks."

He kissed her on the cheek and strode off, staffer in his wake. She slinked over to her new target.

Minister of Defense Wesley Taal did indeed look rather grumpy, standing off to the side of the central mingling space and speaking quietly to a man in uniform. It was a colonel from the Corps, and Breeze quickly assured herself that she hadn't crossed paths with this officer before. Confident that she was free from recognition, she promptly ignored the officer and turned her full gaze upon Minister Taal.

Taal's eyes met hers with a degree of curiosity, then sudden recognition. A politician's smile split his features and he willingly grasped her outstretched hand to kiss it.

"Mrs. Shah, how nice to finally meet you."

"Minister Taal, how good of you to come. It's so important that senior members of Parliament show their support for the revitalization of this region."

"Yes," he said, not quite hiding a sigh. "Especially with all the other matters to attend to."

"Sir," the colonel growled, "I'll get the team working on those numbers for you."

"Thank you, Peter."

The colonel slipped away.

"And how are you enjoying these events, Mrs. Shah?"

"I enjoy supporting my husband, and the good work he does for the State."

A chuckle. "About as much as I do, then."

"Perhaps not quite as much," she offered with a smirk.

"Vijay has been an excellent member of the party for years, but since the attacks last year he's really shown his true form. You have a good man, Mrs. Shah."

"We've been together since not long after those attacks—he wasn't even minister yet when we first met. I'm very proud of how all of Parliament has rebounded from the attack"—she smiled—"but Vijay has been truly exceptional. Thank you for supporting him."

Taal was the senior member of the Progressive Party in Parliament and in a sense Vijay's boss. The Progressives were the largest group in the five-party coalition that formed the current government, but alliances sometimes shifted and few positions in Parliament were secure. With all the newbie members elected after the attacks, Vijay's promotion to minister had been as much due to his relative seniority as it had his competence. Breeze's job in the political world was to ensure that her husband remained in everyone's good graces.

"I understand you served in the Astral Force," Taal said. "So did I, although years ago."

"I served in my own, small way," she said carefully. "Nothing as important as what you did."

"We all do our parts, and every veteran is important. Thank you for your service."

"Thank you, Minister, for yours."

He laughed, eyes scanning the room.

"We're both veterans—can we cut the political formalities?"

"Gladly."

"I'm Wes. May I call you Charity?"

"Of course. You can call me Breeze, if you want—it was my nickname when I served."

"They called me Skip—you don't want to know why."

She laughed, surprised at how relaxing it was to speak to a fellow veteran. It wasn't company she'd ever sought, but the military had been a big part of her life for years, and she couldn't deny the bond created by service. For a remarkably long time she stood at the edge of the factory floor swapping war stories with Wes and genuinely enjoying his company.

Their chatter was interrupted by an announcement that the President was about to begin his address. An obligatory hush fell over the room and all eyes moved to the dais where De Chao Peterson, the President of Terra, was taking his position.

Peterson had been vice-president at the time of the attacks, thankfully away on holiday when the President had been killed in her State residence. Always a hawkish influence on government, Peterson had used the Centauri attacks as justification for doubling the budgets of the police and the Ministry of Internal

Security, cracking down on any suspected dissidents with ruthless speed.

Breeze still gave thanks to whatever god existed that her own court-martial had taken place right after the attacks, and been overshadowed by the political jockeying that had consumed all government energies in the vacuum of power. By the time Peterson had consolidated his position and started his putsch, Breeze's lawyers had worn out the State prosecutors, who fell under pressure to go after higher-profile targets.

She'd slipped through the net, and now she stood in the very presence of power as an invited guest.

Peterson's public persona hardly matched his actions over the past year. Of middling height with the stocky, powerful build of a scrapper, he looked out over the assembled crowd with a kindly expression. His hair was cut very short—a testament to his years in the Army—but it was a glittering silver that somehow softened his square features. His suit was modest and his manner was gentle. To the people of Terra he gave the impression of a favorite uncle—humble and fair, but firm when necessary. From her distant vantage point Breeze could barely see the man himself, but a screen broadcast his speech, larger than life. The screens outside were also broadcasting to the people in the streets.

His speech was typical. Praising the hard work of the Munich people, he declared the opening of this new factory as a triumph, and lauded the continuing technological advances of Terran industry. New weapons were coming on line, which would stop the rebels in their tracks.

"You should see some of the new tricks we've developed," Taal said. "Technology we didn't even know could exist a year ago."

If he was talking about the Dark Bomb, Breeze was only too familiar with it—but drawing attention to that fact was never a good idea. If he was talking about anything else, she didn't really care.

No speech from the President was complete without a combative statement toward the rebels.

"It is with great satisfaction," Peterson boomed, "that I can report another victory in the war against terror. A recent assassination attempt by the rebels was thwarted by our brave security forces. One rebel was captured, and he has admitted to his treason. Justice will now be served." The screen overhead suddenly shifted to the familiar scene of an execution chamber. An interested murmur rippled through the crowd.

"Who was the attack against?" Breeze whispered.

"Sheridan," Taal replied. "In his hotel room after a fund-raiser. Thankfully we had Special Forces operatives embedded. Otherwise I think we'd be looking for a new leader of the Opposition."

Breeze shivered. No one was safe these days.

The execution chamber was a clinical steel and plastic, with the chair located in the center. The prisoner was led in from the left. Breeze had seen enough public executions over the years, but something about this one captured her interest. Who was this terrorist? What kind of person could infiltrate Terran security, and come so close to killing one of their leaders?

The prisoner was a man, tall and clearly fit under his orange coveralls. His hands and feet were shackled, forcing him to shuffle toward the chair. He did so on his own, though, angrily shrugging off any attempt at guidance from the guards. He sat down in the chair, head high and face pointed defiantly at the camera. His lips moved as he said something, but the State never transmitted audio from the execution chamber. The prisoner was clamped into the chair.

"For crimes against the State," an off-screen voice boomed, "this rebel, John Ford of Centauria, is sentenced to death."

Blades shot from the sides of the chair, sliding into his torso, followed immediately by a deadly surge of electricity through the metal. The prisoner's defiant expression collapsed in overwhelming pain before sagging in death. His body continued to jerk as the last of the electrical charge shot through him.

"Justice is served," the off-screen voice declared.

A round of applause erupted from the gathered crowd in the factory. Breeze instinctively joined in, but her eyes searched for her husband. Vijay was next to Sheridan—the assassin's target—and neither man displayed any sense of satisfaction as they dutifully clapped. Even from her distance, she saw Sheridan cringe slightly as someone patted him on the back.

"Sheridan's a good man," Taal commented. "I'm glad we didn't lose him, even if he is the biggest threat to our ruling coalition."

"Is he?" Breeze heard herself ask.

"Of course he is."

She looked up at the Minister of Defense.

"He's a good man," he repeated. "Like your husband."

Breeze suddenly wanted very much to be back next to Vijay, political tactics be damned. This was a cold, dangerous world, and she felt the need for some warmth.

17

The singing studio was nothing more than a hollowed-out, dressed and pressurized chamber in an asteroid, but to Katja, it was pure release.

The thunderous opening strains of the recorded orchestra washed over her in the darkness. It was a particular aria from Mozart's *The Magic Flute*—the aria she'd always dreamed would be the jewel in the crown of her graduation performance with a Fine Arts degree. Her first notes were low and powerful, the melody of German words flowing from her lips with the ease of years' practice.

Her pitch rose as required, and she felt her throat and lungs come alive as they released their power. Oh, it was glorious to be able to truly sing again! She knew what was coming—the famous staccato refrain—but the passion was in her and she felt no fear. The music countered her voice, she paused... and let the heavenly notes fly. The darkness in the room was banished by the full power of a restored coloratura soprano at the height of her ability.

She paused the recording. Silence fell in the studio as she brought the lights up again. There was more to the aria, she knew, but having finally conquered the staccato she knew the rest would be anticlimactic. She'd sing the whole piece another day. There were no demanding professors or senior classmates sneering at her now.

Queen of the Night *this*, she thought smugly.

She'd fought to regain her true singing voice for months in her time off at SFHQ, and the sheer pleasure of exploring her old repertoire had been exhilarating, but now she'd done something she'd never mastered in her training, and she'd done it on her own. It was a good feeling. It helped her to forget about the real world.

<Katja.>

She sighed. But the real world never left her alone for long.

<Sir?> she replied to Korolev's polite query.

<Please join me in control room two.>

<Yes, sir.>

She'd been promised a break. After the penetrating debrief of the last mission had left her mentally exhausted, she'd been assured that she'd done her job as well as could have been expected, and been granted some time off. This time, she really needed it.

Shutting down the studio, she walked out into the wide boulevard of the hobby wing. Tall trees lined both sides of the main path, and beyond them the street was lined with boutique "shops" designed to cater to any interest or fancy an operative might express. The studio had been built especially for Katja as soon as she'd arrived last year, but if ever she wanted to try her hand at something else, the options seemed limitless. Pottery, archery, and even snorkeling had all been welcome distractions at various times, but the singing was her own private obsession.

The climbing wall loomed high behind one of the boutiques, and a sudden twinge of sadness struck her. That had been Chang's latest interest, she knew, before that Centauri bitch dumped him, exposed, into the Bulk. Sorrow morphed into anger, as it so often did, and Katja quickened her pace. If Korolev wanted to interrupt her private time, he'd better have a damn good reason.

Operatives were never permanently paired up, and she'd done half a dozen missions either alone or with another operative. But Chang had been her rock, always there to listen as she unloaded after each mission. He'd never been anything but honest with her, and never anything but supportive. Just like when he'd been her sergeant back in the Corps. He would bail her out of a scrape, and then let her take all the glory. He'd been a constant in her life, *the* constant in her life, and now he was gone.

She absently touched the spot in her chest where the quantum entanglement had screamed his death. It was as if the very fabric of the universe had captured that agony, and then lodged it in her heart.

Somebody was going to pay for that.

Hopefully Korolev had a new target for her.

It was strange to enter the operational section of SFHQ in her civilian clothes, but Katja didn't feel intimidated by the uniforms around her. She was an operative, and her actions were beyond question. She was unhindered in her approach to control room two, and inside she found Korolev alone, his eyes watching the large screen on a console before him. He looked up.

"My apologies for disturbing you," he said.

"I assume you have a good reason."

"Always."

"Word on Moretti?"

"No," he replied. "She's gone underground, and isn't moving, but she's still on Earth somewhere. Our exposure campaign will either keep her buried—and ineffective—or get her spotted. We have assets in position to move the moment we see her."

"Are you sending me back in, then?" She heard the relish in her own voice.

"No, this hunt requires patience."

"So what do you want me for?"

He gestured toward the screen in front of him. "We've been training a new operative, and I want to pair him with you for your next mission."

Curious, Katja walked over to see. Until now she'd always been paired with operatives who were senior to her. It was quite a compliment to be trusted with a new recruit.

The screen before her was a feed from one of the physical training rooms, and the karate sensei was drilling a white belt. Obviously not a recruit from the Corps, then—troopers trained in karate, then judo, then aikido from basic training up into the senior ranks. Katja herself had possessed a black belt in the first two disciplines, even before she joined Special Forces, and her progress in aikido had accelerated over the past year.

"Someone from the Fleet?" she asked.

"A pilot. I think you know him."

Her stomach tightened. Katja didn't make a habit of getting to know pilots. She looked closer, and recognized the shaggy brown hair dripping in sweat as the recruit worked through his drills.

"You're fucking kidding me."

"You don't approve?"

She bit down her instinctive response, forcing herself to see the issue from all sides. Jack Mallory wasn't a trooper, but not every operative lived at the pointy end like she did. He was crazy smart, true, and young enough to be malleable. But still...

"I don't know."

"I think you two will be paired well together," Korolev said evenly. "You have complementary skills, and an existing rapport. There is a critical mission I want you both to conduct."

Katja stiffened, aware that the brigadier was watching her in that all-seeing way of his.

"Sir... I've never shied away from duty before, but it's only been a few weeks since the last mission, and that one took its toll."

"I'm not asking you to deploy this afternoon," he said. "Jack still needs more training, and the time for your mission isn't here yet, but I want you to get reacquainted with him now so that he can get used to the idea that you're still alive, and that you'll be working together."

"You haven't told him about me yet?"

"He's had a lot to take in these past few weeks. If I'd told him about you before now, he'd just have been distracted, and most likely he would have wanted to see you."

"So you want me to just wander down to the dojo and say hi."

"Pretty much, yes."

"I'm not sure I approve of your method."

"Well, I thought with me being commander of Special Forces, and all..."

He was right, and she knew it. Who was she to question him? So she pushed down her objections, and looked back at the monitor. Jack was desperately trying to block the sensei's careful strikes.

"How's he adapting to the implants?"

"His ability to maneuver in the Cloud is unprecedented. It's as if his mind was always wired to exist in a wider space. He's been poring through the depths of Terran knowledge like a fish in water." Korolev sighed. "I've been tempted on occasion to implement some sort of parental controls on his access—do you know how many porn sites are out there?—but he's a young man and I wanted to let him explore uninhibited."

Katja smiled. Jack was still Jack.

"I'll arrange a pretty playdate for him," she said. "Someone sultry."

"You're welcome to do the job yourself."

"Oh, please." Katja frowned. "It'd be like fucking my kid brother. Besides, if we're going to be partners, I want to keep things at a certain distance. I don't sleep within the chain of command." It was an automatic statement, and she knew it wasn't universally true. Korolev knew it too. She glared at him. "Shut up."

His expression was maddeningly noncommittal.

"I guess I should go and reintroduce myself," she said.

"There's plenty of time to get reacquainted. You'll be taking over the majority of his training from now on."

She paused. So much for off-time—but she could always make Jack listen to her sing. That might be fun. *And*, she realized as she left the control room, it was actually kind of exciting to see an old friend. Her pace quickened as she approached the dojo.

The lesson was just ending, and Katja slipped off her shoes at the edge of the mats as Jack bowed to the sensei. She stepped onto the padded surface, watching him closely as he grabbed a towel and mopped his face and hair. The flush of blood in his features highlighted the faint scars of his reconstructive surgery, but otherwise he looked much the same as she remembered him. He noticed her approach without recognition.

Her hair was still black from the last op, she realized, and he'd rarely seen her in casual civilian clothes. She stepped closer, toying with the idea of actually pretending to be someone else. But, she decided, if he was an operative now, he'd better be able to handle shocks.

"How's the training?" she asked.

"Oh, great," he said with a grin, half-glancing at her as he gathered his gear. "I'm doing well with my white belt of purity. Soon I'll be promoted to yellow belt of humility. Then eventually orange belt of servility…"

"Jack," she said, standing carefully at arm's length. "Please look at me."

He did, and she watched his young face morph from the mild surprise of her request through confusion, then realization, then shock. He stared at her in silence.

"I'm still alive," she said.

His eyes flicked across her features, looking her up and down before boring into her.

"Are you a clone?"

"What?" She took a half step back. "No, I'm Katja… for real. I wasn't killed in the attack on Longreach, and I've been in Special Forces ever since."

"But… your family thinks you're dead."

"And officially I am."

"But *I* thought you were dead!"

"I'm sorry, Jack."

His face twisted in anger, and she saw the punch coming. She knocked it away, stepping back to keep her distance from Jack's follow-through. Then, remarkably, he lowered to one knee and bowed his head, his body shuddering…

…with laughter.

He chortled quietly at first, then tilted his head back in a guffaw that filled the dojo. He rose back to his feet and sized her up again with bright eyes.

"You, madame, are a bitch."

Relief flooded through her, a sincere smile spreading across her face.

"It's good to see you again, flyboy."

"If I try to give you a hug are you going to bat me aside again?"

She responded by stepping toward him, arms reaching out to wrap around his shoulders. He was radiating heat, and the fabric of his gui was unpleasantly damp, but she didn't care. He was Jack Mallory, boy wonder, and he was here in the flesh. Life suddenly took on a little more meaning.

* * *

<How's this?>

Katja braced her mind against the flood of data Jack pushed toward her, following as many lines of thought as she could but still not keeping up. The connections he'd made between commuter movements around the Pacific Rim, energy spikes, consumer downloads, State transport schedules, and even the damned weather... they were remarkable. It made her head hurt just trying to grasp the overall conclusions he presented.

"Very good," Korolev said, seated next to her, "but remember to filter out the irrelevant data when you share it with us."

"I'm not always sure if something is going to be irrelevant," Jack replied.

"At first, no," Korolev countered, "but when you present to us, you should've already figured out what info we need. If you bombard us with everything you've investigated, it gets confusing."

Jack nodded, frowning thoughtfully. "I guess sometimes I'm still working through possible connections. I'll have a solid web of analysis for you, but I'm still chasing secondary ideas."

"It's great stuff, Jack," Katja said. "I've been living the Cloud for over a year, and I'm having trouble keeping up with you. You're a natural."

"Too bad there aren't black belts for Cloud analysis," he said with a wry grin.

"You'll get there," she said, jabbing at him and easily beating his late block.

"Stop that. I have a beautiful mind."

Korolev rose from the table. His amused expression encompassed both of them.

"You're coming together nicely as a team. Not long now, and I'll send you on a field exercise to see how well you interact in the real world."

Katja glanced at Jack, watching his expression stiffen. Korolev departed and they were alone in the briefing room, facing each other across the table.

"You okay?" she asked.

"Taking this stuff into the real world," he said. "Sounds a little scary."

"It'll be something routine, probably on Earth."

"Why Earth?"

"We won't have to worry about environmentals, and the Cloud is busiest there." She rose from her seat and beckoned for him to follow. "Let's get out of here—I need to breathe fresh air."

He followed her out into the corridor, and she headed for the elevator to take them back up to the main living chamber.

"What sort of missions have you done?" he asked as they stepped into the lift.

"All sorts," she replied. "My last one was to protect a senior politician against Centauri assassination."

"I haven't heard of any politicians dying lately, so I assume it was a success."

She glanced over at him. "The politician lived, if that's what you mean, but we lost two operatives in the fight."

"Oh." He pondered that for a long moment. "I kind of thought you guys were invincible."

"Unfortunately not, and 'you guys' includes you, now, Jack. Do *you* feel invincible?"

"Nope."

The elevator door opened onto the wide walkway and Katja stepped out, breathing in the cool air and looking out across the park that stretched below them. The ceiling illumination indicated late afternoon, and as she strolled over to the stone railing she spotted a group of suntanners relaxing by the pond. She'd never been one for lying down and cooking her skin, but a nice swim might be just the thing.

"I think I'll head down to the water," she said. "You feel like a swim?"

He made a show of rubbing his shoulder.

"The sensei has beaten the strength out of pretty much every muscle I have. I don't know if I could even doggy paddle."

"You need to keep at it, if you want to look like the rest of us." She patted the soft belly under his coveralls.

"Yeah, I get the feeling that it's always bikini season here." His eyes flickered up and down her form, as they often did. She wasn't interested, but still flattered by the attention.

"How else can we pull off our sexpionage missions?" she smirked.

"You really do that?" His expression wasn't quite as pantingly sophomoric as she'd expected.

"If required." She shrugged, not particularly proud of the fact, and regretting her attempt at humor.

"Hmm." He patted his belly. "Then I guess I better ease off on the cookies."

"The ladies will love you," she said, leaning forward on the cool stone of the railing.

"So what other kinds of missions do you do?" he asked.

"Oh, all sorts. Why?"

"Do you often execute ship captains?"

Her blood froze in her veins. And there it was. She'd always wondered if Jack had known it was her under that helmet.

Turning to fully face her companion, she folded her arms and stared at him. To his credit, he didn't drop his own gaze. If anything, his eyes became as cold as hers. There was a question in his face, she could see, but there was also something else. Was it judgement?

"That was my first mission. It was intended to test my loyalty to the State."

"I stood there," he said quietly, "and watched as you put your gun to my captain's head and blew his brains out. Then you tortured my science officer..."

"I didn't torture her."

"You twisted her arm behind her back until it snapped, and then you beat the crap out of Thomas Kane and dragged him out under arrest."

Kicking Thomas in the gut was one of the more satisfying things she'd ever done on a mission, but she really didn't like being reminded of her actions. If they were in the past, they didn't matter.

"My mission was to enforce the verdict of a Fleet Marshall Investigation. Those are rarely pretty."

"So you were just following orders."

"Yes." She definitely sensed disapproval from him. "Do you have something to say about that?"

His lips parted, but no words came out. He studied her anew, with none of the eager youth she'd always known.

"I'll follow orders," he said finally, "but I'm not going to sacrifice my humanity."

This was dangerous ground and she wanted nothing to do with it.

"We're servants of the State, Jack. The State carries the burden of our actions."

"I don't know if I can give up that burden."

"Then you'd better learn, and fast." Her mind unwillingly flashed back over that first mission, as she'd carried out her orders with brutal efficiency. She pushed down the memory, but in its place rose the faces of the dozen or more Terran civilians she'd killed. By order of the State. And the—*no*. She wouldn't think about it.

It wasn't her responsibility.

"It was in almost this exact spot," she said, "where another operative named Shin Mun-Hee once questioned my actions. Shin is dead now, and I'm still alive, so which one of us made the right choices?"

"I want to stay alive, too," he said. His expression changed again, as he withdrew from her. "I'll have your back, just like I know you'll have mine, but I don't know if I can do what you do."

She forced her arms down, adopting a more relaxed posture. It seemed to work, and Jack's stance loosened.

"You don't have to do what I do," she said. "As a team we work toward the same goals, but we have different jobs. You're the support, and I'm the pointy end—but our loyalty must be beyond question."

He nodded, still pondering before finally meeting her eye.

"The State has my loyalty, Katja. I'm here to serve, and to make a real difference."

She watched him carefully, almost feeling his emotions as he grappled with the issue of what their job entailed. It clearly troubled him, although it had never troubled her. Or so she always told herself.

"Good." She looked over at the distant pond. "You still up for a swim?"

"Yeah, sure, sounds good. I'll meet you down there."

She left him, stalking away without a backward glance. She'd always remembered fondly Jack Mallory's youthful earnestness, but being faced with it head-on, as he questioned her actions, was suddenly uncomfortable. Entering her quarters, she automatically made for the armchair, but paused behind it, fingers gripping into its soft material. The anger was boiling up, and she embraced it.

Damn him and his pathetic questions. Who was Jack Mallory to question the will of the State? If she didn't like him so much she'd be tempted to mention his doubts to their commander.

Tears began welling up in her eyes, the horror buried deep in her heart trying to burst free. As always, her anger fought them down, but Jack's honest features and blunt questioning kept intruding into her mind, almost making her anger into a negative. She didn't want to think about her past actions.

She didn't *have* to think about her past actions.

The armchair was too cumbersome to lift, so she lashed out and grabbed the nearest dining chair. Hefting it over her head she smashed it down against the hardwood table. The legs cracked off cleanly—not enough damage. She swung the chair down again and felt the grim satisfaction of the frame snapping. For a second she wished it was Jack's head.

Damn him, damn him, damn him. How dare he question her? How dare he impose morality on their mission? It wasn't his *place*.

But he was new, she said to herself through deep, calming breaths. He was still learning the life of an operative. They were relieved of all responsibility for their actions. He needed to understand that he was going to be taken care of—completely—in exchange for his loyalty. Maybe he needed a pleasant reminder of that.

She linked up to the Confidential Requirements of SFHQ.

<I want to order a pretty playdate for Operative Jack Mallory.>

<Yes, ma'am,> came the polite reply. <Any preferences?>

<A little voluptuous—he's a bit sensitive about his own weight. Have her come down to the pond in thirty minutes and casually meet him.>

<Certainly, ma'am.>

Nothing could distract a young man from his troubles better than the attention of a beautiful woman. He'd learn soon enough to stop worrying about the outside world, and focus on his job. No judgements—no consequences.

<I also need a furniture repair crew to the quarters of Operative Katja Emmes.>

<Right away, ma'am.>

A momentary image of Jack's impending pleasure filled her mind, and she felt a sudden need herself.

<And make sure one of the repairmen is available for a playdate afterward.>

<Yes, ma'am.>

Feeling the anger course through her, blocking out all other feelings, Katja finally began to calm down. Everything was going to be all right.

No judgements. No consequences.

18

The new security unit assigned to the destroyer *Singapore* incorporated the entire strike team from a fast-attack craft which had been shot down while they were on the ground conducting their assault. Thomas didn't ask for details on how they'd survived being stranded on a hostile planet, but the fact that all ten of them were still alive spoke to their abilities.

His briefing, therefore, had been short. Aside from learning the specifics of their new vessel, they already knew what they were doing.

The lieutenant in charge didn't seem that interested in small talk, and Thomas found himself dismissed and wandering the flats of *Singapore*. The damage his own team had done defending this ship had been mostly repaired, but he ran his hand absently along one of the black scars on the bulkheads. In the haste to get ships back in action, Fleet maintenance had repaired all the airtight doors but ignored the cosmetic effects of his battle. Glancing at his watch, he wondered if the XO was also ahead of schedule.

He activated his headset, pinged, and received a quick response.

"*Lieutenant Perry.*"

"XO, sir, strike officer. I've completed my briefing and I'm ready to go when you are."

"*I'm still busy.*" There was irritation plain in the reply. "*I'll call you when I'm ready.*"

"Yes, sir."

Severing the connection, he continued strolling forward. He obviously wasn't welcome at strike stores, and he doubted the bridge would appreciate his presence. The wardroom? Making idle chit-chat with strangers didn't appeal, especially since the topic of careers inevitably came up. So he continued forward and found himself at the open door to the captain's cabin. Part of him wondered if it was a bad idea.

At his knock, Commander Sean Duncan looked up from his chair.

"Thomas, come on in." Duncan motioned him to a seat and set down the tablet he'd been studying. Thomas sat stiffly.

"Your strike team has been briefed, sir. I have no concerns about their ability to defend this ship against boarders."

"Yeah," Duncan said with a smile. "She's a tough bitch and her troopers worship her. I hear every single one of them was wounded during their last action, but no one was left behind, and they carved a wake of destruction as they cleared to the evac point."

"Good to hear that the Corps is upholding its reputation."

Duncan sat back, studying him. There was a moment of silence between them which Thomas didn't enjoy, but had expected all along.

"Thomas, what's up with all this? I never understood in the first place why you did a crossover tour with the Corps. You could have done support, like I did, and here you are again." Duncan seemed to be groping for an answer to his obvious question. "Is this some sort of special mission, you hiding out as a subbie trooper on a ship?"

"I wish it was, but in fact I'm the luckiest guy in the worlds to be here."

"Why?"

"Because the other guilty parties in that Fleet Marshall Investigation were forcibly retired, put in jail, or killed. I think I got off lightly."

"What Fleet Marshall Investigation?" Duncan frowned. "You mean the one a year ago in the Research Squadron?"

"I was the XO of the ship in question," Thomas said, jerking a thumb at himself.

"I'm sorry, man."

He shrugged, settling back heavily in his chair. "I'm still alive, and I'm still in uniform—those are good things. Being forced to start my career over again does wonders for a man's humility."

Duncan snorted. "In other words, you're a changed man—but at least as a subbie you can be a skin hound again. I can't really do that now that I'm CO."

"But I'm still married, Sean, subbie or no."

"Wow, you *are* a changed man."

Thomas considered those words, even if his old friend had meant them in jest. It was strange, he realized, sitting here in a CO's cabin with his old classmate, friend, and rival. Duncan had won the race and had achieved a major command—their shared dream since the Astral College. But Thomas knew that with senior rank came political challenges, new threats. He wondered if his straight-shooting friend Sean was properly equipped to deal with them. Thomas's own dabbling in that world had led to disaster, and this past year he'd enjoyed the lack of responsibility.

"I'm just a simple trooper these days," he said. "I do my job, I look after my team. Oh, and I keep the other subbies in line."

"Sounds like fun," Duncan offered, his smile almost wistful, "but I'm sure you'll be back soon enough."

"I don't care."

"Really?" Duncan's gaze sliced right through the defensive walls Thomas had erected.

"Okay, whatever," he confessed. "I do care, but there isn't shit I can do about it."

"No, but I think somebody else is doing something about it."

"What do you mean?"

"Your CO told me about that commendation that came down for you last week. Apparently it came all the way from Parliament."

Commander Hu had presented Thomas with a bar for his Distinguished Conduct Medal—in effect presenting him a second DCM. In front of all the other officers, Hu had praised Thomas's brave service and upheld him as an example of consistent professionalism for all others to follow.

At the time it had been nice, but didn't seem to make any difference.

"I didn't know that." But now that he thought about it, he quietly suspected where the initiative had come from. Maybe Breeze had been telling the truth when she'd declared a truce between them.

"I don't think you lack for supporters, Thomas," Sean said. "I saw Admiral Chandler last time we were in, and I mentioned how you'd saved my ship. He looked genuinely pleased, mostly I think just to know that you're still alive and kicking."

Admiral Eric Chandler had been the XO in the first ship aboard which Thomas and Sean had served, right out of training. What had been scheduled to be a routine patrol of Sirius had exploded into a desperate battle for survival as the Sirian civil war had erupted around them. Sublieutenants Kane and Duncan had learned from their XO and had served well. Chandler had never forgotten them as his own career path continued to climb.

"That's good to hear, thanks."

"Your CO doesn't know what to make of you," Duncan said suddenly. "He sees your obvious ability, but he also figures there's a good reason why you were busted down to subbie."

"He's a fair man," Thomas said. "I'm happy to earn his respect."

"That's a solid approach, Thomas. Always has been, in our business."

Was that a criticism? Thomas had always been the more politically minded of the pair, always the one to look for underlying opportunities in every situation. Duncan had always been the earnest one, the *take-me-as-I-am* boor of a line officer. Thomas had seen that as a weakness, and yet... here they sat, Sublieutenant Kane in the cabin of Commander Duncan.

There was a knock at the door. Thomas looked over and saw his own XO peering in. Perry's face registered surprise, then darkened in anger.

"Excuse me, sir," Perry said to Duncan. "I've finished my discussion with your XO and I'm ready to depart at your convenience. Although I see Sublieutenant Kane has decided to impose upon you."

"I actually requested his presence," Duncan replied evenly, "as I wanted to hear his assessment of my new security team. I'm sure you agree that Mr. Kane's experience is very relevant here."

"Of course, sir. It's why I brought him along. I appreciate you taking the time personally."

Duncan rose to his feet, and Thomas followed suit.

"Give my regards to Commander Hu," Duncan said. "My Hawk is standing by to take you home."

"Thank you, sir," Thomas said, nodding to his friend and slipping out past Perry. He heard the XO say some parting words, and then march up alongside him.

"The senior officer speaks, Mr. Kane," he growled as they headed aft for the hangar. "Commander Duncan's comment was addressed to me."

"Yes, sir."

"And don't you go sneaking around behind my back. If you're summoned by *Singapore*'s CO, you call and tell me."

"Yes, sir."

Perry's hand grabbed Thomas's coveralls and pulled them both to a stop.

"Look at me when I talk to you, Sublieutenant."

Thomas turned, every muscle in his body tensing, but he ignored the fist gripping the fabric at his shoulder, and glanced down the passageway to ensure that they were alone. Then he met his XO's eyes.

"We're off our ship, so just for a second let's drop the facade," he said, keeping his words measured. "I am older, more qualified and more experienced than you are, Lieutenant Perry. I have commanded both ships and troops in battle, and I am twice decorated for my service. So get your fucking hand off me."

Perry released his grip, expression tightening in a fight-or-flight conflict. He stared back with an intense uncertainty fueled by growing outrage.

"I don't give a shit what you've done in the past, Sublieutenant Kane," he said finally. "Because whatever good you did was obviously wiped out by your crimes. You are a bad influence in my ship, and your presence threatens the required hierarchy. I don't trust you, and it's only because we are so short-staffed that I don't get you shipped off to a front-line platoon."

Was that supposed to be a threat? Thomas would welcome the brutal simplicity of life back in the Corps—at least then he'd be free of all the Fleet bullshit.

"I'll do my job to the best of my ability," he said, "wherever that is. And if it's decided that I should serve aboard *Admiral Bowen*, then so be it. You can trust me to do my job. Now leave me free to do it."

"And leave me free to do mine," Perry snapped. "I know that the officers resist my demands for routine and protocol, and they do it because they see how *laissez-faire* you are about proper conduct and discipline. I am trying to maintain an exhausted crew at wartime readiness, and they need the consistency of regulations to stay focused."

"What they need is respect."

"Which you have none of, for anyone."

Thomas bit down his response, watching the fear and anger flashing through Perry's eyes. This man was totally overwhelmed, and his view of reality was skewed beyond all recognition. There was nothing Thomas could say to alter that view, or even help him.

"I'm sorry, sir," he said, dropping his eyes and pushing down his frustration. "I will cause no further trouble."

Perry exhaled sharply. Finally he raised a finger and stabbed it in the air between them.

"Don't talk to me, don't talk about me," he said. "Do your job and nothing more."

"Yes, sir."

Perry stormed off, and Thomas followed a few paces behind.

He thought back to the old days in the destroyer *Victoria*, when he and Sean had felt crushed under the burden of still earning their bridge qualifications while their ship fought in a messy, brutal, and confusing war. Their XO, Eric Chandler, had taken it upon himself to guide them and train them, keeping them focused on the essentials and cutting out any peacetime nonsense which their training packages had demanded. He'd rewritten the rules of training, basically, and produced two of the fastest-qualified young line officers in Fleet history.

And then there was Lieutenant Perry, and the subbies of *Admiral Bowen* who were all brilliant, but floundering. Following his XO back to the Hawk, Thomas realized what part of his job was. He wasn't just the strike officer. He was also the Bull Sub, and if the XO wasn't going to help the subbies in training, there was only one person who could.

Perry wasn't going to like him. Not at all. But it was for the good of the ship, and the good of the Fleet. And most importantly, it was for the good of the subbies.

19

Jack allowed himself a moment to admire the handsome man in the mirror. It was the first time since his promotion that he'd worn his full dress uniform, and the second silver bar on each shoulder certainly added to the bling. The pilot's wings over his left breast would always be the most important, but he had to admit that the trio of medals just below added an impressive dash of color.

The Colonial Uprising Medal had been renamed the Colonial War Medal. Pretty much everybody had one these days, but not everyone had four combat bars clasped to it. Next to it were the Distinguished Conduct Medal and the Military Medal, each awarded for actions performed in the cockpit and deemed particularly dangerous, heroic, or important.

The wound stripe on his left wrist caught his eye, and he brushed his fingers over the gold braid. With his face rebuilt and his body healed, this little gold stripe on his uniform was his only remnant of the true horror of war. The only visible one, at least. He'd been banged up enough times now not to obsess over a particular injury, but he still sometimes had nightmares, and he still hated Sirians. Way deep down, he hated every last one of them.

He looked at the wound stripe for a long moment, reminding himself that it was for this that he had joined Special Forces. To join Korolev's plan to stop the war, and to stop other young people from getting stripes—and nightmares, and prejudices—of their own.

The door opened behind him and he turned to face his new Special Forces mentor and partner. Often he wasn't sure if it was fondness or fear that made his heart beat faster when she was around, but either way she had his full attention.

Katja's appearance was striking in how little she actually looked like herself. Her hair was black and hung perfectly straight to the middle of her back, and her pale skin had been tanned to a deep olive. The change was so dramatic that her large, dark eyes—normally so prominent a feature—blended perfectly into the overall look. What Jack noticed most, however, was that those eyes were now level with his as she glided across the room to face him.

"What are you wearing?" he said, looking at the conservative gown which flowed down her slender body to brush the floor. "Stilts?"

"Killer heels," she said with a smirk, lifting the hem of her dress to reveal stylish platform boots.

"Are you hiding a hover tank in each shoe?"

"Not quite," she said, and she laughed, "but they do have some mobility augmentations that I want to try out. Some Centauri spies we've gone up against have had augments, and we need to keep pace."

"Sounds like we're kitted out for the trenches," he said. "I thought this was just an exercise." He glanced at his own uniform, feeling the extra weight of the body armor. That plus the visual implants were quite enough for him.

"No Special Forces mission is ever pretend. We're really on the job today, but we don't expect anything to go wrong, so it's more a chance for you to get comfortable with your gear and use it without attracting attention."

There had been something odd about her voice since she'd arrived, and it was her use of the word "without" which finally clued him in.

"Why are you talking with a Canadian accent?"

"Because Finnish accents tend to stand out in this part of Earth," she replied with a glint in her eye, "and today my job is to blend in. I've been listening to you jabber on for the last few weeks and I think I have it down. Wouldn't you say?"

"It's weird, but yeah, it sounds pretty normal."

"Well, let's go. It's time to get out and about."

"We don't say that," he sighed.

"Don't say what, eh?"

"I mean it." He jabbed a finger at her. "Misusing the local slang is the fastest way to get caught out—and that sounds just painful."

"Sorry."

"That's more like it—very natural."

She faced him, smoothing his tunic. Her eyes were bright—but with affection for him or anticipation of a mission? He couldn't tell. Watching her chameleon skills in full force, coupled with his certain knowledge of the terrifying power that hid beneath that gown, kept his emotions firmly on the side of fear. This was a very dangerous person. Hopefully the woman who'd once been his friend was still in there, too.

"How did you get your skin so dark?" he asked.

"A sophisticated, tactical material applied manually."

"What?"

"Make-up." She reached into her bag and showed him a small container. "It's actually really good—rubs right into the skin for longer wear and a natural texture. Too much sweat can stain it, though, so I always carry a touch-up supply."

He nodded, wondering if he'd ever be called upon to become a chameleon.

"You comfortable with your role?" she asked.

"Stand on the stage and look pretty."

"And…?" Her eyes iced over.

"Act as close defense to the VIPs, in case of an incident. I have this"—he patted the ornate leather pouch attached to his ceremonial white belt—"for shielding… and this"—he patted his holster—"for engaging targets." He tapped the hard surface beneath his uniform and then gestured at his eyes. "I'm capable of taking hits, and I can see the invisible."

"Good," she said, and it sounded as if she meant it. "That's the extreme situation. Now what will you *really* be doing this afternoon?"

"Monitoring all transmissions in the area, and looking for any unusual patterns."

<Are you comfortable speaking this way?>
<Yes.>
<I'll be coming and going on the stage, carrying the awards, so we'll be close enough to do this the whole time.>
<Easy.>
She took his arm and led him toward the door. Her new height really was alarming, but he couldn't help but notice the way her gown flowed down over her breasts. Fear and lust, he thought to himself. It was a deadly combination.

The State limousine delivered them to the university at precisely quarter to the hour. Media were already lined up along the driveway, and Breeze remained comfortably in her seat as the security team opened the door from outside and her husband stepped out into the maelstrom.

Their PR team had done an excellent job, she thought, at making sure Vijay's name kept popping up in the news, often enough to be remembered and always connected to something positive. It wasn't enough to steal the limelight from the President or the senior members of the government, but it was having a slow, steady impact.

As planned, Vijay smiled and spoke to the media only briefly before bending slightly and gesturing to her. She slid across and took his hand, stepping out onto the pavement, turning her most dazzling smile toward the cameras. Then she looked to her husband with an expression of deep affection. Images were captured of the earnest, long-serving Minister of Natural Resources and his beautiful, war-veteran bride. If there was a better tale of humble success, Breeze couldn't think of it.

She cast her gaze upward at the gorgeous facade of the university's main building, red brick covered in ivy and sporting white pillars. Similar buildings formed a wide square around the main driveway, with leafy parks snaking through the open spaces that lay between. On Vijay's arm she was escorted through the front doors and into a towering foyer teeming with excited young graduates and their families.

As a VIP Vijay could certainly have requested to slip into the ceremonies through a private entrance, but this mingling with the crowd would further his growing reputation as a man of the people. He wasn't such a household name that people instantly recognized him, but Breeze noticed with satisfaction the large number of curious stares as their little entourage casually made their way through the foyer. If those students and their families didn't yet know who Vijay Shah was, they certainly would by the end of the ceremony.

The auditorium was already starting to fill up, the broad chamber rumbling with the excited hubbub of the guests. Breeze followed Vijay up onto the stage and took her assigned seat near the podium. As one of the scheduled speakers, he was quickly briefed by the university's technical staff, and Breeze had a moment to glance around the room.

The ceremony today was the graduation for students in a special interplanetary geology program, and Breeze idly tried to identify members of the audience based on their fashions. Amid the huge range of outfits, it was still quite easy to spot the cultural influences of each region of Terra.

The most preening were undoubtedly the Jovians. Next she could spot three different kinds of understatement—the severe sleekness of the Mercurians, the efficient practicality of the Martians, and the cold minimalism of the Tritonians. The Earthlings showed the most skin, and the Loonies—no, she chided herself, the Lunar Citizens—wore the most make-up.

Her own choice of outfit was quite conservative by Earthly standards, as befitting the wife of a minister, but the braided fabric of her sleeves revealed enough bare skin to titillate a Mercurian. The Jovians would dismiss her as frumpy no matter what she wore, so for them she just had to rely on her brilliant smile.

Vijay, she noticed, hadn't yet sat down next to her. A new figure had arrived on stage and was chatting with him. She immediately recognized Christopher Sheridan, and found herself on her feet.

"Mr. Sheridan," she said, extending her hand, "what a nice surprise."

"Mrs. Shah," he replied smoothly, kissing her hand. "You look stunning."

"Thank you." She glanced at her husband. "Shall we expect the President, as well?" Under his easy laughter, she could see that Vijay was perturbed. His style of public speaking was low-key and dignified—and flat next to the charismatic charm of Sheridan.

"I've been a presenter at this graduation ceremony for years," Sheridan said. "Perhaps you didn't know, but I was a geologist before I took up public service."

"I didn't know," she said, feigning interest. "Are you a graduate of this program?"

"No, but I helped to establish it when I was chair of the Martian Geological Society. This program," he added with no small amount of pride, "was the first to provide students with field work on every inhabited world in Terra."

"One to which the government provides generous funding," Vijay added.

"And for that I'm grateful," Sheridan said. "Today I'm happy to put aside any partisan politics, and just enjoy being in my professional field again."

"What I'm looking forward to," Vijay said, slapping Sheridan's arm, "is hearing you bring that oratory power to discussing rocks. If anyone can bring glamor to our field, it's you, Christopher."

Sheridan laughed and nodded his thanks.

Aware that they were on stage and being watched by hundreds of people gathering in their seats, Breeze kept her smile firmly in place, hoping her attachment to Vijay would take some of the shine off Sheridan. This man was a threat, and she needed to figure out how to minimize him.

With a smile, Katja handed off the last tray of graduate scrolls to the other assistant. The younger woman had been quite excited at the idea of carrying the trays onto the stage during the ceremony, and thus getting so close to the limelight. Katja had been more than happy to stay back in the wings.

With both Christopher Sheridan and Charity Shah-*née*-Brisebois on the stage, she doubted even this disguise would have kept her anonymous. In her new life she rarely interacted with any citizen long enough to be remembered. Having two familiars in the same small space was awkward.

Jack had blended in perfectly with the two rows of special citizens seated on the stage as a backdrop to the main events. A mixture of uniforms, suits, and academic gowns made up the "heroes gallery" that had become standard for any major public event where State officials were in attendance. He'd been happily monitoring the waves of electronic communications that teemed forth from the audience, and his analysis of the social media patterns was quite entertaining—especially as he tracked the reactions to the Dean's rather pompous speech.

<There's a count going on for how many times he says "change.">

Katja glanced out at the audience. A few polite faces were still turned up toward the speaker, but most eyes were down on their devices. One or two people had left their seats, and there was a quiet but unmistakable restlessness. If she'd been listening to the speech she'd probably be bored, too, but bored people got careless.

By habit, she scanned the room again.

<He's starting to wrap it up,> Jack said. <There's new optimism in the crowd.>

<Sheridan is up next,> she reminded him. <He was an assassination target barely a month ago, so stay sharp.>

<Roger.>

Even in the Cloud communications she sensed the shift in Jack's tone, and with her eyes she saw him sit up slightly straighter and scan the room anew.

The Dean's speech finally tumbled to a conclusion, amid enthusiastic applause. Katja listened vaguely as Christopher Sheridan was introduced—noting with interest the huge ovation he received—and she reached out again with her senses. There was nothing military she could detect.

<Any unusual movement?> she asked.

<No. Some media people are moving down the aisle to get closer, but the audience is still.>

In the backstage area all was quiet, so Katja stepped to the edge of the stage and casually glanced down at the reporters. Past experience made her suspicious of anyone with media augmentations. Switching to quantum-flux she scanned the six individuals who crouched near the apron. There were two head-mounted cameras that she interrogated immediately, and another optical device built into a pair of sunglasses. Nothing unusual. The other three reporters each held up tablet devices, and beyond a direct data stream feeding up to their network satellites there was nothing of note.

<The media look clear,> she said.

<Those sunglasses are pretty cool,> Jack replied. <Oh, looks like chickie has a problem.>

Katja watched as the sunglasses-wearing reporter stopped watching Sheridan and reached down into her bag. She appeared to be adjusting something when—

<What was that?>

Jack's sudden alert froze Katja in position. She went to pure passive, listening for any sudden changes in the Cloud. There was a ripple through the audience, but she heard with her ears more than anything.

<What happened?> she asked, still frozen, eyes vaguely trained on the reporter with the sunglasses. The woman was reaching up to her glasses, and on either side the other reporters were all quickly studying their own cameras.

<An interruption,> Jack said. <Something just blanked all the devices.>

Sheridan continued speaking, unaware of the invisible interruption, but there was a distracted murmur from the crowd.

The reporter flicked her fingers toward the stage.

<Movement,> Jack reported. <Something very small just came at us from the audience.>

<Shield!>

Katja exploded into motion.

Jack fumbled at his belt, activating the local energy field. It crackled into life over most of the stage, a shimmer of light falling into a dome shape. Gasps erupted all around him, and Sheridan's speech died away as the politician looked up at the shield.

Sudden movement to his left. He leapt to his feet, chair

tumbling backward amid shouts from those around him. The movement was Katja, bounding across the stage and down onto the media cluster. Her tiny form crashed across three reporters and sent the entire group scrambling. Beyond the glimmer of the shield, he saw audience members frozen in shock. There were a few shouts, and screams of fear.

The reporters were inside the shield! He ripped the leather pouch from his belt and tossed it down on the stage behind him. The shield shifted obediently with its projector. Jack lunged forward, grabbing Sheridan's arm and pulling him back.

"Sir, get down!"

Sheridan ducked immediately and retreated toward the chairs. Jack gestured to the other veterans and VIPs.

"Make a ring around Sheridan," he ordered. Then he spun around and scanned the rest of the stage. Katja had pulled her weapon from her purse and was training it on all six of the prone reporters. Someone to his left was down. He scrambled over.

It was Vijay Shah. The minister had slumped out of his chair and sat collapsed on the stage, his face frozen in shock and one hand on his chest. Jack checked for breathing: none. He checked for blood: none. He checked for pulse: none.

"Medic!" he shouted.

Shah's dark face had paled, his open eyes staring dully at nothing. Jack lifted the unresponsive hand from the chest, looking for any sort of wound. He pushed aside the fine wool of the suit jacket, and against the thin cotton of the shirt he saw a speck of blood. Tearing open the shirt he saw a matching red spot in Shah's chest, right over the heart.

"What's wrong with him?" He heard a female voice in his ear.

"Some kind of projectile," he said. "I need a medic."

The woman repeated his call for help then leaned in again.

"Can we move him?" she asked.

"I don't know." Jack did a quick check for any head injury, then slid his hands down Shah's neck to feel for any unusual bumps. Nothing seemed to be broken. "Here, help me get him down on his back."

Together they eased Shah's limp form to the floor.

"Do you know CPR?" he asked.

"Yes," she replied, pushing him aside.

He climbed to his feet again and did another quick survey. Sheridan was crouched behind the chairs, the veterans facing outward in a defiant ring around him while the other VIPs cowered. Shah was mostly surrounded by his official security detail and Jack saw one of them approaching with a medikit. The woman—it was Breeze, he realized—still desperately conducted CPR.

Katja was on the floor below the stage, pistol pointed down at the sprawled reporters. Jack surveyed them, noting the various expressions of shock. He blinked slowly to activate his quantum-flux and carefully swept his gaze over them. Each one of them carried an array of electronic devices, and he could see the biofeed devices linking the brains of the two head-mounted cameramen with their equipment. Not true implants, then, but a common "hands-free" technique for controlling external appliances.

Then, in the reporter with the sunglasses camera, there was a flash of Cloud activity.

"You!" he barked, looming over her from the stage. "Who are you?"

Darkness consumed the auditorium as all the lights were extinguished. Amid the sea of screams Jack watched in his quantum-flux vision as the reporter ripped off her sunglasses, reached into her bag, and then flicked her fingers at him. Something tiny thudded against his chest, the force of the blow dispersed by his body armor.

<Sunglasses threat!> he babbled into the Cloud. <Take, take, take!>

Shots rang out in the blackness. Jack saw the quantum-flux form of the reporter stagger as Katja's bullets struck home—but the woman didn't fall. From her crouch she sprang into flight, colliding with Katja and sending them both tumbling to the floor.

<Protect the prize,> he heard Katja say, even as the two combatants scrambled to their feet.

Jack drew his pistol and stepped back toward the fallen form of Shah, spotting Sheridan still crouched behind the human shield. He was suddenly glad of the darkness, as no one could see how his hand was shaking.

* * *

Katja lashed out with a jab, clipping the enemy's ear. The target was inhumanly fast, and Katja desperately blocked another barrage of fist strikes. Fighting in quantum-flux made distances hard to judge, but she already feared that this fighting disadvantage was the only thing keeping her alive.

Her pistol was somewhere in the darkness, knocked clear by the thundering impact as her attacker had slammed them both to the floor. Katja had managed to get herself between the enemy and the nearest escape route, however, and they squared off again.

Ignoring the screaming around her, she blocked another strike at her face, but grunted as a blow cracked against her ribs, the force only partially deflected by her armor. She backed up two steps, then launched a front kick with her augmented boots. Her attacker's gasp of pain made the impact sweeter, but the triumph was short-lived. The opponent charged forward again, literally flying as both knees smacked against Katja's blocks. A crushing blow came down on Katja's head and she staggered backward, dodging left to avoid another strike from above.

Her right hand was in close and she grabbed desperately at fabric, then felt her fingers against the soft skin of a throat. She squeezed with all her strength, grabbing the back of the neck with her left hand and pulling herself tight against her opponent. In the haze of flux-lit darkness she could almost make out facial features, could see the gasping expression as she tightened her choke hold.

<Surrender!> she blasted out into the Cloud.

A forearm smashed up against her wrist like a steel pipe, but she kept her grip on the throat.

<Surrender!> she repeated.

The attacker's legs left the ground and swung around her torso like pythons. Her own legs buckled under the sudden weight of two bodies and she toppled forward, slamming down on her enemy even as they both tightened their holds. Katja felt her body armor buckling under the strain, felt her insides burn, but still she throttled.

<Surrender!> she said again.

<I'm going to kill you,> came the reply.

In that moment, with the Cloud conduit open between their minds, Katja suddenly confirmed with whom she grappled. Valeria Moretti's mind burned with images of a blasted street. Houses torched and half-collapsed. Bodies of children being pulled from the wreckage. Not just any children—her children. A son and a daughter. Marco and Roberta. Their broken bodies laid on stretchers, tortured expressions burned into her memory before they were covered by blankets.

Katja felt a rage smash into her, a burning fire of vengeance like she'd never felt before. A mother's children had been killed—innocent victims in a pointless battle. She recoiled from the tidal wave of emotion, screaming inside at pain she'd never known could exist.

<You did this,> she heard.

A flurry of defenses welled up in her mind.

<I didn't pull the trigger that killed them—I was doing my duty—I was under attack—you attacked us—this is your fault.> But none of her frantic arguments could overcome the single, fiery accusation that beat her down.

<You did this.>

Katja turned toward the assault, pushing back with her own rage.

<I did what I had to.>

Moretti's thoughts dissolved into incoherence. Katja felt the constriction of her torso tighten, and she leaned into the choke hold with all her remaining strength. Moretti's life energy pulsed in the quantum-flux, as civilian screams continued in the darkness around them.

Then, suddenly, the pressure on her body eased. Moretti's feet pounded down on Katja's thighs, knocking her over and shaking her grip. Moretti rolled, slamming Katja's arms with impossible force. Katja was on her back, left arm numb and right arm knocking away a new barrage of strikes. She pulled in her legs and kicked with all the power of her boots.

* * *

Light poured into the auditorium once again, and Breeze blinked in shock. She still held the limp hand of her husband. The illumination revealed a series of packs laid out across Vijay's chest, and the security guard who frantically operated them.

Vijay's heart would start, but after only a few beats it would cease again. The mask over his face pushed oxygen into his lungs, but his body refused to respond. Aside from a single pinprick in his chest there was no sign of violence, but any ability to live seemed to have been stolen away.

"Is there an ambulance coming?" she asked.

"Yes, ma'am," another guard replied. "Two minutes away."

"Come on, darling," she whispered, squeezing his hand again.

Around her, the stage was under siege. She and Vijay were surrounded by security, and through the black legs she saw Sheridan protected by another ring of guards. The young veteran who had first helped her with Vijay was standing at the edge of the stage, pistol pointed down at a group of people lying on the floor.

Near the first exit from the auditorium, she saw a woman suddenly fly upward into the air. Another woman—one of the certificate carriers in her long, black gown—lay on her back, booted legs thrust upward. The first woman crashed down to the floor, but was on her feet again so fast Breeze blinked to clear her vision.

Then the exit door was open, and the woman was gone. The olive-skinned certificate carrier leapt to her feet and took off in pursuit.

Breeze looked again at her husband's still form, watched it jerk as the guard attempted to start the heart yet again. She'd seen enough death in her military career to know that it was too late, that no amount of medical help could bring Vijay back. She slumped where she sat. Everything had happened so fast. A lightning courtship and a quick wedding, and the sudden promotion to minister. And now, just as fast, it was all over. Her husband was dead, and with it her political ambitions. There was no way she could pull off that trick a second time.

Tears trickled down her cheeks. She brushed them away, trying to hold back the surge of frustration and disappointment. This had been a terrible year, with one setback after another, and she was too young to just be put out to pasture.

There was a bony hand on her shoulder. Looking up, she saw the Dean gazing down at her sadly.

"He is a strong man," he said quietly. "He'll be all right."

The old coot was offering her sympathy. It was the last thing she wanted right now. She dropped her eyes, wanting simply to disappear, then she felt something warm and soft drape over her shoulders. It was a blanket, and she noticed that a new team of medics had arrived, along with a troop of armored police officers who kept the audience in their seats while investigator drones began scanning the crowd.

Strong hands took her arms and she let them lift her to her feet.

"Mrs. Shah," one of the security guards said with deep sadness in his eyes, "we need to get you to a safe place."

They were still treating her like a VIP, she noticed absently. Like someone worth protecting. But she was just the new wife of a minister—why would she matter?

Because, she suddenly realized, their careful PR campaign had *made* her into someone who mattered. The shock of the moment suddenly vanished, and she saw the situation with new clarity. The medics worked on Vijay, there were guards all around, and there was an entire audience watching. She had performed CPR to try to save him, before staying loyally by his side when the first medics arrived.

Oh, this was gold.

"What about my husband?" she asked.

The guard hesitated, glancing down at the limp form.

"We'll do our best, ma'am."

She nodded solemnly, then allowed herself to be led away to safety.

Her mind was already racing. There was much to do.

20

Thomas flopped down on the couch in Club Sub, loving the feeling of falling onto the soft surface. Gravity was back on, and life was just that much better. With *Bowen* so close to the jump gate and scheduled to hold station until the arrival of another Terran warship in two days, the mood on board seemed almost like a working port visit.

Jobs got done, but the tension was down.

The lights in the mess deck seemed permanently on these days, despite the XO's insistence on day, evening, and night lighting throughout the ship. None of the subbies seemed to be sleeping much, anyway. Chen had the mids, but his bunk was open and he was watching some show. Hayley Oaks had just finished a shower and she strolled through from the washplace wiping down her hair with a towel.

It was uncommon for men and women to share mess decks, but a single subbie female didn't warrant her own cabin. Sometimes mixed quarters caused troubles, but as Bull Sub he'd enforced the rule from day one—no nudity in the main mess. The subbies were free to get changed in their bunks with the slides closed, and if Hayley was in the shower the washplace was out of bounds. No exceptions, else the wrath of the Bull Sub would descend.

Hayley hung her towel and glanced over at Thomas, who suddenly realized that he'd been watching her. She was bundled up in her coveralls, but her bare feet and the slightly lower swell of her chest suggested nothing underneath. She smiled absently under damp, curly brown hair that was surprisingly long. She always wore it tied up, he realized, and she was a different woman with this look.

"Enjoying the sprawl, Guns?" she said, strolling over to flop down on the couch opposite him.

He gave her a smile, but didn't dare hold her gaze. He was old enough to be, if not her father, then at least her uncle, and he was a married man now. Those days were long gone. There was another reason besides regulations, he knew, which had made him take such a strict stance on decency.

"When I lounge," he said, staring up at the deckhead, "I like to feel it."

Hayley stretched—he definitely kept his eyes averted for that—and shouted over toward Chen.

"Get to sleep, fuckbrain. I need you awake enough to remember to shake me at three."

"Bite me," he responded playfully.

"Blow me," she muttered, grabbing one of the tablets from its pouch on the bulkhead. She lifted it to Thomas. "Thanks for putting together those lists of dates—it must have taken you hours."

"It would have taken *you* hours, but I knew most of it from memory."

"Really? You like that history shit?"

"Well, some of it I lived through, kid, so it's easy to remember."

"Thanks anyway. Now we can get a couple more reqs signed off by the XO."

"My pleasure."

There was a knock at the door. Hayley reached up to open it, watched John Micah walk through, then returned her focus to the tablet.

"Attention on deck," she sang.

John noted the complete lack of movement, and nodded with approval.

"Relax, please."

"What's up, Shades?" Thomas asked. Micah shrugged, swatting Thomas's feet clear to give him a perch on the arm of the couch.

"Bored," he said. "The evening brief's about to start, so pretty much everyone who's awake is headed for the bridge."

"That'll make the XO happy," Hayley said.

"Yeah, but the wardroom's kind of lame when you're there by yourself."

"Well," Thomas said, shifting to make more room, "as an honorary subbie, you're always welcome in our home. Are you liking the gravity?"

"Yeah, it's comfortable—but as an ASW guy it makes me a little nervous. We really stand out in the Bulk, you know."

"I know, but Astral Intelligence says the stealth threat is low."

"Uh-huh."

"Oh, fucking get over yourself, Shades," Hayley said. "There aren't any rebel stealth ships this side of Sirius. Our threat is those pesky little attack craft the Valhallans use. They seem to have an infinite supply of them. We had to chase off another pack today while a convoy was jumping back to Terra. They're just hanging around out there, right at the edge of sensor range. What a fucking pain—like mosquitoes you can't reach to swat."

Thomas watched idly as John and Hayley chatted, knowing it would do them both good, but never for a moment thinking they'd be a lasting match. She was too harsh and he was too earnest, but the simple act of flirting could do wonders for a person's morale.

Tuning out their banter, he stared upward at the bulkhead, letting his thoughts wander.

The AF had concluded that the attack on *Toronto* had been made by the rebel attack craft, swarming the close-in defenses and boarding the destroyer. A single hand-held gravi-bomb thrown onto the bridge could easily have caused the destruction Thomas had found, and the rest of the crew would have been taken prisoner without a fight. It had been *Bowen*'s quick response to the attack on *Singapore* which must've protected that destroyer from the same fate.

Yeah, that explained it, but it still didn't sit right. There wasn't any intelligence suggesting that the rebels had developed hand-held gravi-bombs. And while a destroyer might have been overwhelmed, if the rebels got in some lucky shots early on, why hadn't there been any emergency transmissions from *Toronto* when the boarding began?

"Hey, Chen," he called suddenly, "were there any special comm conditions here in Valhalla when *Toronto* was attacked?"

"What?"

He repeated the question, and John and Hayley went silent. They both stared at him.

"Uhh, not that I recall," Chen said. "Valhalla hasn't been under any special restrictions at all in the war. It's been a backwater theater the whole time."

"What are you thinking?" John asked.

"Just wondering why *Toronto* didn't send a tactical update on the attack, or even a distress signal when things started to look bad."

"Maybe they never had the chance."

"We're a little faster on the uptake than that," Hayley said, picking up on Thomas's line of thinking. "It takes all of five seconds to switch the beacon to SOS."

Thomas sat up, all thoughts of lounging gone. "I've seen the Centauris block entire areas of space, cutting them off from external comms. Maybe the rebels brought that technology here."

"Then why didn't they use it during the *Singapore* attack?" John countered. "We were far enough away to have been blocked."

"True," Thomas admitted. "Plus the small craft can't be carrying something like that. The amount of power needed would be beyond them."

"What about a stealth ship?"

Thomas shook his head. "It'd have to re-enter the brane and stay there in order to maintain the block. No, I don't think it's blocked comms."

"Well, it was your fucking idea," Hayley protested.

"Shut up, I'm thinking."

Ignoring the stares, Thomas cradled his head in his hands and struggled to grasp the wisp of a thought he knew was eluding him. *The enemy somehow gets past the close-in defenses and clamps on*—hard enough. *The enemy gets aboard the ship and makes it to the bridge, a sealed sphere, without being stopped or even confronted*—very hard. *The ship never even switches the beacon to SOS during the entire attack—*

Impossible.

"The only way the attack on *Toronto* could have succeeded," he said slowly, "was by complete surprise. The bridge had to be neutralized first. With no bridge, there were no sensors being watched, no weapons being controlled, and no comms being transmitted."

"But no torpedo is that accurate," Hayley said, rising to her feet. "You can't navigate in the Bulk with that kind of precision."

Thomas looked up at her from where he sat on the couch. He remembered how, on one of his first nights aboard *Admiral Bowen*, another woman had loomed over him exactly where Hayley stood, as he'd sat exactly where he was now. He remembered the crackle of air as the Special Forces operative had appeared directly in front of him.

"Yes," he said quietly, "you can. Or at least some people can."

Chen climbed down from his bunk and moved to stand next to John and Hayley. All three of them stared down at Thomas, and he knew each one of them believed him.

"What time of day was the attack on *Singapore*?"

"We got their call at eighteen-fifty or so," Hayley said. "I was just prepping for the evening brief when she reported the attack craft inbound."

"At the edge of her sensors?"

"Uhh, yeah, I think so. We were able to close the distance almost as quickly as the rebels did."

"Our ships have improved their sensor ranges in the past few months." Thomas stood. "I bet they don't know that. They probably didn't expect to be picked up until they were closer." He looked at Hayley. "You said those bandits are sitting right at the edge of our sensor range. Right now?"

"Yeah, they have been for a few hours."

"They know the convoy's jumped, and we're alone out here. They can detect that we've switched our AG on, too, suggesting that we've stepped down an alert level. And if they know our daily routine—which is hardly top-secret information—they know when our entire command team is assembled in one place."

John figured it out first. "The evening brief."

Thomas grabbed the nearby handset and punched up the bridge.

"*Bridge.*" The response was clipped. "*Second officer of the watch.*"

"Alex, it's Thomas. Stop the brief. Get all non-watch people out of there."

"*Say again?*"

"Do it!"

The line went dead, just as the deck heaved violently. Thomas saw the handset rip out of the wall as he clung to it, then realized that he was falling forward, as if a giant hand had tipped the entire cruiser up onto its bow. Something hard smashed into his head. He lay against the cold surface for a moment, staring up at the aft end of Club Sub, then felt gravity shift again as he slid down to the deck.

Hayley was next to him, curled up in a ball as she gripped both hands against the top of her skull. Blood trickled between her fingers. John was sprawled in the open door to the washplace, Chen slumped against the forward bulkhead next to the sink.

Thomas sat for a moment, instinctively waiting for the general alarm. There was nothing except for the soft cursing of Hayley beside him, and shuffling sounds as John pulled himself to his knees. In fact, he realized, he heard *nothing*. No rush of air through the ventilation, no distant hum of the accretion drives spinning up, no clatter of boots or shouts in the passageway outside.

In Thomas's world—both as a warrior and a spacefarer—silence was terrifying. He leapt to his feet, stabbing at the speaker controls of the comm set and calling the engine room.

The voice at the other end was anything but calm.

"*Machinery control.*"

"This is the strike officer—status!"

"*There's some kind of incident forward, sir, but we can't make sense of it. The bridge isn't answering. We've gone to airtight conditions and put the drives to safe mode. You can have power anytime, but a lot of systems in the forward half of the ship aren't responding.*"

Airtight explained the silence—engineering had shut all ventilation in case of a breach.

"Good work. Have your senior person meet me in DCC."

"*Yes, sir.*"

Thomas looked down at his colleagues. John was on his feet and helping Chen rise. Hayley was sitting cross-legged on the deck, still holding her head. He grabbed the first-aid kit off the bulkhead and tossed it to Chen as he approached.

"Check her head wound. John, you're with me."

He cracked open the door to test for pressure, then slid it wide and stepped through. Debris littered the passageway. Looking forward, he could see the most distant handrails bent forward against their anchors. He didn't need to look beyond to know what had happened to *Bowen*'s bridge.

John appeared next to him. "Holy crap!"

"Check forward. See if there are any survivors."

"What are you doing?"

Thomas looked over at him, wishing he felt the humor of his next words.

"Being the ace in the hole. I'll be in DCC."

John raced up the passageway. Thomas ran aft three frames and down a ladder to deck three. He slowed amid the gathering crowd. Engineers piled into DCC and troopers headed into the strike storage. He poked his head into the latter.

"Armored suits, full weapons, but impact-only rounds! Deploy to repel boarders. Bring my suit and gear to DCC."

"Yes, sir," Buns snapped, not pausing as she donned her own suit. Two other troopers were also dressing, and another was already slapping magazines into the unlocked assault rifles. At Thomas's order the loader paused.

"Impact-only, sir?" he asked.

"We're fighting on our own ship, trooper. I don't want holes blown through the hull every time you pull the trigger." The trooper nodded and yanked the seated magazines free, opening another locked drawer to grab a new array of ammunition. Thomas paused for a second to admire the efficiency of his team—not a single order had been broadcast, but they were all prepping for the worst.

He crossed to DCC, noting that the main damage control display was lit and engineers were starting to man their consoles.

"Who's senior here?" he bellowed above the noise.

"I am." Chief Petty Officer Ranson stood from where he'd been manipulating a side console. His massive form was reassuring.

"Good," Thomas said, striding up to the main display.

"We don't know what the fuck's going on, sir," Ranson said quietly, leaning in so close Thomas could smell the beer on his breath. "The after half of the ship looks normal, but forward of frame fifty-seven, here"— he gestured at a frame just forward of midships—"nothing makes sense. We've lost sensor readings in this entire area, but then everything looks normal right up here at the bow." Another gesture. "Pressure is low in this forward area, but stable. No sign of a hull breach."

Thomas took in the symbols on the display, imagining the vast, circular hole that had just been torn out of *Bowen*'s heart.

"You and I know exactly what's going on, Chief. Don't pretend otherwise."

Ranson's eyes were afire, but Thomas knew the anger wasn't for him.

"How the fuck did they do this, sir?"

"This is just the first step. We're in a lot of trouble."

Thomas stepped away from the display and surveyed the room. Most of the stations were occupied, but there was no longer any chatter. All eyes were on him. He looked around for the main broadcast handset, and activated it.

"All positions, this is the strike officer in DCC, sitrep." His voice echoed in the passageway, as he knew it did throughout the ship. "*Bowen* has suffered an attack by gravi-torpedo which has destroyed most of the forward end of the ship on decks two, three, and four. There will be structural damage on all decks forward of frame fifty-seven, and all crew are to evacuate to positions aft of that frame, using decks one and five only. If you cannot reach your usual station, report to the after manning pool."

Some soldiers were more capable than others of improvising in crisis situations, but all responded well to a drilled-in command like the general alarm.

"This is the strike officer," he said again. "Bring the ship to battle stations."

Damage Control Center was one of the few places on board with full access to shipwide communications, and one of the engineers immediately sounded the general alarm, then repeated the order. Through the open door to the passageway he heard an immediate rumble of renewed activity.

Engineers backed aside as Sergeant Bunyasiriphant clumped into DCC, her armored form looking extra massive as she carried Thomas's suit in her arms. She lowered the torso and offered him the legs.

"I've split the squad into pairs to guard the airlocks aft of frame fifty-seven, sir. However, there are six entry points and we can currently only cover four." Her dark eyes lit up. "But I have a lot of extra weapons."

"I'll get more troops for you." Thomas stepped into his suit and took the torso from her, sliding it over his head and locking it into place. "Hold your current positions."

"How long 'til the attack?"

"Don't know. Maybe twenty minutes, maybe longer."

"Yes, sir." She left his helmet and assault rifle on the nearest console, ignoring the protest of the engineer who was manning it, and returned to strike storage. As she departed, Thomas noticed Chen and Hayley slipping into DCC in their emergency vacuum suits. Hayley was holding a bandage against her head. Thomas motioned them over.

"See anyone else on your way down here?"

Chen shook his head. "Just a few stunned crew, heading to their stations."

Thomas reached for the broadcast handset, but fumbled with it in his armored glove. He passed it to Chen.

"Sublieutenant, make the pipe—all officers report to DCC."

Chen duly repeated the order, then his eyes moved expectantly toward the door.

"And talk to the hangar," Thomas added. "I need to know the status of our Hawks." He turned to Chief Ranson and calmly asked a few routine questions about engineering status. They had the desired effect, and the chief regained his usual composure, answering the questions and barking a few orders at his team. Reports began to come in from damage control teams, and a sense of normalcy slowly returned, at least for a battle situation.

A distant voice came from the passageway, getting rapidly closer with demands of "make a hole!" and "coming through!"

John Micah burst into DCC, eyes wide, warbags still contained on his belt.

"The whole fucking bridge is gone!"

Thomas marched toward him, servos whirring as his feet thumped against the deck.

"I went to see what happened," Micah shouted, "but the air sucked me down and I barely hung on. There's just a big fucking hole in the center of the ship!" He was staring wildly at the engineers and was about to bellow again when Thomas grabbed his face with a gloved hand. He knew his armor well, and squeezed just enough to freeze Micah's jaw.

"Shut the fuck up, Lieutenant Micah," he hissed. "We know what's happened, and we're dealing with it." He lessened his grip, but didn't remove his hand. "Are you calm?"

"I saw it," John whispered back, tears in his eyes. "It's all gone."

"I know. I've seen it too, in *Toronto*. But we're going to fight."

"How?"

"I need your help," he said carefully, ignoring the question and staring at his colleague. "Will you help me?"

John was shaking, but a semblance of calm returned to his eyes.

"Yes."

Thomas smiled, nodding as he released the anti-stealth director and motioned for him to follow. He returned to his position by the main display, flanked by the other officers.

"The ship is at battle stations," Chief Ranson reported, "from a damage control point of view, and with all personnel confirmed aft of frame fifty-seven."

"You've searched the forward end?"

"Thermal scans indicated certain spaces with life forms, and the manning pool sent teams to evacuate them. Everyone's clear now."

"What's the count?"

"Ninety-seven, including twenty-two wounded." Ranson glanced past Thomas, then back. "No other officers."

Ninety-seven crew remaining, a quarter of whom were wounded. Over fifty lost in the attack. Thomas nodded to the chief, then regarded his officers. Chen stared wide-eyed. Hayley winced as she adjusted the bandage against her head.

John started to regain his composure. He looked around slowly.

"I guess you're it... Captain."

"You ready to help me?"

"Yes, sir."

Thomas took the handset from Chen and carefully pressed down on the talk button.

"This is Sublieutenant Kane. I have assumed command of *Admiral Bowen*. Sitrep: the current threat is rebel small craft who will be attempting to board our ship. We will maintain personnel in engineering and DCC, and strike team will hold their positions. All other personnel report to the hangar. I will need twenty volunteers to take up arms and join our front line of defense. Make yourself known to Lieutenant Micah in the hangar."

He paused, knowing that the crew would be disoriented by his strange orders. Clarity was essential to focus them—and perhaps a touch of inspiration.

"We will keep the unarmed and wounded in the hangar, clear of the fighting," he continued. "Those who are armed will defend our ship from this attack. We will kill every rebel who boards us, and we will chase their craft away. We will ensure that all the colonies understand that they picked the wrong cruiser to mess with."

He heard an approving rumble from the crew around him, and then he uttered the words he'd never expected to say again.

"This is the captain. That is all."

He handed the set back to Chen.

"Lieutenant Micah, you're the XO. I'm going to leave all ship systems as they are, including gravity, just in case the rebels are monitoring us for major engineering changes. I want them to think we're headless and confused. Go to the hangar and sort our people out. Send the twenty volunteers to strike storage for weapons and armor."

"Yes, sir." John headed for the door.

"Sublieutenant Wi, status of the Hawks?"

"Two are fueled and armed with missiles, the third is being prepped, but it only has one engine and can't sustain interior atmo." He frowned. "We've lost comms with Spinner-Three, who was on patrol when the attack happened."

Thomas nodded. He'd hoped their patrolling Hawk could have been their eyes and ears.

"Sublieutant Oaks, I want you on the damage control net. DC is the only shipwide comms system we have that's already manned and can't be hacked by the rebels. You'll keep me posted on enemy incursions based on hatch movements." He raised his voice. "Medic!" He patted Hayley on the shoulder. "Get that head glued back together first."

"Yes, sir."

"Sublieutant Wi," he said, motioning Chen to follow him a few steps away from the main display. "I need your brains. Is there anywhere else on the ship that can act as a central control for sensors and weapons?"

Chen thought hard. "No, sir. All the weapons can be controlled locally, but there's no way to access the warfare nets other than via the bridge. We couldn't coordinate the weapons."

"We could have relays through the DC net," Thomas thought aloud, "but it'll be cumbersome—and too slow for anti-attack."

"There's nowhere to access the sensor feeds," Chen added morosely. "All readouts were on the bridge. Why aren't there backups?"

"I guess," Thomas replied, his mind still searching for possibilities, "the ship designers figured that if the bridge was taken out beneath all that protection, the entire ship would have to have been destroyed first, just to reach it."

"Each sensor can be read locally," Chen suggested.

"Yeah, but it's just raw data—not much good for tactics. Still... The ASW sensors are still working, right?"

"Yes..."

"They can be read by a Hawk's systems." His face split into a grin. "And we have three of them sitting back aft, doing nothing." Thomas felt a plan snap into place. He turned back to Hayley, who was standing by the main display with a headset held up to one ear while a medic wrapped a bandage around her head to secure the fresh dressing.

"Get two ASW techs back to the towed array space," he ordered her, "and make certain it's still feeding data into the combat system. Then get two other ASW techs down to the big dipper and deploy it."

"I'll get the Hawks flashed up," Chen said, grabbing another headset.

Thomas moved back to the main display, trying to think as both a line officer and a strike officer at the same time. Even if the Hawks could get him info on the approaching rebel ships, he doubted he could use the weapons to effectively engage them. And if he tried, the rebel ships could just stand off and pummel *Bowen* to pieces. If they boarded, though, it became a ground war, and he was much better equipped for that.

Hefting his armored helmet up, he snapped it into place. The earpieces extended from the inner shell to hover beside his ears and he heard a quick exchange between his troopers on the strike net. His vision blurred momentarily as the vision field generator moved in front of his eyes, ready to provide infra-red or quantum-flux on demand. He left his faceplate up in order to hear the chatter around him.

"Bravo-One, this is Alpha-One."

"*Bravo-One,*" Buns replied.

"Status of arming additional troops?"

"*Twenty souls prepped. Ten equipped with surface armor and assault rifles. Ten equipped with pistols. Standing by to deploy them.*"

Thomas examined the damage control display, noting which airlocks were currently covered by his troopers. There were two more still unguarded, located aft of frame fifty-seven. Anything forward of that he was going to abandon. He quickly issued orders to split his nine troopers between all six after airlocks, augmented by the heavily armed crew. The pistol-bearing crew he assigned to the hangar to protect the rest of his people.

"Bravo-Two," he concluded, "you command the forward units. Anything that comes through either of those airlocks you smash. If we get indication of entry forward of frame fifty-seven, I'm going to jettison atmo on them, so keep that frame airtight."

"*Bravo-Two, roger. What's your position?*"

"I'll be in DCC, ready to cover the hangar if required. Out."

He turned to Hayley.

"Status of ASW gear?"

"Tail and big dipper both deployed and operational, passive only," she replied.

"Can the Hawks read the data from them?"

"Unknown."

Thomas paused. Info on the rebel ships—before they mated with *Bowen*—was valuable, but not essential. Really he needed to know which airlocks the rebels boarded through. It was a ground war, he reminded himself.

But not if those rebel ships could detach, he realized. Even if they lost their boarding parties, they could just pull back and start firing at *Bowen*. He frowned. Not only did he need the rebels to board his ship, he needed to keep their ships attached to it.

This was still a space battle, too, even if he had no way to fight one.

21

"Indication of airlock seven access," Oaks reported.

Thomas loomed behind her, aware of the slight tremble in her voice. It was the only sound through the silent DCC as all operators watched their consoles, waiting. All ventilation was shut down to protect against breach. All chatter on the nets had ceased. Throughout the ship, he knew, his crew waited in silence.

The enemy had arrived. On the main damage control display he watched as the indicator for airlock seven switched to red as the rebels forced their way through the hull. Moments later, three other airlocks revealed compromise.

"ASW," Chen said into his commlink, addressing John back in the hangar, "airlock incursions at positions three, four, seven, and eight."

"*Roger,*" John replied on the speaker, "*starboard hangar airlock is decompressing, Spinner-Three will be ready to deploy in ten seconds.*"

Spinner-Two was already primed for launch in the port hangar airlock. Micah had taken station in the damaged Spinner-One, which remained in the hangar to relay instructions on the anti-stealth warfare comms.

"Indication of enemy movement at airlock seven," Hayley reported.

"Let them get on board," Thomas cautioned. "Let all four teams get on board." Hayley relayed his instructions over the DC net.

"Do all four rebel ships appear to have solid clamps engaged?"

Chief Ranson nodded, pointing at detailed readings next to the airlock indicators.

"Yes, sir," he said. "They've matched atmo and are holding the doors open."

"ASW"—Thomas turned to Chen—"launch the Hawks." Red lights on the main display indicated both hangar airlocks opening. Thomas waited. The lack of direct combat information was maddening, but he trusted his crew. The strained silence dragged out, all eyes and ears waiting for some signal of the Hawks' success.

"Fire at airlock eight!" Hayley reported.

"Spinner-Two reports destruction of rebel ship at airlock eight," Chen echoed.

Thomas frowned. The explosion had sucked in all the air through the open airlock, causing a fireball inside *Bowen*. That was certainly one way to take out the attackers.

"Status of our team at airlock eight," he demanded.

"No response," Hayley replied. He could hear the distant chatter of weapons fire, impacts vibrating through the hull as his troopers engaged the rebels. But the Hawks were loose and soon there would be more airlock explosions.

"All units pull back one airtight frame from the entry points."

Hayley relayed the order, and he saw clusters of lights quickly change as his teams opened airtight doors and withdrew. The rebels followed, and he heard more weapons fire. Red warning lights flashed to life at airlock seven.

"Fire at airlock seven," Hayley said.

"Status of our troops there?"

"They'd withdrawn..." She paused, listening on the net. "Engaging hostiles."

Thomas shifted in his stance, hating the fact that his troopers were facing the enemy without him. There was still no word from the team at airlock eight—they had to be presumed dead. He studied the display for indication of movement.

A hatch opened on deck five, not far from airlock eight. Someone was moving down to deck four. Moments later, another hatch opened, toward deck three.

"We have movement on deck three at frame ninety-eight," he said to Hayley. "Have Bravo-Two and her team move to intercept."

His orders were passed, but moments later she looked up at him.

"Bravo-Two reports a... a milly? She's pinned down and can't move until the forward threat is neutralized. She wants a team to flank them to port."

Thomas kept his face neutral, but barely. There was a milly loose in his ship. A battle robot like that could wreak havoc in tight quarters—but at least it had made the mistake of picking a fight with Buns.

"No can," Thomas replied. "All troops are engaged. Tell her to hold position and keep that damn thing contained. Don't let it get into the venting."

"What about frame ninety-eight," Chen asked at his side. "It might be survivors from airlock eight."

"But ours or theirs?" Thomas countered. He studied the display for another moment. The unknown movement wasn't far from DCC itself. He was loath to send any of his armed crewmen from the hangar to investigate—they were untrained, unarmored and carrying only pistols.

Looking down at his own armored suit, he realized there was only one person who could investigate.

"I'll check out frame ninety-eight," he said, hefting his assault rifle and flicking off the safety. Before anyone could respond, however, John's voice sounded over the speaker.

"*DCC, this is ASW—new contact poss-high shadow bearing two-zero-zero mark one-niner-zero!*"

Thomas froze. An enemy stealth ship had been detected—no doubt the same one which had singularized *Bowen*'s bridge. No matter how cleverly he fought his battle against the rebel small craft and their boarding parties, that stealth ship could singularize *Bowen* itself in a heartbeat. He had no doubt that it would, if the attempt to capture the cruiser seemed to be going poorly.

"Break engage target at airlock three," he ordered. "Spinner-Two take hostile shadow."

Chen repeated the order, then looked up at Thomas again.

"Sir, what about frame ninety-eight?"

Leaving his position of command during a stealth attack cried out against every instinct Thomas had, but there was an unknown strike threat inside his ship, and the only available asset was himself.

A door on deck three—only two frames forward—indicated open, he noted. There was no more time to consider.

"I'll investigate," he said. "Sublieutenant Wi, you have control of the ship. Give ASW weapons free on all hostile contacts. Maneuver as required to defend against ASW attack."

"Yes, sir," Chen responded. As he turned to leave, Thomas heard Chief Ranson reminding Chen that they still had full maneuvering control, directly through the engine room, and that all ASW battle stations were manned.

Leaving DCC, Thomas shut out all other thoughts. There was a potential threat forward, or it might be friendly survivors, and he needed to be a trooper—nothing more. Slapping down his faceplate, he bounded forward in the deserted passageway, rifle up, passing through one frame and approaching the next airtight boundary. There was no cover against the straight bulkheads— nothing to protect him against enemy fire.

The door up ahead cracked open, then slid aside.

A large figure in a gray spacesuit jumped forward, raising a compact, two-handed launcher. Thomas aimed for the armored plate in the center of the suit's chest and fired a single round. The rebel staggered, clutching at his chest. The launcher sagged downward and fired. A slug smashed down into the deck. Thick smoke billowed forth and visibility dropped to zero.

Thomas gasped as bullets pinged off his suit. He fired a single shot again, then remembered that he was loaded with impact-only rounds. He switched to automatic and sprayed into the thickening smoke. Stepping into the swirling gray cloud he scanned for movement. Spotting a dead combatant, he noted that the enemy suits looked soft. With the flick of a thumb he snapped out the bayonet under his rifle's barrel.

Movement to the left. He swung even as bullets pounded against him. His rifle slammed against something that grunted, but his own shots went wide. The smoke cloud rang as the bullets punched into the bulkhead.

Weight crashed down on his shoulder from behind and he staggered. A gray-suited hand reached to grab into his faceplate, blocking his view. Another hand wrenched at his rifle. Thomas threw himself backward, toppling with the massive weight of the attacker on his back. Together they crashed down to the deck. Thomas felt the sickening squish as the full mass of his armored suit flattened his attacker. The hands grabbing at him went limp and fell away.

Still on his back he fired another spray of bullets upward into the smoke. A responding flash indicated the location of his foe even as his suit's status lights glowed yellow in his peripheral. He fired at the flash and scrambled to a crouch. Shots cracked past him. He activated quantum-flux and quickly scanned right to left. Two more figures lurked behind the shroud of smoke, barely an arm's length away, both crouched and seemingly blind. He couldn't take both of them without being shot again, and a quick glance at his suit's status indicated multiple punctures already.

He wouldn't survive another barrage of hits at this range.

Stabbing outward at the nearest target, he pushed the bayonet at the shape of the suit's throat, into the tough outer material between faceplate and chest armor. The blade sliced through until it hit bone. With a twist Thomas tore the wound open and wrenched back.

The attack was silent, and the second enemy figure remained unaware. Thomas leaned back in his crouch and lined up the quantum-flux image in his sights. He fired a short burst and the target slumped back.

Scanning again with quantum-flux, he then shifted to the longer-range infra-red. Five bodies were scattered on both sides of the airtight opening. No movement.

Then he noticed a deep rumble coming from the deck itself and up through his suit, followed by the tell-tale sway of the artificial gravity fighting against the vectors of heavy maneuvering. *Bowen* was at speed and turning sharply, which could only mean one thing—stealth attack. He rose to his feet and stepped back through the door, breaking into a run as soon as the smoke began to clear.

He'd barely made it ten steps when darkness swallowed the

entire passageway and he felt himself falling forward in a sudden gravity well. The deck slammed into him and he slid along the smooth surface. Ignoring the warning lights of his suit, he hung onto his weapon and braced as the twisted gravity pulled him to rest against the next hatch combing.

Slowly, slowly, gravity returned to normal.

Emergency lights flickered on. Thomas picked himself up heavily and pushed open the airtight door. His armor felt heavy as he walked, the servos on his left side wheezing in emergency mode. The computer would reallocate nanoparts and energy to keep him moving for a while longer, but his suit was effectively cannibalizing itself to obey his commands.

DCC was a shambles of broken displays and injured bodies, but some of the systems were still working. Snapping open his faceplate, he stumbled up to where Chen, Hayley, and Ranson huddled around a desk display. Smoke burned at his eyes as he surveyed their pale faces.

"Close ground threat neutralized," he stated with forced calm. "Damage control status?"

Neither subbie was able to speak. Chen stared at the damage to the armored suit. Hayley gripped her headset against the blood-soaked bandage on her head.

"Damage control system is stable," Ranson growled. "We evaded the torpedo attack, but the near miss took out primary electrical."

"Boarding status?"

"All threats dead or retreated," Hayley said without looking up. "The forward groups pulled back to airlock three and the rebel ship broke away. Spinner-Three was destroyed during the attack."

"ASW status?"

"Unknown," Chen said.

"Explain."

"The singularity wave tore us up back here. It rolled the Hawk in the hangar. All connections to ASW were cut. More than thirty casualties back aft." Chen pointed down at the panel, which displayed the overall ship status. "We've gone to best possible speed and we're running for the jump gate. If we can stay ahead of the stealth far enough, it won't be able to take another shot."

"Very good," Thomas nodded. ASW was a world of very slow speeds, but in extreme cases there was nothing wrong with high-tailing it away from a threat. *Bowen*'s gravimetric signature at high speed would be the size of an asteroid, but nobody was trying to hide now. Their best hope was to outrun the stealth.

"What about Spinner-Two?"

Chen glanced at Hayley before responding.

"Unknown. Last comms we heard was the torpedo flash transmit—we've been blind and deaf pretty much since then."

"Oaks, get down to the tail compartment and report those sensor readings directly up to DCC."

She struggled out of her seat and headed for the door. He hated to send her in that condition, but her line officer eyes would be able to interpret the raw data from the tail sensors, at least enough to give him some idea of what was going on out there.

Thomas glanced around, frustrated at the lack of a tactical display. If Spinner-Two was still out there, he'd be doing something useful. Thomas just needed to figure out what, and then see if he could help. But anti-stealth warfare was impossible without a way to assess relative positions. Then he spotted a blank sketch board lying on a dead terminal.

"Chen, do you remember the last reported ASW positions?"

"Yes, sort of."

Thomas grabbed the sketch board and a light pen.

"Draw it for me."

Chen took the pen and, after a moment's thought, began sketching symbols on the board. Manual combat plotting was a useful tool for teaching new operators the principles of tactical positioning, but it was never used when real combat systems were available. It had been nearly twenty years since Thomas had used the technique himself, but young Chen was fresh out of training.

Thomas studied the rough diagram, which placed *Bowen* in the center and showed the relative positions of Spinner-Two, the enemy stealth, and the lone remaining rebel ship. Chen drew in the vectors of each, as they'd been before he sent *Bowen* to full speed.

"This will have changed now," Chen said, "based on our new velocity."

"Okay," Thomas prompted, "so draw in new vectors for us and see where it places the stealth."

Chen did so, then connected the vectors into a relative motion triangle.

"Chief," Thomas said, looking up at Ranson, "come hard left ninety degrees and then stop the engines."

Ranson barked orders and Thomas felt the AG field shudder as it compensated through the high-speed turn.

"We're turning to fight?" Chen asked.

"I need us to stop accelerating so that we can get a clear picture again, and I want full bearing spread for the tail." He handed Chen his headset. "Get linked up with Oaks and put this on speaker."

Thomas checked the time, waiting as a single, agonizing minute passed. Then he queried Hayley down in the tail compartment. She reported up a series of possible bearings and Chen plotted them on his board. Most likely the stealth was at speed, trying to keep pace with *Bowen*, and hadn't realized yet that her target had slowed. The cross-section of bearings from the tail wasn't enough to give him an accurate range to target, but sometimes bearing was enough. This was a very long-distance shot, and it would re-expose *Bowen*'s position, but Thomas could visualize his assets in the four-dimensional game of chess, and he saw an opportunity.

"Port torpedo tubes," he ordered via Chen, "down a relative bearing of two-six-eight mark two-eight-zero, salvo size three, set peets one, four, and seven—*fire*."

A trio of thuds echoed through the silent hull as his orders were carried out. In his mind he envisaged the three weapons vanishing into the Bulk, each one headed to a different level of peets. He didn't know how far into the Bulk the stealth was hiding, but he knew it wouldn't be too far in if it was hunting *Bowen* here on the brane.

"Three torpedoes, sir?" Chen asked.

"This is called 'firing a spread,' Mr. Wi. All three weapons will go active, and one of them will find our target."

"*New transient down target bearing,*" Hayley reported over the speaker, "*three peets in.*"

The stealth was maneuvering to evade the attacks. *Bowen*'s torpedoes had gone active and the stealth had plenty of time to launch countermeasures and evade. But Thomas never expected his own weapons to score the kill.

"*Second transient,*" Oaks shouted, "*new torpedo closing on target!*"

Chen stared up at Thomas, confusion in his eyes. Thomas pointed at the symbols on the board.

"All I had to do was flush the stealth out. Spinner-Two will do the rest."

"*DCC,*" John's voice crackled on a different speaker, "*this is ASW. We just got comms with Spinner-Two. Assess shadow zero-one destroyed!*"

It was done.

There was no spontaneous cheer in DCC, no sudden hugs or handshakes. Thomas glanced around at the drawn, pale faces at the consoles. He saw the wounded braced against the deck, and the shattered equipment. His ship and crew were still alive, but not by much.

"Roger, ASW. Bravo-zulu to Spinner-Two. Recover the Hawk and secure for jump as best you can." He turned to Chen. "Plot a course for the jump gate. We're heading home."

22

There were eyes on her, Breeze knew, but she studiously ignored them. At least in the VIP lounge of the Longreach skyport, the clientele had enough courtesy to leave her alone.

She kept at least some staff around her at all times now, just to act as blockers from the public. This entire trip to Triton had been a marathon effort of making herself accessible enough to the media to satisfy the public's demand for drama, while keeping enough distance to retain an air of tragic mystique.

After much discussion with Vijay's PR staff she'd finally decided to speak at her husband's funeral, but amid all the genuine outpouring of grief from his family and long-time friends, she knew her own words had sounded stilted. The PR team framed it as a brave attempt by the devastated widow, but she knew she could do better.

The real problem, she considered as she glanced around at her fellow wealthy passengers, was figuring out exactly what her next move should be. Did she use her newfound celebrity to make the jump into media, or did she slip quietly into the background as a senior advisor to one of the big firms?

To be honest, she'd genuinely liked Vijay, and there were times when real tears did take her. Maybe she just needed a bit more time to figure things out. Whenever one door closed, she knew, another would open—and until she saw her opportunity, she had to be very careful what she said and did in public.

At least she was back on Earth. The trip out to Triton had been too long, and that dark world with its grim people had been a lot to take. She looked forward to hitting the beach tomorrow, and working on her tan under the real heat of Sol's direct rays.

Her assistant Susie rose from the chair beside her, and after a moment moved into Breeze's view and crouched down.

"Ma'am, there are some gentlemen who wish to speak to you."

Susie knew better than to let just anyone break through the wall of silence, and Breeze lifted her gaze. Standing politely at the edge of her private circle of chairs were two men she recognized well—Admiral Eric Chandler and Brigadier Sasha Korolev. With a sudden, genuine rush of warmth she rose and embraced Chandler in a light hug, then offered Korolev the standard cheek kisses.

"Admiral, Brigadier—what a nice surprise. Please join me."

She retook her chair as the two senior officers seated themselves across from her. They were an odd pair—Chandler with his rugged good looks and easy charisma, Korolev with his plain, unassuming features—but she wasn't terribly surprised to see them together. They'd both risen to prominence at the beginning of the war, when their respective commanders were killed in a surprise attack, and together they'd assumed command of Expeditionary Force 15.

Chandler had been the public face of the attack on Centauria, and over the past two years he had become a frequent spokesperson for the Astral Force. Korolev had shunned the spotlight, but Breeze knew he'd been anything but idle and, last she'd heard, he was heading up Special Forces. Susie had definitely got this one right.

These men were people worth talking to.

"I'm so sorry to hear about your husband, Breeze," Chandler said. "He was a good man."

"Thank you," she replied carefully. "It's been hard, but I'm not going to be defeated by it. I assume"—she turned her eyes to Korolev—"something's being done about it?"

"We know who the attacker was," Korolev said with a reassuring nod. "It's being taken care of."

"Good."

"Are you heading home?" Chandler asked. "Maybe taking a bit of a break?"

"Yes. I think a few weeks on the Mediterranean will help a lot. Where are you traveling?"

"I'm headed topside," Chandler said with a gesture toward the ceiling, and ultimately toward Astral Base One orbiting high above them. "But I heard Sasha was passing through, so I came over to the skyport to meet. Running into you is a pleasant bonus."

"Secret discussions, no doubt?"

"Very interesting discussions, actually." He glanced at Korolev. "For the first time in a while, I'm actually really optimistic."

"Oh? I could use a bit of good news right now."

Korolev held up a hand to pause the conversation, nodding silently toward Breeze's assistant.

"Susie," Breeze said, "would you give us a minute, please?" The younger woman promptly rose from her chair and moved a discreet distance away.

"We have a new military plan," Chandler said quietly, leaning in. "I can't discuss details here, but… Well, I'm optimistic. Sasha and I have been working on the details for quite a while, and the tactics are sound."

"We just worry," Korolev interjected, "that the political will won't be there."

"It's a bold plan," Chandler continued, "and it will change the war. But I agree, it needs full political support."

Both men stared at her expectantly.

"I wish I could help you," she said carefully. "Any new strategy created by you two is bound to be brilliant, but I'm not sure what I can do."

"Your influence among your husband's colleagues is greater than you might think," Chandler said with an admiring smile. "Or did Thomas Kane just earn that second DCM on his own?"

Breeze stiffened, wondering how her subtle words of influence had reached Chandler's ears. But then she remembered that seated next to him, with a bland, innocent expression, was the commander of Astral Special Forces. She allowed herself a confident smile.

"Thomas deserves any accolade offered him—I just gave a nudge in his direction."

"He deserves more than you know. Why do you think I'm heading into space? I have a ride waiting to Astral Base Five to welcome our new hero home."

So Thomas's career was back on track.

Good, that will keep him happy... and silent.

"How wonderful—please give him my best." She watched both men, judging their reactions to her next comment. "But I'm still not sure how I can help you with your new strategy. Especially if I don't even know what it is."

"As you know, we'd never discuss top-secret information with a private citizen," Korolev said. "Not even one with close connections to the government, and a prior career in Astral Intelligence."

"No, of course not," she said, "and in the wake of this tragedy, I'm not sure what my own future holds. There are many... possibilities, but who can say what the best one is."

She waited expectantly.

"Have you considered," Chandler said, "running for Vijay's seat in Parliament?"

A surprised laugh escaped her, dying as she saw the lack of amusement on the admiral's face. The notion was absurd. It took years to gather the sort of resources required to fight an election to Parliament.

"I'm flattered, Eric," she said, "but that by-election is going to be announced in a few days, and I'm not even an official member of a political party. Plus my husband is barely cold in his grave— what would the optics be?"

"They would be of justice," Chandler said. "They would be of strength. Our enemies strike us at the heart, but we rise up from our sorrow and stand resolute. As a veteran yourself, you would represent every one of us who risks everything for the good of Terra."

Breeze felt her mind racing. It was an insane idea. Or, perhaps, it was just an audacious idea. But still...

"No independent has ever won a seat in Parliament," she said. "I'd need the support of one of the parties."

"Knowing the high regard in which the Minister of Defense holds you," Chandler said, "I think Vijay's party would back you."

That might be true, she thought. She hadn't yet disbanded

Vijay's political staff, as they'd been required to guide her through the chaos of the funeral process. The staff was top-notch, and they'd already spent months building her public profile. But could her image as glamorous wife be transformed in a few short weeks to serious political contender?

"I'd need a lot of help," she said. "Building a successful campaign so quickly would take a miracle."

"Miracles have been known to happen," Korolev said with quiet resolve.

She sat back in her chair, considering the idea. Losing Vijay had seemed at the time to be the death knell for her budding political career, but as one door closed...

"We need a strong voice inside Parliament, to support us with our new plan," Chandler said. "And we want that voice to be you."

"I'd like some time to think about it."

"Of course," he said. "I'm heading out for a few days, but Sasha will be nearby."

"I can call on you in two days," Korolev offered.

"No doubt you already know the address."

His expression was neutral, but he smiled slightly.

She returned the smile, and began to consider how best to make her public announcement. True power beckoned, and all she had to do was answer.

23

"All moorings secure, sir."

Thomas nodded his acknowledgement of Chief Ranson's report. Tugs had met the crippled cruiser as soon as it emerged through the jump gate and taken positive control, guiding her carefully alongside one of the battle-blackened docks of Terra's jump gate fortress.

The broken DC display had been converted to show a visual of the port side of the ship, and Thomas had been able to watch as *Bowen* was brought alongside the spar at Astral Base Five, but he'd had nothing to do with the maneuver himself.

"Secure from docking stations," he said quietly.

As Chen began rattling off the routine list of orders that occurred whenever the ship came alongside, Thomas turned to John Micah.

"I don't have any special requirements for the crew, XO. Unless you have anything planned for them, I suggest you contact Fleet personnel and start arranging transports home. *Admiral Bowen* isn't going anywhere for a long time."

"Yes, sir," John replied, making a brave effort at a smile. "I'm just gathering the crew for a final debrief and then I'm going to get them ashore. I've already arranged quarters for each of them in the base until we're told where everyone's being reassigned."

"I'd like to see everyone sent home for leave."

"I agree wholeheartedly, but from my discussions with Fleet, that may not be happening."

Thomas sighed. The pace of the war was unrelenting, it seemed. He could just imagine the conversation at Fleet Personnel regarding the news of *Bowen*'s return.

We have a cruiser that was terribly damaged in battle, but they limped it home.

Casualties?

Half the crew.

The other half—they're still serviceable?

Absolutely.

Well, get them onto new ships ASAP. We have a war to fight.

With pleasure.

Thomas shook his head, looking around again at his exhausted team. They had managed to return home, through a jump gate, with a vessel that was little more than a blind shell surrounding troublesome engines. Technicians had practically rebuilt the sensor control systems to turn DCC into a rough-and-ready bridge, but everything was still controlled from primary units. There was a team of operators around him whose sole job was to relay his orders along various circuits to engineering, the weapons and sensors, the hangar, and—he shuddered at the memories—all the thruster controls.

Aside from the programmable visual on the main DCC display and a single 3D projection stolen from Spinner-One, Thomas had no way of knowing what occurred beyond DCC except for listening to the voice reports of his operators. He felt like the captain of an old water-based ship from centuries ago—all he needed was a hand telescope and a sword on his belt.

DCC suddenly filled up, and within moments he found himself surrounded by a weary but bright-eyed crew. Chen and Hayley moved to flank him, and Chief Ranson loomed behind, arms crossed and his habitual scowl firmly in place. John ensured that a decent space remained clear around them and, noting the last of the arrivals squeezing in the door, motioned for silence.

"I realize," John said to the room's occupants, "that my tenure as the executive officer of this fine vessel is coming to an end, and before Fleet bureaucracy strips me of my authority, I wanted to make sure one last critical task has been completed." He nodded to the subbies, each of whom reached into their pockets.

"It is unseemly," John continued, "for a vessel as mighty as *Admiral Bowen* to remain under the command of a mere sublieutenant, and while it is not in my power to grant field promotions, as XO I have the authority to grant field appointments. And so, with that authority, I bestow upon you, sir… the appointment to sublieutenant commander."

Thomas's eyes darted down to where Chen and Hayley unfastened his epaulettes and replaced his rank with something he'd never seen before—the single bar of sublieutenant, augmented by a star. A roar of laughter went up, and he joined in. Then he forcibly composed himself, making a show of solemnly shaking John's hand as the laughter gave way to thunderous applause.

John stepped back and offered him the floor.

"Thank you," Thomas said, turning slowly to take in everyone crowded around him. "I'll be sure to sign the log with my new appointment—if only to confound future historians. In all seriousness, though, I'm just one person in a team of elite professionals who did the impossible. The honors are due to all of you. I'm proud to have served with each and every one of you. Well done, and welcome home.

"And now," he continued, "if the XO truly has nothing else to say…?" John shook his head. "Everyone get ashore and get some down time. Don't hurt yourselves, don't hurt anyone else, get rested up. We might not have a lot of time before the State calls upon us again."

"Three cheers for Sublieutenant Commander Kane," Chief Ranson bellowed.

The cheers were loud and sincere, and Thomas had to drop his gaze to hide the sudden grin that threatened his stoic countenance.

"Now you heard him," Ranson roared. "Get your shit and get ashore! If I see anybody on board in twenty minutes, they'll be getting my size thirteen boot up their ass." Amid new laughter and a rumble of chattering voices, the crew began to file out of DCC.

Thomas glanced around at his "command team"—a pair of young subbies, a wet-behind-the-ears lieutenant, and a curmudgeonly old engineering chief. He could have done a lot worse.

"Don't wander far, any of you," he said. "And Hayley, you hold Chen's hair back when he needs to puke."

She laughed, but before she could reply her eyes suddenly widened as she looked past Thomas toward the door. She snapped to attention.

"Admiral on deck!"

Thomas instinctively stiffened, and turned to look toward the door. Admiral Eric Chandler gazed back at him, his stern features taking in the entire scene.

"Carry on," Chandler said, stepping forward and letting the last of the crew exit, until only John, Haley, and Chen remained. He approached Thomas, eyes lingering on the unique rank insignia.

"Sir," Thomas said, "I present to you the cruiser *Admiral Bowen*—or as much of her as we could save."

"You've done excellent work," Chandler replied, nodding at the epaulettes, "Sublieutenant Commander."

"A gesture from the crew," Thomas offered. "All in good fun, sir."

"And appreciated. It almost makes the Fleet's gesture seem unnecessary." Thomas searched his memory for any recent gesture from Fleet to *Bowen*. Other than the squad of tugs sent to bring her alongside, nothing sprang to mind. But he could see the glint in Chandler's eye, and he guessed something was up.

"What gesture is that, sir?"

"This new appointment your crew created for you… It's not officially sanctioned and, in my opinion, it's too cumbersome." He nodded to Hayley and Chen. "Remove those epaulettes, please." The subbies silently obeyed, and Thomas saw John frowning in resignation behind the admiral.

"Your crew, in their gesture, took two ranks and pushed them together," Chandler continued. "I say—and Fleet agrees—that it should be one rank or the other. Since you've proven yourself multiple times as a sublieutenant, I think it's time we test you as a commander." He produced a new pair of epaulettes—each bearing three bars—and handed them to the subbies. They took them and fastened them to Thomas's shoulders.

"This is an official promotion, effective immediately and so noted in Fleet records." He extended his hand. "Richly deserved, and far too long in coming, Commander Kane."

Thomas shook hands with his old mentor. Then he took the sublieutenant commander epaulettes and held them tight.

"Keep those," Chandler said. "They're from your crew, and a greater honor than I could bestow."

"Thank you, sir."

Chandler reached over and patted him on the shoulder, then began leading him toward the door.

"Let's you and I adjourn to somewhere a bit tidier. We have a lot to discuss."

It didn't take long for Thomas to learn what Chandler meant by "somewhere a bit tidier." Departing *Bowen*, they walked directly across the spar and boarded another cruiser, *Admiral Moore*, which itself showed the black scars of battle across its hull.

Inside, however, the passageways were bright and clean, and the only crew they passed were technicians completing their work and a caravan of storesmen directing pallets toward the ship's holds. In just a few minutes, Chandler stopped in front of the door to the captain's cabin. He gestured to Thomas.

Puzzled, Thomas pressed the call button. A moment later the door slid open to reveal a middle-aged crewman who glanced efficiently between the two senior officers, and then stepped back to invite entry.

"Commander Kane, welcome, sir."

Thomas entered the cabin and scanned for its occupant—whoever *Admiral Moore*'s commanding officer might be. The large room was empty. He stepped forward to the sitting area, following Chandler's lead as the admiral sat down in one of the armchairs. The crewman, who was obviously the captain's steward, poured coffees and retreated to the pantry.

Thomas looked around the room, then back to Chandler, who was sipping at the coffee and looking back with a spark of humor. There was silence for a long moment, then Thomas remembered the new rank on his shoulders. He took a guess.

"Is this my new cabin, sir?"

Chandler set his cup down and sat back in the chair with a satisfied nod.

"I present to *you* the cruiser *Admiral Moore*, fresh out of refit. Try to bring this one back in one piece."

A startled laugh escaped Thomas's lips. Promotion, and now command?

"Is this how we do things in the Fleet now, sir? Seems kind of low-key."

"We don't have time for pomp and circumstance these days, Thomas. Fleet has a cruiser coming out of refit that needs an operational crew, and you and your battle-hardened gaggle need a ship. You'll be augmented by most of the technicians already on board, and a few more officers I've pulled together from the manning pool." He leaned forward, all humor suddenly gone. "But more importantly, Thomas, Fleet needs this ship to quietly disappear without any fanfare or notice. I have a special mission for you."

Thomas felt the old rush of excitement that came before an operation. Not just a promotion and a command—he was going to do something vital. He'd asked Breeze for his career back, but he'd never expected this. If he ever saw that conniving bitch again, he'd kiss her full on the lips.

Or maybe not.

"When do we leave, sir?"

"In four days. Give your crew tonight and tomorrow to blow off steam, then get them on board for drills. I'll have your new XO and other senior staff assembled by then."

"Has this ship been through post-refit trials?"

"That's what your two days alongside with the crew are for."

Two days. Two days to test a cruiser and all its systems. Two days to gel a new crew before deploying to a war zone. In peacetime it would have been absurd. But in these times of war…

"What's the mission?"

"You remember how much damage we did to the rebels, back when we did our little sneak attack on Abeona?"

Thomas remembered well. It had been a suicidal plan, in his opinion, and most of Expeditionary Force 15 had never come home from it. He nodded silently.

"We've learned from that," Chandler continued. "A frontal assault is too costly, especially with the Fleet scattered and weakened as it is. Yet our strike on the rebel homeworld stopped the war in its tracks for a full six months. We have a new plan, this time to end the war altogether, and I need you and your ship to conduct the reconnaissance."

"So a covert mission to Centauria. Am I going alone, or will there be other Fleet assets with me?"

"Yours is the only ship going, but you'll be delivering Special Forces assets to the system and maintaining a link with them. A second ship—which I'll be aboard—will join you later for the mission conclusion."

Thomas took his cup of coffee and drained it.

"I'll do my duty, sir, gladly," he said, "but my crew will be better prepared if we can have some more time to work up the ship. Even just a week. Are the timings critical, sir?"

"Militarily, no, but something I've discovered since I joined the admiralty is that military considerations don't always take precedence. This mission commences in four days, whether we like it or not."

"Yes, sir." Thomas had always been able to read his mentor's moods, and he could tell that Chandler was in anything but a political mood right now. He decided to test the waters. "Is there a lot of pressure from Parliament?"

"More every week." Chandler refilled his cup. "The loss of our permanent positions in Valhalla doesn't matter one bit, not militarily—in my opinion we're stretched too thin just dealing with the major colonies—but it was seen as a humiliation politically. Parliament feels that Terra should be able to hold all the colonies at once, and isolate each rebel faction in order to prevent another consolidated attack."

"I'm not sure I follow their logic, sir."

"Because there isn't any! They see any territorial loss as a defeat, and they don't listen when we tell them that we're over-extended. They want us to win everywhere, all at once."

"But isn't Parliament mostly filled with veterans? Don't they understand tactical realities?"

"Veterans," Chandler snorted, "who served their minimum obligatory time in uniform before getting out and running for public office. Our government is comprised mostly of spoiled civilians who served in the military just long enough to think they don't need to listen."

"And my mission?"

"Ah," the admiral brightened considerably. "Now that's something I'm proud to be a part of. It's a plan I developed with my old friend Sasha Korolev, based on some good work that's been done over the past two years. Yes, it's driven by Parliament's need for a major territorial gain—and it will accomplish that—but even more so it will send a clear message to the rebels that continuing the war is foolish... for everyone."

"An end to the war?"

"And not a moment too soon."

Thomas sat back in his chair, looking around the large cabin. Habit told him that it belonged to Commander Hu, but then he reminded himself that he was aboard a different—if identical—ship. *His* ship, and with it he had the chance to execute what might be the pivotal mission of the entire conflict. He no longer cared about fame, but to make a difference as a soldier—that still meant something.

"How is the war going, sir?"

Chandler fixed him with a stern look that quickly melted into fatigue.

"Not well. We're hurting the rebels, but they're still doing too much damage to both the Army and the Astral Force. They outnumber us, and in some cases they have the technological advantage. We can probably keep fighting for another year or two, but eventually both sides will be exhausted, and neither will be able to control the other."

"Then they win, because they're free of Terra."

"Exactly. If we keep on this path, the war will end in military stalemate—a political defeat for Terra."

"And millions will have died to get us there."

Chandler sat forward, staring down at his hands.

"It's too late to avoid that," he said quietly. Then he looked up with a new intensity. "This mission is going to be challenging, Thomas. I need loyal officers who will stand firm with me as we act for the good of all humanity."

"You can count on me, sir."

24

"What are you suggesting?"

Jack forced himself to hold Katja's glare. The question she posed had been a challenge. Her dark eyes burned with their usual intensity, and while he was getting used to it he still couldn't decide whether fear or lust was his dominant emotion. It certainly wasn't fondness or affection—she was far too distant for that.

Eventually, though, he broke her gaze and looked around the cruiser's wardroom. He sat with his feet on the coffee table and she sat beside him, legs curled up as she turned to face him. Except for a pair of stewards clearing the dining table, they were alone in the space.

He shrugged.

"I'm not really sure what's real anymore."

"Is it your Cloud connections? That can mess with anyone's mind, and you've been in pretty deep these past few weeks."

He might struggle with the Cloud, he thought absently, but it was the least of his worries.

"No," he said. "It's more that I'm sitting here on a cruiser which looks exactly like the one I used to serve in. She's a different ship, but half the crew are exactly the same people as those I used to serve with. Oh, except *Thomas* is now the captain, and not a subbie. Plus I'm sitting here, talking to a woman who was dead for more than a year. Who I can communicate with in a way most of the human race doesn't even know exists."

<You think this is strange?>

He held up his finger and thumb in close proximity.

<Little bit.>

She shrugged. In her blue uniform coveralls and wearing a lieutenant's rank, she almost looked as he first remembered her. Her hair was longer, but every fiber of her being seemed to whisper a threat. It was strange to see his own rank insignia to match, but he glanced at it to remind himself that she wasn't his superior anymore. On this mission they were equals, and he knew his strengths.

The door opened and a familiar female form stormed in, flopping down on the couch near him.

"Fuck!"

"And good morning to you, Hayley," he said with a smile.

She glared at him, the bags under her eyes giving evidence to the pressure of the past week's drills. Jack and Katja had boarded literally minutes before departure, and in the three days it had taken *Admiral Moore* to move into deep space, this crew had been kept running from one simulated emergency to another.

Jack had never taken Thomas to be a hard-assed line officer, but the way he'd been driving the crew since taking command made him wonder if his colleague's true self had just been hiding in the soft, fluffy guise of a strike officer.

"We're making the jump in ten minutes," Hayley said. "And then hopefully I can get some sleep."

"Yeah, because Centauri space is a real yawner."

"Fuck off."

He glanced over at Katja. "These are my peeps."

Katja gave him a tiny smile, then rose to her feet.

"We should probably get to the bridge."

He followed her lead, resisting the urge to pat Hayley on the head. Line officers could bite if provoked.

The walk forward was quick, and those few crew members they passed barely glanced up, so intent were they on their jobs. No one had questioned the arrival of two new lieutenants, and even those crew who knew Jack didn't seem to have noticed that he'd barely set foot in the hangar. He wondered if he should be insulted.

One of the Hawks had been replaced by what looked to be a high-performance racing launch, and *that* had started lips wagging—but with no conclusions.

Warning lights flashed at the threshold to the bridge, announcing the impending switch to zero-g. Katja slowed to a stop and pressed a hand lightly against Jack's chest. Her fingers tapped against him, almost hesitantly.

"We should check our entanglement," she said. "Now, and then again after the jump."

"Okay," he replied hesitantly, as he realized that she was tapping the spot in his ribcage where that creepy device had been implanted. Katja removed her hand and purposefully looked away from him. Then, deep in his chest, he felt a sharp flare. It was brief, and didn't hurt—he couldn't really say what it felt like—but it was unmistakable.

"It's working," he said with a nod.

Katja barely looked up, pushing the door open and stepping through. *Moore*'s bridge was fully crewed. She and Jack hooked onto the anchor lines, and then made their way to the center of the sphere. All around them the starry blackness stretched away to infinity. One of those stars, nearly dead astern, shone brighter than the rest. Sol was more than ten billion kilometers away, placing *Moore* most definitely in the middle of nowhere.

Perfect for a secret dimensional jump.

Commander Kane sat in his seat at the center of the bridge. He noticed the pair of arrivals and nodded to them.

"Ms. Emmes," he said, "Mr. Mallory. Your timing is perfect. Why does that not surprise me?"

Katja didn't respond, other than to cross her arms and look forward. Things were still a bit frosty—had been ever since he and Katja had boarded. Not only had Thomas seemed unsurprised to see her—given that she was officially dead—but their formal handshake had been less than what Jack expected from old friends. Of course, the last time he'd seen them together she *had* kicked Thomas nearly in half, and then arrested him.

Maybe they were still working through some issues.

"One minute to jump," Sublieutenant Chen announced from his position as second officer of the watch.

"All stations report ready," *Moore*'s XO added. He was a short bull of a man named Lieutenant Duquette, who in very short order had already demonstrated more competence than *Bowen*'s old XO.

Jack glanced around the bridge. Some of the operators he recognized from *Bowen*, but apart from Thomas, two of the subbies, and John Micah, all the officers had been pulled in from the Fleet manning pool, which was generally made up of the survivors from destroyed ships. It was significant, though, that all of these officers were *survivors*—they'd all been through hell at least once already, and lived to tell the tale. It gave him confidence that they would serve Thomas well.

"Thirty seconds to jump."

"Douse the beacon," Thomas ordered. "Switch all sensors to passive." His commands were carried out and reports came back. *Moore* was silent in deep space, poised to do something Jack had never seen before—jump without a jump gate.

"Jump coordinates are locked," Micah reported from ASW. "Projector ready."

This "projector" was a new piece of technology that had been delivered on board—a top-secret device that could create a temporary path into extra-dimensional space and project it around the ship. It tapped, not into the Bulk, but into the even more mysterious spatial dimension known in physics as the Point. Infinitesimal in size, it still connected to every coordinate in five-dimensional spacetime, and allowed instantaneous travel between far-separated areas in the brane by offering a "short cut." In the Point, distances were real, but so small as to be practically immeasurable.

It was the principle behind all the jump gates ever made, and was a proven reality of the universe, but Terran jump gates were all massive, high-energy devices that took years to set up and required a minimum of gravimetric interference. The Centauris had proven the possibility that jump gates could be much smaller, and could be safely operated inside of gravity wells, but even those had been stationary, pre-set devices. This projector was the first time he'd ever heard of a vessel being able to create its own jump gate at will.

"Ten seconds to jump."

"Deactivate gravity," Thomas said. His voice was measured and calm, but he was gripping his armrests with unusual intensity. Jack ensured his anchor line was taut, and then felt the stomach-turning lurch as gravity disappeared. No one moved, but he saw a few grimaces on the faces behind consoles.

"Three... two... one... jump!"

There was a flicker of darkness, accompanied by a strange, wavering slide that might just have been in his mind. He tightened his grip on the anchor line, and forced himself to breathe. All around him, the stars looked the same as they had a moment before. Ahead of him, Katja floated in silence, arms still crossed tightly over her chest.

He reached inward with his mind and activated his entanglement device. She turned wary eyes toward him, and nodded. Entanglement was tied in to the Point, as particles somehow became connected in that dimension and could transmit certain information via the no-distance in the Point to dispersed positions in the brane.

"Officer of the watch," Thomas said, "check our position."

The young officer seated next to him examined his displays.

"All directors," Thomas continued, "report status."

"AAW condition white," the anti-attack warfare director reported. "No detected threats."

"AVW condition white," the anti-vessel warfare director echoed. "No indication of other vessels."

"ASW condition white," John concluded as the anti-stealth warfare director. "No gravimetric anomalies."

"Based on star fixes," the officer of the watch announced, "we are in the Centauri system, approximately eight billion kilometers north of Centauri A. I'll have an exact position in three minutes."

"Very good." Thomas released his grip on his armrests. He took a long look around at the starscape, then pointed low on the bow. "There. Twin suns. That's where we're headed."

Jack followed his gaze down and saw two stars shining much brighter than all the others. He glanced aft to where Sol had shone just moments before, but saw nothing of note amid the sea of lights.

"We'll retain passive sensors and zero-g for now," Thomas announced. "I want to get a good assessment of the rebel strength as we close Abeona."

"Yes, sir," the XO replied.

"And ASW," Thomas called over his shoulder, "have the projector pre-programmed with our escape jump back to Terra."

Katja rotated slowly in place, turning to face the captain.

"How long until we deploy?"

"About forty hours for us to close Abeona, unless you want to spend extra time in your little ship."

"We'll launch at maximum range," she said, as if she was challenging him to disagree. "Three billion k."

"Then it'll be about twenty-five hours." He shrugged. "The bridge can keep you posted on exact timings."

"Make sure they do," she said.

Every officer within earshot appeared to stiffen, but if Thomas took any offence at Katja's attitude, he hid it well. Chen snuck a sidelong look over at Jack, but he ignored the silent communication. These were his peeps, but Katja was his partner. And they didn't have to live with her for the next few weeks.

25

"Just seeing it again makes me angry," Jack said, breaking the long silence in the cockpit.

It wasn't the first time he had piloted a small craft toward the Centauri homeworld of Abeona, and as the brilliant blue-green globe swelled to fill the view ahead, he tried to see the beauty of this Second Earth. Yet this globe had been the backdrop to too many terrors, too many nightmares.

Beside him, Katja turned in her spacesuit to give him an appraising look.

"Good to hear," she said. "I was half expecting you to start gushing about how beautiful everything is."

"When do I gush?"

"Pretty much whenever you like something."

"Yeah, well… fuck you."

Her laughter filled the tiny space.

"Stay angry, Jack. That's what's going to get us through this mission." She gestured forward at the approaching planet. "It is beautiful, and the society we're infiltrating has a lot of appeal. We're going to blend in, going to act like they do. If we're not careful, though, we'll start to sympathize with them. That cannot happen. We're on a mission for Terra, and Centauria is the enemy. Staying angry is the best way to keep it straight in your head."

He nodded. Katja knew him better than most.

"I promise not to meet any nice Centauri girls."

"Don't joke—it happens."

"With you at my side, Katja, I doubt any woman would even risk looking at me."

"You'd be surprised how sweet I can be," she said, blinking her big browns.

"You're right," he said. "It would be a surprise."

Turning his attention back to his flight controls, he listened to the chatter of Abeona Traffic Control as they diligently tracked and identified vessels near the planet. He was trying his very best to stay beneath their notice. The insertion craft he flew was designed to evade sensors, but he'd long ago learned the folly of underestimating Centauri technology. As they entered the crowded lanes he watched the movements of other ships and kept beyond visual range, moving into a high polar orbit that pointed him away from the main starports.

"Any warships?" he asked.

"Three," Katja responded, highlighting them on their shared display. "Looks like two Space Guard cutters and a Navy frigate."

"The cutters are probably diligent, but I doubt the frigate is paying attention. This is a relaxation mission for them, away from the front."

"Yeah, they're perched in geosynchronous over Firsthome. The cutters are maneuvering, and I'd bet they're coordinating their coverage."

Jack watched the symbols in the display for a moment, reassuring himself that their vectors were heading away from him. Returning his attention to the visual, he surveyed the brilliant white expanse at the top of Abeona's visible disk. Traffic over the northern ice cap was practically nonexistent, and he kept the craft pointed at the waypoint one thousand kilometers above the pole. As the planet loomed larger, filling his entire view, he watched as the greens and blues of the temperate zone gave way to the browns and, finally, white of the arctic. Only a single unmanned satellite kept pace with him as he continued north, but it drifted up and ahead as Jack bled off velocity and continued to slowly drop toward the planet. He was closing the entry point.

"Ready for insertion?" he asked.

"Ready."

He closed his faceplate and did one final check of the surrounding area. There were no craft within a thousand kilometers, and no ground-based sensors nearby. Entering atmosphere was hard to do without anyone noticing, but the odds today were in his favor.

Spinning the craft to point its main engines into his direction of flight, he opened the throttle. The acceleration pushed his seat against him and his vector began to drop toward the surface. Abeona's gravity was strong enough to take effect immediately, pulling the craft inward as it bled off speed. For several minutes there was no apparent change in the cockpit—the view of orbital space remained full of the distant blinking lights of spacecraft, and the pressure against his back stayed constant.

Then he felt the first buffet of atmosphere. He couldn't count how many times he'd flown atmo insertion, and he knew what to expect. His hands tightened on the controls, the craft started to vibrate, but he kept his eyes on his instruments as both speed and altitude switched to planetary reference, and steadily dropped.

The vibration grew to a constant shudder. In his peripheral he saw Katja grip her armrests, and the first hints of super-heated air flashed into view. Not good—few things telegraphed the presence of a descending spaceship more clearly than a meteor trail of burning air. He throttled up, taking the strain of deceleration on the engines and away from the surrounding air. To an observer on the surface his thrust would be as bright as a new star by now, but only if that observer was in exactly the right place. With millions of square kilometers of ice below, that was unlikely.

All part of the plan, he reminded himself.

It took nearly ten minutes, but the craft finally dropped to hypersonic speed and flight-capable altitude. One final thrust flipped the craft around, pointing its nose in his direction of travel. He extended the craft's wings and switched from thrusters to flight surfaces. His control stick fought for a moment, then settled into atmo flight. All around, the white expanse of the

Abeonan arctic spread away beneath them.

"Not bad, Jack," Katja breathed. "First atmo entry ever where I didn't want to hurl."

"Thanks," he replied, feeling a smile tug at his lips. A compliment from Katja Emmes was a rare treat, and he swallowed any wry comment which might spoil the moment.

"I've input the RV point, and I'm starting my initial security scan," she said, all business again. A new symbol appeared on the display—the rendezvous point where he was to land the craft and take possession of their ground transport—and he adjusted course. They were still high in atmo for a flier, but here in the quiet skies of the far north there were few dedicated air lanes, and even fewer people likely to complain if he disregarded the recommended routes. Starting a long, leisurely descent he kept watch for other craft while Katja hunted for any threatening emissions or signals.

All was quiet as they sped southward, high over a continent-spanning mountain range and into the temperate zone. Civilian chatter increased in frequency as they entered more populated areas, but no one interrogated them, and there was nothing from the planet to suggest any sense of urgency. It was almost as if the war hadn't touched this place, Jack thought, and the business of regular life just carried on.

The RV point was to the north of the major city of Starfall, nestled among a range of low hills near a lake hidden deep in the dense forest. Jack slowed to his minimum flying speed and did a slow circle of the lake. On one shore the trees fell away to reveal a beach and grassy meadow. That was the landing zone.

"Looks clear," he said.

"I concur," Katja replied, eyes on her console.

"I'm bringing us in."

The winds were light and they dropped nearly to tree-top height as he engaged his thrusters and slowed to a hover over the beach. Ripples spread out across the water, and then he felt the thump of touchdown. The craft's weight settled on the landing gear, but he kept his hands on the controls. He watched the visible shore for any signs of movement.

"We're clear," Katja said.

Jack killed the engines and began his shut-down procedure. The rumble of the craft faded into a close silence broken only by the taps of his fingers on the controls, and Katja unbuckling from her seat. She closed her eyes—he could sense her presence in the Cloud as she did another scan of the area—and then started pulling off her spacesuit. Jack followed and within a minute they were both clad in the latest in casual hiking fashion.

Katja lifted an assault rifle to her eyeline and gestured for Jack to open the door. He did so with one hand, the other gripping the pistol he'd stuffed into his pocket. As the door slid open a gust of cool, moist air rushed over him—his first Centauri breath. It was clean, almost sweet, and he paused to savor another before stepping down to the flattened grass.

<Our equipment bears two-four-zero,> Katja said. <Just inside the treeline.>

Jack glanced at his watch to get his bearing, then walked out across the soft ground toward the edge of the forest. He kept his movements casual—he was completely out in the open and crouching or skulking would only make him look suspicious—but his senses reached out on all wavelengths. With a pilot's eyes he scanned the trees and the flat surface of the lake, seeing nothing unusual.

At the edge of the forest there was a pair of vehicles tucked into what might be an old campsite. One of the vehicles was a civilian hovercar, thoroughly nondescript in color and design, but the other was more interesting. It looked like a flatbed transport truck, but with no cab for a driver, and its construction was robust, even military-hardened. He sent the visual feed back to Katja.

<Both vehicles look secure,> he said, <but I don't see how we'll operate the truck.>

<Look inside the car,> Katja replied. <I'm coming over.>

Jack peered through the windows of the car and, sure enough, saw an obvious control unit sitting on the floor of the back seat. The door was unlocked and he pulled the control unit out. Katja jogged up, rifle cradled in her arms. She surveyed the scene without comment.

Examining the control unit, he skipped past the manual

instruments and linked directly to its electronic brain. Within moments he'd mapped out the capabilities of the truck and was impressed.

"It's designed to stay underwater for months," he said, "and it's strong enough to carry a Hawk."

"So, strong enough for our craft?" Katja asked impatiently.

"Easily." He climbed up onto the flatbed and offered a hand to her. She ignored the gesture and scrambled up to stand next to him. Activating the truck, he smiled as it lifted slowly off the ground. Branches snapped and flicked past him as he drove it clear of the treeline and crossed the stretch of meadow to the beach. Together he and Katja grabbed their gear out of the craft, and while she carried the packs back to the civilian vehicle, Jack played around with the truck's anti-gravity controls.

It was impressive that a vehicle this small could manipulate gravity enough to lift his spacecraft, let alone smoothly guide the awkward load onto the flatbed. Magnetic locks secured the two vehicles together and then Jack—with a final check that the spacecraft was fully sealed—drove the load slowly down the beach and into the water. It was a smooth slope, but steep enough that the truck disappeared underwater within moments, and the craft slipped beneath the surface shortly thereafter.

He kept the truck moving to make certain several meters of murky water covered the craft, then lowered it to the sandy lakebed and locked it into place. Then he jogged back to the car. Katja had loaded the backpacks and hidden her rifle, and was sitting in the driver's seat.

No, he realized as he climbed in beside her, she was in the passenger seat. Centauris drove on the opposite side of the road from Terrans, and their cars were designed in reverse. He looked around curiously at the controls. They were different from standard Terran cars, but not so much that he couldn't figure it out.

"Having troubles, there, Mr. Pilot?"

He gave her a withering glance.

"There's a steering wheel, a pair of foot throttles, and an on-off switch. I'm pretty sure I can make it work, but you're in charge of the stereo." He tapped the power button and the car blossomed to life. Glowing readouts gave him his status and Katja quickly brought up the navigation screen between them. A route traced out over the map and then zoomed in to give him directions.

"You might just have the car drive us," she offered.

"No way," he responded. "I want to get a feel for this little roadster."

"Suit yourself." She sat back in her seat and closed her eyes. A new surge of Cloud presence dismissed any notion that she was settling in for a nap.

Jack gripped the wheel and nudged the car forward, maneuvering slowly through the tiny clearing and picking up the trail through the trees. It was strange to have the majority of his vehicle on his left, but he hooked himself into the car's proximity sensors and quickly got a feel for how much space he really had around him. By the time the forest trail spilled out onto a wide, cropped-grass road, Jack was driving the car like it was an old friend.

Following the navigation system was easy and Jack watched the remote forest landscape gradually give way to farms, and then to small settlements. Centauri policy had always been to spread out the human population as much as possible over its worlds, limiting the ecological impact on any given area. With transport as quick and efficient as it was, there was no reason to cluster large populations together. Thus he noticed a significant increase in car traffic even before they approached the Starfall city limits.

Starfall was one of only three major centers on the entire planet, its population holding at just below one million. It had been the site of humanity's second permanent base here, its role as landing zone and administrative center forcing a certain number of colonists to remain nearby even as arriving settlers were quickly scattered across the northern hemisphere.

Like any human settlement it eventually achieved a cultural and economic critical mass that made it politically impossible to maintain normal population restrictions. Even so, it was impressive how well the city blended into nature as the grassy road led into its heart. The main route dropped below ground into a sprawling series of tunnels that served as transportation arteries. The hard stone excavated to make these tunnels had in turn been used to build an entire generation of buildings on the surface. Following the nav system through the tunnels toward their destination, he felt a twinge of disappointment that he was missing the beautiful, historic city above.

When they finally re-emerged, his impression was that it must be nearing sunset, but the orange tint to the light was normal for Centauri A, hanging high in the sky. Cars and buses moved smoothly along the treelined boulevards and Jack merged with the flow. Spying a driveway between a cluster of low-rise apartment buildings, he turned and slipped into the residential zone.

Pedestrians moved with purpose on broad raised walkways, and the car slowed to a crawl, switching to automatic control. The buildings next to the wide street were low, none of them more than four stories high, though much taller ones rose further back. Their narrow, elegant lines and distance from the street did little to threaten the airiness of the entire locality. It was a stark contrast to the crowded cities of Earth.

"Did we get set up in an expensive neighborhood?" he asked.

"No, we're actually in one of the lower-income areas."

"Wow." He looked around again at the bright, clean buildings, the bustling sidewalks and the grassy street. Growing up working class in Terra, he would never have dreamed of living in a place like this.

The car parked itself in an underground lot. Jack and Katja retrieved their backpacks, as well as the long "fishing rod case" which carried the heavy weaponry. They ascended via an elevator to the apartment that had been arranged for them. Their ID chips released the door locks, and within minutes of arrival they were setting down their bags and exploring their new home.

The front entrance had a small closet on the right before spilling into the main living room. A breakfast bar formed the border with the kitchen. One door led to a bedroom just off the front entrance, and another door led to a bedroom next to the kitchen. The view through the main window was of the pleasant street below.

Katja sent Jack the instructions she had received from the

Terran assets who had arranged everything for them. He was now John Edwards, a v-ware specialist who worked for various large companies on short-term contracts. She was Kristin Magnussen, an independent tour guide for a company that specialized in "extreme" vacations.

Glancing into the nearest bedroom, away from the kitchen, Katja said, "I'll take this one," and she tossed her backpack through the door. Jack obligingly carried his pack over to the far bedroom and set it down by the door. He wandered into the kitchen and opened the fridge.

"We're going to have to do some shopping."

"You can take care of that," she said, sitting down on the couch. "Centauri intelligence has images of my face, so it's best if I stay out of public places. I'll plan to stay in here unless we're doing an op."

"Okay."

Jack was happy to get out and explore the neighborhood. His mission was to infiltrate Centauri security systems and provide cover for Katja as she conducted her operations. The better he understood how Centauri society worked and thought, the easier his job would be. Plus, he thought as he looked out the window at the green, spacious road and walkways below, there were worse places to be.

26

"People on Earth don't know what cold is."

Breeze gauged the appreciative chuckle which rippled through the crowd. All eyes were on her, and indeed there was nowhere to hide in the cozy, circular auditorium. The mood was positive, but subdued in that stern, practical way of Triton. She'd never truly appreciated how much her late husband had been a product of his environment, but these last few weeks of campaigning on Terra's most isolated world had been revealing.

The people of Triton were hardy folk, proud of their isolation and their continued survival in one of the most hostile environments known to humans. Why they bothered to live out here at all remained a mystery to her, but she accepted their rugged sense of community—and, she was pleased to see, the people of Triton seemed to be accepting her.

"Cold does many things," she continued, stiffening her features as she began to pace around the central stage. "It hardens. It secures, and sometimes, it crystalizes. In the same way, the cold-blooded act of the rebel terrorists has brought out the best in Triton. By stealing the life of one of our own, they have only hardened our resolve. They have secured our commitment, and they have crystalized our knowledge of what needs to be done. Terra needs to step up and put an end to this war, once and for all."

Steady applause broke out and washed over her. No cheers,

no hoots, but a steady, determined show of support. Such was the Tritonian way. She nodded grimly.

"There are some voices in Parliament, such as Mr. Sheridan"— she practically spat his name—"who argue for a lessening of violence against the rebels. For a return to a more 'civilized' kind of warfare. But there is nothing civilized about what the rebels do. They sneak in the shadows. They kill civilians. They murder our loved ones, and the time for debate in Parliament is over!" More applause interrupted her, but she raised her voice and bellowed over the swell.

"This is not the time for debate—this is the time for action! As your representative in Parliament, I will throw my full support behind a quick and decisive end to this war. Terra must be protected, and these criminal terrorists must be brought to justice." She paused, summoning tears to her eyes. "They must pay for what they have done."

The ovation was tremendous and, slowly, members of the audience began to rise to their feet. Breeze let the moment ride, pausing in stillness in front of the applause before delicately wiping her eyes. Then she straightened again.

"As a veteran, I understand what war is. As a veteran who fought the enemy in Sirius, Centauria, and here in Terra, I know the horror of war, and it is with a heavy heart that I choose this path. But I know our enemy, and only through overwhelming force will the enemy be defeated. Security and freedom will be returned to the innocent people of Terra. Elect me as your representative, and I will follow this path with cold resolve."

Another surge of appreciation rose from the crowd, and Breeze finally allowed a grateful smile to split her features. She made eye contact with the local councillor in the first row, and as planned he promptly stepped onto the stage and took both her hands in his, beaming in admiration.

"Wonderful words, Mrs. Shah," he said quietly.

"Thank you," she replied, knowing that the audience couldn't hear, but could see the exchange. "I'd love to stay longer, but I have another engagement to attend."

He nodded, and then motioned for the security team to clear a path out of the auditorium.

"Mrs. Charity Shah!" he bellowed to the crowd. More applause.

Guided by his hand, Breeze stepped down from the stage and began her slow walk out of the auditorium. She made eye contact with as many of the clapping people as she could, and noted in those gazes a quiet respect and—more and more—acceptance. Very few actually reached out to her, but she grasped their hands of those who did and quickly thanked them. Such an open show of admiration was a risk among the Tritonians, and she wanted to reward each person who dared to make their feelings visible.

Her car waited outside, door held open for her to slip into the back seat. Her assistant Susie was close behind her, and her two senior campaign advisors were already seated facing her. The car door shut and silence descended.

Her staff knew not to break the silence as the car pulled away from the civic hall and headed for one of the main access tunnels. Despite all her years being the center of attention, Breeze was still getting used to the intensity of the political spotlight, and every speech drained her emotional reserves. Not that she'd ever show weakness in front of the staff, but she'd made it clear that she needed a couple of minutes of silence each time.

The low, utilitarian buildings of the domed city whisked by outside, and as always she marvelled at how the "sky" began to close in as the car approached a tunnel. The dome finally tapered down to meet the ground, and in a flash the warm light of human space vanished behind them, replaced by the dim, starkly beautiful landscape of Triton.

Through the clear tunnel wall Breeze looked out across the silvery plain, broken by jagged pillars of methane ice. High above in the starry sky, Neptune was a blue crescent, impossibly large to her Earthling eyes, and toward the horizon she could see one star outshining all the others. It would be good when this campaign was over, and she could head back a few billion kilometers into Sol's welcoming warmth.

The team kept busy checking their devices, and she knew that they were assessing the social impact of her speech. Her entire staff was already a well-oiled political machine, having been Vijay's staff for years. It was several minutes before they reached the next dome, and when she felt settled she offered her gaze to the advisors who faced her.

"How did that go?"

"More than two hundred clips of your speech have already been shared by audience members," one offered.

"The local news feed has already broadcast your finale," the other said.

"I'm getting a lot of positive feedback on the social nets," Susie reported.

The tide was turning, she decided. It had been a delicate thing, positioning herself both as the sympathetic widow of a beloved politician, and as a strong, capable candidate in her own right. On sensationalist Earth she would have sailed the emotional tack more aggressively, and she would have dressed more like a movie star. Here on grim Triton everything had to be understated and backed by pragmatism.

She primarily wore black, with occasional hints of gray, and whenever she spoke of Vijay it was to praise and honor him. Tears had been kept to an absolute minimum, and it was with a steely resolve that she had built her platform around a stronger military position. That had played nicely to her own Astral Force experience, and it had allowed the idea of vengeance to be implied with ever being stated. The people of Triton had been shaken by the assassination, but open talk of violent retribution would have been unacceptable.

All the other candidates had steered clear of such talk almost entirely, fearing a backlash, but Breeze had stepped into that space with ease, and woven her tapestry of fear, negativity, and revenge, delivered with a beautiful smile and sympathetic story. It was working, too. With four days to go, she was finally edging into the lead.

Criticism over her lack of political experience had dominated the early weeks, but it was being pushed out by the image of a hardened veteran with a love for her husband's homeworld. She hadn't even been certain she would receive support from Vijay's own party—the endorsement from Minister of Defense Taal had been lukewarm at best—but even he seemed to recognize the momentum she'd built, and lately his support had been far more enthusiastic. A political survivor, he wanted to be on the winning team, and that team now appeared to be Breeze's.

Perception was everything, and the winner was usually the one who understood best what the public *wanted* to perceive.

"Any thoughts on fresh content for the final push?"

"Admiral Eric Chandler was in the news again," Susie offered. "Very positive interview, and he emphasized the need for a stronger military solution—one that would be taken to the colonies directly. We might play up your personal connection to him."

"Yes," she nodded. "He'll never give an open endorsement, but I might be able to convince him to make a few extra remarks to Triton media." She glanced at the man who sat across from her. "Get in contact with him."

"I think we still might pick up momentum by bashing Sheridan, too. His position on reducing the conflict is emerging as his party's main platform, and his personal presence these past few days has attracted a lot of attention. Triton isn't really buying the argument, though."

"Very good," Breeze said. "See if you can get me in to speak with a widows and widowers group, or something like that. If we're going to push the idea of violence against the colonies I need to have a human face attached to the suffering here in Terra—and particularly on Triton."

"Yes, ma'am."

"And make sure to get some more footage out there from the assassination, where I was doing CPR on my husband while Sheridan was hiding behind a wall of guards."

"Right away."

Breeze sipped at the hot tea with sweet satisfaction. All around her the staffers were still congratulating each other with hugs and handshakes, but she appreciated their universal respect for her personal space.

Sitting alone on the couch, she faced the main news monitor where the announcement of her victory had just been declared. The Terran Parliament would continue to be represented by a Shah. Or at least, she smiled to herself, a wolf in Shah's clothing.

Susie crouched down in front of her, holding out a headpiece. "Ma'am, it's Christopher Sheridan on the line."

Setting down her tea, she fastened the headpiece to her ear.

"Mr. Sheridan."

His voice was calm and clear on the line, blocking out the celebratory hubbub around her.

"Congratulations on your victory, Mrs. Shah," he said. "I'm sure that Vijay would have been proud."

"Thank you. You and your local rep ran an admirable campaign, but it seems you still have more to learn about the Triton mentality."

"It would appear so. No doubt we'll have many more opportunities to debate once you reach Parliament."

"I look forward to it."

"As do I," he replied. "Enjoy your evening, Mrs. Shah. Your real work is about to begin."

She disconnected and handed the earpiece back. She couldn't tell if Sheridan's final words were meant as an encouragement, a warning, or a threat. Not that it really mattered, she reminded herself. She was part of the ruling government coalition, and Sheridan was just the drum-beater on the outside. She'd seen how Vijay and his colleagues had skillfully deflected any criticisms of their policies, and while making verbal concessions to the Opposition's arguments, they'd in fact rarely made any actual changes to their decisions.

It was all a big game, and now she was a player.

The cold seeped into her from every corner of this iceball world, and the sooner she was back on Earth the better. Breeze drained the last of her tea, enjoying the warmth that slid down her throat.

27

Katja opened her eyes, bracing for a visual chaos which matched the Cloud assault in her mind. Jack was seated across from her at the café table, watching her with maddeningly sympathetic eyes. All around them, the bustle of the busy shopping concourse throbbed with visual advertising messages, audible speech chatter, and the incessant interaction of average Centauri citizens in person and in the Cloud.

She'd thought the Terran Cloud had been busy, but in reality it was still in proto form, comprised of blind electronic messages from an ignorant populace. Here on Abeona, every man, woman, and child could access the Cloud consciously as part of their daily routine. The result was a thunderstorm of noise that made her head hurt. Yet Jack just sat there, looking completely at ease—and even a little sorry for her.

"How can you stand this?" she muttered.

He shrugged, glancing here and there at their surroundings. The café spilled out into the covered concourse, and sunshine streamed in through the glass ceiling high above. Trees formed a line down the middle of the mall, around which hundreds of shoppers padded by quietly on the treated softstone.

"It's neat," he said. "They're so open in their chatter and yet at the same time so sophisticated with their networks. I can really keep my finger on the pulse here."

Most of the tables around them were occupied by students

from the local university, and Jack very much blended in with his boyish looks and casual attire. Katja wasn't fooled by his appearance, though. This kid had come a long way since his days as a pilot. He was smart, insightful and, in his own way, tough as nails. If he could just lose his moralizing, she might actually like him again.

Or, to be more accurate, if he'd just stop reminding her about morality, she'd have an easier time liking herself. His presence was distracting in a most unwelcome way, and she hardened herself against the intrusion. Today was their first major excursion, and she needed them both to be focused.

On the table between them were a large coffee and a disposable news reader, but they were just props.

"Are you sure you'll be able to focus on the mission?"

"Definitely," he said, "and in a crowded place like this no one will ever notice my activity. Even if Centauri security detects what I'm doing, they won't be able to pinpoint me among all this." He gestured vaguely at the hubbub around them.

"Okay," she said, rising to her feet. "Just don't start chatting with the college girls and forget about me."

"Never, dear."

<Can you hear me through the noise?>

<Yep.> He nodded, then gave her a playful smile. <No kiss, to warn off the college girls?>

<In your dreams, flyboy.>

She weaved her way through the tables and out onto the concourse. The noise from the Cloud actually started to give her a headache, and she projected barriers in her mind to fend off the bombardment. Heading for the nearest exit, she gratefully breathed in a deep lungful of fresh air as the shopping mall faded behind her. It was only a short walk back to their apartment, and within minutes she was safely secured in the car. A quick check confirmed that all her gear was still in the rear cargo space. She programmed her destination into the vehicle and let it drive itself, freeing her to focus.

The wide streets of Starfall drifted past, fading eventually to the countryside. Out here the Cloud was much more manageable. Katja dropped the barriers and began examining the live data that was leaking out from her target—a Navy munitions depot tucked discreetly in one of the vast forests stretching away from the city. All security systems appeared to be operating in normal mode, and she located the interrogation from the depot to an approaching convoy. It was an expected resupply shipment, arriving on schedule two days before the departure of a squadron of frigates currently in orbit.

Her hope was that the personnel at the depot would be occupied with the convoy, and not as attentive to other areas of the compound.

Katja opened her eyes as the car pulled to a stop in the artificial clearing of a local hiking hub. She surveyed the smooth grass of the parking lot, noting only three other vehicles nearby. One of them was open and the occupants were busy unloading camping gear. No one even gave a glance in her direction. Shutting down, she leaned forward in her seat, staring at the dark dashboard and focusing her mind on the vehicle's computer brain.

It was still active, although most systems were shutting off in the wake of the power-down. As practiced back at the apartment, she zeroed in on the command channel, giving the computer a series of sharp orders to keep it active for another few seconds. As it processed her signals, she took hold of the locator beacon and severed its connection. Then she commanded the beacon to lock onto its current location, and remain static.

A moment later, the computer shut down completely.

Leaning back in her seat, she looked around the small clearing again. The group had gathered their gear and were heading out along one of the trails. She reached out with all her senses and confirmed that there was no one else around, then started her car again and drove slowly back to the road.

<I'm underway again,> she signaled.

<Roger,> Jack replied. <Traffic sensors still report you as stationary in the campsite parking lot.>

<Good—how does the depot look?>

<The convoy is just entering—no unusual activity.>

How Jack was able to tap into the Centauri Cloud so easily remained a mystery to her, but there was no doubt that Korolev had chosen well for this mission. Mallory might still be a horny, happy-go-lucky kid with far too much forgiveness in his soul, but he'd proven his abilities as they tested the Centauri security systems.

No, she chastised herself, she was being unfair. War *had* changed him, made him grow up fast. His smiles still came easily, and humor laced most of his words, but there was a deep sadness in his eyes. It was easy to remember the young punk she'd met nearly two years ago, who'd drooled after Breeze and then after Katja herself. That boy was gone, she knew.

And although it was hard to admit, he was already better in the Cloud than she was. She'd always be able to kick his ass physically—the thought brought a sudden smile—but it was good to know that he was there, backing her up.

Driving the car on manual another few kilometers down the road, she finally turned off to follow a narrow path through the trees, just far enough to obscure the car from the road. If questioned, she was a solo hiker out exploring some new trails, and *oh my—is there really a military installation so close by?* She'd been practicing her cute face on Jack for the past few days, and his reactions told her she was definitely learning how to charm.

Katja stepped out of the vehicle, slipped on her backpack, and hefted the "fishing rod case" in her arms. A small hatch on the underside opened to give her access to the trigger of her assault rifle. A pair of pistols and a cluster of grenades were also inside the case, weighing it down, but at least she was armed and ready for an ambush.

The trail made for easy progress into the forest. After a few hundred steps she paused, reaching into the Cloud. Confirming her position, she stepped off the trail and into the underbrush, moving slowly over the uneven ground, trying to keep the sounds of her passage indistinguishable from the gentle rustle of the wind through the leaves. The odd chirp or hiss reminded her of the small, indigenous animals scurrying underfoot, but she knew them to be harmless. Through the trees ahead, she could see the sunlight beaming down on open ground.

At the edge of the trees, she crouched down and unlatched the fishing case, senses scanning the long line of military fencing. She donned her pistol belt, fastened each holster to her hips, then hooked the four grenades over the base of her back. Drawing out the assault rifle, she checked ammunition and then slipped the harness over her shoulders, snapping the rifle into place against her chest.

She couldn't remember the last time she'd been so heavily armed, and it felt good. The time for disguises was over.

<In position at the treeline,> she said, flashing her exact coordinates to Jack.

<Roger. The convoy is starting to load up, so a lot of the guards have been pulled into close support around the trucks.>

<I don't see any observation towers from here.>

<No, you're clear. Let me distract the roving patrol.>

Suddenly there was chatter between the depot's main building and a pair of anti-personnel robots hidden off to the left. She shivered as she thought of those silver war machines rolling across the ground on their twin tracks, weapons pods tracking any movement. It had been a long time, but some memories didn't fade.

<Roving patrol moving to the far side of the compound,> Jack reported. <I gave them a minor alert against the fence.>

<Am I clear?>

<Yes.>

Katja rose to her feet and jogged low across the open grass. Her heavy backpack jostled with the movement and the grenades slapped against her back.

<Approaching fence.>

<Sensors disabled,> he replied, <clear to insert.>

Slowing to a trot as the fence loomed before her, Katja activated the anti-grav pockets on her boots. She pushed off the ground and sailed into the air, clearing the top of the fence by an entire body length and still rising. Cursing, she deactivated the AG and let herself start to fall, then activated again to stop her downward acceleration. She thumped down against the ground, the micro anti-grav field shielding her from the weight of her gear, but not the momentum.

That caused her to topple forward, coughing in the dust as she slid on the hard dirt. Shutting off the AG she hauled herself up and dashed for the nearest grassy mound. The depot was dotted with such mounds, grass and dirt providing additional protection against the ammunition stored in the bunkers buried beneath.

Leaning against the soft vegetation, she took a moment to catch her breath. Here at the edge of the compound she could neither see nor hear the convoy loading up, but routine chatter in the Cloud indicated its bearing.

<I'm in the compound.>

<Okay, your target is the mound directly south of you.>

<Approaching now.>

With a quick scan of the field of hillocks around her, she ran across the open ground and crouched down against the door of her target. She examined the security systems.

<Target storage still locked.>

<Stand by.>

The display before her shifted, and she heard a series of heavy clicks behind the reinforced door. It hissed open a crack. She pushed it aside enough to slip in, then slammed it shut.

<I'm in the storage bunker.>

The locks on the door clicked shut again and she was surrounded by darkness and silence. Activating infra-red she scanned the black cavern. Most of the material was almost as cold as the air, but through the vague shapes she detected the power units of the micro-torpedoes stored on their racks. Unfastening her rifle from its harness clip, she brought it up to her eyeline and shuffled forward, scanning left to right. Pausing, she switched to quantum-flux and scanned again. The storage racks nearest to her revealed their forms in ghostly clarity, but the rest of the chamber faded from view.

She did a quick count of the torpedoes, then examined the nearest one resting in its bracket. It was nearly as long as her, and with one hand she could grab the entirety of its slender nose. The body of the weapon barely widened down its length, until the bulges of its engines at the end. She absently ran her fingers along its smooth, hard surface as her mind interrogated its electronic innards.

<This looks like what we came for,> she said after a few moments of study.

<Agreed.>

Through the glow of quantum-flux she examined the bracket and the locks around the weapon.

<Can you get it unlocked?> she asked.

<No,> Jack said after a pause. <I can't access the individual locks—I think they're local.>

<Stand by.>

Katja examined the lock again, reaching into its protocols. She uncovered the trigger to release the lock and examined the signal it was programmed to receive. After a moment she replicated that signal and fired it in.

The clamps snapped open. The torpedo was free.

Slipping off her pack she reached in and retrieved a simple, civilian hover dolly. She switched it on and placed it under the torpedo, feeling the gravity-damping field take hold. The dolly indicated a lock, and she gingerly pushed upward, watching as the entire unit rose out of the bracket to hover in the darkness. With effort she pulled it free of the rack. The dolly might have absorbed gravity's pull on the object, but it still had a lot of inertia and resisted her efforts to move it. Sweat was dripping into her eyes by the time she'd maneuvered the torpedo over to the door.

<Prize in hand—ready to depart the bunker.>

<Wait—there's something activating.>

Katja froze. Around her she could sense the electronic hum of the storage equipment and environmental controls. And... there! A new energy signal on the far side of the dark room. She snapped her rifle free of its harness again.

Amid the gentle rush of air, she barely heard a skittering of metal taps against the floor. Something moved at the edge of her quantum-flux vision. It was low and fast, almost slithering between storage shelves.

<Visual,> she said. <Some kind of robot, I think.>

Data flooded her brain as Jack transmitted the latest info on the recent addition to the Centauri war machine arsenal. It was nicknamed the "milly," and it was bad news.

She fired once. The blast erupted in front of her, sending her reeling backward as the shock wave of her explosive round impacted military armor. The milly charged forward, rearing up in front of her to reveal its underside. She dove behind her captured torpedo as darts pinged off the weapon's hull. Returning fire beneath the hover dolly, she flinched as the dazzling glare of her rounds struck the robot. But as before, they didn't penetrate its armor enough to do any real damage. She reached back to grab a grenade from her belt. It would be a bad idea in such a small space, but dying appealed less.

The milly suddenly stiffened, the chittering of its legs falling silent. The reared body sagged, then lowered to the floor and remained still.

<I hacked into it,> Jack said. <Forced it to restart all systems.>

<How much time do I have?>

<About a minute.>

She jumped up and readied herself by the torpedo again.

<Then get this door open.>

<Roger, stand by.>

The locks released again and a sliver of sunlight blinded her as the door hissed open. Deactivating quantum-flux, she blinked away the tears and forced her eyes up toward the light. It seemed an eternity before she peeked out through the narrow opening at the sun-drenched compound beyond.

<Ready to move for the fence.>

<I've given the patrol another false reading on the far side. They're investigating, but I'm detecting a general increase in overall alert status—do you want to hold position?>

<No,> she said immediately. <The longer I'm here the more likely I'm detected—is my escape route clear now?>

<Yes.>

She pushed open the heavy door and eased the torpedo out into the fresh air. Slamming the door shut she wasted no time turning her cargo to skirt the grassy mound and point at the fence.

<I've resealed the storage,> Jack reported, <but it was noticed. There's new chatter on the security net.>

Katja ignored her own Cloud inputs and leaned into her steady push of the torpedo toward the fence. It gained speed, sailing along at waist height over the hard dirt, until she had to jog to keep up.

<Approaching fence,> she sent him her position again.

<Sensors down.>

Running under the torpedo she wrapped her arm around its body and activated her anti-grav pockets. With just a tap of her toes she felt herself rise slowly into the air, torpedo and dolly ascending with her. The fence loomed. She curled up her legs and whisked over the top, deactivated the anti-grav long enough to feel her own weight start to pull down the weightless torpedo, then used momentum to touch down in the grass and, with barely a stumble, start pushing her prize at a run for the safety of the trees.

Guiding the weapon at speed over uneven ground tasked her every sense, and she couldn't focus enough to send Jack a message. He'd be panicking within moments, though, and she didn't want him to do anything overt to distract the Centauri guards. So she activated her entanglement test signal. A second later she felt the warble in her chest as he responded. Now he knew she was still alive.

Gasping for breath she crashed the torpedo through the underbrush and dug her heels into the soft, loamy dirt to slow her cargo's rush into the forest. Finally coming to rest, she looked back at the broken branches and twin heel-troughs. Leaving the torpedo on its dolly, she quickly smoothed over the troughs and snapped off the few small branches that hung limply. While she couldn't remove all evidence of the passage, she could at least erase the most obvious signs.

A quick scan back toward the ammo depot revealed no immediate threats, but the increased radio traffic was obvious. Hopefully, the security stayed focused on the convoy and hunkered down in defensive positions. If she could complete the mission with zero casualties, she knew it would make Jack happy.

It bothered her that she wanted that.

With a few final heavy breaths, Katja took control of the dolly with one hand and gripped her assault rifle with the other. Time for a slow withdrawal.

28

As captain, Thomas didn't often find himself in the after end of the ship. *Moore* maintained her low-profile reconnaissance of the Centauri system, and most of his waking time was spent on the bridge.

He'd always imagined that he'd be a more personal captain—strolling the flats and getting to know his crew members in situ—but as always, the war seemed to waylay the best-laid plans. He met quite a few surprised glances as he moved aft to the hangar, but at least he was able to greet some of the crew by name.

Thomas floated discreetly to the side of the hangar as the starboard airlock opened to reveal the dark, angular shape of the Special Forces insertion craft. Slung beneath it was the smallest torpedo he'd ever laid eyes on. The first objective of the mission was complete. A mix of flight and ASW technicians clustered around, eager to examine the weapon which had so crippled *Admiral Bowen*.

Though curious as well, he was far more interested in the pair of operatives who emerged from the aft door of their craft. Clearly not re-accustomed to the zero-g, they fumbled to hand their spacesuits off to the waiting ground crew.

"Welcome back, operatives," he said, keeping his tone mild but fighting down the urge to embrace them both in a big hug. Jack and Katja looked healthy and relatively at ease. She gave him a curt nod, but Jack smiled and reached out his free hand.

"Permission to come aboard, Captain?"

"Granted," he replied, shaking the hand. "Good work on your capture."

Jack glanced over to the torpedo, and at the technicians extracting it from the insertion craft.

"I'm sure we'll learn a lot from this little bitch."

Nodding, Thomas motioned for them to follow him toward the forward door.

"How many did they have in inventory?"

Jack glanced at Katja. She considered for a moment.

"I saw twenty-four. Enough to cripple an entire expeditionary force—and that was just the storage bunker I was in. Who knows how many more they have."

"So it's in mass production," he surmised as they moved into the main passageway that led forward. "It wasn't just a prototype."

"No."

The ship was bustling as it approached watch turnover, and Thomas made to weave his way through the crowd. Then he noticed very quickly that no weaving was required—the throng seemed to part before him. He made sure to acknowledge every crew member who tucked against the bulkhead to let him pass, sensing that their actions were made out of respect, not fear. Maybe he didn't get out to wander the ship as much as he'd like, but it seemed his crew still felt that he knew them.

The sitting area of his cabin was immaculate, as always, and before he could even make the request his steward appeared with three bulbs of coffee and a clear ball filled with finger foods. Pulling himself down to the couch, Thomas hooked in and invited his guests to do the same. Jack joined him in the illusion of sitting, but Katja floated free.

"I need to get used to zero-g again," she said. "If I try to tell my body that I'm actually sitting when it can't feel the pull, we're likely to be dodging balls of puke in here."

A sharp chuckle burst from Thomas's lips, even more so as he saw his steward glance back subtly from the servery door.

"Master Rating Stinson," he called out. "Would you please excuse us for an hour or so?"

The steward nodded politely and exited into the passageway.

"Don't worry about the gravity," Thomas said, glancing at his watch. "We're just about to switch it back on for an hour or so—critical maintenance needs to be done on a few mechanical systems which don't open well in zero-g."

As if on cue, the bridge announced the imminent return of AG. After a fifteen-second delay, the gentle tug of the ship's graviton generator began to take hold. It increased steadily toward Earth-normal. Thomas steadied the refreshments as they slowly lowered to the table. Katja lowered with them, and found her footing on the deck. The relief showed on her face.

"Thank you," she said.

Thomas smiled and offered the finger foods to the operatives. Neither hesitated, and Thomas figured it had been a long flight from Abeona.

"It's good to see you both," he said. "How was the mission?"

"Awesome," Jack replied immediately. "The Centauri Cloud is phenomenal, and designed for easy access, so I was able to move through it along multiple lines simultaneously." Thomas had no idea what a "Centauri Cloud" was, but he gathered that it was something of importance to how the operatives did their job.

"The society doesn't seem geared for war," Katja added, looking as if she wanted to change the subject. "Most people are just living their normal lives."

"We've monitored their news channels from here," Thomas said. "There's at least one story per day on the subject of the war, but it's usually buried beneath domestic concerns."

"It's as if the war doesn't even matter to them," Katja said, frowning.

"Actually," Jack weighed in, "I think it's more nuanced than that. The commentary I see on the war is quite balanced—it actually seems like their reporters do their research, and try to give the full picture. The responses from the public are remarkable, too—plenty of strong opinions, but nothing extreme. This is an educated population."

Silence fell in the cabin for a moment. Thomas noted Jack's expression of thoughtful respect, and noted also Katja's narrowing eyes.

"All the more reason," she said firmly, "to take them seriously as the enemy."

"Yes," Jack agreed, "most definitely."

Thomas sipped at the coffee. He was becoming addicted to the stuff again, but at least it tasted better than straight amphetamines.

"Do you two have any combat cocktails in your gear?" he asked suddenly. All Astral Corps troopers were injected with a combination of drugs prior to battle—Thomas well remembered the euphoria from his days as a platoon leader. Katja would be familiar with them, he knew, and he was pretty sure even Jack had been juiced up on "valour valium" after his injuries in Sirius.

"No," Katja said with a puzzled frown. "Why?"

"I can issue you some from my own strike team's store—you might need them for the next mission."

"Oh crap," Jack said, sighing. "I told them I wasn't a combat operative. I only have my yellow belt of humility."

"What?" Thomas laughed, shaking his head.

"Operatives generally don't use combat cocktails," Katja said. "We can dull certain senses, and need to be able to react instantly on multiple levels."

"Well, they're yours if you want them."

"More importantly," Jack said, "why would we need them? Tell us about the new mission, sir."

Thomas met Jack's apprehensive gaze, then shifted over to Katja as she stood nearby and stared at him expectantly. He'd received the orders from Chandler that morning via a needle-beam encoded transmission, and he was still turning them over in his head. Looking again at his companions, he wondered how much he should really let them know.

"There is going to be a Terran attack on Abeona," he said finally, "and your mission is to disrupt Centauri defensive networks from within."

"For how long?" Katja asked. "The last time we attacked this planet, the landing alone took nearly a day. If we're landing Army troops, then this could go on for months."

"We're not landing troops," he replied. "The attack will occur from orbit, and we only need a disruption for a few hours. Ideally you'll infiltrate their networks beforehand, and set up the disruptors to activate automatically based on the schedule I'm going to give you." He paused, then added, "You need to be off the planet when the attack occurs. Part of your mission is to send word to any other Terran assets posted on Abeona, instructing them to evacuate, as well."

Katja nodded thoughtfully.

Jack stared at him with raised eyebrows.

"Why, exactly," he asked, "do we all have to be off the planet? What is this attack?"

Thomas hesitated. They wouldn't need the details of the attack in order to successfully conduct their mission. Yet these weren't just two anonymous operatives—this was Jack Mallory and Katja Emmes. And the knowledge he now possessed wasn't something he could just bury away. He needed to hear their opinions.

"You remember that little science experiment we three did, the last time we were in Centauria?"

Jack and Katja exchanged glances.

"You mean the Dark Bomb?" Jack asked quietly.

"Yeah." Thomas felt the next words try to die in his throat, but he forced them up. "Terra is going to launch a Dark Bomb at Abeona."

"Where?" Katja frowned. "Their orbital stations haven't been rebuilt. Is there a central fleet docking facility we're taking out?"

Jack was speechless, staring with his mouth open. He got it, Thomas knew.

"The bomb isn't targeting anything in orbit," Thomas explained. "It's targeting Abeona."

"Yeah," Katja snapped, "but where?"

"The entire planet." He met her gaze and held it as the realization finally dawned in her eyes. "Terra is going to detonate a Dark Bomb in Abeona's core."

Her face went pale, eyes widening, and a conflict of emotion wiped across her features, but as with Jack, no words emerged.

"In the name of God," Jack whispered, "why?"

"To send a message. To tell the colonies that we have the power. To end the war."

"What's going to happen to Abeona?"

"No one knows for sure," Thomas sighed, rolling his eyes. "At a minimum the shock from the core will set off quakes all over the surface, with enough force to essentially liquefy the crust. At the maximum, the singularization of the planet. It all depends on the gravity generated by the implosion."

A harsh laugh erupted from Jack. He shook his head.

"I wonder if somebody's getting their PhD signed off, if they estimate the damage accurately enough." His expression hardened. "Or do those fuckers in the research squadron just have a pool going?"

Thomas dropped his gaze. He knew he was supposed to say something inspirational or authoritative at this point, but words eluded him. Katja moved to sit on the couch next to him. She was still pale, but her voice was steady.

"Do you have a download for us, sir?"

"Yes," he replied, reaching for the data stick. "It's all here."

"Wait a second," Jack said. "Do I have a say here?"

"No," she said firmly. "We don't make the missions—we carry them out."

"Yeah, but have you noticed what this mission is?"

Thomas listened for her response, but the silence stretched on. He glanced up, and saw that they were staring intently at each other, but not speaking. Was this some kind of operative battle of wills?

Then, with a sigh of disgust, Jack launched to his feet.

"Please excuse me, sir. I need a few minutes. Or hours."

"Jack, stay."

"What the fuck?" he snapped. "What. The. *Fuck*. Since when is it okay to blow up an entire world? Do you know how many people live on Abeona?"

Thomas closed his eyes wearily, not wanting to think about it.

"About seven hundred million," Jack said. "Seven hundred million men, women, and children who are down there right now, just living their lives."

"They are the enemy, Jack," Katja said.

"No they aren't! The rebel military forces are the enemy, and maybe the colonial governments. Tell me that we're bombing the Centauri Senate, and I'm right there with you—but the whole fucking planet? Second Earth? Is that really what we want to destroy?"

"It's not our decision."

Jack pressed his fists against his face, obviously biting down more angry words.

"I'm not sure," he said finally, "that I can do this."

"Then," Katja said slowly, almost as if she was repeating herself, "I will kill you." At that point Thomas knew the conversation had to stop. He kept his face neutral as he looked up.

"Operative Mallory, you have until eighteen hundred to assimilate the download," he said. "We'll reconvene here at that time for a final brief."

"Yes, sir." Jack spun and left the cabin.

Thomas turned to Katja. Her delicate features hadn't changed in a year, and she moved with the same quick assurance as always, but her big, dark eyes regarded him with a luminous strength he hadn't seen in her before.

"Katja..."

She met his gaze, a sad smile playing at her lips.

"Yes, sir?"

"How did we get to this?"

"By the paths we've chosen, Commander."

Her face revealed little, but he could sense that she was being sincere. The mental walls he'd seen her throw up so many times were absent. He reached out and took her hand in his. She didn't resist.

"We've each walked our paths," he agreed, "and we can't go back, but we still need to look ahead at where we're going, and make sure it's the right place."

"My path is clear," she replied. "I'm a servant of the State, and I always will be."

"As am I, but with this level of destructive power, I also have to be a servant to humanity. This mission..."

"Stop," she said, squeezing his hand. "Don't even let yourself think it. You have to be strong to guide your crew through this. They have to be able to look at you and see absolute confidence. You need to be strong for them... just like I have to be for Jack."

"I know you're strong—stronger than I've ever been," he responded. "You have nothing left to prove, to anyone. But—"

"But nothing." Her features hardened and he saw the barriers rising. Her grip tightened further. "We have our orders, and the State carries the burden."

"Do you really believe that?"

She stared at him in silence. Then, suddenly, she pulled herself against him, wrapping him in her arms. He felt her cheek press against his, a trickle of moisture caught against his skin.

"I have to," she whispered.

He held her close, reveling in the feel of her warm body against his, her breath against his ear. She hung onto him for a long time, crying quietly. When she finally pulled back to look at him, cheeks strained with tears, she actually managed a smile.

"I don't know what it is about you, Kane, but you always make me feel human."

"Are you not human anymore?"

"No," she said. "I'm a monster. I hid from that for a long time, but that damn pilot kid just reminds me too much of what life really should be."

"He's a damaged young man, Katja—and war did that to him."

"He may be damaged, but he's stronger for it."

"But is he better for it?"

"Just stop this." She shook her head and wiped angrily at her eyes as tears welled once again. But she still kept her arms around him, body leaning into his. "We are what we are, now. Nothing can change that."

She was so warm against him, so powerful and yet so fragile. He ached with her proximity, unable to hold back the flood of long-forgotten emotions.

"Well, at least we're here together."

"Yes."

"Katja, when the war's over…"

"Thomas," she interrupted him, running her fingers tenderly across his cheek. "Don't live in the past. You don't know who I am anymore—if you ever did. For people like me, the war will never be over." The strength was returning to her eyes, the moment of weakness, of doubt, banished. She was a front-line operative, and he could only guess at what she'd done in the name of the State.

"Only if you so choose."

"I made my choice a long time ago."

"We've all made choices. I made one too, a vow to my wife, and I'm going to honor it forever." He stared into her eyes, feeling his heart tear. "But that doesn't mean I don't love you."

She stared back at him. He waited for her defenses to rise even more, but instead she just offered a sad smile.

"This isn't the time, Thomas."

"It might be the only time we have. I've done enough shitty things in my life. I'm sorry, for everything."

She nodded, still stroking his cheek.

"I'm sorry, too. And even if you're still an asshole"—She smirked at him—"I love you too."

The hole in his heart filled in, just a bit. He was a cruiser commander in hostile space talking to a Special Forces operative on the eve of the most devastating attack in human history. He had no illusions about what the future promised, but he relished this one, single moment that was for just them.

For Thomas and Katja.

29

Breeze had always wondered what true power would feel like. She wasn't surprised to discover that it included comfortable chairs and delicious food. Lunch had just been cleared away by the silent servants and she watched as tea was poured for herself, then President De Chao Peterson, then Minister of Defense Wesley Taal.

Soft jazz played in the background of the private dining room, adding a touch of class but also obscuring any conversations. Not that there was anyone else in the ornate, wood-lined room, but one could never be too careful.

It was only her first week in Parliament, and Breeze was thrilled at the personal attention she was receiving from all sides. She'd been given a thunderous ovation by the assembled members of Parliament on her first day in the chamber, and the media made quite a spectacle of her assuming her late husband's seat. Some voices—undoubtedly fed by the Opposition—had offered criticism at her inclusion in the government despite her lack of political experience, but her military service had come out to save her. No one was allowed to criticize a veteran, especially these days.

As she sipped at her tea she realized with satisfaction that the years of bullshit she'd endured in that fanatical organization were finally paying off. She'd survived her time in uniform, and now that base of respectability was hers forever.

Even so, to be invited to a private lunch with the President was unprecedented for a new member. Either the shadow of her husband was long, or the government recognized her true potential. It didn't matter—she was determined to exploit this opportunity.

Much of the lunch discussion had been about the war, naturally enough. President Peterson had served as a junior officer in the Army decades ago, and Minister Taal had been a ship captain in the Astral Force. Breeze had kept her comments to a minimum while they discussed recent tactical reports from the fronts, but she'd listened carefully to the underlying tones.

Neither man was happy with the progress of the war.

"Charity," Peterson said, setting down his tea. He was an elderly man, but his stocky frame still moved with power. Faint scars were visible on his scalp through his close-cropped silver hair, and set in his rugged face deep-set eyes held her with absolute confidence. "I apologize that we've been nattering on over defense details about which you haven't been briefed. I'm afraid we've put you at a disadvantage."

"No apologies necessary, sir," she said. "Like many veterans, I maintain a keen interest in the success of our troops, and I've stayed as informed as I can." She offered an expression of concern. "Despite what the media is crowing, I gather that our resources are being stretched."

"Very astute of you," Taal commented. "The government's position is clear—we cannot back down on any front, else we risk encouraging the rebels to push harder. One tactical retreat by our forces can be exploited by rebel propaganda, blowing it up into a huge victory for their side."

"It's about perception," she said, nodding. "More than anything, we need to break the rebel will."

"Exactly," Taal agreed. "And to do so we've aspired to have State forces everywhere, at all times, so that the rebels get thumped whenever they so much as move. Unfortunately, this is taking a toll on troops and equipment, which we're struggling to keep up with."

"We need decisive action," Peterson concluded. "A single strike so powerful that it will shock and awe the rebels, and from that position of strength we can call for a cease fire and negotiate their terms of surrender."

Breeze had rarely seen colonists lose heart in the face of overwhelming Terran military force, but it seemed as if something new was in play. It had to be Chandler and Korolev's secret plan.

"I think that could be an excellent strategy," she said, "if it's done properly. But will it cost too many Terran lives?"

"That's the beauty of it," Peterson said. "If it costs *any* Terran lives, it will be a handful at most. And not only will it crush the rebel spirit—it will neutralize their main benefactor, and leave them headless."

"This sounds like an ideal plan, sir," she said. "How can I help?"

"Your last position in the military was as the head of a research project to develop a new weapon called the Dark Bomb."

"It was."

"I confess," Taal interjected, "that the technical aspects of this weapon are beyond my own expertise, and I'm cautious to place all my trust in my admirals for so important a mission. Given how familiar you are with the Dark Bomb, you would be the perfect person to take charge of this project and make certain it's handled effectively."

"I appreciate the minister's honesty in this," Peterson added, "and I'm very glad that we have such an obvious alternative. Charity, I'm offering you the post of Deputy Minister of Defense, with your first responsibility being the political oversight of this critical mission."

Deputy Minister? With an advisory seat in the President's cabinet, a full staff, and a genuine public profile? And all because of the stupid Dark Bomb. At that moment, Breeze saw her whole career come together, and she struggled to keep her smile to a modest line.

"I'm honored, sir," she said. "Thank you."

"We have a chance to end the war, with a victory for Terra," Peterson said. "I'm pleased to know that you're with us."

Taal told her when and where she'd be introduced to her team, and be briefed on the mission specifics, but most of the details flew past her. Her assistant would get her to where she needed to go, she knew, and this was just too sweet a moment not to savor.

As lunch ended and she said her goodbyes to the President and Minister, she did wonder idly what the Dark Bomb had to do with the mission. No doubt the briefing would fill her in, so she pushed it from her mind. For now she was due in Parliament.

It was probably the last time she'd be stuck up on the "back benches" of the circular Chamber of Parliament. As a junior member of the government she was just one in the sea of faces stretching back from the central floor of the Chamber.

The ministers all sat down in the first few rows, and the senior members of the other parties did likewise, in order to have easy access to the speaking floor. Most members of Parliament never got the chance to make a formal speech, and were restricted to hooting their support and cat-calling their opponents from above. No outside observers were allowed into this room, but every word and action was captured as part of the official record.

How much of that record was released to the people, Breeze knew, was decided mainly by a consensus of the party leaders, although occasionally one party would break ranks and leak damaging facts to the media. Such actions invariably yielded repercussions, though, and Breeze watched with interest the high-stakes game of cat-and-mouse played out between the parties.

Her party, the Progressives, was part of the coalition of five political groups that together controlled enough votes to effectively *be* the government. President Peterson was elected independently, and did not sit in the Chamber of Parliament, but his political alignment was very similar to that of the government, and Vijay had told her that relations between these two arms of the State were very good.

Across the chamber sat the representatives from the parties who were not part of the ruling coalition. The largest of these, the Federalists, was run by Christopher Sheridan and therefore held the honorary title of Official Opposition. Anyone among the three hundred members of Parliament was theoretically allowed to question the government, but in practice it was usually the party leaders, led by the leader of the Opposition. For someone who wasn't actually a part of the functioning government,

Sheridan had secured himself about as high-profile a position as possible. His protests against government policy were largely ineffective, however, since the ruling coalition held a majority of seats, and could out-vote any dissenters.

The coalition itself was where the real machinations occurred, as members of the five parties jockeyed among themselves for the plum positions. Minister of Defense Taal was also a Progressive, and Breeze's promotion most likely was an effort to consolidate his position. Whoever controlled the military, she knew, had a real advantage over any rivals—arguably as much as the Minister of Police and even the Minister of Internal Security.

The amount of power in this chamber sent a thrill through her, and she looked down the rows to try to guess where, as deputy minister, she would be seated for the next session.

The day's business began with a series of questions from Sheridan, who stepped out onto the central speaking floor and challenged the government on different topics of rule. The first was on the matter of a series of riots that had been tarnishing the otherwise productive mining camps in southern Mercury. After a scathing series of responses by the Minister of Police, Sheridan switched targets and addressed Minister Taal. Breeze leaned forward with new interest.

"Mr. Minister," Sheridan said with a dramatic sigh, "when is this government going to admit that its current military policy of over-extension across the colonies is costly, not only to the State's finances, but also to the lives of our troops?" The far side of the Chamber echoed with applause and desk thumps from the Opposition members.

Taal rose to his feet, straightened his suit and stepped out onto the floor.

"Mr. Sheridan," he said with a great show of weariness, "this government is well aware that the war against the rebels has been costly, but our actions have been entirely contained within pure necessity. If you don't like the extent of the battle front, I urge you to pose your complaint to the rebel leaders in all ten colonies."

Laughter and applause erupted from the government members.

"Mr. Minister, as my party has been saying for some time, there are more effective ways to defeat the rebels than meeting them face-to-face in battle, wherever they appear." Sheridan stood his ground. "You stretch our forces too thin, sir, and in so doing you unnecessarily endanger our military men and women."

"I assure you, sir, that as a veteran myself I am pained by the loss of every soldier, trooper or crewman. However, I understand perfectly the realities and sacrifices of war, and I know that our military men and women understand them, as well."

"I'm not questioning the reality of sacrifice, but rather the methods employed by this government to wage the war."

"Stop beating this dead horse!" one of the government backbenchers cried out.

"I would far rather," Sheridan declared over the growing hubbub, "beat this dead horse into a pulp than see a single unnecessary dead soldier." An appreciative roar washed over the Chamber from the opposition members. Sheridan basked in it for a long moment, then turned expectant eyes across the central floor to Taal.

"I await your answer, Mr. Minister."

Taal signaled for quiet, and the chamber slowly calmed.

"Security requirements forbid me from speaking openly about military strategies in this honorable venue, but I invite the leader of the Opposition to join me for a private discussion on this matter."

Applause broke out on all sides. Breeze joined in, nodding her appreciation. It was an excellent end to the drama—the government had conceded nothing, but the Opposition could claim to have been heard. Both sides could count the exchange as a victory.

Several other opposition party leaders had a chance to fire questions at a minister, and Breeze watched the show with an amused respect. Every politician here was a master orator, and the chorus of supportive members made for quite a spectacle. In the end, the people would feel as if their representatives were working hard to serve them, and that all opinions were welcome within Parliament.

When the show was over, of course, the government would go right back to doing whatever it wanted.

The question period ended, and it was announced that in twenty minutes a senior civil servant was being summoned before Parliament. This caused a rumble of interest, and Breeze noticed that her desk console lit up with a series of files that provided information relating to the summons. The recent famine in Scandinavia had been caused primarily by the mismanagement of food supplies. The civil servant being summoned, one Deputy Director Laura Robblee, had been responsible for the fiasco.

Vijay had sometimes told her about these "summons" to Parliament. They hadn't been a common event, but had become prevalent this past year. If something truly catastrophic had occurred, for which Parliament risked criticism from the people, a summons ensured that the individual responsible was brought to the Chamber to answer for their actions. Breeze couldn't help but notice the predatory excitement coming from the members around her.

Twenty minutes later, down on the central floor, a pair of armed guards emerged from a side entrance, escorting a middle-aged woman in a sensible pantsuit and leading her to a semicircular podium which had risen out of the floor. She was directed to stand at the podium, and one of the guards explained how the controls worked. Breeze assumed that the files displayed on her own desktop were the same as those Ms. Robblee would have access to.

The Minister of Health took the floor and addressed the entire chamber. He described the terrible tragedy that had befallen the citizens of Scandinavia, referencing hundreds who died from starvation in the frigid northern winter. Thousands more had fallen ill from malnutrition. He then took a moment to remind Parliament of the outstanding record of the Terran food distribution program, and how billions of people across the entire system were kept well-fed every day.

He highlighted a spreadsheet from the notes which showed regular food shipments to Scandinavia in the months leading up to the tragedy. Then finally, he showed the dramatic drop in food quantities that began just as the worst weather in a decade had slammed across northern Europe.

"As deputy director of food distribution for Europe," he

said, facing Robblee, "are you responsible for making certain the citizens of Scandinavia are supplied with enough food to maintain their health?"

"I am." Her voice was very quiet, but amplifiers ensured that her words were heard throughout the chamber.

"Then how did you let this tragedy occur?"

She cleared her throat, then sipped at the provided water.

"I did everything I could to avoid it, but the winter storm grounded our skycraft, and our land transports had to fight their way through impassable conditions."

"Yet surely winter storms are a common enough event in your area of responsibility, that you can plan in advance for them. Did you know that this storm was coming?"

"Yes, but the severity caught us by surprise."

"Weather can still surprise us," the minister replied, with a side nod to his colleague from Environment, "despite our best efforts." The Minister of Environment nodded politely amid muffled chuckles around him.

"But that doesn't excuse any lack of preparedness on our part," Health continued. "Deputy Director, what steps did you take to prepare for this storm?"

"We followed the standing orders of my department," she responded, then listed a series of steps that had been taken. Breeze had to admire Robblee. She was clearly frightened, but she kept her voice steady and answered the barrage of questions without hesitation. She knew her job, clearly, and wasn't just some sacrificial suit thrown out by her department.

The Minister of Health finished his examination, and the picture that had been painted was one of a competent civil division overwhelmed by circumstances. A tragedy had occurred, yes, but only in spite of the best efforts of the State. As a member of the Sol party, he then ceded the floor to one of his government colleagues.

Breeze watched as a representative from her own Progressives rose and began questioning Robblee. A summons was unusual in that each party was free to take its own stance on the matter— there was no requirement to vote as a coalition. As a result, eleven different members rose in turn to have at the deputy director. Questions increasingly became an interrogation, and Robblee began to visibly quail under the assault. Details from her history as a civil servant were dragged up, and at one point the leader of the fringe People's Party brought her nearly to tears.

Among the assembly, the members began to mutter, sometimes even jeering as Robblee struggled to find answers to the questions being hurled at her. Finally, the Minister of Health took the floor once again.

"Members of Parliament," he called out, "you have heard the evidence and have taken the measure of this servant of the State. It is now time to vote on how we will conclude this summons."

On her desk, Breeze saw the screen clear itself of all other files and present to her a list of choices. She was free to vote for execution, imprisonment, work service, warning or pardon. She considered. Robblee didn't seem to be an incompetent, and she clearly wasn't any sort of political threat. Breeze voted for work service.

Her vote was tallied with the rest of those in the Progressive party, and they would announce a unanimous decision based on the majority. It took less than a minute for all votes to be cast and then Minister Taal, as the senior Progressive, stood.

"The Progressive Party," he announced, "votes for execution."

Breeze was shocked.

The Minister of Health then rose to present his party's vote.

"The Sol Party votes for execution."

One after the other, representatives from the ruling coalition voted for execution. Sheridan's Federalists and one other opposition party voted for imprisonment, but the majority in Parliament was clear.

Deputy Director Laura Robblee was led away to be killed.

Amid the animated chatter around her as the session of Parliament closed, Breeze sat back in her chair and surveyed the room anew. This game she'd joined, she now realized, wasn't just for high stakes. It was for the *highest* stakes. All power in Terra was focused into this Chamber and these three hundred citizens—many of whom had been playing the game already for years, if not decades.

In order to succeed, she was going to need all her skills.

Smiling suddenly, she welcomed the new resolve that settled over her. Every other member was now either her potential ally—for as long as they were useful to her—or her enemy.

30

He'd chosen an open-air market this time, given that it was a pleasant day. The air was so clean here in Starfall, Jack took every opportunity to just be outside. As expected there was a busy café for him to settle at, large coffee and news reader on the square, wooden table before him. Folks his age surrounded him, some in groups chatting and others sitting in quiet solitude.

Beyond the café, the market bustled with weekend activity as the local population got out to enjoy what promised to be one of the last good days of autumn. Out on the street it had been cool enough to make him fasten his coat, but here in the market a gentle warmth seemed to emanate from everywhere. It was still appropriately cool, but the edge was gone.

Staring blankly down at his news reader, he reached into the Cloud along the several dozen lines of investigation he'd been pursuing. Military networks had been on much higher alert ever since their theft of the micro-torpedo, but so far it seemed to be mostly an increased vigilance in guarding sensitive locations. There had been a flurry of encrypted activity a few days earlier, centered here in Starfall, but neither he nor Katja had been able to detect a coherent pattern.

They'd made one attempt to contact a known Terran asset in the city, but there'd been no response. With the extra activity by Centauri intelligence, they considered it best to stay silent whenever possible.

The mission had actually been scheduled for yesterday, but Katja had postponed it to allow the Cloud to settle. Jack would have preferred to wait even longer, but they were on a tight overarching timeline, and further delays were unacceptable.

There was no unusual activity on either the military or police networks as he tracked Katja's car pulling into the parking lot beneath a government building. Called the Pierce Building after some civil servant of note, it housed the Centauri Department of Finance. The building itself was quiet, and except for the usual security personnel it gave the appearance of being unoccupied. Except for the very faint, highly encrypted pattern of signals they'd detected coming from the sub-basement.

<I'm on foot,> Katja reported. <No contacts here in the parking lot.>

Jack checked the view from the various security cameras. By taking control of the device watching the entry, he'd overwritten its live feed with a thirty-second clip devoid of activity while Katja drove in. Now he picked off the various viewers that were anywhere close to her and did the same thing, interrupting their real-time feed and replacing it with imagery from just a few minutes earlier.

<I've deactivated the sensors in HVAC trunking two,> he said.

<Roger,> she said, <entering now.>

Jack plugged into the sensors in the ventilation system, following Katja's careful progress through the ducts and carefully masking the quantum-flux sensors for ten meters around her. He couldn't actually *deactivate* the sensors—that would risk an alarm. Here again he had to replay previous, innocuous sensor readings which he'd recorded over the past half hour. It was the same game as with the cameras, just a lot harder to get right.

Katja paused, he noticed. Holding the sensors steady, he eased his perceptions back to better assess her position. She was at the first insertion point.

<Room below me is clear,> she said. <Ready to enter.>

<The grill isn't sensored,> he said. <You can lift it straight off.>

Moments later, she dropped out of the ventilation duct and drifted to the edge of the quantum-flux sensors. The room she entered showed no other security systems—nothing Jack could tap into directly to watch her progress—but just as she trusted him to keep her hidden, he had to trust her to get the job done.

<This definitely isn't financial stuff,> she commented, and images from the room flashed into his mind. Just the look of the consoles revealed their military design. Katja hacked into one of them and sent a summary of information back to him. The sub-basement of the Pierce Building was a major node in the planetary defense network.

A short time later she climbed back into the duct, and replaced the cover.

They repeated the drill three more times. He covered her movements as she skulked through the venting and planted pre-programmed devices intended to disrupt the Centauri network. After she left, he couldn't detect the disruptor pods—they were completely inert until remotely activated. Hopefully this would keep them hidden from Centauri agents until the time came.

The mission continued smoothly, and Jack kept an eye on the faint signals which periodically flashed from a series of rooms even further down in the sub-basement. He assumed they were military transmissions and he began capturing what he could. The encryption was very sophisticated, but the more he studied them, the more a pattern emerged.

There was also a standalone signal that reminded him of the alert system on the milly they'd encountered in the ammunition depot. Was there a milly somewhere in that building? It was exactly the sort of environment for which the mechanical beasts had been designed.

"Excuse me!"

His head snapped up, eyes blinking in the sunlight. A woman was standing in front of his table, hands on the chair across from him, staring down at him with a puzzled expression.

"What," he stammered, barely remembering to use an Abeonan accent. "What was that?"

"I asked, are you using this chair?" the woman said slowly.

"Oh, uh, no. It's all yours."

"Thanks." She offered a strange smile as she moved it over to her own table of friends. Feeling his heart thump in his chest, Jack released his grip on the pistol nestled inside his coat. He didn't even remember reaching for it. The efficiency of military training really frightened him sometimes.

<You good?> he asked into the Cloud.

<Yes—starting my way back to the car.>

Jack settled back into his task of covering Katja's movements. It took a large part of his concentration to mask discreetly the quantum-flux sensors, and now he kept his eyeline a bit higher and watched the woman and her friends. They didn't seem to be paying him any attention. The heat of the café was suddenly stifling, though, but he didn't dare remove his coat.

As soon as Katja exited the HVAC system, he collected his cold coffee and untouched news reader. It was easy enough to fool the parking lot cameras as she made her way back to the car, and Jack turned more of his attention to his own surroundings.

There was Cloud activity all around him, chirps and hearts and cat videos galore. It was all perfectly normal. The tables around him were full of merrymakers, and the market stalls were overflowing with local goods. He took a deep breath, trying to calm his heart.

<I'm in the car,> Katja said. <Clear of the building.>

<I'm leaving my position,> he said, rising to his feet.

<What's wrong?>

He eased his way between the seated patrons, keeping one hand close to the pistol in his coat. No one reacted other than to give him more room, but he had the inescapable sense that he was being watched.

<I don't know.>

<Give me visual.>

He transmitted his own sight into the Cloud, scanning slowly left to right as he made his way out to the market.

<Look back across the café,> she ordered.

He turned, standing still and making the motions of stuffing his news reader into his coat's inside pocket. His eyes drifted over the tables again, lingering on the empty chair he'd just vacated and again on the group of women who had taken his spare. One of the women—indeed, the one who'd asked for the chair—peered at him with large, dark eyes. She was probably forty, he guessed, with an angular face and a lean figure.

<Ops red!> Katja said. <Turn and walk quickly away. Do not look back. Do not slow down.>

He did as commanded, pushing into the crowd and retreating. <What's going on?>

<Centauri agent—get the fuck out of there. I'm en route at best possible speed.>

He kept his eyes up enough to avoid collisions, but his main focus was reaching backward, scanning for any sign of pursuit. Amid the maelstrom of signals, he noticed one device suddenly begin to move out of the café in his direction. He recognized it as a typical civilian device, but behind its signal he detected something else. Something very subtle.

Something searching. For him.

He pulled back, withdrawing all his links from the Cloud, and fought the urge to break into a run. Slipping past casual shoppers, he muttered apologies and quickened his pace. Then he scanned ahead for an escape path. There was nothing but the vast market sprawled out in front of him. The stands and tents were laid out in a rudimentary grid pattern on the flat, grassy field, so any of the side alleys would at least get him out of sight.

He darted to the left, stealing a glance over his shoulder as he did. The woman was two stalls back, eyes fixed on him. He started running, ignoring the cries of protest from people who began jumping out of his way.

<Who is that?> he shot out into the Cloud.

<Valeria Moretti.> Katja replied.

<Yes,> came a new voice in his head. <And who are you?>

Jack bolted to the right, hoping a vague zig-zag path would obscure him from view.

<I'm coming to find you, young man,> the voice said. Jack ignored it, lengthening his stride to a full sprint as he saw the edge of the market up ahead. He fired a quick scan behind him, and saw the signal from Moretti's device. It was approaching fast. Much too fast.

He spun around, gaping in shock at the huge, bounding strides she took. She was practically leaping over the shoppers who scrambled out of her way. Three more strides and she'd be on him.

<Shoot her!> Katja ordered. <Shoot her!>

Grabbing his pistol he drew it out. He fired at the center of mass, then twice more in quick succession. Moretti staggered as she hit the ground, leaping sideways for cover behind a stall. Jack fired again, the crack of the bullets punctuating the screams all around him.

<I'm at the street,> Katja said. <Withdraw!>

Jack turned and ran, spotting a familiar beige car hiss up to the edge of the field. The driver's door opened and Katja emerged, pulling a long, dark object after her. She raised it to her eyeline—it was her fucking assault rifle—and Jack felt a rush of heat sizzle through the air as an explosion rocked the market behind him. She stepped clear of the door and motioned him in.

He leaped into the seat, ears ringing as he heard at least three more rounds launch down her railgun barrel, and new explosions in the market beyond. Movement on his left grabbed his attention. It was Katja climbing into the passenger seat.

"Go, go, go!" she bellowed.

Jack stomped the throttle to the floor and peeled out onto the road. He cut across the lanes of traffic and diagonally through the first intersection. The dashboard flashed in protest at his unsafe speed, but Katja had disabled the safeties and he kept control. Dodging left and right past the slower cars, he sensed Katja reaching out into the Cloud.

Up ahead, the traffic signals had just switched to red, but then they flicked back to green to give him right of way. Under her electronic influence, they put a dozen blocks behind them in just over a minute.

"Pull over," she ordered. "We have to lose this car."

He veered onto a side street and found a service alley behind a line of stores. The loading bays were quiet for the weekend and he swung the car to a hard stop, then was out and running for cover even as Katja grabbed her gear. Seconds later she joined him next to the cover of a large recycling bin, rifle in her arms as she scanned the nearby buildings.

"Tell the car to drive itself," she said. "All the way to Firsthome."

Jack locked onto the car's navigation computer and gave it a destination more than seven thousand kilometers away.

Reactivating the safeties, he told it to drive the route at best, safe speed. It pulled out of the alley and signaled its way back onto the main road.

Katja hid her rifle in its case, but her hand disappeared through an opening. She stayed perfectly still, eyes scanning their surroundings and mind focused on the Cloud. He was breathing hard, adrenaline coursing through him like it would after an atmo drop or a stealth attack.

Following her lead, he reached out tentatively. There was nothing unusual in the immediate vicinity, but an overarching emergency call blanketed the city. Fire crews and ambulances were rushing to the scene of the combat, and a cacophony of distant voices cried out in shock and panic.

"Here," she said, thrusting a small make-up capsule at him, "get this on your skin." He popped the lid and rubbed the brown paste onto his hands and forearms, then onto his face, ears, and neck. Katja did the same, eyes darting in all directions. Within moments she'd transformed into an olive-skinned shadow of herself, just like on their first mission as operatives, but her blonde hair glowed in contrast. Reaching into her bag she wrapped a blue hijab over her head, hiding her hair under its long, silk train.

Then she examined him closely as he finished applying the make-up, strong fingers pressing against his neck and ears as she completed his work.

"You look different enough," he said, nodding at the close-framing scarf which now masked her head and softened her features, "but facial recognition might still nab me."

"That's why I have this," she said, hefting a hair-lengthener in her fist. "Hold still." Jack struggled to keep from wincing as the device hummed to life. Katja pressed it down, not on his hair, as he'd expected, but his chin. He grunted in pain as the follicles of his beard burst to life. Searing heat seemed to fry his skin as Katja carefully moved the tool along his cheeks. His eyes watered from the pain, but he forced himself to remain still. Finally she leaned back, scanning the alley again before quickly assessing her work.

He brushed his fingers against the new beard that covered his face, wincing as his lightest touch sent shivers of pain through his tortured skin. He sat back, slick with sweat. Trying to distract himself from the pain, he reached out into the Cloud again.

The Centauri government was asserting control, issuing a statement that there had been violence in a public market, and that police were already investigating.

"To the government of Centauria," Katja said suddenly, in a perfect local accent, "the attack today on the Starfall city market is our message to you. Your reckless pursuit of war against Terra is killing innocent civilians in all the systems—except yours. That will now change. You will no longer be protected behind your war machines, and your worlds will no longer be safe. We, the... Alliance of Hope, have demonstrated to you the horror you are causing in other systems. End this war, and we will end our attacks. Continue this war, and more innocent Centauris will die to match their brothers and sisters in other systems."

She pursed her lips, then uploaded her message to one of the main social media sites.

"That ought to fuck 'em up for a while," she said, pulling him to his feet.

Her line of thinking clicked in his mind. If the authorities started looking for home-grown terrorists, they wouldn't be looking for Terran operatives. And public outrage was a powerful, mindless force, difficult to distract with facts once opinions had been formed.

"How did you think of that so quickly?"

She pulled him along with her into a brisk walk.

"It's my job." She led him by the arm back to the side street. Her grip was like iron and her smooth hip brushed against his as they walked.

"Act natural," she said as they emerged onto the main road. "We're walking back to our apartment. Keep your weapon hidden, but handy."

She closed up her case and slung it over her shoulder. Then she reached into her coat, no doubt to check on her own pistol.

"We're just a local couple," she said, "out for a walk."

Jack took another deep breath, then gave her an obedient nod. It was a long walk back to their place.

* * *

Katja set a relaxed pace, so it took more than an hour, and Jack often felt himself getting ahead of her as his body screamed at him to take action. Eventually she took his hand in hers and held it tight, and they strolled with the appearance of just another young couple out in the street. His beard and her hijab were probably enough to fool any visual scans, but facial recognition programs still might see through them.

The sheer number of images that the Centauris would have to search was their best line of defense. Katja's arsenal of weapons was their last.

Slowly, slowly, he began to relax, and as she loosened her grip he almost enjoyed the walk. Neither of them looked happy, but then, with news of the terror attack spreading, nor did anyone else on the streets. Jack probed into the city security systems and noted that all exits from Starfall had been placed on lockdown—but their car was already dozens of kilometers to the south and speeding happily along a lonely right of way carved through the forests.

They both scanned the area around their building from as far out as they could manage, and the only Cloud activity they discerned was the chatter of the residents as they learned of the terrorist "bombing." No police cars loitered nearby. No individuals seemed out of place. Moving with swift but casual-looking purpose, they entered the building and climbed the stairs.

Their apartment was the same as always, and Jack retreated to his room as soon as they confirmed that their residence was clear. He threw his sweat-soaked clothes into the laundry and climbed into a hot shower to scrub himself down, washing away the stress and fear he always felt after combat. It was never a pretty thing, but he recognized sadly how used to it he'd become.

Just wash it away with soap and water, he sighed to himself. The make-up took some effort to remove, and his skin was too sensitive to even try shaving the beard. Rubbing his sore muscles he admitted to himself that, during his time as an operative, he had bulked out nicely. Months aboard ship, with three squares and no shortage of desserts, had made him bulk out in a less attractive way, but those days were gone.

Throwing on some clean, comfortable clothes good for lounging, he re-emerged into the living room and sat down next to Katja, who was slouched on the couch. Her blonde hair was loose and stark against her still-darkened face. Tiny, bare feet rested on the table, her boots and socks lying on the floor beneath her legs.

She turned to look at him, dark eyes lambent as they reflected the deep orange glow of sunset through the broad window.

"You okay?" she asked.

"Yeah, just shaking it off."

He could never tell if she was baiting him, or asking a sincere question. She was so closed, and her exterior was so hard, but he knew what was within, deep down, and he wished that the old Katja would return.

"They'll figure out that the explosions were caused by Terran bullets," she said, "but hopefully by then we'll be long gone."

"If we're long gone," he said, "then this mission will be over, and there'll be nobody here to figure *anything* out."

"True." She nodded. "Then we're good."

Her words were casual—so much so they filled Jack with horror. He'd tried to shove it aside for days, but all of a sudden it overwhelmed him. He turned on the couch to face her.

"Are you for real?"

She turned slightly toward him. Her features barely shifted, but a swirl of different emotions welled up from the depths of her eyes. She didn't reply, and he could see her defenses locking down, but he wasn't going to be intimidated this time.

"Doesn't it *bother* you? The fact that we're planning to destroy an entire world—the one we're sitting on right now?"

"Oh, Jack," she shook her head. "Not this again."

"Yeah, this again. I understand we have our orders, so you don't have to worry about having to kill me. I'm not arguing that. What I guess I want to know is this—who are you, really, Katja?"

She sighed angrily, looking away.

"What are you talking about?" she said.

"How can it not bother you that we're going to kill seven hundred million people?"

"We're not the ones doing it."

"We might as well be," he snapped, brushing aside her attempted deflection. "We're making it possible for the Astral Force to do it."

She stared at him, silent in her defiance.

"Doesn't it bother you?" he repeated. He stared at her for a long moment, trying to read her expression. She held his gaze, but with less power than before.

"It doesn't matter if it bothers me," she said, her voice nearly a whisper.

"Of course it matters," he said. "As officers we're obliged to think about the morality of our orders. It's our duty to do so."

"I'm not an officer anymore, Jack. I'm an operative." She stabbed a finger into his chest. "And so are *you*." She rose abruptly to her feet, turning away from him and walking toward her bedroom. He rose to follow, pausing at the open doorway.

"And what does that mean, Katja? Nobody told me that being an operative meant abandoning my conscience."

She pulled off her sweater and tossed it on her bed. The motion bared her flat stomach before her T-shirt slipped back down into place. She unbuttoned her jeans and moved to slide them over her hips, then paused and stared at him.

"Do you mind? I'd like to take a shower."

He turned away, leaning his back against her doorframe and looking out across the living room to the darkening street beyond the window.

"I'll look away," he said firmly, "but we're still talking."

"Can't it wait?"

"No, Katja, it can't. I'm not going to be brushed aside."

"I don't want to have this conversation again."

"Well, we're having it!"

There was a long pause. He kept his eyes pointed toward the living room during the silence. Then he heard the clink of her jeans dropping to the floor.

"Fine," she said, voice calm again. She padded into the bathroom.

"Why did you use your assault rifle to cover me?" he asked suddenly. "Your pistol would have worked just as well."

"The rifle is better at long range," she called back, "and I knew you were up against Valeria Moretti."

"But why did you fire into the crowd?"

"I didn't. I was shooting at Moretti and she was behind one of the stalls. The civilians got in the way." The sound of water running from the shower masked her last words somewhat. Jack wasn't sure if he heard regret or not.

"So they're just collateral damage?"

"What?" she called. "Come to the edge of the bathroom so I can hear you."

Jack stepped across her discarded clothes and glanced into the bathroom. The shower doors were closed and obscured with water droplets, but her sleek figure was vaguely visible as she put her face under the stream and soaked her hair. When she stepped free again, he raised his voice to be heard.

"So the civilians who died today, as you fired at Moretti. They're just collateral damage."

"Yes." She paused, scrubbing her face with ferocity. "Unfortunate, but worth it to Terra if I was able to kill the most dangerous Centauri agent in this war."

Jack's impulse was to argue the point, but he knew he couldn't. He had enough blood on his own hands, and whether they were military or civilian, it didn't matter.

She was washing herself down with soap, the shower doors blurring her form just enough to suggest the erotic, and Jack had to force his eyes to turn away. It was hard to remember where he was even going with the conversation.

"I guess," he finally said, "that I'm feeling betrayed by this mission."

"Why? Because things went to shit today, and I busted you out? It happens."

"No, not today—thank you for that—I'm talking about the whole mission."

"You said you wanted to make a difference, Jack." The shower splashed as she turned in the stall to wash off the soap. "The results of this mission may be terrible, but consider the alternative. Years of war to come, millions more dead in every system as we fight ourselves to exhaustion and sacrifice an entire generation of humanity."

Maybe having this conversation while she was in the shower wasn't the best idea. He forced himself to focus on the argument.

"But couldn't we just blow up one of their uninhabited planets? That would send a pretty strong message."

She shut off the shower and reached for the glass door. He forced himself to retreat across her bedroom again.

"Maybe," she called as he heard her step out and grab a towel. "But maybe not. You saw how many micro-torpedoes the rebels have—enough to wipe out the entire Fleet. What if our leaders know something we don't? What if they've learned that Centauria is developing a similar Dark Bomb weapon? What if this attack is the only way to stop the enemy from hitting us first? We just don't know, Jack."

She emerged into the bedroom, towel cloaked loosely over her petite form. Blonde hair dark with water clung to her neck and powerful shoulders, and his eyes were drawn to the smooth lines of her arms as she absently rubbed at the towel to dry her skin beneath. It preserved her modesty, but it wasn't wrapped all the way around her. Pausing in the center of the room, she looked up at him with genuine interest in her eyes.

"Why do you feel betrayed?" she asked.

"When Brigadier Korolev approached me about joining Special Forces, he said that he had a mission especially for me. He said that I could help to end the war quickly, and save millions of lives." He knew he should say more, but he was having trouble keeping his thoughts straight with so much of her skin showing.

"Is he wrong?"

"What?"

"Is what he said to you wrong?"

"No, but..." His voice trailed off as she lifted one end of the towel to dry her hair. Her thighs were revealed by the movement, decency just barely preserved. He really had to think to remember the point of his argument. "But he didn't tell me that to do so I'd destroy Second Earth."

She studied him, brushing stray hair from her face. He tried to figure out what could possibly be going on in her mind. Why could she not see the obvious clarity of his argument? And since when did she carry on conversations in nothing but a towel?

"When I was recruited into Special Forces," she said finally, "Korolev made quite a different promise. He told me that by becoming a servant of the State I would be exempted from any responsibility for my actions, as they weren't really mine but rather an extension of the State's will."

He stared at her. At the peaceful expression that was settling over her features.

"That's why you're always saying that," he said. "Always talking about us being servants of the State."

"Yes." She stepped closer, hands holding the towel across her body. "And it's true. We will never be called out for our actions. We are forgiven all, and we are free from guilt."

His insides were churning. Her body was so close, her dark eyes staring at him with a clear intent he'd never seen before. His stomach was like ice even as he felt himself rising to the occasion. She took another step closer, eyes locked to his.

"Are you even human?" he whispered, unable to look away.

"Oh, yes." She reached out one tiny hand to rest across his shoulder, and one side of the towel fell away. "Very much still human." He could feel the heat of her naked body pressing against him, felt her other hand let go of the towel and reach down to press against him.

"One of the beauties of being an operative," she purred, "is that we're free to do whatever we want. No judgements, no consequences."

He shuddered as her hands roamed over his body, nudging his own hands onto her bare hips. She reached up to kiss his neck, and began to slide off his pants. He gasped, savoring the heat of her breath against him. It was like that woman, Angela, at the lake at SFHQ—who'd appeared out of nowhere and given him the most amazing night of his life.

And now, it was Katja Emmes on offer.

He stepped back, banging sharply into the doorframe. She moved into him, lips pressing against his. No judgements, no consequences. But he moved his hands from her hips to her stomach—her smooth, sweet skin and taut muscles beneath—

And shoved her away.

She staggered back a couple of steps, and stared at him in

surprise. It was the first time he'd ever seen her naked, but any lust was washed away by his sudden realization of what was actually happening.

"No," he gasped. "Not like this. I'm not going to pretend like nothing matters. Or that this"—he gestured between them— "wouldn't matter. I thought my night with Angela mattered, until I figured out that she's just a Special Forces prostitute. I'm not going to do the same here."

"But, Jack," she said, stepping forward again, "that's the beauty of it. It doesn't matter. Nothing does."

"It would matter to me," he said, seeing through the spell of seduction and recognizing Katja's clinical advances for what they were. "Just like those people who died in the market—they matter. Just like every crew member I've ever lost matters. Just like this mission *matters*."

She stared up at him, hands still resting on him. Then, suddenly, she stepped back, collecting her towel and tying it around her again. Her knuckles whitened as they gripped the material. Her muscles tensed visibly. For a moment, watching the expression on her face as she stared downward at the floor, he was terrified. She could kill him in seconds if she really wanted to—of that he had no illusions.

But when she truly looked at him again, he saw only fatigue.

"We can't change what we are now, Jack, whatever you choose to think. And we will carry out our orders, or die."

He shook his head, rubbing it where he'd slammed into the doorframe.

"I told you that I'll do this mission—you don't have to worry about killing me. But after this one, I'm done."

"That's what you don't understand," she said, new intensity firing her features. "We're never done. Operatives don't retire, Jack. We know too much, and we're too damaged to be cut loose in civil society. All those implants in your brain—do you think they can be removed?"

"Can't they?"

"Our brains have adapted to them, come to rely on them. I've seen footage of one operative who had her implants removed, years ago. She's a vegetable, and there's nothing anyone can do."

She shrugged. "Besides, the State will never let any of us go—we're too much of a security risk. If we try to leave they'll hunt us down and kill us."

Jack slumped back, feeling the strength flow from his body. He thought of all the things he'd wanted to do with his life—cozy images, lofty dreams, the visions of a youth with many decades of adventure ahead of him. Then he tried to process the horror Katja had just shown him. An operative for the rest of his life?

"Nobody told me that."

"Welcome to the State," she said. "Our lives are no longer our own, but we are freed from any consequences."

He raised his eyes to look at her. She stared back defiantly, but as he continued to study her he saw tiny cracks in her resolve.

"We may be free of consequences," he said, "but we can never abandon our conscience. If we do, we're not human anymore—and that's one sacrifice too many for me."

"You better start examining the new reality, before you go insane."

"I think you should start looking at the old reality. If you can't, then you've already gone insane."

She stared back at him, unable to speak. Then she shoved him aside and slammed the bedroom door.

31

"**C**ommander Kane is here, sir," the steward announced.

"About damn time." Thomas heard the response from the CO's cabin of *Singapore*. As the steward moved aside, Thomas floated into the space.

Commander Sean Duncan pushed his way over, grasping Thomas in a handshake that came very close to a hug. In zero-g, it made for awkward positioning, but Thomas took it with good humor.

"And," Duncan said, grinning, "you just *had* to get a bigger ship than me, didn't you?"

"We're always just compensating," Thomas said with a smile, then he noticed Admiral Chandler hooked into a seat at the forward end of the room. "A pleasure, Admiral."

"If you two boys are finished your love-in," Chandler growled with good humor, "I have a mission to discuss."

Thomas glided over to the settee and pulled himself down, while Duncan returned to his own chair. Through the portal, the contour lights of *Admiral Moore* could be glimpsed, faint illuminations designed to stop the warships from actually bumping each other at such close quarters. She was a beautiful vessel, he was proud to admit—and yes, she was bigger than Duncan's *Singapore*.

Any more good-natured banter remained absent, though, and Thomas saw gravity in the expressions of Chandler and Duncan. It matched his own. *Singapore* had jumped to Centauria earlier that day, with the admiral aboard and a very special cargo primed for launch. H-hour was less than three watches away.

"So you both know the goal," Chandler began without preamble. "All of us have seen Abeona's orbital defenses before, and while they haven't rebuilt their orbital platforms, don't for a second think they've lessened their vigilance. Terran assets on the planet have been trying for months to ascertain what kind of surface weapons they have, but it's been impossible to secure the full picture.

"Thomas," he continued, "your role in this operation, I'm afraid to say, is to draw Centauri fire. A cruiser like *Moore* can take a hell of a pounding and give back twice as hard, and I have every faith in her captain's ability to fight her well."

Thomas nodded his thanks to the praise. It hadn't always been so.

"Sean," Chandler continued, "your role is simple—get within range and deliver the Dark Bomb. We have to get within ten thousand kilometers of the surface if the weapon is going to penetrate all the way to Abeona's core."

"What sort of danger zone do we expect upon detonation?"

"Worst case," Chandler replied, "is thirty thousand kilometers, so as soon as you launch we have to turn tail and scramble."

Duncan nodded.

"We have assets on the surface who will disrupt the Centauri defensive network," Chandler added, "so ideally we'll have a clear window to get in and get out before they can mount a coordinated defense. But... we just don't know how many backups they have, or how effective our assets' efforts will be."

"Is *Singapore* going to try and sneak in with *Moore* distracting at a distance?" Thomas asked. "Or am I providing close escort?"

Chandler gave him the expectant look he remembered well from their days long ago, aboard *Victoria*.

"What do you suggest, Mr. Kane?" XO Lieutenant Chandler had never just given his subbies the answer without forcing them to take a stab at it themselves.

"I recommend close support, sir," Thomas replied immediately. "*Moore*'s fate is ultimately irrelevant, but if *Singapore* doesn't make it to the launch point, this whole mission is for nothing. If

I'm half a world away, and one sharp Centauri operator spots *Singapore*, I'll be in no position to assist. If I'm nearby causing a ruckus, you can still sneak in like a hole in space, but then run for cover if required."

"I agree, sir," Duncan said. "With all the orbital noise, we can stay very stealthy even if *Moore* is nearby drawing attention. But if things go to shit, they'll do so very quickly, and our chances of making the launch point are greatly improved if there's a big cruiser nearby."

Chandler nodded thoughtfully, a sparkle in his eye as he glanced between the two men.

"Very well—close support. And allow an old man a moment of pride. I'm very glad to have both of you here with me. This mission is our century's Hiroshima, and it's hard, but we are servants of Terra and what we do is for the good of all humankind."

"I'm glad to have you at my side as well, sir," Duncan said, with none of his usual bravado. "I'm not going to lie to either of you. When I learned what this mission is for, I felt my heart tear in half."

Thomas sharply exhaled the breath he suddenly realized he'd been holding. So he wasn't the only one struggling with the moral quandary. He glanced at Chandler, hoping to see empathy for Duncan's admission. He was disappointed.

"I hear you," Chandler said, face stoic. "War is a terrible business, and whether this mission happens or not, we three will all suffer nightmares for what we've done in the service of the State. But war is *our* terrible business, and it is our duty to obey."

"I understand, sir," Duncan said, "and we will. I just wish, in this case, there was another option."

"So do I, but if we want to end the war quickly—before Terran forces are exhausted and our economy is ruined—we need to act boldly, and now."

Duncan's resolve was strengthened, Thomas could see. His old friend hated what he was about to do, but he was going to do it anyway.

"Sir," Thomas said slowly, "I feel that it is my duty to ask—*is* there any other way? Is there another, less populated target which we could hit?"

"Why do you feel it's your duty to ask that?" Chandler demanded, eyes suddenly hardening. "Your duty is to obey."

"Yes, sir, and I always have. I will suffer those nightmares you speak of for the rest of my life—and I accept that. As officers, however, there's one instance when we are not only permitted but *required* to question our orders, and that's when we are given an immoral order. As an officer—of whatever rank I may be—it is my duty to question an immoral order."

"This is not an immoral order, Mr. Kane. Horrific, yes, but not immoral." Chandler's jaw tightened. "Abeona is the headquarters of the entire rebel movement. It is the factory of war machines and the nest of spying vipers which so assault us. If there was an obvious, isolated surface target for us to hit, we'd do it—but there isn't. The Centauris scatter their bases across the planet, hiding beneath civilian populations because they think we won't strike there. That entire planet is the brain and brawn of our enemy, and it became a legitimate target the day the Centauris opened jump gates on Earth's surface and started laying waste to our greatest cities.

"If you want to talk about immorality, Mr. Kane, I suggest you consider the actions of our enemies. Terra is the victim in this war, and we have done nothing but defend ourselves. This mission, this single, decisive act, will decapitate the rebels and demoralize their scattered network of resisters. This act we are about to perform may be horrific, but it is for the good of all humanity. It will bring peace."

"The good of the State is the good of all," Thomas quoted easily from his school days. He'd heard that phrase every day growing up. He'd enforced it as a young platoon commander when his troops questioned their actions against irregular Sirian fighters. He'd believed it in his heart for as long as he could remember. Until now.

"Exactly," Chandler said. "The good of the State is the good of all."

Thomas looked over at his friend Sean Duncan, but saw only a resignation to following orders. He looked back at his mentor Eric Chandler, and saw the fire of righteous justice burning bright. He thought of his wife, Soma Kane, and her blissful acceptance of whatever the State told her.

Then he thought of Katja Emmes, and remembered the hardness in her eyes as she accepted this mission without question. But she'd given her soul to the State, he knew, and as much as he knew he loved her he couldn't follow her there. She was lost, both to him and to her own humanity.

Jack Mallory, at least, had gone kicking and screaming. But Thomas knew that Jack was too afraid of Katja to defy her. He'd hate himself forever, but he'd do his job. Of all the people involved in this genocide—for there was no other word for it— Thomas actually found himself most impressed with Breeze. She had clung to the Dark Bomb right from the beginning, and now she'd landed herself the position of Deputy Minister of Defense.

She was ultimately responsible for this mission. He didn't believe for a second that she thought it would bring peace, or that she believed she was serving humanity. She was out for herself, and the death of seven hundred million people was just a means to an end. She'd publicly deny that to her grave, but at least she'd be honest with herself about it.

That took real strength, and Thomas had been humbled enough over the past year to realize that it had been a trait sadly lacking in him for far too long. What did that say about Terran society if its most admirable representative was Charity Brisebois?

Thomas finally decided to be honest with himself, but as he looked back at his mentor and his oldest friend, he took another page from Breeze's playbook.

"I'm sorry for making this an issue," he lied with perfect sincerity, "and for threatening to place doubt in all our minds. Thank you for clarifying it for me, sir. This mission is essential to the safety of Terra and the welfare of all humanity. I know that we three will all do our duty."

"Duty is the great business of an officer," Duncan said with a hint of relief. He was quoting the brilliant Admiral Horatio Nelson. "All other private considerations must give way, no matter how painful it is."

"Struggle is the father of all things," Chandler echoed, quoting the martyr Adolph Hitler. "It is not by the principles of humanity that man lives, but solely by means of the most brutal struggle."

Words upon which the Terran State had been built, Thomas knew. Words he'd been taught at the earliest age. The struggle was never against one's fellow citizen, but against anyone who threatened society as a whole. For centuries this had been the struggle against the environment of hostile worlds, and for recent generations on Earth it had been the struggle against the MAS virus, which had killed billions before finally being contained and subdued.

He had experienced the primal thrill that came from combat, the struggle to keep one's own life and take another's. It had been years since he'd been conscious of it, but he knew the sense of almost orgasmic triumph when he emerged victorious in battle, when he still lived as his foe fell. He knew the deep urge to fight that rested within humanity's soul, and this war was an outlet for all of Terra's citizens, whether they fought in person or just cheered from the home front.

This mission was Terra's jaws closing on the jugular of its greatest rival, Centauria, and from this would come domination of the pack once again. No other colony had the resources to fight humanity's home system, and the natural order would be restored. But first, seven hundred million innocent people had to die.

Chandler reached out to clasp hands with his old subbies.

"Stay strong in the next few hours, my friends. History will be the judge of our triumph here today."

Thomas looked at the three young officers who stood before him. It wasn't quite like the old days in *Victoria*, but then, his career had taken a radically different path from that of his mentor. Just as Chandler had earned the unswerving loyalty of two young subbies all those years ago, Thomas could only *hope* that he was worthy of even greater loyalty now.

John, Chen, and Hayley stared back at him, their expressions displaying mixtures of confusion and horror. Thomas had just revealed to them the purpose of the mission.

"There's no way anything will survive on the surface," John said. "No matter what happens, that planet is going to be shredded."

"Correct," Thomas said, watching them all closely, "and this is why I've called the three of you here. I need to ask you each to do something for me, which may go against your personal beliefs. But I need your help."

Chen was pale, and speechless. Hayley's face was locked in a frown. John dropped his gaze momentarily, but managed to keep himself composed.

"What do you require of us, sir?" he asked.

Thomas glanced at the door to his cabin, reassuring himself that it was closed. He'd sent his steward down to the galley. There were no witnesses.

"I require you to assist me... in preventing this mission from succeeding."

All three stared at him in new shock.

"I remain loyal to Terra," Thomas said, "but this mission goes beyond nations. This mission is about the future of humanity. I cannot, as an officer of good conscience, allow it to succeed."

"You're talking mutiny, Captain."

"That risk is mine alone," he admitted. "I will go to my grave saying that none of you were complicit, and that you were merely pawns in my... evil plan." He offered a wry smile. "But the truth is you're all too smart to fool, and when the time comes I'll need you to act without hesitation."

"So you're asking us to choose between our loyalty to the Fleet, and to you personally?" Hayley snapped.

"In this one instance, yes I am."

"Well, then, fuck the Fleet," she growled. "I always wanted to be a pirate queen."

"I'm not suggesting we go buccaneer, Hayley... just stop this single mission from succeeding. Then we go home and report the failure like loyal Fleet officers."

"So the rest of the ship won't know?" John asked.

"Correct. I think I know how we can do this, but it'll take the four of us to pull it off."

John nodded thoughtfully, glancing at the subbies before looking back to his captain.

"Sir, I'm in."

Thomas fixed his stare on Chen, who'd been silent since

he'd learned the mission's true purpose.

"Chen, what are your thoughts?"

The young man was still pale, but he finally looked up with certainty.

"I signed up to defend Terra, sir, but now it looks like the rebels aren't the real enemy. I won't join the rebels, but I'm happy to help stop this madness. I'm in."

Thomas took a deep breath, looking around at his three loyal colleagues. He was asking them to commit the ultimate military crime and, despite his assurances, he had no guarantee that he could truly protect them if it came to a Fleet Marshall Investigation. By agreeing to help him, they might be signing their own death warrants.

Looking into their eyes, he saw reflected back what he knew was in his own. If this mission was allowed to succeed, he'd never be able to live with himself. It would be better to die knowing that he'd tried, than to live with seven hundred million murders on his conscience.

"Thank you, my friends."

"What's the plan, sir?" John asked.

If he was honest with himself, Thomas had to admit that he'd been devising the idea since the moment his true orders had been revealed.

"We'll never be able to launch one of our own weapons against another Terran warship—not without some record making it back to Fleet. But it just so happens we have a Centauri weapon on board, and I think we can make use of it..."

32

Korolev picked his people well. Initially Katja had wondered at his choice of Jack Mallory for Special Forces, but she saw now that the kid was far more than just really smart. He was strong, in ways she'd never imagined him to be. In ways she'd never been herself. He deserved a future, and she would do everything in her power to give him one.

Her gear was packed and rested by the front door. Small weapons were distributed over her body beneath her loose-fitting clothing. Everything was coming together as usual for another mission, but over the thunderous beating of her heart she knew it was all just a cover for her real purpose.

Jack crossed the living room toward her, hefting his own backpack. He glanced at her, but offered none of his usual smiles or good humor. His young face was surprisingly devoid of any emotion—almost as if he had slipped on his war face early. He set the pack down next to hers and cast his eyes around the apartment.

"I have everything of mine," he said. "Are you ready?"

"Yes."

Her heart ached to see him so withdrawn. Her seduction attempt had backfired in ways she truly hadn't expected. She'd been ready for awkwardness between them the next morning, no matter how it had played out, but Jack's cold distance was unsettling.

Not that she didn't deserve it. Her actions had been a cold-blooded attempt to distract him—and herself, honestly—from the powerful truth about their mission. A truth they both knew in their hearts, but which only he had the courage to face. His surprising strength hadn't just deflected her manipulation. It had also, finally, made her face reality.

Looking up at him now, as he diligently avoided her gaze to check the straps on his pack and confirm the contents of his pockets, she wept within at the trap they found themselves in as operatives. She wanted to tell him—wanted him to understand that she saw the truth of his words. He was right, about everything, and she had decided to act for what was right.

She couldn't tell him—couldn't even hint at it. Because he had to go back to Terra and report to Korolev on what happened. He had to believe, for his own safety.

He finally noticed her hesitation and looked down at her.

"What is it?"

"Slight change of plan, for me anyway."

"Oh?" He froze in place, tensing as his eyes searched hers.

"I've been thinking about our disruptor pods in the Pierce Building. Given the ruckus that occurred there, we don't even know if they're still in place, and even if they are, we don't know how long they'll be effective before Centauri cyberguards find them and shut them down." She crossed her arms, giving him her fiercest stare. "Disrupting the enemy security network is much too important for the mission to leave in the hands of remote machines. I'm going to go there in person and make sure it happens. Thomas and everyone else in orbit is counting on it."

Jack couldn't hold her angry gaze. He looked away, taking a deep, thoughtful breath. Then he turned back.

"How are you going to get to the escape point?" he asked. "It's more than a hundred kilometers outside the city. I might be able to fly in and pick you up somewhere close, but—"

"That's too risky," she said. "You stick to the original plan, and get yourself off-planet. Don't worry about me."

"But, Katja..." he said slowly, "if this attack succeeds, there won't be any second escape route."

"I know." Her heartbeat was pounding in her skull, but she

kept her face stern. "I'm a servant of the State, and I will do my duty."

It was exactly what she'd be expected to say. By Jack's expression she knew he wasn't surprised, nor would Korolev be when Jack reported back. It was bullshit, but she had to make Jack believe it just one more time.

"This mission," she added, "is too important to leave with such a variable still in play."

He made to speak, but stopped himself, mind clearly racing through possibilities. Then he glanced over their gear, as if some new solution would suddenly present itself.

"You can't throw your life away," he said finally.

"I'm already dead, Jack." At another time her statement might have been a joke, but as she spoke she realized that truer words had never passed her lips. "I've been dead for a long time."

"Katja…" His face melted into compassion. After a moment's hesitation he dared to reach out and grip her arms. "Don't do this."

She knew she should shrug off his touch with a show of anger, but his strong hands felt too good against her, and she couldn't find the will.

"The mission," she said, "is too important. It's my duty to ensure that it succeeds."

His eyes shut tight as he fought back emotion. Finally he nodded in understanding.

"Then I guess," he said, "I'm coming with you."

Oh shit, shit, shit. No, that wasn't part of the plan. Her mind raced. "Not a chance, Jack," she snapped. "You'd just slow me down, and there's no need for both of us to be sacrificed."

"How could I abandon you to this?" he asked, eyes opening to reveal glistening moisture. "After everything…" His voice trailed off as he grasped for words. "You know, everything."

He really wasn't making this easy. She fought down the emotion welling up within her, forcing herself to become the operative once again. "You're still valuable," she said coldly. "Terra will need you in the future that's coming. You have to survive."

"And what about you?"

"I will do my duty… to Terra. I need you to honor that, and make sure my actions aren't in vain."

His hands dropped away from her. He stared at her in sad disbelief.

"I can't help but admire you," he said, "but I'll never understand you."

And you will never, she prayed to herself, *become like me.*

"You know I'm right," she said.

"Yeah, and now I just hate this mission even more."

"Get yourself to safety, and make sure that bastard Kane gets to safety, as well."

He tried to laugh, but it died in his throat and he looked away sharply, wiping his eyes. Without another word he grabbed his backpack, and opened the apartment door. Katja took up her gear and followed him out.

They'd already selected a vehicle for their actions today. The big car was owned by an elderly couple in the building who used it only once a week, regular as clockwork, and certainly wouldn't miss it for the next few hours. Jack reached into the Cloud, opened the locks, hijacked the ID system, and disabled the navigation even before he'd placed his pack in the car's storage compartment. He moved with such casual efficiency—both physically and in the Cloud—that she could only shake her head.

"So am I giving you a lift to the Pierce Building?" he asked as they climbed in.

"If you could drop me a couple of blocks away, that'd be great. I'll walk from there." The banality of their exchange belied the simmering tension she felt, but at least Jack wasn't arguing anymore. He pulled out onto the street without further comment. She welcomed the silence, even if she hated what he must think of her. His feelings might very well save his life.

A short time later he pulled over on a quiet side street, exactly two blocks from her target. A scattering of pedestrians moved past on the walkway, but no one seemed to notice a car parking alongside the others. She unstrapped and turned to him.

After a moment he turned to her.

"It's ninety-five minutes to H-hour," he said. "I'll be airborne by twenty. If things are going well here, and you want a pickup, you just let me know."

It was a noble gesture, and just like him to offer. She half climbed out of her seat, leaning into him and wrapping her arms around him tightly. He didn't hesitate in returning the hug, squeezing her close. She let herself bask in the embrace for longer than she'd intended, suddenly not wanting to let go.

The first time she'd said goodbye to her life had been easy. This time, not so much. She pressed her cheek against his and gave him a long, slow kiss on the jawline.

"Goodbye, Jack."

He didn't answer, other than to hold her tight for another long moment. Then, reluctantly, she pulled herself free and exited the car, not looking back.

Thomas sat in his command chair, listening to the professional murmur around him on the bridge as he watched the red symbols drift near the visible disk of Abeona, low on the bow. The blue symbol of *Singapore* was high to port, slowly drawing left as *Moore* overtook her.

The two ships moved on slightly different courses and at different speeds. No doubt they both were being tracked by Abeona Traffic Control, although they were still too far out to have been challenged. Orbital contact density increased up ahead, which would be very helpful in the coming hour. Thomas glanced at the clock.

Seventy minutes to H-hour.

Next to him the officer of the watch, Lieutenant Overvelde, completed his checklist to bring the ship to battle stations. Thomas heard the voice of the XO through the local speaker, reporting the disposition of the damage control system. Overvelde acknowledged, then glanced up.

"Captain, sir, officer of the watch," he declared. "Ship is at battle stations."

"Very good," Thomas replied. The bridge was fully manned around him, all personnel in their emergency spacesuits with helmets strapped to their belts. Each warfare area was ready for the action to come.

Abeona grew larger up ahead, and Thomas remembered only too well the last time he'd done battle here. He cast his eyes over the bridge crew, wondering how good the AAW and AVW directors really were. He needed them to keep his ship in one piece long enough for the final maneuver, but he also needed them to be distracted enough to not see what was really going on.

Over in ASW, John Micah paced as he watched his displays.

Chen and Hayley were secured to the deck in front of him. Hayley was second officer of the watch, but Thomas had designated Chen as "officer at large" for this battle. He had explained to the XO that he wanted a trusted set of eyes and ears at his disposal, but since all the lieutenants already maintained official positions, it would have to be a subbie. The XO had not argued.

"Sublieutenant Wi," he said. Chen unhooked from Hayley's station and floated over, gripping the command chair armrest and leaning close.

"Check in with Shades," he murmured, too quiet for Overvelde to hear on his other side. "Confirm which tube he wants to designate, and then get down there to load up."

"Yes, sir." Moisture beaded on Chen's young face. "Do you want me to come back to the bridge afterward?"

"No. Stay there in person and guard it."

"Yes, sir."

"Good luck, Chen. I'm counting on you."

The subbie pushed away carefully and moved across the bridge to John's position. Thomas watched them exchange quiet words before Chen maneuvered back to the command chair.

"Captain, sir," he said to Thomas across Overvelde. "ASW reports a possible malfunction in the port-side forward countermeasures battery. Shall I get a maintenance crew down there?"

"No," Thomas replied. "This close to combat I want them to stay at their stations. Get down there yourself, Sublieutenant Wi, and have a look—see if it just needs a reboot. If not then report to the XO and then we can detach techs."

Overvelde nodded in acknowledgement as Chen accepted the order and moved off. As officer of the watch, Overvelde was responsible for the overall running of the ship and was the person most likely to notice what Chen was really up to. He'd proven himself far too competent for Thomas to think he'd miss the impending changes to the port-side forward countermeasures battery.

Chen used his anchor line to glide aft to the bridge doors. Thomas watched him go, then glanced over at John. The ASW director met his gaze, nodding once.

Thomas sat back in his command chair, scanning his display and then gazing out at the view projected all around him. The lights of other craft were becoming visible, moving against the starry backdrop, and Abeona loomed ahead.

Katja crawled along the ventilation duct, moving slowly enough to minimize the potential for the metal to shift under her weight, but knowing that she worked against the most important deadline in human history.

It had taken longer than she hoped to get past the security systems, and a quick glance at her watch reported less than thirty minutes to H-hour. She'd had to tackle the quantum-flux field by herself, but a clever manipulation had left the sensors on bare minimum power—not actually disabled, since that would have tripped the status alarms. They were too weak, however, to detect her movements amid all the airflow of the ventilation.

A careful observer would probably still spot her, but she doubted there were any humans involved in this sort of security. Sometimes the Centauris trusted their machines too much.

She'd already checked one of the disruptor pods—it was still in place—and she'd hoped to verify at least one more before activating them. But she was running out of time, and if one disruptor was still ready, then they all were. No, she had to get *herself* in place.

Pulling up into a sitting position at a junction of ducts, she reached out, scanning quickly for any active detectors. There was nothing unusual, and with a single micro-burst she transmitted the activation command. Four automated acknowledgements came back, but otherwise she detected no changes.

The disruptors were designed to be subtle, slowly building their interference in a way that would degrade, but not destroy, the enemy's tactical picture. It would take at least fifteen minutes for the degradation to really kick in, and she could only guess at how long it would be before the Centauris figured out the problem and corrected it.

The first part of her mission complete, she braced herself against the sides of the duct and lowered herself down a level. The orbital network stations were no longer of any interest to her—her next prize was even deeper. Reaching out again, stilling her mind and really listening, she could just make out the tell-tale signal of Centauri agents.

The ship was being hailed by Abeona Traffic Control, and the tension level on the bridge rose significantly, but silence surrounded them.

Overvelde responded with his best Centauri accent, indicating that *Moore* was the private courier ship *Bear Seven* en route to Starfall. Such vessels often failed to log flight plans between worlds, having little interest in being formally tracked in their daily business, but it wouldn't take Traffic long to figure out that there was no such vessel registered to any courier company.

Not that it really mattered, Thomas thought, glancing at the clock again. Twenty minutes to H-hour. All he had to do was keep the Centauris busy for a little while longer.

An alert ignited on the status board between him and Overvelde. The officer of the watch noted the warning lights, which connected to the port-side forward countermeasures battery.

"Looks like something's really wrong down there, sir," he said. "I'll get the XO to send a team."

"Just wait," Thomas said quickly. "It's probably Chen rebooting the system. I don't want DCC distracted right now."

"But, sir, the countermeasures—"

"And I don't want you distracted, either," Thomas snapped. "Transfer system status to your second officer of the watch—I need you focused on driving this ship into battle, Mr. Overvelde."

"Yes, sir." Overvelde dutifully manipulated his console and simplified the display so that only ship movement and tactical information were displayed.

"I have control of system status," Hayley called from her station just forward.

Thomas looked at Overvelde, and got a determined nod in return.

Singapore had fallen astern, maintaining her plodding course toward the launch point. She would likely be hailed any moment, as well—it was time for *Moore* to smack the hornet's nest.

"Officer of the watch," he declared, "increase to attack speed."

Above her there was a sudden flurry of activity. Secondary network nodes activated as additional security stations flashed to life. Comms traffic exploded outward, and Katja recognized the machine responses from Abeona's scattered array of surface weapons.

Thomas had made his move.

Her disruptors were already confusing the tactical picture—she just hoped they would do so enough to give his ship the edge.

Below her, she sensed new chatter from the Centauri agents. She'd identified at least four separate individuals, even if she couldn't make out their messages. Three of them were in a single, large compartment less than two hundred meters away from her, and the fourth was rapidly closing that location. From the amount of encrypted data that was sizzling through, she suspected the compartment was a central control station. Special Forces had plenty of similar setups.

She increased her pace through the vents, figuring all eyes were looking spaceward, and she doubted the quantum-flux sensors would highlight her movement amid all the commotion.

More alarms sounded, both above and below her. She ripped off her jacket, abandoning it behind her and slipping down another tube, and smiled to herself at just how many people Thomas was frightening right now. She could feel the surprise, in some cases bordering on panic, as the defenses tried to make sense of what they were seeing in orbit.

Her feet slammed down on the metal trunking, her smile broadened as she scrambled forward along the vent.

He really could be a bastard.

Then behind her, she heard another slam against the metal, couched in a hiss of tapping feet. Spinning around, she gasped as the awful length of a milly revealed itself down the tube she herself had used. It scanned the vents and locked onto her, scuttling forward even as its body continued to descend from above.

Snapping a grenade from her belt, she threw it back at the beast and launched herself into motion. The explosion thundered through the venting, a wall of air knocking against her as she scrambled away. The clatter of mechanical feet resumed behind her, and she didn't even spare a glance to confirm that the milly was still in pursuit. Reaching another vertical intersection she dropped down the tube, her body crashing against the next trunking below.

She released another grenade in her wake as she moved on all fours, toppling into a forward roll as the blast impacted her and rattled the entire tunnel. Leaping into a crouch she looked back, saw the milly slithering past the wreckage toward her. They were in a long, straight vent now, with nowhere to hide.

Drawing both of her pistols, she unleashed a hail of bullets. Sparks flew off the nose of the robot as it raced toward her, forward claws extending. Both of her pistols clicked empty. She tucked into a ball and held them up as shields.

Abruptly the milly collapsed, going limp as all power fled its body. It slid to a halt, unmoving.

Katja stared in shock, dimly aware of her hands going through the motions of reloading her pistols.

<You didn't really think I'd abandon you?>

Jack!

<Where the fuck are you?> she asked.

<Airborne, en route to your position—get outside anywhere and I can pick you up.>

<There's no time! If you don't head for space right now you'll never clear before H-hour.>

<Impossible odds haven't stopped us before—they won't stop us now.>

No… That heroic jerk was ruining everything. Why couldn't he just understand that she didn't *want* to be rescued? Against the thumping heartbeat in her chest, Katja reached up and felt for where she knew her entangled particle device was. Jack was never going to stop this fool's errand, so long as he thought she was still alive.

That left one option.

She pulled up her shirt and quickly felt for the tiny incision scar. There. Her knife was in her hand and without allowing herself to think she dug the point of the blade into her chest, just under her right breast. Grunting through the searing pain, she probed with the knife between her ribs.

<I'm not going to make it,> she said. <There's too many of them.>

<I see you as clear.>

<No—there are agents on either side of me.>

<Where?>

<Right here—they must be cloaked.>

As he no doubt burned through the various sensors in the Pierce Building, she felt her knife click against the tiny capsule attached to the top of her rib. With a sharp twist she cut it free, then reached in with her fingers, past the torrent of blood, to pull it out of the hot gash she'd made in herself.

<I'm not going to make it,> she said as she put the capsule on the metal by her feet and pointed her pistol at it. <Get out of here, Jack.> She pulled the trigger, obliterating the capsule and sending a clear signal of trauma. She just heard Jack's cry in the Cloud before she shut down all of her implants.

Tears streamed down her face as she ripped open her medikit and sprayed her wound before pressing a bandage against it. She sat back against the wall of the vent, gasping for breath and waiting as the blood trickled hot down her stomach and the cocktail fought to seal the breach. Her head spun with the pain, but pain was like an old colleague, and she weathered it stoically.

Finally, she blinked open her eyes, clearing her vision. Her mission wasn't over yet, but now she had to proceed without using her implants. No one—least of all Jack—could ever know what she was going to do next.

33

"We're being illuminated," the AAW director called out.
Ten minutes earlier one of the Space Guard cutters had broken from low orbit. Now it was closing on *Moore*, and had just activated its fire control radars to closely track the interloper. Yet the second cutter had not been baited, and was stubbornly sticking to its patrol pattern. The lone frigate in orbit had just started to move out of its geostationary perch.

With all of *Moore*'s active sensors on standby they were building the tactical picture based purely on passive input. It made for an eerie quiet.

Well, Thomas decided, so much for the cutter.

"Take hostile zero-three," he ordered.

There was a flurry at the controls over his right shoulder in AVW, and then four dazzling orbs appeared in space outside the hull, blasting away from *Moore* in a slow spread before angling inward on their target. The Centauri cutter was so close that he doubted they even had time to activate defenses. The four missiles smashed into the bright hull, tearing through the frame as fires gasped through the escaping oxygen before dying in the vacuum. The wreck spun wildly, breaking apart.

The encounter lasted barely thirty seconds, but now Abeona knew there was a warship in orbit. Passive sensors all across the bridge sphere lit up as tracking radars bloomed to life on the planetary surface, filling a quarter of his view. On the local display Thomas saw the vectors of the remaining cutter and the frigate both increase, and they turned toward him.

Dead reckoning placed the silent *Singapore* a good ten thousand kilometers away and approaching the first inbound traffic lane—far enough to be clear of close combat, but not so far as to be out of *Moore*'s reach. Ideal.

"Go active on all sensors," he ordered. "Target the frigate first and fire as soon as it's in maximum effective range."

Moore's powerful search sensors came alive, flooding the displays with new information. Symbols burst to life across most of the starscape, computers and operators frantically trying to assign and classify all the objects. Two red symbols were immediately obvious ahead—the two fighting ships now accelerating to intercept *Moore*—but otherwise any identification was lost amid the sea of civilian craft. Including *Singapore*.

"Get an ID on Raffles," he barked. "I don't want to lose her in that mess."

"ASW will track Raffles," Micah called out, earning an appreciative acknowledgement from the anti-vessel warfare director. Thomas nodded. John had to maintain that track—and the less the other warfare areas knew, the better.

"Hostile zero-four is launching weapons," called AAW.

Wow—their range was longer than intelligence thought. Thomas rechecked his own display. At this distance even *Moore*'s long-range missiles would fall short, running out of fuel and becoming mere ballistics.

"Vampires are not locking on!"

The enemy missiles were still distant, but as they approached their relative bearing took them clearly to starboard. They weren't closing *Moore* at all. Thomas sat back in his chair and watched. The plan had called for the operatives to spoof the Centauri defensive systems. It appeared as if Jack and Katja had succeeded in their mission.

"Stay sharp for a small, inbound contact squawking Special Forces ID," he shouted for the entire bridge to hear. "Our operatives will be trying to approach us at some point in the next two-zero minutes."

At least, he hoped so.

His display indicated that the Centauri frigate had moved into missile range. At his order, long-range weapons loosed from their launchers embedded in *Moore*'s flanks, and rocketed into the darkness. Given the range, and against such a sophisticated enemy, scoring a hit was unlikely, but it would help to focus an entire world's defenses on one ship. *His* ship. Thomas felt a rush of adrenaline. For the next five minutes, he and his cruiser were taking on the entire rebellion.

A blue symbol appeared on his display, just aft of the port beam. It was nearly lost in the swarm of civilian contacts.

"Positive ID on Raffles," Micah announced. "She's increased speed and is closing the launch point."

Thomas checked the distance to *Singapore*. The gap had opened.

"Get us within eight thousand k of Raffles," he said to the officer of the watch. "Maneuver as required to protect the ship, but stay inside that boundary."

"Yes, sir." Overvelde gave the order to turn *Moore* to port. On his display he created a sphere around *Singapore* to indicate his new zone. Thomas watched the relative vectors begin to converge, then turned his attention back to the battle.

"Status of our long-range strike?"

"Hostile zero-four knocked down all our missiles."

"Re-engage hostile zero-four, salvo size eight."

More weapons flashed free, the glow of their rockets quickly lost against the looming orb of Abeona. The first planetary missiles came blasting up through the atmosphere, but their aim was scattered by the Special Forces spoofing.

The sphere around *Singapore* enveloped *Moore* at the center of the display, and Thomas felt the faint accelerations as Overvelde weaved the big cruiser through a series of defensive patterns to throw off enemy targeting. Thomas glanced back to John, who gave him a quick thumbs-up, face grim.

Ten minutes to H-hour.

Katja peeked down through the grate. The Centauri ops center was crowded with people. Most were in uniform but four civilians stood out from the rest. The four were scattered along the rear of three rows of consoles, each hovering near a senior officer who clearly commanded a different area of warfare. The mood among the military personal was professional, but agitated. Even as Katja lifted the grate she heard the nearest senior officer curse in frustration as he slammed the back of an operator's chair.

"Why are we not *hitting* anything?" he demanded.

Katja lowered herself through the opening and dropped to the floor of the ops center with a soft thud.

"Because you're being spoofed," she declared.

Dozens of heads snapped over at her voice, shock and confusion blossoming. She met the eyes of the nearest civilian woman, who was without question one of the agents, and placed her hands on her head.

"I surrender. Now let me save your planet."

The agent stared back at her, not speaking—at least, not out loud.

"She's a Terran operative! Take her down!" Down the long row of consoles she saw Valeria Moretti leap into the air, clearing half a dozen operators as she broke into a run. Katja dropped to her knees, hands firmly on her head.

"I surrender," she repeated, imploring the nearest agent to listen to her. "We are all going to die unless you listen to me."

The agent threw up an arm to block Moretti's charge. All around them, military weapons were raised, and Katja flinched as every barrel was aimed at her.

"Speak, Terran," the agent said.

"Your network is being spoofed by four disruptor pods placed two floors up in this building." She rattled off their frequencies and locations. "If you can spot those signals, you can deflect them and get a clear picture of orbit."

Moretti met the eyes of her fellow agent in a Cloud exchange. Moments later, the imagery on every display in the ops center jerked and reset.

"There is a Terran cruiser engaging your forces," Katja said, her voice carrying through the room, "but it is not your target— it's the distraction. Your target is another Terran warship which is moving silently through your civilian traffic, closing Abeona."

"A stealth ship?"

"No. Probably a destroyer."

"Why?"

"Because it can slip through your defenses more easily than any other kind of warship, yet still keep the brane picture crystal clear."

The senior officer spoke into his handset, and Katja heard voices raised further down the line of consoles. The general din of an active ops center returned, but Katja watched as the two agents conferred again, both staring down at her.

"We know who you are," Moretti said finally.

"And I know who you are," Katja replied, fighting the aggression which boiled up in her veins. The time for fighting was over, for many reasons. She felt the anger slowly drain out of her taut muscles, and grasped for whatever might take its place.

"I'm sorry," she said.

Moretti's face hardened like stone. Behind her, operators reported a suspect vessel in descending orbit at the edge of the traffic lanes, less than eight thousand kilometers from the Terran hostile currently engaged in close combat with their frigate.

"That vessel," Katja said, "is carrying a Dark Bomb, and its target is your planet's core. That vessel is coming to destroy Abeona."

She glanced at a nearby clock.

"You have four minutes to stop it."

The Centauri frigate pulled back, reeling from *Moore*'s last barrage. For a small warship it was putting up a good fight, but Thomas could tell that he'd battered it into submission. As it turned and retreated he let it go, thankful for the pause in the action.

Unhooking from his chair, he floated swiftly over to John at ASW. The director's face had an ashen coloring, but he met his captain's eyes.

"Are you still solid in tracking Raffles?" Thomas asked.

"Yes, she's here"—he pointed—"at speed and heading straight for the launch point."

"Are you sure this contact is Raffles?" Thomas subdued a wince at the sudden tightening of his gut. "We can't be wrong about this."

John nodded, bringing up a side screen with a list of detailed characteristics for the contact.

"Every vessel has a unique gravimetric signature, caused by shape, mass, and certain pieces of equipment. We've been recording and analysing Raffles' signature for the past day, and this is definitely a match."

"Okay," Thomas said, pushing away from ASW. "Keep me posted."

"Yes, sir."

"AVW, captain," he called out. "Status of hostiles?"

"The frigate's in retreat, sir. The cutter is rising in orbit but not closing us."

"Very good." He reached the second officer-of-the-watch station and touched Hayley's shoulder.

"System status?"

"All vital systems operational," she declared loudly, for all to hear.

"Very good." He picked up a handset and tapped in a particular number.

"*Port forward countermeasures*," Chen responded.

"This is the captain," he said very quietly. "Is the package loaded?"

"*Yes, sir. Tube six is loaded with the package and ready.*"

Thomas scanned the tracking info on Hayley's tactical display, noting that *Moore*'s sensors were easily pinpointing *Singapore*—even through the immense clutter of orbital traffic—as the destroyer raced for its launch point. He saw that countermeasures tube six was indeed showing green status, and John had assured him that his tweaking of the Centauri micro-torpedo meant it would respond to the launch commands of a Terran ship.

The command—which Chen had pre-programmed with help from John—was to track down *Singapore* and destroy its bridge. When that weapon fired, Thomas knew that both his mentor and one of his oldest friends would die.

Hayley's hand was near the launch button, and she looked up at him in dread-filled questioning.

He motioned her aside.

"I've got this."

"Thank you, sir." She glided to the other end of her console, busying herself with other duties.

"Captain, sir, AAW! A new wave of planetary vampires has launched—assess thirty or more!"

Thomas glanced up. "Time to intercept?" His finger still hovered over the countermeasures fire button. There was a pause from AAW, and Thomas turned his focus back to the personal mission. He rechecked the firing solution one last time, then reached for the button.

"Sir! The vampires aren't aimed at us—they're firing at Raffles!"

Thomas moved his hands away from the console, staring up at the symbols moving across the face of Abeona on the forward half of the bridge sphere. A swarm of red hostiles were coming up from the planet, and he could see that both the frigate and the cutter were vectoring toward the blue symbol of *Singapore*.

"Flank speed," he shouted. "Engage hostiles zero-four and zero-five with missiles—salvo sizes six!"

The volleys of missiles launched forth, and the Centauri frigate maneuvered wildly as it launched countermeasures and engaged its defenses. The cutter was farther away, and didn't seem to notice the sudden attack until almost too late. The frigate survived the assault but continued to drop toward lower orbit, no longer attempting to close *Singapore*. The cutter took the brunt of the missile strike, and despite the distance Thomas saw the visible explosions momentarily light up the sky.

He felt a moment of grim satisfaction, then realized the absurdity of it. Was he going to protect *Singapore* from enemy fire, just so he could destroy her himself?

"Raffles is maneuvering," AVW reported. "Looks like she's trying to evade the surface missiles."

Thomas noted the clock. It was sixty seconds to H-hour. If *Singapore* appeared to be doomed, Chandler might very well fire the Dark Bomb early, and hope for the best.

He slammed his hand down.

The console lights shifted to indicate that the package had launched.

"Captain, sir, AVW. We're tracking the Special Forces craft on approach."

The planetary missiles swarmed *Singapore*—she had no chance, and there was nothing *Moore* could do to save her.

"Recover the Special Forces craft," he ordered. "Break for open space and then prepare for jump."

The view on the sphere shifted as *Moore* turned away from Abeona, but Thomas spun around to keep his eyes on the single blue symbol of *Singapore* as she fought valiantly against the overwhelming attack. As his friend Sean Duncan fought to survive, and his mentor Eric Chandler tried to impose the will of Terra on all of humanity.

The blue symbol flashed, then winked out.

Thomas dropped his eyes, unsure whether he wanted to scream, cry, or vomit. His insides churned and sweat soaked his uniform beneath the emergency suit. He noticed Hayley hovering near him, the subbie's pale face fixed on his.

"I'm sorry, sir," Hayley whispered. "We did our duty."

Thomas forced himself to nod, then pushed back over to his command chair. Hooking in, he automatically surveyed the tactical situation around him. His crew was entirely focused on keeping *Moore* safe, and even as he watched a pair of anti-attack missiles fired from the after launchers, taking down a lone Centauri missile that was chasing the cruiser.

Otherwise, though, it seemed as if the enemy—no, the Centauris—were willing to let him go.

"Have we recovered the operatives?" he asked.

"Yes, sir—now inside the hangar and secure."

"ASW, any gravimetric changes to Abeona?"

Beside him, Overvelde cast him a curious look.

"No change, sir," John reported.

He assessed the tactical situation once more, assuring himself that there were no immediate threats.

"All stations, stand by for jump to Terra."

Moments later, Overvelde nodded.

"Ready for jump, sir."

"Start the countdown."

"One minute to jump," Hayley announced.

Thomas watched the retreating tactical situation, telling himself over and over that it had been the Centauri missiles that had destroyed *Singapore*. Very likely his efforts had contributed nothing to the mission's failure.

"Thirty seconds to jump," Hayley said.

"Jump coordinates locked," John said, "projector ready."

Thomas looked back over his shoulder at the brilliant orb of Abeona, wondering if he'd ever see it again. The planet would survive, but Thomas wasn't too sure of his own fate when he returned to Terra. He saw Jack Mallory entering the bridge and hooking to an anchor. His friend pulled his way forward to stare grimly up at Thomas.

"Welcome aboard, Mr. Mallory," he said. "We're just about to head home."

"Sounds good to me." Jack looked ten years older, his features drawn and haggard. Yet if there was anyone in the universe Thomas knew he could trust, it was this young pilot. He could guess at the reason for Jack's somber look, and realized that he might have a cure for it.

"I need to debrief you on the mission," Thomas said, leaning in close. "And I might need your help in... correcting a bit of data on board."

"Yes, sir."

Thomas suddenly realized Jack's partner hadn't appeared.

"Where's Katja?"

Tears appeared in Jack's eyes. Thomas felt his own heart wrench.

No... He pulled Jack close against the command chair, wrapping an arm around the young man's shuddering form.

"Three... two... one..." Hayley called. "Jump!"

Katja watched the tactical screens on the walls, translating the Centauri symbology and tying it to the snippets of reports she could hear nearby. She was still on her knees, hands clasped on her head, but beyond assigning a pair of guards to flank her, the Centauris didn't seem in much of a hurry to deal with her. Their attention was still very much on the orbital situation. As was hers.

To their credit, the Centauris had acted on her words, and without delay. The second Terran ship had been exactly where she'd directed them. Indeed, their military response had shocked her with its speed, accuracy, and strength. From what she could make out, the ship had responded effectively at first to evade the attack, but was quickly overwhelmed by the missiles.

Seven different observers confirmed that the Terran vessel had been destroyed.

There was discussion about launching a system-wide alert to hunt down the Terran cruiser which was even now fleeing Abeonan orbit.

"Don't bother," Katja said. "She'll be gone within the hour."

"We'll find her," the senior officer growled.

"No, I mean she won't be here anymore. She'll have jumped back to Terra."

That got their attention.

Moretti turned to Katja, crossing her arms.

"So, Lieutenant Operative Katja Andreia Emmes, why are you telling us all this?"

"Because this mission was wrong. We all do a lot of bad things in war, but nothing can justify what Terra was about to do. I had to stop it."

"A Terran operative with a conscience? That's a first."

Katja looked around at the gazes turning once again in her direction. There was some doubt, still some fear, but most of all an overwhelming hostility. She doubted this day was going to end well—but at least it would end.

"They don't want us to have consciences," she said, "and for a while I didn't. Or at least I ignored it. I can't do that anymore. Now, because of what I've just done, I can never go back."

"So what," Moretti scoffed, "you're switching sides?"

"No. I just want to make you an offer."

The agents exchanged glances, all four of them gathered around Katja.

"We're listening," Moretti said.

"I have the ability to erase everything in my brain—all the classified data, all the plans, all the State secrets with which I've been entrusted. We're designed that way, in case we're ever captured." She took a deep breath, moving her eyes from one face to the next. "But I'm willing to give you access to all of it—everything there is in my brain—in exchange for one thing."

"What?"

"When you've extracted everything, I want you to wipe my memories, so that I never again know who I was or what I've done. I want nothing to do with this life."

Moretti's fists clenched at her sides.

"So you want to just walk away from all your crimes? You want us to pretend they never happened?" The rage burned in Moretti's eyes. The impotent rage of someone who sought justice, but found only empty vengeance. Katja knew the feeling well. She knew the abyss that hate could burn into a heart.

"Valeria," she said, "there's nothing I can do to change what happened. Yes, I killed Kete Obadele—and you killed Suleiman Chang. Yes, Terran forces killed your family in our attack on Abeona—and Centauri forces killed my father in your attack on Earth. We can keep this game going, but I hope you can understand that today, if it wasn't for me, Terra would have played that game for keeps. Your entire planet would be gone."

She turned her gaze to the other agents.

"I am willing to surrender all of my classified information to you, and I am willing to have your surgeons remove whatever implants they feel are necessary to render me forever harmless. All I ask is that you let me go in peace." She remembered Kete's words to her, when she'd held his life in her hands, and she took one last gamble.

"I'm surrendering myself to your mercy, and to the mercy of the Centauri state."

Moretti swore quietly, turning away in disgust.

Katja watched the other operatives, and awaited their decision.

34

"Deputy Minister, ten minutes until the summons."

Breeze ignored the voice of her chief of staff, keeping her eyes on her screen for an extra few moments. She wasn't reading the words there—she just wanted everyone in her office to see that she moved on her own schedule. She was still getting used to the size of the staff assigned to a deputy minister, and hadn't bothered to start learning their names yet. They did the grunt work, and she took the credit. That was how things operated now, and she reveled in it.

Finally, and without warning to anyone, she rose from her hand-carved chair and crossed the woven rug for the polished doors. Her assistant scurried to catch up, a pair of flunkies swiftly opening the doors ahead of her.

Life as a senior government official suited her, she decided as she strode down the main corridor toward the Chamber of Parliament, entourage trailing behind. She was never expected to arrive at work before mid-morning, and by then her staff had assembled the day's briefings. She listened, read and signed as appropriate, and then it would be time for lunch in the exquisite dining room.

As a deputy minister Breeze was usually sought after by other members of Parliament, and over lunch and drinks she would hold court with whomever she felt might be useful to her. The networking opportunities were without equal, and already she had some ideas about how to improve her private portfolio.

Everything in good time, though. She was young, and the world of opportunity lay before her.

By far the most interesting task had been supervising Eric Chandler's Dark Bomb mission, although word had reached her this morning that the mission had failed. That was the subject of this Parliamentary summons—Breeze was to lead the government's questioning of the senior surviving officer, and it was with vicious delight that she prepared to interrogate Thomas Kane.

Entering the Chamber she breathed in the cool scents of wood and stone, noting the murmur of voices all around her as the other members took their seats. The session hadn't been on the schedule, and no doubt many of the members were irritated by the imposition. Breeze intended to direct this ill-will toward Thomas, and let the Parliamentary mob decide his fate.

Taking her seat in the second row, she quickly brought up her notes. From the analysis she'd received, Thomas had directed his ship, *Admiral Moore*, in a textbook distraction-and-deceit maneuver, drawing Centauri fire while Chandler and *Singapore* had snuck in to launch the Dark Bomb. It would have been easier if Thomas had made some critical error, but it was results that mattered, and the mission had failed.

Someone had to take the fall.

Since everyone in *Singapore* was dead, that left Thomas.

Breeze allowed herself a tiny smile.

Christopher Sheridan took his seat across the floor from her, greeting his colleagues but largely absorbed with the upcoming summons. She'd made a few overtures to him this past week, and hoped that his cutting wit would assist her in today's questioning. Minister of Defense Taal sat down in front of her, turning back to give her an encouraging smile.

"Good luck today," he said quietly. "Don't be intimidated by the summoned or the Opposition leaders—they may try to confuse the issue. Stick to the facts of this mission, and stand firm behind the rightness of it. You're the expert here. This is your first big moment, Charity—make it a memorable one."

"Thanks, Wes," she replied. "I'm looking forward to it."

With a nod he turned back to greet the last of the members who were taking their seats in the first row around the central floor. The doors to the lower corridor opened and, flanked by a pair of guards, Thomas Kane walked out to his podium. Standing tall in his full dress uniform, glittering with rank, medals, and qualifications, he certainly cut an impressive figure—but Breeze looked straight through that to the damaged, conniving, lecherous man she'd known for years. This was going to be fun, and then he was going to die.

She rose from her seat and stepped out onto the floor, knowing she cut an impressive figure in her own right. Her dark dress was modest in hem and neckline, but it hugged her figure in a way she knew would subtly draw the eye. She wore minimal jewellery, but had pinned over her heart a small cluster of military decorations, miniature versions of the real medals and awards appropriate for civilian wear. Her heels were high enough that she barely had to look up to meet Thomas's eyes.

As she approached, he remained stoic.

"Commander Kane," she said, hearing her own voice carry through the augments to every corner of the Chamber, "as the commanding officer of the warship *Admiral Moore*, were you responsible for the protection of the warship *Singapore* on your recent mission to Abeona?"

"I was." His voice was loud and steady, head up and eyes meeting hers.

"Then please explain why *Singapore* was unable to reach her launch point and complete her mission. A mission which, I might add, was deemed of the highest importance to the security of Terra."

"My ship's role in the mission was to draw the fire of the Centauri defenses, taking all their attention in order for *Singapore* to sneak in amid civilian traffic and launch her weapon. I did that, and my ship has the scars to prove it."

A few appreciative chuckles from the assembly irked Breeze.

"Scars or no," she countered, "*Singapore* never reached her launch point and the mission was a failure. Terra has lost a valuable warship, a hero in Admiral Eric Chandler, and a golden opportunity to end this war in a single stroke. As the senior surviving officer, you carry that responsibility."

"I executed my part of the mission with great effect. The responsibility for its overall success rests with you, Deputy Minister."

A murmur of surprise rippled through the chamber. No one ever talked back like that at a summons. Breeze noticed a few front row members shifting in their seats. All eyes were on her.

"I will remind you of your place, Commander," she said coldly. "You were charged with executing this mission, and it failed."

"I executed my orders to the letter. If my orders were flawed, then the responsibility rests higher than me."

Breeze strolled slowly around the floor, offering a beseeching gesture to the members around her. Thomas obviously intended to fight, so it was time for the drama.

"It appears the commander is invoking the defense of incompetent leadership. I would like to remind the distinguished members of Parliament that the overall commander of this mission was Admiral Eric Chandler, hero of both the Sirius and Centauria campaigns and one of the most renowned tacticians of our times. The weapon *Singapore* carried was the result of years of development by the top minds in the Astral Force. In my last posting in uniform, I was personally responsible for its development, and I do recall"—she spun to face Thomas—"that I was forced to remove then Lieutenant Commander Kane from his position as executive officer of the research ship in charge of the project."

She stood across the floor from him, staring him down.

"I suggest you rethink your manner of defense, Commander, as you are on very shaky ground." She guessed he would try to turn this around, and bring up the court-martial, but she was ready for that. She'd been found not guilty, after all, whereas he'd been demoted and banished. She prepared herself for a quick retort, waiting as he gave the appearance of checking his notes.

"You declared earlier, Deputy Minister," he said finally, "that this recent mission was of the highest importance to Terra." He paused expectantly. Breeze stood in silence, not sure of his new approach.

"You said," he continued after the silence, "that this mission was a golden opportunity to end the war in a single stroke. Do you genuinely believe that?"

She stared at him, feeling the sudden shift of three hundred gazes as they fell onto her. The lights shining down on the floor seemed to burn hotter.

"This summons is not to discuss military philosophy," she snapped. "This mission was of paramount importance to Terra, and you failed. Do you deny this?"

"The mission failed, yes." He fell silent, and Breeze let his words hang in the Chamber for a long moment. "But had it succeeded," he added unexpectedly, "seven hundred million people would now be dead, and we'd still be at war."

"Don't presume to tell the Chamber of Parliament whether our decisions are right or wrong," she said, feeding upon the shock of the members around her. "We rule for the good of the people, and as a servant of the State you must obey."

The next voice came from her right.

"Point of order."

She looked over and saw Christopher Sheridan rising from his seat. The leader of the Opposition wore a look of deep concern.

"I'd like to ask for clarification on the commander's last statement. There's nothing in the files that have been provided to us that refers to seven hundred million deaths. What deaths are these?"

"The details are classified," Breeze said quickly, before Thomas could speak. "I'll be happy to brief you on what I can… at a later time."

"But is the commander speaking in error? Did the mission you authorized have this sort of destructive potential?"

"The commander is speaking in hyperbole," Breeze said dismissively. "I'm not at liberty to openly discuss the mission, as a matter of strategic security."

"Hyperbole or not, that is a rather specific—and horrific—figure."

"War is horrific, as I know personally," she barked, using her advantage as a veteran, "and this mission was an attempt to do exactly what you've been screeching at the networks for months. 'Strike at the heart of terror'—isn't that your favorite saying?"

"My concern is that you, as Deputy Minister, perhaps did not understand the full implications of the mission you authorized."

Breeze felt herself flush. She looked to Minister Taal for support, but his expression was set in stone. Then she recalled his advice about not being intimidated, and realized that this was her first test on the big stage. Sheridan was playing his role to the hilt, and she was expected to rise to the challenge.

"I remind the honorable leader of the Opposition that I am a decorated veteran with wartime service in Abeona, and that I led the research program into the weapon which was at the center of this mission. I resent the implication that I was unaware of its full potential, and I demand a withdrawal of that last statement."

She'd seen this sort of personal attack before. As soon as it was challenged, the insult was withdrawn. Yet Sheridan didn't adopt the expected pose of withdrawal. Instead, he stepped fully onto the central floor and raised his voice.

"I am invoking the Privilege of Parliament, to determine the exact details of this mission." Immediately a new murmur rumbled through the assembly, and Breeze saw the lights go black on every member's desktop. The air crackled with a faint hum, and every door into the Chamber locked loudly. The Privilege of Parliament cut off the Chamber from all outside information links to create a secure space, in order that classified or otherwise sensitive information could be discussed openly.

It was rare for a government leader to invoke the privilege, and practically unheard-of for an Opposition leader. The truth was rarely pretty for anyone, and whatever was said could never be repeated outside of the Chamber. Breeze wasn't sure if she'd surrendered the floor or not. She kept her position, but Sheridan ignored her and stepped forward.

"Commander Kane," he said, "you are now protected under the Privilege of Parliament, and you are both permitted and required to answer in full any question or statement put to you, regardless of security clearances. Do you understand?"

"Yes, sir."

"Explain what you meant by 'seven hundred million people would now be dead.'"

"The mission," Thomas said, looking over at Breeze, "was to detonate a weapon known as the Dark Bomb in the core of the planet Abeona. None of us knew exactly what the results would be. Best case was worldwide earthquakes powerful enough to transform the crust into sludge. Worst case was the singularization of the planet."

Silence fell over the Chamber. Sheridan took another step.

"By singularization," he said, "you mean destruction? As in the destruction of the entire planet Abeona?"

"Yes, sir."

Breeze felt a new surge of energy as she sensed the horror forming in many of the members. Thomas was going to hang himself and save her the trouble.

Sheridan spun to face her, face twisted in incredulity.

"And you, Deputy Minister Shah, authorized this mission?"

His question caught her short, and again she felt all eyes shifting to her.

"Yes," she said automatically.

Sheridan's eyes were wide, turning away from Breeze to stare at Minister Taal.

"And you, Mr. Minister?" The sharp tone in his voice was jarring, and Breeze suddenly realized that this was more than just Parliamentary drama. Sheridan's shock—and, she now saw, growing outrage—was real. Taal rose slowly to his feet, his face bereft of expression.

"This mission was delegated to Deputy Minister Shah. I knew I lacked the expertise to direct it effectively, and I trusted her specific military experience to provide the correct oversight." He pursed his lips and exhaled slowly. "It appears I may have been wrong to do so."

"More than just wrong," Sheridan said. "This mission could have threatened all of humanity with its consequences, and destroyed Second Earth."

"The responsibility," Taal insisted, "lies with Deputy Minister Shah."

Breeze felt as if she'd been punched in the stomach.

Why wasn't he defending her? Where was the support he'd shown just before this session began? He'd told her to stand firm behind this mission. What he meant was to stand up and take the blame for it, she realized with a sickening twist in her heart.

"We'll see," Sheridan said, stepping back out to the center

of the floor. "This attempted act, fully authorized by the government, is the most heinous war crime ever conceived. I have no faith in the wisdom of this current leadership, and I call for a vote of no confidence in the ruling coalition of Parliament."

Breeze took an involuntary step back.

"What about the summons?" she said.

"It will be placed on hold," Sheridan said. He turned to the guards standing watch over Thomas. "Take the commander to the Parliamentary holding cells until further notice." Grim-faced, Thomas was led away without another word.

Minister Taal stepped forward.

"Before answering the honorable leader of the Opposition's call for a vote, I propose that we further examine the issue in question." With no protest from Sheridan, he turned to address the entire Chamber. "The government summons Deputy Minister of Defense Charity Shah."

She felt her lips part, but she couldn't form any words. Sheridan glared at her expectantly, and Taal motioned her to take position at the podium which Thomas had just vacated.

Jack sat alone at the bar, absently sipping at his beer while the merriment of a Friday evening swirled around him. It was nice to be back in Vancouver, among his tribe, and he leisurely sifted through the electronic chatter of local news and gossip. For a few hours he'd been able to pretend that life was simple, and that he was just a regular Joe among the people.

There was plenty of chatter about the recent upheaval at Parliament, with the government having suffered an unprecedented vote of no confidence. No one in the media seemed to know what this really meant, and Jack had heard no end of theories being argued by the drunken patrons around him.

Beneath it all, though, in the cryptic messages flashing between State agencies, Jack sensed that the truth was much more damaging than anyone imagined. The media screens all through the bar were currently lit up on local sports, but in less than five minutes an official announcement would be made.

A man sat down on the stool next to him, and Jack didn't even have to turn his head.

"Honestly, sir, can't a guy just grieve in peace?"

Korolev ordered a beer to match Jack's, and leaned his elbows on the bar, staring up at the nearest screen.

"Sometimes misery loves company. I wanted to see how you were doing."

"You know *exactly* how I'm doing," he spat, fighting off the nightmare memories. "You led the invasion of my brain."

"We had no choice, Jack," Korolev said without a hint of remorse. "An operative was lost in a major Centauri headquarters, with no eye witnesses to confirm what happened. All we have is your mental records—so we needed to be sure. We needed to know whether Katja was alive."

"Well, she's dead." He tapped his chest. "I felt it right here." Jack turned back to his beer, taking another swig. Korolev's unflappable calm was really beginning to annoy him.

"Yes..."

He ordered another drink, trying to avoid Korolev's gaze, but even silent and immobile, the man was impossible to ignore.

"Sir," he asked, "is there something I can do for you? If not, I'd really rather be left alone for a while. I appreciate your concern for me, but I just need to get away from everything."

"I know you had doubts about the mission," Korolev said. "That you even questioned whether or not you could carry it out."

Jack held his tongue. An operative of questionable loyalty was a useless operative—and a useless operative was a dead operative. Not for a minute did he doubt Korolev's devotion to that truth.

"But you did carry out your mission," Korolev said finally, "despite your doubts. That shows real strength in you, real courage."

There was no point in trying to hide anything from this man.

"I thought we weren't allowed to have doubts—servants of the State and all that."

"Of course we can. Everyone has doubts from time to time, but that's when your loyalty is most tested." He nodded toward the screen, where the official State seal had replaced the hockey. "There are more challenges ahead, a new situation which will test us all."

The seal dissolved to show nine men and women sitting at a long table, facing the camera. He recognized Christopher Sheridan immediately, and a quick search of the government databases confirmed that the other people were each leaders of a party in Parliament. Five of them were part of the government— no, recent government, he corrected himself—but surprisingly it was Sheridan who spoke for them all.

"My fellow citizens of Terra, we, the leaders of Parliament, come before you today with good news regarding the war. After considerable discussion with the representatives of various rebel factions, today Terra has generously agreed to a cease fire." A rush of emotions exploded around Jack, a mixture of cheers, groans, and expletives.

<What discussion?> he shot at Korolev. <I never heard of any.>

<There weren't any. It's a sham—we basically told the rebels today that we're pulling back to defensive positions.>

"While our many grievances have not yet been resolved," Sheridan continued, "we wish to avoid unnecessary bloodshed, and we are willing to hold in our current military positions and commence official talks.

"We are also aware of the rumors floating around the media, indicating a collapse of Parliament, and my colleagues and I are here today to assure you that no such thing has happened. There was a momentary crisis yesterday, when it was revealed that a servant of the State had attempted a rogue action which had imperiled millions of lives. However we in Parliament have put aside any political differences and come together in condemnation of this heinous act. The perpetrator has been identified, and judgement will now be carried out."

A new rush of excitement rippled through the crowd in the bar, all eyes on the screens as the view shifted to the familiar sight of an execution chamber. The chair sat ominously in the center of the room, and being led in from the side was a woman of middle height, brown hair falling flat past the shoulders of her orange prison coveralls.

She was handcuffed and barefoot, and even through the screen Jack could tell that she was heavily sedated. The guards sat her down in the chair and strapped her arms, legs, torso, and head with frightening efficiency. Jack watched closely, trying to make out the face of the woman. Her thick hair was unkempt and strands fell across her features, but even so he recognized her exquisite features.

<What the hell is this?> he demanded. <Are they talking about *our* mission?>

<It was always a huge risk,> Korolev said. <And the government knew they would never survive if the mission failed.>

<So they made sure they had a scapegoat.>

Korolev gave him a sidelong glance.

<They made certain they had several—but Mrs. Shah presented herself as the most politically palatable.>

A voice boomed from off-screen.

"For crimes against the State, Charity Brittany Delaine Marie Brisebois-Shah is sentenced to death." Amid a roar of cheers from everyone around him, Jack watched as the blades shot from the sides of the chair into her torso, and her entire body spasmed against its restraints as electricity coursed through her. Most likely the death was instant, but the execution continued for nearly ten seconds. He lowered his eyes, having already seen enough death to last many lifetimes.

"Justice is served," the voice intoned, as it always did. Applause broke out across the bar. Jack closed his eyes, sighing at the sudden revelation which struck him. The world he lived in was a terrible place—and he was an active part of it. Sheridan spoke again on the screen, but Jack couldn't stomach the political rhetoric.

"Another loose end tied up," Korolev said to him.

He looked over sharply, shocked at the mild words and the neutral expression that stared back.

"That's all she was?" he heard himself ask.

"No, she was also a conniving, manipulative, ambitious monster. None of that is relevant to why she was executed." Korolev's smile could have frozen the sun. "But it does take the sting out of it."

Jack shook his head.

"And Thomas Kane?"

"In jail, being kept quiet."

"And me…?"

Korolev's smile returned, marginally warmer than before.

"You're still very valuable, Jack, and as an operative you're not responsible for the orders you carried out. You had no official involvement with any of this."

"So we just go back to work?"

"The politicians have a few days of horse-trading now," Korolev said, "and it looks like Sheridan's party is going to come out on top. None of that matters to us, though—because nothing changes about what we do. What's the most important quality in an operative, Jack?"

"Loyalty, sir."

"Loyalty. If the politicians can't get their act together, remember that we serve the State, not any individual or party." He drained the rest of his beer and stepped down from his stool, patting Jack on the shoulder. "Get some rest, son, and I'll see you soon. We still have a lot of work to do."

Korolev slipped away into the crowd.

Jack tracked him out the doorway and onto the street, idly noting the three other operatives who were positioned around the bar. None of them seemed to notice his probes, and as he listened to their Cloud chatter he detected a pattern he'd never noticed before, about the way operative signals were exchanged. He tucked that tidbit away, knowing he'd spot it again the next time someone was watching him.

He looked around the bar, watching as the patrons returned to their drinks and conversations. All was well again in their lives. The State had identified the problem and swiftly dealt with it. No one he could see or hear seemed to think it was worthwhile asking any questions, except perhaps to debate whether Terran forces should break the cease fire and surprise the rebels with a crushing assault, or whether they should actually let the talks proceed.

Either way, the consensus formed around him in dozens of conversations. Terra was still in charge, and all was well.

Jack Mallory finished his beer, realizing that his time here was done. These weren't his people anymore, and he could either leave them behind, or drag them along to where he was now going. He glanced around, considering.

A few networks hacked, a jailbreak, a bit of media manipulation, and a way to stay completely hidden from view. He'd been able to do that sort of thing routinely in the Centauri Cloud. He figured it would be child's play here in Terra.

As he walked out of the bar and began shedding all his forms of identification, Jack knew that Korolev was right.

To safeguard Terra from its true enemies, there was a lot of work to do.

ACKNOWLEDGEMENTS

Creating a book is always a group effort. To my agent, Howard Morhaim, and my editor, Steve Saffel, thank you for all your expertise and support. To the good folks at Titan, thank you for producing such a beautiful book. And to my own teammates at Promontory Press, thank you for giving me the time to work on this when I really should have been doing my day job.

ABOUT THE AUTHOR

Bennett R. Coles served fourteen years as an officer in the Royal Canadian Navy and earned his salt on all classes of ship, from command of a small training ship to warfare director of a powerful missile frigate to bridge officer of a lumbering supply ship. He toiled as a staff officer in the War on Terror, and served two tours with the United Nations in Syria and Lebanon.

He has maintained an interest in military affairs since his retirement from active service in 2005 and he makes his home in Victoria, Canada, with his wife and family.